BLOODCHILD

THE GODBLIND TRILOGY, BOOK THREE

ANNA STEPHENS

TALOS

First published in the UK by Harper Voyager
First Talos Press edition published 2020

Talos Press books may be purchased in bulk at special discounts for sales promotion, corporate gifts, fund-raising, or educational purposes. Special editions can also be created to specifications. For details, contact the Special Sales Department, Talos Press, 307 West 36th Street, 11th Floor, New York, NY 10018 or info'skyhorsepublishing.com.

Talos Press® is a registered trademark of Skyhorse Publishing, Inc.®, a Delaware corporation.

Visit our website at www.talospress.com.

10 9 8 7 6 5 4 3 2 1

Library of Congress Cataloging-in-Publication Data is available on-file.

ISBN: 978-1-945863-42-4
EISBN: 978-1-945863-44-8

Cover design by Domonic Forbes © HarperCollinsPublishers Ltd 2019
Cover images © Shutterstock.com

Printed in the United States of America

For Mark.
For everything.
Forever.

RILLIRIN

Sixth moon, first year of the reign of King Corvus
Fort Four, South Rank forts, Western Plain, Krike border

WHEN THE FORT'S WARNING bell began to toll, Rillirin knew they were all dead. Rilporin had fallen and the Mireces—and Corvus—were coming. Her luck had run out and she was going to end up back in her brother's hands. It was over, all the running, all the fighting and freedom, the moments of joy. Her hands went to her belly and she stiffened her spine and found her courage. No. It might be over, but it wasn't over without a fight.

She snatched her spear from its place by the door and sprinted from the infirmary where Gilda was having the wound in her shoulder checked, out into the drill yard. Soldiers were spilling from the barracks and donning armour.

"What's happening?" she demanded.

"Scouts are back. Enemy force—big one—heading our way, but from the east not the north."

"Listrans? Reinforcements?" someone muttered. "Please, Dancer, please let it be reinforcements."

"Tresh, maybe," someone else said and was shushed. Officers were shouting the Rank into line, so she slipped free and ran into the corner watchtower and up to the allure before anyone could stop her. On the eastern wall stood Colonel Thatcher, commander of Fort Four, staring through his distance-viewer at the approaching dust cloud. Four was the fort closest to whatever was coming for them; Four was where the battle would begin.

Thatcher took his time and Rillirin was about to scream when he lowered the distance-viewer. "Rilporians. Palace Rank in the lead, what looks like Personal Guards at the rear. Civilians in the centre." He turned to a captain. "Sadler, flag it over."

The captain complied, whirling red and yellow flags through a complex series of gestures that was repeated on the wall of Fort Three and on to Two and then headquarters. The bell began ringing the all-clear even as the news travelled and Rillirin leant forward and put her forehead against the stone of the parapet, breathing deep to channel the adrenaline flooding her. Rilporians. Did that mean they'd won? The thought stood her up again so fast she stumbled. Below, the drill yard erupted into excited speculation quickly curbed by the junior officers in charge.

Fort One sent a heavy mounted patrol out to greet the advancing troops, General Hadir himself leading them. Within minutes word came back to open the gates and prepare the infirmaries and kitchens for a mass influx.

Rillirin could make out the army now, or what was left of it, marching in weary time. A mass of civilians in the middle just as Thatcher had said, and more Rankers behind to protect them. And to one side, tramping through the dry grass of the Western Plain, a loose, flowing group in boiled leather and chainmail. The Wolves. Her breath caught in her throat. They were here. Dalli and Lim and Isbet and Ash and all the rest. They were here.

She watched until the formation split, groups peeling off to each fort with the Rankers shepherding the civilians in, watchful to the last. As soon as she knew the Wolves were coming to Fort Four she ran back down into the drill yard. Her heart was yammering in her chest, her head swimming with fear and excitement.

Dom.

Would he be here too, among his people or maybe in the Rank's custody for his . . . actions? It would be hard to see him in chains, of course, but once everyone understood what had happened, that the things he'd done hadn't been his fault, not really, it would be different. It might take even Gilda a while to forgive him, but she would, all the Wolves would. They had to.

Her thoughts stuttered to a halt as the gates opened and people began streaming in. Civilians, hundreds of them rushing with glad relief into the nearly empty fort that had once contained the South Rank's Fifth Thousand, soldiers who'd marched to Rilporin to aid the king and now, maybe, if they were lucky, marched back. A babble of voices rose from soldiers and refugees alike as Rank physicians and any soldier with healing experience hastened towards the newcomers, and a sergeant with a voice that could crack stone directed them to form up in lines before half a dozen hastily assembled tables and chairs to give names and be allocated quarters.

Rillirin hopped from foot to foot, desperately trying to see over and through the press to the Wolves who'd been trailing the group. And then . . .

"Dalli! Dalli!"

The short woman turned when Rillirin screamed her name. Her eyes nearly popped out of her head. "*Rillirin?* Fuck the gods, girl, get over here!"

Rillirin sprinted around the edge of the throng, shoving between people with muttered apologies, and flung herself bodily into Dalli's arms where she burst into tears. "You're alive, you're alive," she sobbed.

"*You're* alive," Dalli countered and there was a wobble in her voice Rillirin had never heard before. She pulled back and took in Dalli's face: sunburnt, freckled, green eyes rimmed with red and sitting in shadows so deep they look bruised. "How the bloody fuck are you still alive? You fell off the ship."

"Long boring story," Rillirin said, wiping her nose on her sleeve, other hand still clutching Dalli in case the Wolf suddenly vanished. "I made it to shore, found Gilda in the Dancer's Fingers and—"

"Gilda?"

"Gods, yes, Dalli, Gilda's alive! She's here, wounded . . . but, but recovering; she's fine. In the infirmary. I can take you there, you and Lim and Ash and Dom." Her voice got quieter on the last name, with a rise at the end that made it almost a question, something of a plea.

Dalli's face went colder than Rillirin had ever seen it, colder even than the mask she donned for battle. That face would not entertain forgiveness or weakness. That face knew nothing of light. "We don't know where Dom is. Nor Ash. They disappeared when Rilporin fell. Lim is dead."

Now Rillirin did let go. She stumbled back, hands to her mouth and nausea coiling up her throat. "Rilporin *fell*? You mean we lost?" Her words were too loud and carried to the nearest South Rankers. They'd have found out soon enough, but still; they needed the official version, not some overheard panicked gossip.

Dalli's expression closed even further. "Yes, we lost, and yes, Lim died. So did thousands of others. Doesn't mean it's over though. Come, take me to Gilda. She should hear the fate of her sons—blood, adopted and fostered—from me." She licked cracked lips. "The Wolves voted me their chief."

Rillirin blinked away tears and managed a shaky smile. "I'm pleased for you, Dalli, truly. You deserve it. I . . . The infirmary's that way. I'm sure you can find it."

"No," Dalli said, flint in her voice. "You need to hear it all."

I don't want to hear it all. I don't want to hear any of it! But when Dalli began walking in the direction Rillirin had indicated, she followed, and then slid ahead of her and led her to the priestess.

She was unable to take any pleasure in their reunion, knowing some of what was coming next. Was Lim's death somehow Dom's fault, too, as Gilda's wound was, as Rilporin's betrayal was? She rubbed her belly, beginning to round outwards now and obvious when she was undressed. When Dalli broke the embrace, Rillirin plucked at her shirt to make sure it wasn't tight over her stomach. She already knew she didn't want to tell the other woman about the babe, and who its father was. Not now, not ever, maybe, and if that meant hiding it for however long the Wolves were in the forts, so be it.

Gilda sat stiffly in her chair, back unbending despite her age and the toll the wound had taken on her. Her eyes were dry and her hands folded tightly in her lap; she didn't invite contact, didn't want emotion. "How many?"

Dalli gave a single nod, as if to say, *If this is how you want it, this is how I'll tell it.* "Too many. Including Lim." Her voice cracked and she cleared her throat; she didn't look away even though agony crossed the old priestess's face, there and gone like summer rain. "In battle against the Mireces, defending his people, defending the city. It . . . was Corvus himself, Gilda. But it was quick, and I'm not just saying that."

Gilda flicked a finger for her to continue, not looking at Rillirin even though her gasp at mention of her brother must have been audible to them both. Dalli's eyes filled with tears but her voice was steady now. "Strike to the neck and then . . . decapitation. He had the charm he'd made in memory of Sarilla. Kept it with him the whole time. She'll have welcomed him into the Light."

"His father too," Gilda murmured and Rillirin flinched. Gilda had lost so many and still she kept going, bearing the weight of pain without complaint. She nodded once, with the air of someone excising a wound. "Who else?"

"Dom was—"

"Dom is a Darksoul who betrayed his people and his gods. He tried to kill me; he failed. Who else?"

"He's your son!" Rillirin burst out, unable to contain herself any longer. "You might all hate him, you might think that what he did was of his own free will, but I don't. I know he was forced. I *know* it. And I want to know where he is even if you don't."

Dalli rose from her seat, gaze fixed on Rillirin's hands curled protectively across her belly. Rillirin blushed and let them drop to her sides. "He put a child in you?" She whirled to the priestess. "You have to do something, Gilda! Crys is the Fox God—yes, I know how that sounds but it's true—and Dom betrayed him to Corvus. He tortured him on the Mireces' orders. Cut him open, beat him, ripped out his fingernails for all to see. Rankers saw it happen; they saw him do it! Whatever abomination he's put in her can't be allowed to live. He's brought all of us to the brink of destruction and I don't care if he did kill the Dark Lady afterwards, I won't allow some Blood-infected babe to come into this world and push us over the edge! End the pregnancy or I will."

None of what she said made sense, none of it. Dom torturing Crys? Torture? Killing the Dark Lady? The new Wolf chief was still shouting but her face, pale with fright and fury, vanished into a sea of buzzing black dots, her words drowned beneath waves of roaring.

Rillirin retched and stumbled, lurched against the table and fell back from Dalli's seeking hands, unable to take a full breath through the tightness in her throat.

She pointed a shaking finger at Gilda. "You said . . . you said it was innocent; the babe is innocent. I don't . . . You stay away from me. Both of you stay away!" Her head was too light, her limbs heavy and not under her control. She took two steps backwards on legs wobbling worse than a newborn fawn's, and fainted.

MACE

G ENERAL HADIR, YOUR HOSPITALITY is gratefully received," Mace said, wincing at the formality of the words when what he wanted to do was hug the wiry old soldier until his ribs creaked. Still might, once his people were settled.

"Commander Koridam, whatever you need," Hadir said. "I don't mind admitting that when you appeared I thought you were the enemy and we were all dead. Can't tell you my relief when we spotted your uniforms. You'll have my quarters, of course. How many staff are with you?"

Mace hacked a cough from a dry throat before answering. "Me, Chief Dalli of the Wolves and a handful of valiant captains who'll bed down in the barracks as normal."

Hadir blinked. "That's it?"

Mace coughed again and the general belatedly handed him a cup from his desk. His office was small and neat, much like its owner, and Mace felt like a ragged beggar in its midst.

"That's it. My father is dead, as is Colonel Yarrow. Colonel Edris has gone east to Listre with a small company to tell Tresh he is now our king and to raise an army to take back his throne and country. While he's only distantly related and I don't believe he's ever even visited Rilpor, he's legitimate at least and the best we've got. The rest of my officers and army are captured or presumed dead." The water did nothing to prevent his voice hoarsening with the last words.

"Gods," Hadir murmured. "My condolences, sir. Do you know the number you bring with you?"

Screams rang in Mace's ears. So many losses. "Almost two thousand Rankers and Wolves who need rest and healing, though the badly wounded were left behind or died on the journey. Nearly four thousand civilians. I know rationing will be a problem, but I wasn't leaving them to the Mireces."

Hadir just nodded, a crease between his eyebrows as he no doubt calculated what they had in stores against the number of mouths they'd be feeding.

"We got on to the Tears and made it look as if we were sailing for Listre, then sent the boats on and doubled back, through the great forest. Colonel Dorcas and Major Vaunt had another, slightly smaller, group and were going to storm the King Gate and join us. They never showed up."

There was a long silence and Mace got the sense Hadir was giving him time to collect himself. He made the most of it, closing his eyes and leaning back in the chair, feeling some of the tension run out of his shoulders for the first time since they'd fled. No, since the whole godsdamn mess of a war had started.

"We'll hold a full council at dusk, General," he said eventually, focusing on Hadir again. "All your staff and those among my people who have taken on such responsibility in the last weeks. In the meantime, here's the quick and dirty version. Let the whole Rank know—we're a long way past keeping secrets from the men who'll be doing the fighting."

Hadir nodded, refilled their cups with water, and began to take notes.

MACE HADN'T SLEPT; HE hadn't even closed his eyes, waiting for the uproar that would signal the remains of the South Rank learning what had happened in Rilporin. What he had allowed to happen.

It hadn't come. Oh, there'd been noise and disappointment and the bravado of men saying what would have happened if they'd been there, but those men had been stared at by Mace's surviving soldiers, just stared at, all the horror and carnage they'd been involved in bleeding from their eyes, and the bravado had dried up. Mace had been prepared to break up brawls; this was much more chilling. And far more effective.

Still, the sense of failure was acute, even days after the abandonment of Rilporin. Now he sat in stiff silence while the council room filled up, absurdly grateful that Dalli had taken the seat next to him and given his knee a surreptitious squeeze beneath the table. It took him a moment to recognise Gilda and what-was-her-name, Rillirin, Corvus's sister, and a moment more to wonder why they were sitting as far from Dalli as they could get. One look at the tightness around his lover's mouth and he decided not to ask.

"Thank you all for coming. For those of you who marched with me, I hope you find some ease behind the South Rank's walls. And officers of the South Rank, let me be frank: the Wolves and civilians in this council are people I trust, people who co-ordinated and led the evacuation with me. They may not hold high office, but they have as much right to be here as you do. I know you will treat them as you would any officer. The royal physician, Hallos, travelled with us, but declined my offer to attend this council in preference to treating those who still bear the wounds of the siege. Though he is not here, I consider him a member of my staff.

"As for high priestess Gilda and King Corvus's sister, Rillirin, I am glad to see you both still live, and am most keen to learn what has befallen you since last we met." Gilda was tired and haunted, made no attempt to hide it. "Your son Chief Lim was a great man, high priestess, and he led his people with honour and fortitude. I grieve with you for his loss."

"Thank you, Commander, that is most kind. Especially as we both know how intractable he could be. But I take your words to heart."

Hadir tapped the table with his forefinger. "Commander Koridam, it will be as you say. These people have seen more of war and bloodshed than many of my own; they will be treated accordingly. And if I may, this is Colonel Jarl of Fort Two, Colonel Osric of Three, and Thatcher of Four. We thought it best that this first council include the full staff so that there is no confusion."

Mace nodded at them in turn. "A pleasure to meet you all. Let me begin by thanking you for your hospitality. We bring numbers these forts were never designed to hold, and coexisting is not going to be easy. Both my soldiers and the civilians need time and rest and food to recover from the siege and the journey here. Not to put too fine a point on it, General, but you and your Rank are all that stands between Rilpor and disaster for the next few weeks while the rest of us recuperate and formulate a country-wide offensive to end the Mireces threat once and for all."

Hadir gave a single sharp nod. Mace put both his hands on the table. "Let me be clear: this is not over, not by a long way. We mauled them, and they mauled us, yes. Our king and former Commander of the Ranks are dead, and many, if not most, of our senior officers, but they lost the Dark Lady Herself." *Just don't ask me how I know or who did the killing—or why.*

"The claim is incredible, if you will allow me to say so, Commander," Hadir said. "We are all faithful followers of the Gods of Light, but to suggest one of the Red Gods is dead . . ."

"Dom did it. The Wolf calestar. Forgive me for speaking out of turn, I know I wasn't there but I've spoken to some of the witnesses, sirs. Dom allowed himself to be captured by the Mireces and—and he fed them certain information in order to become trusted by Corvus and the Blessed One, and then there are rumours that he killed Rivil in a duel to the death. Later on, when the Dark Lady appeared in Rilporin, he killed Her too. Well, stabbed Her so the Fox God could kill Her."

All eyes turned to Rillirin and she flushed under their scrutiny but raised her chin, defiant. The story wasn't hers to tell and she'd put a spin on it that didn't sit easy with Mace, but they were certainly the facts as he understood them.

"Aye, maybe he did kill Rivil, and that's a job well done, but why was the Dark Lady there in the first place?" Dalli demanded, shoving to her feet and knocking her chair over. "Because your precious Dom was torturing Crys! Torture, on the Mireces' orders. Don't try and make him out to be the hero of this tale. He did nothing but betray us at every turn and cause the deaths of thousands of people. He turned to Blood and you say we should thank him for it!"

Rillirin stood too, shaking off Gilda's restraining hand. "You don't know what you're talking about," she started and Dalli's eyes bulged.

"I don't know what I'm talking about?" she raged. "*You said yourself you weren't even there!* Well, I was there and I saw what happened. You think you know Dom because you fucked him, because you're carrying his poisonous seed? You don't know the first thing about him, about any of us.

You were a Mireces slave for ten years, your brother is their godsdamned king—of course you'll forgive Dom for turning Mireces himself, it justifies your own weakness, your own treason! Maybe we should be asking about your faith instead of allowing you to sit here in council with us."

"Enough." Mace slammed both fists into the table hard enough to rattle the cups and cut off whatever Rillirin had been about to scream. "Sit down or get out." Dalli shot her a triumphant look. "Both of you." She gaped at Mace and her expression turned murderous; he stared her out and, slowly enough to promise that this wasn't over, she retrieved her chair and sat. Gilda hauled on Rillirin's arm and dragged her back into her own seat.

"General, Colonels, forgive me. The wounds from the siege are still raw for many of us. But let me reiterate—this is a war council. We confine ourselves to the facts and to the plan for victory. If you want to argue allegiances, do it elsewhere. My own thoughts on Dom Templeson's actions are mixed, but no one can deny that without his aid, the Dark Lady would not have been destroyed. We cannot change his past betrayals and I do not expect that last action of his to make those of you who were there forgive him; I certainly haven't. But he is not here and arguably he is no longer important. What is important is what we do next."

The silence was thick with suspicion and burgeoning embarrassment. Mace found Dalli's leg beneath the table; she moved it deliberately from under his hand.

"The . . . ladies do bring up a valid point," Colonel Thatcher said. "Would someone explain this information about the Fox God and how it relates to Major Tailorson again, please?" Rillirin and Dalli glared at each other some more. "And what the high priestess thinks of it all, perhaps, as the authority on such matters?"

"Captain Kennett here may be best placed to answer that," Mace said and pointed. Kennett flushed under the scrutiny and sat up a little straighter. "Tell the council what you know, Captain."

"Yes, Commander. Kennett, Palace Rank, sirs. I served alongside Captain Crys Tailorson as he was then before the war, and again during the siege when he was promoted to major. Great leader, sirs, talented and brave. He had command of the southern wall. He found his, ah"—Kennett broke off and licked his lips, shot a desperate glance at Mace who kept his face perfectly neutral—"his *friend* dead, pinned up to a door in a deliberate provocation by the Lord Galtas Morellis, he suspected, who he'd had some sort of feud with and who had infiltrated the city. Morellis was Prince Rivil's co-conspirator."

"Slimy, one-eyed bastard," Jarl muttered. "Wouldn't be the first soldier he's provoked."

"Anyway, he found his friend and, well, I mean I was there, but it's hard to explain. He started shouting about doing whatever was needed to bring Ash back from the dead, screaming at the Dancer for allowing him to die and then . . . well, he broke all the glass in the district and cracked the paving stones beneath his feet. There was a sort of silver light that shone out of him, brighter than sunlight, and then Ash wasn't dead any more and Crys—Major Tailorson, that is—was the Fox God."

Kennett broke off and wiped sweat from his upper lip. His face bore the expression of a man who believes he's made a terrible mistake but is determined to see it through to the bitter end. The silence was pregnant with scepticism.

"I was there, too," Dalli said, backing him up; Mace let out a silent huff of relief. "We thought you'd prefer to hear it first from a Ranker, but I was there and everything the captain has said is true. I found Ash and I know a corpse when I see one. He was dead and then he wasn't and Crys did it. He did other things too, after that, during the siege. Held the breach almost single-handed through the night, rallied troops on the verge of breaking. Killed the Dark Lady after Dom wounded Her." Her voice was level again and her thigh bumped Mace's in what might have been a silent apology. "Fought Gosfath, too. Crys is the Fox God come to aid us."

There was a snort of something like derision from Osric. "And where is this so-called god now?" he asked.

Unfortunately, that's a good question.

"We don't know," Mace admitted. "He vanished during the retreat."

"The Fox God lives, and lives inside Crys." Gilda's tone held all the calm assurance of a woman who'd spent most of her life being the voice of authority among powerful people. "I felt the god's awakening even from here. He will return when we need Him."

"How convenient," Osric muttered, though not quietly enough.

"You have something to say?" Dalli snapped, her temper fraying again. "Because while you were sitting here with your cock in your hand, the rest of us were fighting and dying. Why don't—"

"*Enough*, Chief," Mace said, and the use of her new title was just enough to bring her down again. Gods, he loved her fire, but sometimes he could throttle her. "My father ordered the South's three Thousands to remain here and that decision was the right one."

Jarl cleared his throat. "The enemy will be consolidating its hold not just on Rilporin but the whole country, and as it stands we don't have enough soldiers to break that grip. What are our next steps?"

Mace shot him a grateful look. "You know that Colonel Edris has gone to Listre to recruit King Tresh and an army; we hope and expect to hear from him in a matter of weeks. Until then, we need to infiltrate the major towns and gather intel on the enemy's movements and intentions. With luck, the Mireces don't know that we doubled back and will believe us to be in Listre, but keep sending out scouts to watch the approaches as you have been. If our presence does go unnoticed, then when we get word that Tresh is coming at the head of an army, we can pour out of here like ants and catch the bastards in a pincer, end them once and for all."

"And the Mireces' numbers?" asked Colonel Jarl.

"No definitive idea," Mace said. "It was hand to hand in the streets for the last part of the siege. Before that, it looked as if they had six or so thousand, maybe more. More than us." He took a deep breath. "We need more troops and although I have confidence in Edris reaching King Tresh and raising an army, I'm not willing to risk the country and its inhabitants on anything less than absolute certainty. As such, I intend to send emissaries to the Warlord of Krike and negotiate a deal for their aid. It is my hope that Tresh will forgive my actions, but the survival of Rilpor is more important than lines on a map. With that in mind, I plan on offering the Krikites—"

"Forgive my interruption, Commander," General Hadir said, "but that's not an option. Commander Koridam, that is your father, Commander Durdil Koridam, sir, at the time he sent orders for our two Thousands to reinforce Rilporin, he also asked me to explore the potential for aid from Krike. The Warlord was . . . less than forthcoming."

"He said he looked forward to our forces wiping each other out so the Krikites could expand north into Rilpor," Jarl added in an acid tone.

"If they wouldn't agree to supply us with troops when we were, ah, winning, Commander, I think it's unlikely they will now we have suffered a reverse," Hadir added in an apologetic tone.

Suffered a reverse. At least he's phrasing my crushing defeat tactfully.

"That is not news I was hoping to hear, gentlemen. And there's no way we can go back to them with an offer—say, half the Western Plain—in return for aid?"

"The Warlord and his witch, the Seer-Mother, threatened to kill any envoys they came across, regardless of whether they carried the flag of parley, Commander. Once a decision is made in Krike, it's made."

"Shit," Mace said. "So we wait for Listre and pray King Tresh is eager to claim his kingdom."

"Train the civilians," Colonel Thatcher said. All eyes turned to him. "I'm a commoner, sir, rose through the ranks to where I am now. Always dreamt of being a soldier. These civilians we've got, they've been through a siege, they've seen death and destruction and been unable to prevent it. Put weapons in their hands now, get commoners like me training them, and you'll see their spines. Not just a chance to fight back, but the ability, too? We need forces—these might be all we get. Best to start working with them now."

"Women too," Dalli said before anyone else could speak. "I'm chief of my people and we know the importance of recruiting warriors whatever their gender. There'll be women amongst this lot who spent every day of that siege waiting to be raped and killed, by their own as well as the enemy. It's what war does. Tell them they can protect themselves and they'll jump at the chance. I've spoken to dozens myself on the journey here. Give them the chance, Commander. They won't let you down."

"I agree," he said. "We're not just fighting for our lives; we're fighting for our way of life, for our children and their children. We're fighting for freedom and the Light. I won't deny training and weapons to anyone who wants to stand at my side."

"You had that woman captain, didn't you?" Osric muttered.

"Major Carter, yes," Mace said in a bland tone. "Your point?" It appeared Osric didn't have a point. "Right. General Hadir, I want your rested three Thousands on patrol. I want them scouting Rilporin to see what Corvus is up to and visiting Yew Cove and Pine Lock, Shingle too if the bridge over the Gil is intact. Maybe even Sailtown if the roads are clear of Mireces and you've men who'll risk crossing hostile territory. Let the civilians see you're alive and you haven't given up hope or given up on them. Tell them aid is coming, but don't specify from where. Tell them to stay alive. And for the love of the Dancer, buy as many supplies as you can or we'll all starve.

"But"—Mace raised a finger to stress his point—"no one—and I mean not a single Ranker—is to confirm the presence of anyone from Rilporin within these forts. The longer Corvus believes us to be in Listre, the more likely he is to leave us alone and let us plan our next move. If he knows we're here . . . well, let's just say I for one have had enough of being besieged."

"And we're sure he thinks you're in Listre, are we?" Jarl asked.

"No," Mace said, "but let's not hand definitive proof to him on a platter, eh? Meanwhile, let it be known across the forts that we're taking volunteers for a militia and that it's open to women. We'll start training them in a week. Until then, they rest and they eat. We all do—with our safety in your hands."

"Understood, sir," Hadir said. "All right, gentlemen, let's show Commander Koridam what the South Rank is made of."

CRYS

Seventh moon, first year of the reign of King Corvus
Green Ridge, Southern Krike

TWO OUT OF THE three of them woke screaming—again.

By the time Crys flailed upright out of the nightmare, sweat sticking his shirt to his back, Ash was stoking up the fire and the calestar was huddled by it, gaunt and rocking. Dom's nightmares were a product of him killing the Dark Lady. Crys's were the result of Dom nearly killing him.

"Morning," Crys croaked, scrubbing sweat from his face and reaching for the waterskin. Ash grabbed his hand, grazed a kiss across the knuckles. Neither of them looked at Dom. Despite the Fox God's insistence that he should accompany them, Crys's skin crawled every time the Wolf came near.

It will fade.

Crys grunted and drank. Weeks of running and hiding from Mireces and their own people to get over the border into Krike hadn't improved his mood much, but at least now they were here and safe. Unless the Krikites decided to kill them. *An archer, a god and a one-armed madman walk into Krike . . . Worst joke ever.*

They picked through the remains of the previous night's meal, slung weapons and blankets scavenged from a burning Rilporin over their shoulders, and began to walk. Dom was silent. Dom was always silent and that was just how Crys liked it. He and Ash walked a few steps apart from him, unwilling to forgive—and unable to forget—what he'd done. Everything he'd done.

Not all the choices were his. Not all the betrayals were willing.

And not everything he did to me was felt by you, Foxy, Crys countered. *But I felt it. All of it. I looked into his eyes and saw joy.*

I looked into his soul and saw despair, the Fox God said. Crys told himself he didn't care.

"So, this Warlord," Ash said, picking up the threads of the conversation they'd been having for the last few days, perhaps in response to the faraway look Crys got whenever the Trickster within spoke to him. "Rules all of Krike?"

"Sort of. He's the military and secular arm of the government. They have a seer—Seer-Mother or Seer-Father, depending on who's elected—who leads the priesthood and arbitrates those disputes that can't be settled by local priests. When I served in the South Rank, the Warlord was Brid Fox-dream and the seer was a woman."

"Fox?" Ash asked.

"No relation," Crys said and grinned, the change of subject blowing away the last tendrils of memory and nightmare. "They're quite particular about it, though. They have some ritual, performed by the priesthood once a year, I believe, when they take children of a certain age on some sort of spiritual journey and they are confronted with a . . . creature that they're particularly attuned to."

"Ridiculous," Ash snorted. "Mine would be a majestic wolf, of course, with a silver pelt and noble aspect."

"Flea-bitten badger, more like," Crys teased him. "But maybe we'll get to find out when we meet her."

"Riders," Dom said and pointed.

Ash's hand went to his bow and Crys gripped the axe he'd taken from Rilporin. Not a favoured weapon, but all he had. Dom just cradled the stump of his arm—hand severed by the same axe—and watched them come. The Fox God rumbled wariness but not danger.

The small band cantered up and encircled them, spears pointing down at their chests. Ash twitched again but then Crys was stepping forward. "Greetings, warriors. May the Fox God shine His light upon you and the Dancer bless you with plenty." He dropped his axe into the grass and raised both hands, shirt sleeves falling back to expose the scars on his forearms. "You have heard of the war in Rilpor, the invasion by the Mireces and their Red Gods? We've come to see if you will fight alongside us—fight for your gods—to repel the heathens? May we speak with your clan chief?"

"I am Cutta Frog-dream," a woman said. "I am war leader of Green Ridge and clan chief. We know of your troubles, Rilporian, but they trouble us not. We have already answered your emissaries and promised to shed the blood of any more who came."

"Well, that's awkward," Ash muttered. "This is no normal emissary," he shouted and nearly took out Crys's eye with his pointing finger. "This is the Fox God Himself, the Great Trickster in a mortal's flesh. He fought—and killed—the Dark Lady of the Mireces! He brought me back from the dead! He healed thousands of wounded soldiers and civilians! You owe him your allegiance."

Crys waited for the laughter followed by the spears. Neither came.

"The Two-Eyed Man," someone whispered. "The old tales . . ."

"You make a bold claim for your friend, Wolf," the war leader said. "Yes, we know your clan by your look. A bold claim and one that will see you all dead if it is untrue. You think us savages and wild, our beliefs childlike, but you are wrong. If you think to trick us, it will be the last thought you ever have."

"Thanks for that, Ash," Crys said as the Krikites turned their horses and clicked them into motion back the way they'd come, the three men in their midst.

"May as well start as we mean to go on," Ash replied with a tight smile. "You never said this would be easy, after all. But I'd quite like to live, if it's all the same to you."

"Wouldn't we all," Crys muttered. "Come on then, Foxy. No pressure."

IT WASN'T EXACTLY A private audience with the war leader and her priests, but the Fox God didn't seem to mind. Crys stood on the green at the centre of the town, where a single finger of rock twice his height had been erected. Something about its outline, its presence black against the sky, called to him. Before anyone could speak—and it looked as if the whole town had been summoned to bear witness—he found himself drifting across the grass towards it, goats and chickens ambling from his path. Inside him, sharp teeth grinned with anticipation.

"This is where you come to soul-dream with your priests," he said, his voice lifting across the green.

"It was," Cutta Frog-dream replied. Crys frowned. "Now all soul-dreams are performed at Seer's Tor, our capital, by the Seer-Mother herself."

"You don't dream without her?" Crys called. "Why not?"

"It is not done any more," the war leader replied. "And how do you know of our magic?"

"Because I am the Two-Eyed Man," he said and the claim spoken aloud caused a susurrus of disbelief and outrage. None of them believed him, not yet anyway. But they would. They had to.

They will.

Up close, the surface had been carved with whorls and spirals and sinuous connecting lines that dizzied the eye and drew it upwards. Lightheaded, heart speeding, Crys placed both palms against the carvings. The hair on his forearms stood up as if he was in the centre of an electrical storm. He'd moved before anyone could question him or tell him what to do, and over the rushing in his ears he just made out the muttering and shifting of the crowd. Part of him wondered if he was committing sacrilege, but the stone and its patterns didn't care and neither did the Trickster.

Some of the carvings called to him and he traced them with his fingertips, aware of the tiny trails of silver light he left in their grooves as he made his way around the rock, touching here and there, wonder and rightness and homecoming and duty and the Fox God expanding until he could feel fur brushing the inside of his skin.

"Two-Eyed Man," someone shouted and he ignored it, ignored all but the carvings and the guiding instinct within.

"This is home," he whispered. "This is us."

When the pattern within the pattern was done, Crys stepped back. The middle of the stone glowed, the carvings bright as starlight in winter. The air hummed. Ash had already knelt and bowed his head and Crys opened his mouth to tell him to get up, silly bollocks, and stop embarrassing them both. The Fox God stopped the words.

"Two-Eyed Man," Cutta shouted. "Our legends tell of you. The teachings of our old priests talk of your appearance and how you will lead us."

"To death and beyond," Crys muttered, though none heard him. "I do not lead you," he shouted back. "I do not seek to take command, but the Gods of Light need you. I need you. If Rilpor falls, the Mireces will come for you next. Your faith and your way of life will be forbidden. Krike will drown in its people's blood unless we stop them in Rilpor. Unless you help me stop them."

The war leader walked forward into the empty space between them. The stone at Crys's back was still humming, as though a million sleeping bees fanned their wings as they dreamt inside it. "Is this magic? Blood magic?" she asked quietly, loosening the knife on her belt.

"This is me," the Fox God said and she took a step back, awe and fear chasing across her features. "This is the fate of Gilgoras and the part you may play in it."

"May?"

The Fox God spread His hands. "I do not command."

"You killed the Dark Lady?" she asked. A tiny frog was tattooed in front of her left ear.

"I drank Her and destroyed Her," the Fox God replied. "But She seeks a way back and Her followers aid Her. If they succeed all will turn to Blood and madness. While I can stop the Dark Lady again, I cannot stop Her forces alone."

"You are not alone, Two-Eyed Man," Cutta Frog-dream said, and knelt at his feet. "Green Ridge is with you and together we will convince all Krike, including the Warlord."

That was easier than expected, Foxy.

There was a rustle of amusement from within. *Don't get used to it.*

CORVUS

T HE THING ABOUT CONTROL that you Rilporians have never quite understood is that if you don't believe in it, neither will those you rule."

Corvus examined the nobleman kneeling on the marble before his improvised throne, the original now a charred heap of wood and gold leaf. "Take us, for example, and them." He pointed at the fresh corpses. "I have control over you, because I have proved beyond doubt that if you disobey me you will die. As such, our relationship is established and both of us can be content within it—me as owner, you as slave. Oh, don't look so horrified. You're alive, aren't you, still in possession of your limbs, your tongue, your eyes and your cock? So you have to serve me instead of others serving you. You'll get used to it. And when you place your feet upon the Dark Path, you'll be freed and can buy slaves of your own. The sooner you understand that, the sooner we can all get along."

Lord Silais shifted, clearly unused to the discomfort of kneeling on cold stone.

This is the breed of man who ruled this country? Corvus allowed a sneer to twist his mouth. *No wonder Rivil was weak.*

"Your Majesty, I am a child of Light. I will never walk the Dark Path—but that does not mean I cannot be of assistance to you. Advise you," he added quickly. "There are many things you will encounter as you consolidate your rule. Rebellions, laws, heirs to the throne who may seek to seduce loyalty away from you."

Corvus looked at Valan, his second in command, and rolled his eyes. "I know about Tresh in his little castle in Listre," he said. "You're beginning to bore me, Slave Silais." He grinned as the man twitched again—it really was too much fun.

The former noble met his gaze with an expression of earnest surprise. "Oh no, Your Majesty, there are many more heirs than just Tresh. They're like rats, Sire—kill one and another rears its head. It's a shame so much of the palace burnt, really. All the records of the full line of the Evendoom dynasty were in the royal library."

Corvus's humour vanished. "Let me guess—you know who these heirs are and you're bartering your freedom in return for the knowledge?"

Silais's smile was silky-smooth. "It appears we can assist each other, does it not?" he asked, straightening a little, feeling he was on firmer ground.

"It does," Corvus said and jerked his head. Valan stepped down from the dais and held out his hand to help the lord up. Silais nodded his thanks and was on his feet before he realised Valan had ducked behind him, snaking his arm around beneath his chin and grasping his ear firmly. Valan tucked his elbow and pulled Silais's head into his chest, stretched his ear out further, and sawed it off with his knife.

Silais was screaming like a bloody woman by the time it was done, legs treadling and hands slapping uselessly at Valan's constricting arm. Corvus wandered down from his throne and bent to look into his face, still tucked lovingly against Valan's chest.

"Control," he whispered into the bloody hole where his ear used to be. "I have it, and you don't. And you're going to tell me the names and locations of Rastoth's heirs, aren't you, my lord Earless? Or Valan here will show you just what an artist he can be with that knife."

Silais tried to nod, snot bubbling from his nose. "Y-yes, Your Majesty. Anything. I'll tell you anything."

Corvus patted his head. "Not anything," he clarified, straightening up with a wink at Valan. "Everything."

BLOODCHILD

THE PROBLEM, OF COURSE, despite his fine words to the contrary, was that Corvus didn't have control. Or not as much as he'd have liked, anyway.

Oh, Rilporin was mostly peaceful as the slaves adjusted to their new way of life and any uprisings were put down with the usual brutal efficiency, but the rest of the country was kindling awaiting a flame. And Mace fucking Koridam, General of the West Rank, was running around out there somewhere striking sparks.

Best guesses put him in Listre, but in the chaotic aftermath of the fall of Rilporin and the days afterwards with Mireces and East Rankers struggling to come to terms with the loss of the Dark Lady, the man could have marched past the city with drum, flute and flag and no one would have noticed.

Corvus had never had this much territory to control before and his influence—or lack of it—had never extended so far from his power base, and he'd never had to function with his heart torn from his chest.

The Dark Lady's absence was madness clawing at the edges of his mind, questioning his every decision, whispering at him to lie down and die. Every night, when he pulled a blanket around him, the temptation was there, at the tip of his dagger. Every morning, the grief mocked his cowardice. Corvus survived by packing the hurt down inside himself to fester, like an abscess beneath a tooth, buried and stinking.

It was different for the common Mireces and East Rankers—all they had to do was follow the orders given them by their leaders. For Corvus, his surviving war chiefs, Lanta and General Skerris, it was like trying to stand against an avalanche to make sure others survived. And what should have united them was driving them apart.

Two weeks after Rilporin's conquest, Skerris and the East had left the capital, flooding west and north to occupy the major towns along the Gil and the Tears to take control of supplies, stores, wealth and crops. It made military and economic sense, and it left Corvus with an altogether unfamiliar sense of loneliness. Despite his mild contempt for the fat general, Skerris was a talented commander and a faithful son of the Red Gods, and he needed someone he could trust in Sailtown. On the other hand, aside from the one-eared, snivelling Silais, Skerris was the only other who truly understood the workings of Rilpor. And he needed to restore order as soon as possible. The question was how—and which sort of order. Rilporian laws and customs, or Mireces? Prisons or executions? Persuasion or forced conversion?

It was a new way of life, requiring new thinking, and Corvus hated it.

Now that parts of the palace were habitable, he'd taken up residence there, as befitted the King of Rilpor and because he thought he should. There was a suite for the Blessed One, though she never used it. She never left the temple district or the shrine that she had constructed on the flagstones in the great temple square that were stained by the black splats and sweeps of divine blood. The site of the Dark Lady's manifestation and destruction.

Valan lived in the heir's quarters, both because they were close by and because he was, until Corvus produced a son, his successor. War chief Fost had a suite of rooms and so did the other surviving or newly made chiefs, but there was no communal living, no longhouse camaraderie like back home in Eagle Height. The palace was empty and Rilporin was too big. Corvus hated that, too.

Outside, the endless sounds of hammering and of dragging stone, the shouts of slave labourers and their Mireces overseers, painted a backdrop of noise both like and unlike his home village. *This is home now,* he reminded himself firmly. They had thousands of slaves, soldiers and civilians, though the number of deaths since their victory was far higher than the usual attrition rate as Mireces offered their wealth to the Red Gods, seeking to fill the voids in their souls with Rilporian blood.

In the last weeks they had cannibalised entire sections of the city to gather enough stone to fix the walls and wood to repair the gates, and while they weren't pretty, they were high and sturdy once more. Holy Gosfath had left them more than enough shattered stone after His rampage through the city to fling it at any enemy who approached, using the East Rank's trebuchets. Those slaves who were carpenters were attempting to fix the catapults and stingers, too. When Listre came, when any enemy came, they wouldn't find him unprepared.

They'd scoured the city: every house, alley, building and cellar had been looted of people and goods both. Corvus had given every Mireces two slaves, more wealth than some of the lowest warriors had ever had, but all were expected to lend them to the great rebuilding of the city. The remaining slaves were awarded to those who'd fought hardest. Corvus had accepted only six, three strong men and three pretty women, though the surviving war chiefs and most of the warriors had clamoured for him to take more. He declined; he had an entire country, and enough riches had survived the burning to tempt the greediest of men, something Corvus had never been, despite what his enemies said of him.

And so by seeming to take less than his due, his men cleaved still more closely to him. He would need such loyalty in the months to come. Rilpor might be beaten, but it wasn't subdued, not by a long way. More Mireces would die in the next few years than in an entire generation of raids. Perhaps more than they could afford to lose.

The marketplace that had once stood in the killing ground in First Circle was operating again, albeit run by the victors now, and the flesh trade was brisk as men bartered slaves for goods and goods for slaves. The sealing of the gates had done much to curb the escape attempts and the city was loud with Mireces voices, sullen with fear and pregnant with violence.

It almost felt like home—unlike the echoing palace.

"It's time to send Fost to fetch our women and children, Valan. It'll do much to steady the men, having their consorts and legacy back with them, and once the women are running the households and keeping the slaves in check, we can look to the rest of the country. There is still much work to be done. Besides, it will be good to hear more Mireces voices than Rilporian. The consorts will make the city our home, and this country ours too."

Valan grinned. "It will be good to see Neela and my girls again, I admit. I've been too long from them."

"That we could all find such contentment in the arms of a single woman," Corvus said, feeling his mood lighten. Teasing Valan for his unusual fidelity never got old.

"There's only one Neela, Sire. But perhaps you will find some pretty Rilporian who will walk the Dark Path at your side. The Lady's . . ." He faltered, tongue tripping over the words.

Corvus swallowed against the spike of hurt and he found the healing cuts on his left arm without conscious volition, wounds he'd carved into himself in the moments after Her destruction, blood that hadn't been enough to save Her.

"The Lady's will," he said deliberately, pressing against the stitches and offering the pain to the gods. "She's coming back, Valan. The Blessed One and high priest Gull work tirelessly. Whatever happened, She is still our Lady. Our pain calls to Her, the Blessed One calls to Her, and She will come back. She must."

"I pray it is so."

The old banter was swallowed by the new world and the loss of Her, and Corvus strode restlessly to the window. The fine glass was missing, but the view was one of industry and scars being repaired, and besides, the weather was warm down here in the flatlands and the breeze soft against his face, unlike the ice-edged winds of the Gilgoras Mountains. Everything down here was soft—the women, the weather, Rilporian courage.

A world rebuilt in honour of the Red Gods. Washed clean in blood. It would be hard, but it was his sacrifice to the gods. He would build paradise in Gilgoras for Them. His will—Their will—crystallised. "She will return, and She will look down on this new world we have dedicated to Her, and She will be pleased. All Rilpor will worship. And all Gilgoras will follow our example."

"Our feet are on the Path," Valan murmured and Corvus's mood lifted again. "Sire, the food situation isn't what we hoped. Some of the fires we set when taking the city burnt grain stores, and more was ruined or consumed by the defenders before they fled or were captured."

Corvus's mood dropped. He squinted out at the blue sky and strove for calm. "We've felt lack before, Valan. I know we expected rich bounty, but war is different to raiding. It'll be a lean harvest and a hard winter, but when Fost returns, they'll bring any stores they have left and all the livestock. If it's still not enough, we take more from the towns. Let winter cull the slave population so that when spring comes our people have plenty of land each and the optimum number of drudges to work it for them."

He turned back. "In the meantime, we need to deal with these fucking Evendooms. How many did Silais name?"

Valan consulted the papers scattered across a small table. "Fourteen, Sire. Women and bastards, mostly, but he's right: the Rilporians will be so desperate they'll rally to anyone with a drop of royal blood who might be able to save them. Simultaneous attacks?"

"I don't know if we've the numbers to spare," Corvus admitted; then he grinned. "Bring the royal women to me instead of killing them outright. Perhaps one of them will be pretty enough to rival even the luscious Neela. A consort of royal blood could legitimise my rule in the eyes of some, including Listre and Krike. If it allows us time to consolidate our hold and recruit more warriors from converted Rilporians, as well as crush any surviving rebellion within our borders, then I suppose I can lower myself to fucking a princess, illegitimate or not."

"A noble sacrifice," Valan said and chuckled.

Corvus returned to his throne. "Speaking of princesses, any news of my sister? She's a few months gone now, isn't she? The Blessed One is beginning to devise the ritual to bring back the Dark Lady"—another pain in his heart, hinting at the depths of agony rolling like a slow swell deep within—"but it would be better to have Rill in our possession in good time. With proper instruction, by the time she births the vessel that will hold our Bloody Mother, she'll have come round to our way of thinking." *And if not for your loyalty to skinny Neela, you could have had her, Valan. Then if I don't sire an heir, at least my blood still sits the throne when I am gone.*

"Nothing yet, Sire. The East Rank is consolidating its grip on the main towns and villages, recruiting from or replacing the local watchmen. There've been uprisings, of course, but nothing serious. They've all got a description of your sister, though."

"Tell them to keep looking and to send me those royal women," Corvus said, "and then get me Fost. It's time to make Rilpor a true home for the Red Gods and all the Mireces people." He stretched and gave a self-satisfied grunt as Valan's face lit up. "It's time to show our women and children the wealth of their new land."

TARA

*Seventh moon, first year of the reign of King Corvus
South barracks, Second Circle, Rilporin, Wheat Lands*

TOMAZ? TOMAZ, MY LOVE? Call to me, darling. Tell me where you are."
Tara rushed along the rows of beds with their manacled,
staring occupants, easily outstripping her guard, skirts bunched
in a sweaty fist and praying none of the soldiers outed her as one of them.
She passed an open-mouthed Captain Salter, a man who'd served under
her for a year and had never once in that time heard Tara call anyone "my
love." He looked down and away.

Too many weeks of eyes-down, mouth-closed hard labour and a ded-
ication to duty that would have astounded Mace, and Valan, her *owner*,
had finally allowed her to visit the makeshift prison and her husband.
Valan himself stood by the entrance with the other barracks guards, the
door open to clear some of the miasma of sweat, shit and sickness from
his delicate nostrils. Tara barely noticed it, both out of respect for the
Rankers chained here and because if this went wrong, she could measure
her remaining life in breaths, not years.

You better figure out the ruse fast, Tomaz my lad, or we're both dead.

"Slow down, wench," Bern, the barracks guard escorting her, grumbled, a note of warning in his voice.

Tara gritted her teeth and complied. "Forgive me, honoured, I am
anxious to see my beloved after so long. I've been so worried . . ."

"He's a heathen traitor, an enemy of Rilpor, and a bastard," Bern grunted. "You want to get anywhere in this life, you'd be better off finding yourself a real man. Your so-called marriage laws count for nothing now, remember. It's only because you belong to Second Valan that you haven't been fucked seven ways from midsummer already. Though I bet he's done a good job of showing you what a real man can do, hasn't he?"

Tara didn't answer. Instead she hurried for the row of small rooms at the rear of the barracks, the officers' quarters, where word had it that the captive high command were imprisoned. Not dead. Not dead yet, anyway.

"Tomaz?" she called again, and this time a bearded face appeared at the barred window in one of the heavy wooden doors. "Darling!" she shrieked, running to the door and pressing her face to the bars. "I'm your wife," she hissed. Major Tomaz Vaunt blinked once in confusion and Tara's stomach threatened to exit via her throat, and then the guard was unlocking the door and she shoved her way inside and fell into his arms, showering his face with kisses and clutching his unresponsive body to hers.

"Oh my love, my love," she said breathlessly, "I never thought I'd see you again. Oh, my darling Tomaz, my husband, my Tomaz."

Please, please, you fucking idiot. Play along.

She could feel the disbelief in Vaunt's rigid frame and dug her fingers hard into his back. He coughed. "Tara?" he said hoarsely and squeezed her to him. "You there," he added a moment later as Tara was swallowing tears of relief, "any chance you can piss off for a while? This is my wife."

The man staring through the door sniggered and made a few comments, but they heard the turning of the key in the lock. "One hour," Bern said, "and if you come out of there with a babe in your belly, you'll still work until you drop it. No light duties, no extra rations. And if Valan wants to put one in you, you'll abort it and thank him while you do, understand?" He spat at them, the thick glob of saliva clinging to the window bar, and left.

Tara gave it a few more minutes, murmuring endearments and pressing kisses to Vaunt's face and neck. He thawed quickly and soon enough was playing the part of loving husband with vigour.

Eventually, Tara pushed him away. "Put a curtain up over the window, my love," she said huskily and he grabbed up a blanket, hooked it awkwardly over the frame; they heard a cheer, and more ribald jests that made even Tara blush. As a soldier, she'd thought she'd heard them all. Apparently not. Fucking pig.

Vaunt sat cautiously next to her on the bed, close enough to drag her into an embrace if needed. "You're alive."

Tara snorted. "Of course I'm alive. What do you think I am, some soft Palace Ranker?"

Vaunt's mouth quirked. "No. Though you do appear to be married to one."

She shrugged. "I didn't fancy being passed around the Mireces, thought a high-ranking husband'd be my best bet. Working so far."

Vaunt shook his head. "What the actual bollocking fuck are you doing here, Major?" he hissed. "I mean here, in Rilporin? Last we heard, you were cut off in the city, no idea if you were dead or not. Why didn't you get out?"

Tara took a second to rub the taste of him off her mouth, her chest suddenly tight at his use of her rank. A reminder of who she really was, not this, this drudge, this *slave*.

I'm a soldier. An officer. I'm a godsdamned West Ranker.

"Assassination, rebellion, insurrection. The usual," she said flippantly, but Vaunt wasn't taken in by her act.

His face paled. "Assassination? Corvus?" he guessed and she blinked acknowledgment. He ran distracted hands through his hair. "That's a big ask, Carter."

She waved it away. "First things first: what do you know?"

He looked ready to argue, then slumped. "Not much. I haven't been out of this room since they caught us at the King Gate, even though the rest labour from dawn to dark every day repairing the walls and gates."

"All right, listen up. You're the only captives who haven't been sold as slaves yet," she told him. "You and any soldiers still alive in the north barracks, but as I have no reason to go there, I can't find out who's left. Everyone else, every other civilian, now belongs to someone. You belong to the city itself, or the Mireces as a group, maybe. I don't know why they haven't sold you, but it can't be out of a sense of fair play. So they've got something planned. I'm trying to find out what, but no luck so far. I'll keep digging."

"And you?"

She tapped the heavy metal collar around her neck. "Oh, I'm special, I am. I was *a gift* to Valan the king's second himself. Hence the need for a husband, though he's . . . got a sort of honour, in a way. Hasn't touched me yet, anyway."

"Carter—"

"I'm your wife. Get used to calling me Tara. And don't worry about it."

Vaunt was grim, but he didn't press and she was glad. "What else?"

"The East Rank has been sent up the Tears and the Gil to subdue the towns and villages and take a tax in food and goods to send here. So that means there're only Mireces guarding this place. That could give us an advantage."

"You want to start a riot?"

"I want to start a fucking war," Tara snarled and then interrupted herself with a string of endearments and a giggle she could tell by Vaunt's face he never expected to hear from her. The footsteps outside the cell paused and then carried on. More than one guard now, ready with their fists and clubs no doubt.

"My orders are to kill Corvus and Lanta too, and for that I'm going to need a distraction. I'll ready the palace slaves to fight and if we co-ordinate with an uprising among you lot, we can take this city back and kill every Mireces Raider we find, those two included."

"Shitting hell, Cart— Tara. You want to ghost Lanta and Corvus? That's insane. Don't get me wrong, it's a decent plan, but the risk is huge," Vaunt said; then he pressed a finger to her lips and listened hard. Tara held her breath until he shook his head slightly and gestured at her to continue.

"I think we're past worrying about risks. Besides, no one knows I'm a soldier," Tara said with more confidence than she felt. "I'm in a good position as Valan's property. There're a lot of logistics to work out, but it's doable. I wouldn't be here if it wasn't. But it's not just my orders. That Blessed Bitch Lanta has apparently come up with some insane plan to bring the Dark Lady back from death, a plan that involves Corvus's sister Rillirin, who's at large somewhere in Rilpor. Yes, I know how it sounds. The woman's touched by the moon, madder than a frog in a skillet, but she *believes*, so if it comes down to it, I reckon she needs killing more than

Corvus does. He's just a man, after all; she's got the power to resurrect a goddess."

Vaunt scrubbed his fingers through his short beard. "Maybe I'm the one who's gone mad," he muttered, "because that's the craziest bloody story I've ever heard."

"Try being on this side of the slave collar," Tara muttered and then threw Vaunt back on to the bed and followed him down, a leg over his hips. A sudden rattling of the door, shaking it hard enough to dislodge the blanket, and faces crowding the window.

Vaunt shouted a curse and tucked Tara behind him against the wall as if to shelter her. His acting was good, and she felt a sudden urge to stay there with him and let him protect her for real. *Just for an hour. Just a little while. Please, gods. Please.*

Colonel Dorcas's voice rose loud from the next room—cell—along, and the guards drifted reluctantly from the door again. Vaunt replaced the blanket, threading it between the bars this time to hold it firm.

He came back to the bed and managed a smile. "Good ears," he whispered approvingly, "I'd no idea they were there."

"You learn to sense it," she said and an involuntary shudder rippled down her back.

Some of the gleam went out of Vaunt's face. "Are you really all right? Have you been hurt?"

"Yes, I'm all right and yes, I've been hurt. What did you think would happen, I'd be showered with gifts? I'm a *thing*." She waved away his concern and her own scalding bitterness. "Sorry, ignore that. It's nothing I can't handle."

Again, he didn't press and again, she was grateful. "All right, I'll let this lot know we've got someone on the inside and to be ready to fight. With luck and the Dancer's grace, they'll get word to the soldiers in the north barracks too. Anything else?"

"Code words," Tara said. "Something to identify friendlies. It needs to be—"

Three metal-on-stone taps on the wall from the next room interrupted her and this time it was Vaunt who jumped on her, pinning her to the cot and forcing her legs apart with his knees.

Tara heard a mumbled "sorry" against her mouth before his hand was inside the neck of her gown and fumbling at her breast band. She stiffened, hooking her fingers into claws to drive at his eyes, when the lock rattled and the door swung open without so much as a knock.

"Godsfuckingdamnit, sir!" Vaunt roared, leaping up off Tara and leaving her thoroughly dishevelled, one breast peeking from its restraint and her skirts halfway up her thighs. Vaunt stalked towards the guards smirking and staring and poked Bern in the chest with his finger. "One hour, you said. One hour of privacy for myself and my wife. Get the fuck out of my quarters immediately!"

Tara scrunched against the wall next to the cot, tidying herself and not having to fake the shock and anxiety on her face. She held out an imploring hand. "Tomaz, darling, don't. They'll hurt you."

"Listen to the little wifey, soldier," Bern snarled, "or you'll lose that fucking finger and more besides." The flat of a dagger slapped Vaunt between the legs and he grunted, twitched and took a halting step back.

"Hour's up," Bern added and Tara slid off the bed.

"No, it bloody well isn't," Vaunt snapped and this time the guard sheathed his knife and then slapped him so hard across the face it spun him around. His eyes narrowed to murderous slits and Tara stepped quickly past him.

"Your will, honoured," she said quietly, eyes downcast.

"It isn't," Vaunt insisted, but Tara turned and put her palms on the sides of his face.

"Hush now, don't make them angry. I'll be back soon." She kissed him, and even meant it this time, wanting something of warmth and softness to remember. Something real. It seemed Vaunt wanted the same, because he wrapped his arms around her and his mouth parted under hers and his tongue flicked, gentle as a butterfly's wing, over hers.

And then he pushed her away. "Stay safe, Tara," he murmured. "Do as you're told and no harm will come to you. I love you."

"I love you too. I'll visit again soon, I swear it."

Vaunt kissed her knuckles. "I'll be ready," he promised, his eyes telling her they all would. She stepped back, nodded once, and then walked to the open door and the waiting Mireces.

"Touch her and I'll kill you," she heard Vaunt promise as she left the room. It didn't matter that the threat was empty; it comforted her nonetheless.

Bern fell in beside her, the other guard behind, as they walked the length of the barracks through the shit-stinking, red-stained gloom of a thousand shackled, despairing men. Salter gave her the barest nod, which she ignored.

"Get yer wet, did he?" Bern asked as they reached the exit; Valan was just outside. Tara didn't answer. "Asked you a question, bitch," he grunted.

"I am an officer's wife," Tara said, "and that is no sort of question to ask a lady."

Bern's hand was big enough to encircle her throat and he slammed her back-first into the wall next to the door. "You are a fucking slave," he muttered, teeth stained and cracked and foul breath blowing in her face. "You are fucking nothing."

"You're right," Tara gasped, struggling to prise his fingers away. "I am a slave. I am Second Valan's slave. I belong to him, not you." Her collar was biting into her neck under his hand and she could feel the sting of skin parting.

"Asked if he got you wet," Bern grunted. "You don't answer, I got to find out for myself. Don't need no fucking permission for that."

"Stop," she choked. "Please. Please, honoured."

The worst of it, she thought as Bern's fingers dragged up her skirts and she pushed at arms thicker than her thighs, wasn't even what he was doing. It wasn't that she couldn't kill him without revealing herself as more than a simple slave woman, even though she could practically taste his death she wanted it so badly.

No. The worst was that she could just make out, over his shoulder, the faces of both Major Vaunt and Colonel Dorcas at their windows. Dorcas turned away, unable to watch, but Vaunt was bellowing threats and curses in their direction. Tara closed her eyes.

You die first, Bern.

Believe me, shithead, you die first.

"What is this?" The voice was soft and cold and very, very lethal. Bern disappeared, to the sound of flesh smacking flesh and tearing cloth. Tara looked down at a long rip in her skirt. Her thigh was visible, as were the red fingerprints Bern had left in her skin. The man himself was sitting on his arse and clutching his bleeding mouth.

She fell to her knees in front of Valan. "Forgive me, honoured, forgive me. I didn't want . . . but he insisted and I, I was afraid. My husband is so angry, but . . ." She let the tears come, tears from weeks of fear and responsibility and grief. "I told Bern that I belong to you now." She whispered the last, casting a guilty glance in Vaunt's direction, and then dared to look Valan in the eye. "Although my heart forever belongs with Tomaz. Please don't hurt him for my error, lord."

Valan hauled her to her feet, not unkindly. "The error was not yours. The error was Bern's, who failed to realise that a slave collar means a woman is *fucking claimed by another*." He roared the last in Bern's face and all of them flinched.

Bern fought his way to his feet. "Just checking that fucking Ranker hadn't had a go at her," he whined. "Didn't want you raising no bastard of a Rilporian."

"Touch her again and I'll cut your cock off, roast it and make you eat it—do you understand?"

Bern spat blood. "Aye, Second," he said, tone sullen and eyes defiant. "I understand."

"Get out." Bern and the other guard sidled through the barracks entrance and Valan glared at the men chained closest. They turned away. He put a finger beneath Tara's chin and raised her head. "Did he hurt you?"

She looked into his face and let a hint of fire show through. "Yes. But that is the lot of a slave, isn't it? To be hurt."

Valan's mouth twitched, as though he appreciated her answer even as he didn't deny its truth. "Bern won't bother you again, but if he does, tell me. Work hard, do as you're told, and you can visit your husband again."

"Yes, honoured," Tara said and followed him from the barracks, absurdly grateful for his intervention. Vaunt's kiss was still on her mouth, but it was Valan who'd kept her safe.

THE BLESSED ONE

Seventh moon, first year of the reign of King Corvus
Red Gods' temple, temple district, First Circle, Rilporin, Wheat Lands

Sire, how may I serve?"

If Corvus resented having to trek through the city to the temple in order for her to "serve" him, it didn't show on his face. Nothing showed on Corvus's face but what he wanted people to see.

She padded out of the shadows of the temple and watched him drink in the sight of her, the godblood adorning her skin, the marks and the wisdom they imparted painting her in truth and promise and hope. The blood of the Dark Lady, stained forever in swirls and sigils on Lanta's body, tingling and whispering like the breath of a lover.

She curtseyed and he offered a stiff nod in return, declined wine or water or food. Annoyed, then, and straight to business. Lanta suppressed a sigh.

"We have thousands of slaves and not enough food to feed them all," Corvus said. Lanta blinked. What did she care about stinking Rilporians? "You said we would offer a mass sacrifice to bring back the Bloody Mother, and yet there is still no date set for the ritual. May I know the reason for the delay, Blessed One?"

"You think hungry slaves determine when a work as great as this will be carried out?" she asked. "This is why you come to me, interrupt our devotions, our ritual-crafting?" She stood in a swirl of skirts. "I don't have time for this."

"Hungry slaves are rebellious slaves," Corvus said doggedly, staying her with his voice. "I have sent Fost to bring home the women and children from the mountains; soon the city will have even more mouths to feed. You told me to spare as many lives as possible for your great rite and there are two prison barracks bursting with angry, hungry soldiers and I cannot keep them alive indefinitely. Would you have me take bread from our young to give to them?"

"I would have you do your job as king and sort out such matters. Do you need me to wipe your arse for you as well?" She was tired and frustrated—the ritual they needed didn't exist and she and high priest Gull had no previous lore to draw upon—but still, she shouldn't have said it. The temperature in the room plummeted, chilled by the ice in Corvus's expression.

Lanta inhaled through flared nostrils. "Sire, forgive my hasty words. I am very tired. I thought I had made myself clear—the slaves will be needed in the great rite that restores the Dark Lady to us in the body of your sister's child."

Corvus thumped the arm of his chair. "You want me to keep them alive until—when, Yule? Another half-year? Impossible!"

"This is the richest country in Gilgoras, Sire. Are you telling me you cannot find enough grain to feed slaves a starvation diet? I need their bodies and blood and fear, not sleek muscles and healthy minds. They can be raving skeletons for all I care, just keep them alive."

"We trampled through most of the Wheat Lands during the siege. We have ruined half the crop." Corvus was standing too now, anger gleaming just below the frustration.

"Then it is a good thing we only need to feed the half of the population that walks the Dark Path," Lanta snapped. "Sire, please. I don't have time to come up with all the answers for you. Back in Eagle Height you made it clear that I should confine myself to spiritual matters while you dealt with the rest, and now you come here expecting me to magic bread out of the air and take control of those very matters you have excluded me from. I cannot. I will not."

"We will have a rebellion on our hands, Blessed One. Slaves and Mireces will die in that rebellion."

Lanta gritted her teeth. "You swore that everything you did was for the glory of the gods. They need more than glory now; They need an act of faith so enormous that it returns the Dark Lady to us. All other considerations are as nothing in the face of that. What we are attempting has never been done and I will not have you jeopardise it. I will not, so I don't care where you get it from, just find the food and keep my sacrifices alive until I need them."

Corvus's hand was squeezing the hilt of his dagger, but not in threat, she thought. "You ask too much."

"The gods always ask too much, Sire," she said softly. "And we always provide Them with what They demand. We are Mireces; sacrifice is in our blood."

He had no answer to that, of course, as she'd known he wouldn't. It furthered his frustration and added another crack in the bond that had united king and Blessed One thus far in their great conquest. Corvus stalked from the temple without another word, and when he was gone Gull detached himself from the shadows and joined her.

"You are concerned?" he asked.

"He was the perfect king to lead us to victory—even a victory such as this, that cost us our Bloody Mother. But is he the king to rule Rilpor in the gods' names? Is he the king who will do all that is necessary to see Them ascendant?"

"You doubt his loyalty?" Gull was surprised.

"Never," Lanta responded instantly, and was a little surprised to find it was the truth. "I doubt his . . . ability. Corvus is a killer and a leader of men, but is he a governor? Can he provide for his people and keep the slaves in their places? When he killed King Liris, he took over an established and stable world. This one he is building from scratch and I don't think he knows how. I don't think he really wants to."

"He wants to go to war."

Lanta rocked her head from side to side. "He knows war, but he knows subjugation too. Sending the East Rank rather than Mireces to occupy the towns and villages was a master stroke—it's easier to give up your liberty to people who look and sound like you. But taxes and crops and laws? Where's the glory and excitement in that?"

"Do you want him removed?" Gull asked.

Lanta pursed her lips. "Not yet: we need stability, at least for now. Corvus understands the importance of keeping the slaves alive; despite his frustration here, he will not risk the great rite out of pettiness. But he needs aid, someone who can teach him what he needs to know, provide answers to the questions he doesn't know how to ask."

"I may be able to help with some of the governance," Gull offered. "I was a silk merchant here in Rilporin for a decade. I understand trade, supply and demand."

Lanta turned away from the door through which Corvus had exited. "Your offer is generous, but I need you here. Corvus will monopolise you if he thinks he can pass such things into your hands. But if there are others among the slaves who would suit . . ."

Gull nodded and left her, understanding her moods well enough, and Lanta wandered through what had once been the Dancer's temple and was now sworn and blooded to Holy Gosfath and His absent Sister-Lover. Not dead. Absent. It was the only way she could bring herself to think about it despite the great work they were preparing, despite her every waking—and some dreaming—moments being dedicated to it.

She passed the godpool, sanctified now with the blood of scores of sacrifices so that the once-clear water was red-tinged and thick, clotted and reeking. It was unpleasant, but the last of the Light needed to be chased from this newly hallowed place. Besides, it served as a potent reminder to any slave who thought to raise the defiant eye to their betters.

As always, her footsteps led her outside and into the temple square, to the wooden, open-sided shelter that had been erected over the place where the Dark Lady had been taken from them, the ground still stained with Her divine blood, much as Lanta was herself. There was someone in the shrine, kneeling on the unmarked stone and staring fixedly at the black droplets just in front of him. He looked up at her approach, and scrambled to his feet.

"Second Valan, forgive me. I had no wish to intrude on your prayers."

He bowed, his eyes running hungrily over the marks on her skin. He wanted to touch them, as he wanted to touch the stains on the stone. He didn't dare. "It is I who should beg forgiveness. If this place belongs to anyone, it belongs to you."

Lanta sat on one of the benches circling the shrine and gestured for him to join her. "It belongs to us all, Second. You are welcome here whenever you wish, but if you are looking for Corvus, he has left."

Valan was silent for a while. "I was not," he said. "I came here to pray for my family. Their journey is long and may be perilous, and Ede is only three." He met her eyes briefly and Lanta noted the flash of indecision. She gave him a reassuring smile. "I worry my daughters won't remember me," he confessed in a rush. "What will they have been through while I was here fighting? What trials or sicknesses that I could not comfort? They might not even be alive now."

Lanta was surprised. Valan rarely spoke of his family and she couldn't even remember his consort's name. Such open love was rare among Mireces men, such loyalty even rarer. "Their lives will have been what the gods decreed for them," she said. "Be at peace knowing that if they suffered, they did so to prove their devotion. But there is no saying they did," she added.

They sat in silence for a while longer. "You are a good man, Valan," Lanta said and he blinked in surprise. "I hope Corvus knows how lucky he is to have you as his second."

"The honour is mine," Valan said automatically. "My life to serve."

"Yes," Lanta said, examining him in light of the idea sitting fresh and a little shocking in her mind. "We are all put in Gilgoras to serve the gods and do Their will, whatever it may be." She stood and he rose with her. "I will pray for your family," she said and strode back towards the temple before he could respond.

DOM

Seventh moon, first year of the reign of King Corvus
Green Ridge, Southern Krike

THEY'D GIVEN THE THREE of them a small house to sleep in, the Two-Eyed Man and his faithful companions. Or faithful companion, singular. Dom wasn't sure he qualified. Dom wasn't sure Crys and Ash would allow him to qualify, regardless of his own opinions on the matter.

As the sun went down, the others had gone to the town's council house and Dom had stayed behind. He lay on the floor, head pillowed on a pile of blankets, and watched the flickers of orange light dancing among the roof beams and spiders' webs. He'd managed to untie and retie the laces of his trousers eleven times, each one a victory against the memory of the crushing embarrassment at asking Ash—a man he'd once considered a brother and who now hated him—to help him in the first days after the loss of his hand.

But being able to take a piss unaided and being able to fight were two different things. Dom hadn't managed to scavenge a weapon when they'd fled Rilporin, but he'd found a reasonably sharp knife in the kitchen that might break the skin of an enemy if they didn't mind holding still for a while.

He snorted and spun the blade awkwardly in his fingers, his right hand so less nimble than the one he'd lost, and fumbled it so the hilt knocked against the stump of his arm and sent a bolt of lightning through the twisted nerves and flesh. He yelped at the pain, and then did it again because it felt, in some indefinable way, good, opening a well inside him he hadn't realised was there and demanding he jump in.

Dom sat up. Holding his breath, he jabbed the tip of the knife into the scar tissue this time. More lightning, searing up his arm and into his heart until it seemed to skip in his chest and pump delight and darkness. A bead of blood formed along the knife tip and he stared at it with unblinking intensity, fascinated by the firelight reflected in miniature in the crimson. He pushed harder, a little deeper, more blood welling and with it relief. Purpose. All the promises he'd told himself and Crys—all the lies—fell away to reveal the red, sharp-toothed truth.

The words came of their own volition, words of power and ecstasy and glorious surrender. "Dark Lady, beautiful goddess of fear and death, accept this my offering. Holy Gosfath, Lord of War . . ."

And there He was, the God of Blood looming over Dom in the sudden echoing darkness of the Waystation between Gilgoras and the Afterworld. Dom's breath stuttered, mingled longing and terror freezing his thoughts. How was he here? How had Gosfath summoned him with such ease, such swiftness? And for what?

Yet Gosfath ignored him, sitting in the flames of His own burning, wrists resting on His bent knees as He watched His own shadow writhe and dance across the cavern's wall. Tongues of red fire licked His red skin; He paid it no more attention than He did Dom.

Dom took a stealthy step backwards, and then another, but however he'd arrived, that path was closed to him. He was here until Gosfath said otherwise. Trapped. Bladder clenching, Dom eased himself to his knees. "I am here, Lord." The god didn't respond. "Holy Gosfath, Red Father, what is your will?"

Now He did move. The great horned head rose ponderously in his direction, and small black eyes, dancing fire reflected in their depths, met Dom's. If the god recognised him as the murderer of His Sister-Lover, Dom had no doubt he'd be killed, slowly, over months or years, for Gosfath's pleasure.

"Gone."

The word was so loud and huge, the meaning behind it so vast, that Dom struggled to process it. All the loss and hurt that filled Dom to the brim was as nothing; Gosfath's pain would drown the spaces between the stars, His rage hotter than those distant points of light, His loss a winding-sheet black enough and big enough to cover the face of Gilgoras itself.

Gosfath raised both hands, palms up in an expression so human, so lost and bewildered, that Dom's throat constricted with shared grief. "Gone."

"We'll bring Her back," he said impulsively, his hand extended towards Gosfath's, finger to black talon. It was razor-sharp and Dom sealed the oath with blood.

"Gone," Gosfath repeated, as though Dom hadn't spoken, and the pain tore his heart into shreds.

"What are you doing?"

Ash's voice was so sudden, the return to the firelit room in Green Ridge so unexpected, that Dom yelped and the knife scored a deep cut through the remains of his arm as he stumbled to his feet. He yelped again and dropped the blade.

"Gods, you scared me," he said shakily, pressing the hem of his shirt to the cut and backing rapidly behind the table.

"I said, what are you doing?" Ash demanded, following him. "Who were you speaking to? You were making promises. Which lord?"

Dom blushed and retreated again until his back was against the wall. "I didn't, it wasn't, it's not what you think," he tried, but Ash reached out a long arm and hauled him close so that Dom was forced to look up at him.

"You better not have been doing what it sounded like you were doing," he snarled. "I came back because Crys sent me to fetch you, because he wants to find a way forward, a way for you both to live with what you did to him—aye, and what he did to you. Though if he hadn't cut that hand off, it would've killed you. But he sent me here because he's not healing and neither are you and we need you both if we're to have any hope of winning this. And I was starting to think we had a chance, that today was the beginning of something, and then I walk in here to find you cutting yourself and praying to the *Red fucking Gods*."

Dom couldn't meet his eyes. Shame and the hollowed-out emptiness of grief churned uneasily together. His vision blurred with tears and he kept his head down, blinking savagely. *He brought me into His presence. So desperate is He for companionship that He'll snatch at anything offered Him. Even me.*

Ash's arms came around him, one hand pressed to the back of his head, an embrace Dom neither expected nor deserved. He hesitated, snatched out of his thoughts and into this most surprising of moments. Gingerly, he hugged Ash back. More tears, and a wrenching pain deep inside that would never go away.

"I'm broken, Ash," he whispered, and the confession was a catharsis. "There's nothing left of me, nothing inside but hurt and hate and death." He tightened his arms, wanting to hold Ash to him even though he knew the archer must be disgusted. "I crave Her, Ash, Her touch, the . . . delight of the agony She brought, as wrong as I know that is. I don't know how to live without Her. Everything the Dark Lady did to me was cruel, evil, but . . . I still love Her. I always will."

He heard Ash swallow, felt him lean away, just a finger's width, but one that threatened to become a chasm they could never bridge. "But you have to live without Her," he whispered. "Because She's gone and She's not coming back, no matter what crazy plans that blue-clad bitch has. We're going to stop the Mireces, stop Lanta, and then send Gosfath into death after His Sister. And you're going to help us do it, because that's what we do, it's who we are." He pushed him away to arm's length, hands on his shoulders. "It's who you are, as well, deep down."

"Is it?" Dom whispered, the remembered expression in Gosfath's face mirrored now in his own. "When all I can think of are ways to help the Blessed One? When every night is haunted with dreams of Her even though every day all I long for is to see Rillirin again? There's even a part of me that would offer up her and our child if it would bring back the Dark Lady, and I hate it, I hate myself, but I can't stop."

Revulsion flashed across Ash's scarred face and now he did let go, took a decisive step away. To the other side of that chasm. "Yeah? Well, we don't always get what we want, do we?" He touched the notch in his jaw, another scar just visible through the open neck of his shirt. "I got killed by Galtas; didn't want that. Crys got tortured—by you; he didn't want that. The man I love above all others is a fucking god, and one that you prophesied would have to die to end this war, or have you forgotten your own words? 'And the godlight will lead us, to death and beyond'. Do you really think either of us want *that*? Because Crys knows this will kill him, he knows there's no coming back from this, and he's doing it anyway. Because he understands."

"Understands what?" Dom whispered across the gulf, trying to reach his friend. Failing.

"That sacrificing his life to save Gilgoras is worth it. That doing everything he can to spare innocents from the horrors of the Dark Path is worth it. That"—Ash swallowed again, thickly this time—"that me losing him is worth it."

He cleared his throat and blinked hard. "You killed Her, which was the only good thing you did in those months of your madness, and you're not going to return there no matter how much you want to. I'll kill you myself rather than see you lost to Blood again. So you're going to help us make sure She stays dead, and you're going to repent for the lives you took and the betrayals you perpetrated, because otherwise—" He broke off, perhaps knowing that no threat he made could ever scare a man who wanted to give himself, body and soul, to madness.

"And believe me, you have no idea how much courage it's taken Crys to send me here with the prospect of forgiveness. It's certainly not something I suggested, because I have seen every last one of those scars you put into him, and those that live only on the inside, too, that even he might not know are there."

Ash paused to get his voice back under control. "Those are the scars we'll have to deal with when this is all over, if any of us are alive to do so. Those are the ones that will define the rest of his life, his ability to sleep peacefully, our chance at happiness. Those are the ones I don't want you to ever forget inflicting. And with all that said, he's still trying to find a way to forgive you."

Dom's chest was heaving with repressed sobs. "Can he? Can you?" he choked out.

Ash's face twisted. "No. Maybe. I don't know. But I do know he's the one you pray for," he added, jerking a finger out at the night. "Pray for Crys, and pray to the Fox God. Not Her, never again Her. Got it?"

"Got it." Dom licked his lips and nodded, looking away. "Are you . . . going to tell him?"

"Are you going to do it again?"

Dom shook his head—and meant it.

"Then no. But don't let him down like that again."

Ash picked up the knife Dom had used and examined its edge, then shoved it deliberately through his belt. Dom fidgeted, wanting to ask for it back, knowing how it would sound. No hand, no weapons, no way to hurt himself or others. Bitterness rose in him to mingle with the guilt, the hope, the grief.

Ash wiped his hands on his shirt as though they'd touched something foul. "Come on, then," he said in a voice cold as an axe blade. "He still wants to see you."

CRYS

Seventh moon, first year of the reign of King Corvus
The Belt, Krike

GREEN RIDGE COULD FIELD two hundred warriors, and all of them followed Crys when he left the town three days later. He'd expected to leave them behind, pick them up on his way back through towards Rilpor, but they elected to follow him instead.

"And by follow," Crys hissed to Ash on the fourth day out of Green Ridge and through the thick pine forests known as the Belt, "I mean everywhere. I'm pretty sure I saw one watching me have a shit yesterday."

Ash glanced behind at the Krikites; Crys didn't. He knew what he'd see. Cutta Frog-dream walked half a dozen paces behind with Dom, and behind them were ranged the warriors. They watched his every move like stoats watching a rabbit burrow. Unblinking.

"Yeah, that's creepy," Ash said when he turned back. "But they'll get used to it. I have, despite the yellow eyes lighting up the night when I'm trying to sleep."

"You think you're hilarious, don't you?" Crys demanded, tapping his fingers on the pommel of his sword; he'd traded the axe he'd brought with him and the new blade was decent quality, well weighted. However curious about him they were, the Krikites at least boasted some talented smiths. The pine needles underfoot were springy, lending energy to his steps, the rich scent sharp in his nose. He had an urge to sprint off ahead and leave them all behind—leave everything behind. Prophecies and legends and the prospect of war.

Ash pressed his lips together but couldn't suppress a hoot of laughter. "It's not their fault," he said with an air of implausible seriousness, "they've never actually met a god before. I don't think any of them expected you to be so handsome. Oh yes, I've seen the women—and a fair few men— eyeing you up, don't think I haven't. Should I be jealous?"

"Hilarious," Crys muttered again, blushing. "You have no idea how weird this is, though. Half the time I think I've just gone mad and no one's had the heart to tell me."

"Crys, my love, you've gone mad. We just didn't have the heart to tell you."

"Stop it," he snapped. Ash raised his eyebrows. "I'm not who they think I am. I mean, I am, but I'm me too. No one wants to know me; they just want to see Him. *I'm* invisible."

"You looked pretty visible when you were getting dressed this morning," Ash teased. "I remember it distinctly. The manly sweep of shoulders, the pale curve of your arse—"

"This is serious," Crys almost screamed, fingers curling into claws in his hair. "I don't know who I am any more."

We're us, the Fox God said, as if it was simple.

"You're you, you're Crys, heart-bound to Ash." Ash echoed the internal words so closely it was eerie. The laughter fell from his face. "You're mine," he added, "and you were mine before all this happened. You'll be mine again afterwards."

"I'll be dead afterwards," Crys said and the silence between them then was so profound he nearly fell into it. He caught Ash's hand in his, waiting for his lover to denounce his words. He didn't and Crys's gut twisted within him. Every time they'd skirted the subject before, Ash had been vehement in his denials. Now, maybe because of what had happened with the Fox God and the stone in Green Ridge, his opinion had changed. He believed Crys was going to die and that meant Crys believed it too, bone-deep for the first time. Nothing could save him.

And the godlight will lead us all, to death and beyond. Thanks Dom, you always were a cheery fucker even before you tried to kill me.

Crys glanced back to where the calestar walked alongside Cutta Frogdream. The knowing that had meant nothing for so long, that had been empty words easily forgotten, was coming true. The Fox God brushed against him, reassurance and gentle mockery, humour and love. Crys pushed Him away, feeling as if he was an intruder in his own body.

"Maybe none of this would've happened if you hadn't brought me back," Ash said and Crys registered the guilt in his face. "I mean, you made that promise in return for me. If you hadn't—"

"If I hadn't I'd already be dead," Crys said, squeezing his hand hard and feeling a flush of guilt himself. He'd never considered how Ash must feel. They stopped walking. "I'd have got myself killed during the siege. Nothing mattered to me in those minutes when I knew you were dead, love. Nothing. I'd have made any promise, done anything, to have you back. And . . . the Fox God was always here, I know that now. He'd have found a way out when He needed to, no matter what. This way I got you. I got a whole life to cram into however long we have, and I intend to make the most of it. If you want?"

Ash wiped at his eye with a thumb, his palm sweaty in Crys's grip. "I want," he said in a scratchy voice. "I want it all, but I'll settle for this. For you and these next . . ." He trailed off.

Crys swallowed and forced a smile. "Days. Weeks. Months. How about we don't count?"

"Numbers are overrated," Ash said, and although it wasn't funny, they laughed anyway.

The snake of warriors had come to a halt behind them instead of carrying on, waiting in a respectful hush. Crys faced Cutta. "We'll catch you up," he said. She paused; then she nodded and led her warriors on.

"What's wrong?" Ash asked before he caught the glint in Crys's eye. "Oh. *Oh.* Catch you up. Got it." His smile was hot. "Well, you know what they say: a bow long bent grows weak. Some time off should do us both some good."

They wandered off the main track and Crys could feel eyes on them as they went, knowing they were seen. He squeezed Ash's hand. He didn't care.

YOU REALLY NEED TO stop saying 'gods' when we make love," Ash said later, leaning on one elbow to pick pine needles from Crys's hair. "It's like you're talking to yourself."

Crys felt a flicker of annoyance at the words and suppressed it ruthlessly. Instead he arched an eyebrow. "Didn't hear you complaining about my godlike abilities," he said.

Ash screwed up his face and slapped his bare shoulder, laughing. "Damnit, you're not supposed to join in the teasing. I don't have an answer to that one. As long as my merely mortal prowess is enough for you."

"Oh, it's enough," he murmured, "believe me."

Ash ran gentle fingers over the myriad silver scars in Crys's skin and Crys relaxed, enjoying the caresses in the aftermath of their urgency. "Not sure when we'll have time to be together again," he murmured eventually, knowing he was breaking the moment, unable to stay quiet. "Especially not once we're back in Rilpor. Just because Mace didn't arrest us when he found out doesn't mean we can shove it in their faces."

"I have no intention of shoving anything in Mace's face," Ash protested and Crys smiled. "But you're right, I suppose. Let's just hope your godhood means we don't get arrested at all."

"Godhood? Is that a more impressive name for man—"

Ash clapped his hand over Crys's mouth. "Worst. Joke. Ever," he warned, though he was struggling not to laugh. Crys kissed the palm against his lips, moved it aside and replaced it with Ash's mouth.

"Hate to say this, but we need to get back," Ash said after another breathless few minutes. "Unless you want Cutta's warriors spying on this too."

Crys grunted, horrified by the thought, and that's when the attack came.

The Fox God screamed warning and Crys was up and on his feet, scanning their surrounds, an instant before the first warrior sprinted from the trees into the glade. "Up!" he roared at Ash and leapt in between him and the assailant, naked and shining silver. The attacker, stunned by the nudity or perhaps Crys's strange markings, missed his strike. Crys slapped the spear down and this time the warrior didn't hesitate, driving the butt end towards him in a flat trajectory that just skimmed the flesh of his belly as he jumped backwards.

Four more pounding out of the trees, and Ash's arrows took three but missed the fourth, who ducked and threw himself on to the archer. Crys's new sword was somewhere beneath their clothes with his belt and dagger and the rest of Ash's weapons, and the spearman was fast. Very fast.

Surely he could just let himself be skewered and then heal?

Move, the Fox God barked. Crys moved. He couldn't get inside the spear's reach, so he led his attacker further into the trees where the weapon's length would be a hindrance. Jabs came fast and hard, aiming for his naked chest or gut, and Crys was feeling backwards with his bare feet; if he tripped, he was dead.

A grunt ratcheting up into a scream from the clearing and Crys's blood turned to ice. If that was Ash . . . The spearman attacked, sensing his distraction. Crys jinked right and the spear tip scored a hot, ripping line through the inside of his upper arm. He bellowed hurt and got the tree between them, a second's rest, wasted it looking for Ash instead of a weapon.

The spear came around the bole and Crys leapt high, left hand closing around a branch. Tucking his feet, he pulled himself into the tree, on to the branch—too thin to support his weight—skipped out along it and threw himself off the end even as it began to crack.

He landed in a tumble, came up on to his feet and burst into the clearing. Ash, on his back in the leaf-litter, brawling.

Sword. Crys dived forward, scooped up the weapon by its scabbard and clubbed Ash's attacker between the shoulder blades as though he was splitting wood, reversed the blade and ripped it free, spun to deflect the spear thrust with the scabbard and punched the sword into the spearman's ribs.

His attacker dropped his weapon to clutch at the wound and Crys spun again, almost dizzy with it, but Ash rammed an arrow in his enemy's thigh, fishing for and finding the main artery, and people rarely think about killing someone when their life is pumping out of their leg.

Ash heaved the man off him and staggered to his feet, gasping and wiping blood out of his eyes. Two of the three he'd put down with arrows were dead, the third wounded and trying to crawl to safety. Ash went over and stamped on his back, shoving him into the dirt.

"Start talking," he growled as Crys finished the other two, who were dying already, and then crouched at the injured man's side. One side of his head was shaved and tattooed with a stylised hare.

"Shit," he breathed. "Krikites."

"Fucking Rilporians!" the man raged. "The Seer-Mother has forbidden you to set foot in Krike! All Rilporians to be killed on sight. We'll lend you no aid in your war!" He had an arrow in his shoulder, through and through, and he was pale with shock and blood loss.

"The Seer-Mother made this pronouncement, not the Warlord?" Ash demanded. "Who is she to give such orders?"

"The Seer-Mother sees all, knows all," the Krikite snarled, hand clamped around the arrow. He groaned. "The Warlord bows to her wisdom."

"Wisdom?" Crys spat as the Fox God rumbled discontent. "This is not wisdom. Has the Seer-Mother forgotten her oath to Trickster and Dancer? To me?"

"You?" the Krikite tried, but then he squeaked as Crys's eyes flared yellow. "Rilporian demon," he muttered. "Please. Don't hurt me."

"I'm not going to hurt you, Hare-dream," Crys said, touching the tattoo. "But the Seer-Mother is wrong in this. Rilpor needs aid and sends me to garner it. I am no demon, Krikite. I am the Fox God and you will lead me to your people."

"You what?" the man asked, and then gasped as Ash snapped the tail from the arrow in his shoulder.

"Waste of a good shaft," he murmured as he bent the man forward and and drew it on through and out, fighting the sucking pull of the flesh. The man screeched and thick pulses of blood leaked from the entry and exit wounds. Ash batted his hand away. "Go on, then. Do it."

Crys put his palms against the wounds and let the light rise. The man's pain became terror, became awe, and by the time it was done, the fervour of belief shone in his face. He looked at the place where the arrow had been and flexed his arm, then at the newly sealed scar in Crys's own arm from the spear thrust.

Ash helped him to his feet. "When they ask, you tell them the Fox God Himself spared your life and then saved your life. Wait here."

The Krikite's jaw was slack and he held out a wondering hand, brushing it gently over the scars on Crys's chest. "I see you, Lord."

Crys straightened his shoulders. "And I see you."

They dressed hurriedly and Crys looked at those they'd killed, wondering whether he should have tried to save them.

There have to be consequences, the Fox God told him.

Ash buckled his belt and winced as the adrenaline faded and the hurts made themselves known. "One way to start a legend," he sighed. "No healing for me," he said, slinging an arm around Crys's shoulders and pressing a kiss to his temple. "I don't know if you've got a limit on that silver light, but use it for something more important than bruises. Besides, sometimes we should hurt. Keeps us sharp."

Crys squeezed his waist. "You're wiser than you look, heart-bound," he said. "One of the reasons I love you. But let's catch up with Cutta before anyone else decides to try and kill us."

"Once this one tells his tale to all who'll listen, we'll have even more warriors on our side. At this rate we won't even need to meet the Warlord," Ash said as they began walking, pointing to the Krikite now following so closely he almost trod on Crys's heels.

Crys frowned. "No. There's something I can't quite put my finger on, but I have to go to Seer's Tor. There's something wrong in Krike. All those stories I learnt in the South Rank, everything I told you before Green Ridge about the Krikites and their way of life . . . well, we haven't seen any of that, have we? No, there's something going on here." He shrugged. "Besides, it's only fair to meet the man we're stealing warriors from and give him the chance to join us."

"Think he will?" Ash asked.

"I really don't know."

T HE KRIKITE'S NAME WAS Sati Hare-dream, and when he burst into Belt Town shouting news of the Two-Eyed Man, Crys was relieved to find Cutta and her warriors already there. He didn't much fancy explaining having killed four of their number and then asking them to ally with him and Rilpor.

Cutta's relief at seeing them again was palpable, and it was clear she'd already spent some time trying to convince the town elders of Crys's double identity, because they didn't fall about laughing at Sati's pronouncement.

"Where is the rest of your hunting party, Hare-dream?" an elder asked and Ash tensed.

"In our ignorance we attacked the Two-Eyed Man and his lover," Sati said. "It was the Lord's will only I survived."

I wouldn't say will, exactly, Crys thought. *More like terror.* He decided it wouldn't be particularly godlike to tell them that, though.

"I would be happy to speak with your priests," he said instead. The elders exchanged mutters and embarrassed looks. "You do have priests?"

"The Seer-Mother dispenses wisdom from the tor," Cutta said when no one would answer him. "I told you this."

Crys rounded on her. "You mean there are no priests left in the whole of Krike, not just Green Ridge? What did you do, kill them?"

"Of course not," Cutta protested. "But when the Seer-Mother's gifts made them obsolete, they were given other work."

"Horseshit," Ash muttered. Even Dom looked shocked and Crys couldn't remember an expression other than self-pity on the calestar's face since they'd left Rilporin. He swallowed bitterness and put him out of his mind.

"What is a community without priests?"

"The Seer-Mother dispenses judgement," Sati ventured.

"I did not say judgement; I said community. Your priests are still here—you have just stopped recognising their wisdom. Bring them to me."

As war leader of the region, it seemed Cutta outranked even the elders, for soon enough an old woman hobbled towards Crys, labouring along the rutted road from a dark, ramshackle house on the outskirts of town. Ostracised. Crys favoured them all with a disgusted look and jogged to meet her; he could hear her whistling breath from ten paces away. He stopped her with a gentle touch and stooped to meet her eyes.

"Priestess of Trickster and Dancer, I am the Two-Eyed Man and I see you as the vessel through which wisdom passes. Tell me, how can I prove my identity?"

She examined him for long enough that he started to get uncomfortable and doubt began to rear its head. "It is for the Seer-Mother to say who you are and who you are not," she said in the end, her voice thin as paper. "It is she who sees and knows all."

Crys took her hand, dry as a bundle of sticks, in his and straightened up. "Thank you, priestess, but no one is the arbiter of my identity. I ask how you would have me prove it, not whether someone else allows me to be who I am." She flinched and he raised her hand to his cheek, acting on instincts that weren't quite his, despite his fine words. "The fault is not yours, priestess. Can you tell me what has happened here, why the Seer-Mother has broken up the priesthood?"

"I said," the old woman began, her voice quavering.

"And only I am here to listen. I am not Krikite, priestess. You can tell me the truth."

She sucked her remaining teeth, cheeks hollow, as she examined him. "The Seer-Mother has . . . she has broken our people's connection to the land and the gods. All prayers must pass through her; all decisions come from her. There is no truth here any more, no reverence. She is the dam that separates us from the river of divinity."

Her thin chest was heaving under her rags; the grip of her hand was fierce. "Save us, Two-Eyed Man. Save us all."

And there it was, another burden for Crys to bear. And yet how could he say no? If he could do it, then he had to do it. "I will go to the tor. I will do all I can to fix this so that you are recognised as priestess again and the land remembers its people and its people the land." He kissed her hand. "I see you, priestess. There is no dam between us."

"I see you," she whispered. "I see. He is the Two-Eyed Man," the priestess called out in a wavering voice. "He will restore the gods to us. Follow him."

A storm of muttering rose from the gathered Krikites, abuse hurled towards the old woman. Crys held his arms out in a barrier as a few began edging forward with clenched fists. Would they tear her apart for daring to speak out? Was this how far their faith had fallen—or been claimed by the Seer-Mother?

Crys headed towards the crowd and they fell back before him. "War leader, you will guarantee the priestess's safety. I want three warriors you trust to look after her while we are gone. This behaviour towards the priesthood—regardless of the Seer-Mother's pronouncement—is unacceptable."

She withered beneath his anger and the noise of the dissenters faltered. Wordlessly she pointed to three Krikites and they shoved out of the crowd and passed Crys with bowed heads, taking up position around the priestess. One of them murmured reassurance to her.

"Does some distant woman's word mean more to you than decency and respect for those in your community? Does it mean more than the harmony of the land and the voices of the gods? Is this how you show your allegiance?" Crys was disgusted and made no effort to hide it, uncaring whether he alienated those who were wavering in their decision to follow him. In light of their inability to think for themselves or treat each other with respect, he wasn't sure he wanted them at his back when it came time to face down the Red Gods.

Ash and Dom fell in on either side as he stepped forward and then Cutta and her warriors behind, with Sati sliding into their ranks. Crys didn't look back to see whether any others joined him as they marched through the parting crowd. He had a war to win but, first, he had to get to Seer's Tor and cut out the rot that was infecting Krike.

Seer's Tor? the Fox God barked. *No. My tor.*

RILLIRIN

Seventh moon, first year of the reign of King Corvus
Fort Four, South Rank forts, Western Plain, Krike border

RILLIRIN SQUINTED INTO THE approaching night and jabbed her spear at the pell, pulling back, stepping and then striking upwards with the butt. It skittered off the wood and past, but if it'd been a person, it would have broken their knee, she was sure. She spun to the imaginary enemy behind her and lunged; Dalli's spear parried and then the shorter woman had her weapon at Rillirin's throat.

Rillirin froze in shock—she hadn't even known the Wolf chief was there—and then sidestepped, batting Dalli's spear down.

"You're dead," Dalli said. "Never hesitate in battle because you're surprised; train until defence is as instinctive as breathing." She flipped her spear around her head and drove it for Rillirin's temple; Rillirin staggered back, her parry clumsy and weak.

"You're dead," Dalli said again. "Don't get distracted by your opponent's words."

Rillirin gritted her teeth and lunged, then feinted left and snapped the head of her spear towards herself, driving the butt in a flat arc. Dalli knocked it up and countered with a strike that finished a hand's width from Rillirin's eye.

"You're dead. You need to commit to a feint, otherwise your opponent knows what you're doing and will ignore it to prepare for your true strike."

Growling now, Rillirin lunged hard for the centre of Dalli's chest; the Wolf sidestepped and snatched Rillirin's spear, jerking her forward and finishing with a short jab towards Rillirin's gut. She shrank back, dropping the spear to protect her belly and the child nestled within.

"You're dead. Don't let anger make you clumsy. If you over-extend, you're off balance and your enemy will take advantage."

Rillirin snatched up her spear by the end and flailed it for Dalli's knee, then backed away, trying to set her hands. Dalli slammed the shaft of her own spear down and ricocheted Rillirin's spear tip off the flagstones. As it bounced back up in Rillirin's stinging hands, Dalli skipped past it and put a knife against her cheek.

"You're dead. If you lose your weapon too close to the enemy, draw another. Don't step into their range to pick it back up."

Panting, Rillirin eased away from the knife and then raised her spear and lifted the fingers of both hands from where they wrapped the wood to signal she wasn't going to attack. Dalli sheathed her knife and stepped clear anyway.

Rillirin grounded the butt and let it take some of her weight. "Is that what I am then?" she asked as sweat trickled down her back. "Your enemy?"

Dalli shrugged. "I don't know. Are you?"

Rillirin wiped her free hand across her face. "We were friends not too long ago, or I thought we were."

"People change. Loyalties change. Yours is quite clear."

"And Gilda made it quite clear that my baby is innocent. Even if you won't believe me, you should believe her. Everything Gilda's been through and you think she'd lie about something like this?"

Dalli spat. "Everything she's been through, aye. Like Dom trying to kill her. Like him betraying Rilporin and everyone inside it. Like him being a Darksoul."

"He didn't choose any of those things!"

"How do you know?" Dalli flared. "You haven't seen him in months. You've just got a memory of him you've put up on a pedestal and you can't see past it to the truth."

"Neither have you. All you've got is rumour and hearsay and things glimpsed during battle that have been distorted or misremembered."

Dalli shook her head in disgust. "Gods, but you're naive. Will you damn us all, that child included, by believing he can be saved?"

Rillirin slammed the butt of her spear into the stone, the flat crack echoing across the drill yard. "Yes! Because he taught me that anyone can be saved, including me." Dalli flinched but Rillirin held up her hand. "No, you've said enough. Just, just fuck off, will you? I don't need your poison poured in my ear. Dom's the only one of your precious Wolves who saw past my accent and the things I was forced to do and loved me despite it all. Who understood not everything that happens to us is a choice. If you can't see that, then just leave me alone. There's talk of sending the civilians away somewhere safe—if there is such a place. I'm sure you know more about it, being chief, as well as the lover of someone *respectable*. You've made it clear I'm no warrior, and I'm pregnant too, so I'll stay out of your way until it's time and then I'll leave with the other civilians, go wherever Mace thinks I won't be able to infect anyone with my treason."

Her face twisted with bitterness. She turned on her heel and stalked across the drill yard. When Dalli called after her, tentative and too quiet, it was easy to pretend she hadn't heard, to pretend there were no tears clogging her throat. She wouldn't cry for Dalli's spite. Rillirin stalked up the southern watchtower's steps and out on to the allure, staring into the night. Krike was out there somewhere and for a mad, intoxicating moment, she thought about slipping out of the fort and crossing the border, losing herself in a foreign land and never coming back.

There was a fluttering in her stomach, a weird shifting. Rillirin leant her spear against the wall and put her palms on the small mound. *Is that you in there, little warrior? Is that you? Do you want to go to Krike?* Nothing. *Or do you want to stay in Rilpor?* Another flutter.

Rillirin huffed. "All right then," she muttered to the first stars and the stirring life within her, "that'll do. Rilpor it is. But if we're staying, I really hope we win."

C OLONEL THATCHER?" RILLIRIN HURRIED to catch up as the officer crossed towards the mess. He paused and waited, giving her a distracted smile. "Colonel, I'd like to volunteer."

He glanced sidelong at her spear. Despite general Rilporian attitudes to women fighting, her status as a sort-of-Wolf had guaranteed her a weapon when she and Gilda made it to the forts. "Volunteer for what?" he asked.

"Anything, really," she said. "Anything that gets me out of the forts. Or a transfer to one of the others."

He paused by the mess hall door. "Transfer? I know we're tightly packed in here, but the other forts are just as crowded."

"Away from the Wolves," she said in a rush. "I'll go when the civilians go, so it won't be for long, but I'd like to help out. Riding patrols, perhaps?"

He gestured her into the mess and followed and they joined a line of people waiting for breakfast. "You're pregnant, aren't you?"

"Yes, but I can still ride and fight and scout," Rillirin said, annoyed at how everyone assumed she was incapable. "I'm barely even showing," she added.

Thatcher frowned. "Pregnant women get extra rations," he said and pointed at the soldier doling out bread and porridge. Rillirin blushed, stammered an apology. "As for volunteering or moving barracks, let me see what I can do. Ride and scout and hunt, you say?"

"Well, I've done it before a few times," she admitted and took the bowl offered, added a spoonful of honey. "I want—I need—to be useful. I can't just sit here doing nothing."

"I appreciate your enthusiasm, but I need experienced people performing those tasks—the security and provision of the forts isn't something I can trust to a novice. But I'll sign you up to train with the militia, and we might get you out on a foraging party or something. There are lists of things that need doing, if you don't mind hard work."

"I don't mind," she said. "I just need to be busy." He nodded, already distracted by another soldier waving a sheaf of papers, and slipped away into the press. Rillirin examined the long trestle tables packed with soldiers and civilians. A knot of Wolves eyed her from a corner; Isbet beckoned with a wave.

Rillirin took her bowl outside and ate in the early sunlight. Two hours later, she joined three hundred civilians in the drill yard and began to learn to fight like a Ranker. In the afternoon she rode out with a firewood party, and by nightfall she'd been transferred to Fort Three.

It was exactly what she wanted, so it had to be the pregnancy that made her cry herself to sleep.

TARA

Seventh moon, first year of the reign of King Corvus
Marketplace, First Circle, Rilporin, Wheat Lands

ARA DIDN'T KNOW WHAT to think of the shopping list Valan had given her, didn't want to examine what it said about the man who owned her, who lived a life of brutality and violence, who only three days before had flogged one of his other slaves for breaking a plate.

The very first of the Rilporian merchants had arrived, those bastards who didn't care who they sold to or what it was if it turned a profit. The same merchants who sold opium to the rich or the desperate, or stolen goods to the unsuspecting poor, had arrived in a small, wary group outside the gates and Corvus had allowed them entry.

Tara had to admire their ingenuity even as she cursed their greed. Livestock and grain, jewellery and weapons, fish and information: all were for sale. Some merchants were even accepting slaves as payment and then bartering those for more goods and reselling on again, a loop of wealth that gained them a few copper knights more with each transaction.

She stared at their bare necks with hungry intensity. Rilporians without slave collars—how was it they were allowed to walk free? She stopped at a stall holding thin bolts of cloth, all of them dyed an uneven blue. The quality was poor, but the price was high and it was the only stall selling material in the required colour.

"How much for eight yards?" she asked.

The man leered at her, brown teeth in a pockmarked face. "For you, pretty? Depends on what you got to offer. Knock a bit off the price if you're a good girl."

"I'm not a good girl," Tara said and then cursed as the merchant winked and leered some more. "No, is what I'm saying. How much?"

"No? Say no to your owner too, do you? Bet you don't. How'd it be if I told him you offered yourself to me in exchange for your freedom, eh? How'd that be?"

Tara rounded the stall and grabbed the man by the front of his shirt, hauled him close until they were nose to nose and she was enveloped in the stink of his breath. "How'd it be if I choked you to death with your own shitty linen, you traitorous little wank-stain? I want eight yards and I want a good price."

"Royal a yard, royal a yard and no less," the man croaked.

Tara shoved him away. "I'm not paying you eight silvers. I wouldn't pay two silvers for this quality of dye."

The merchant spat at her. "Fucking Mireces can afford it, why shouldn't I make a profit serving scum like that?"

Tara could've told him why not, could've mentioned the fact many of the slaves here in the market would be beaten, starved or executed either for failing to purchase the goods or for buying at too high a price. She knew none of that would matter to this man.

She put her back to him and snatched up the tailoring shears, started measuring the linen. When he tried to stop her she shoved the shears towards his face and he fell back squealing, though not loudly enough to attract attention.

Tara hacked off eight yards and threw two silver royals on to the table. "And just so we're clear," she snarled in his face. "You're all scum." She stalked away before he could reply and made it twenty yards before she remembered to drop her head and slow her steps, kill the fire in her eyes.

A slave was watching her, standing with a couple of others. A big man, huge in fact, with a beard halfway down his chest. He had a trowel in his hand and was supposed to be shovelling mortar on to the inner face of the wall, right about where it had breached. Where Durdil had died. She blinked and looked away, looked back. The man went to wipe his face, then tapped his fingertips quickly against his heart. Tara faltered, then kept walking. When she was almost past she glanced back, gave him the tiniest nod. A Mireces overseer snapped something at him and he bent to his task again.

A mason. That could be useful, either to bring the wall down or to blow the fucker up, maybe. Somehow. Failing that, he's as big as an ox and if he had a shield he could hold a stairwell indefinitely.

It wasn't much, but it was a start. Tara checked her list and bought those items she could find. Combs and hair ribbons; four fine cups and plates with a matching pattern of flowers around the edges; linens and breast band, linens for children. The underwear was the only thing she got for a good price, there not being any free women or children in the city who might need such things. So cheap, in fact, that Tara took the enormous risk of buying fresh ones for herself and then, on a whim that could see her executed, she bought two painted wooden horses.

The slave woman who was selling them wept with silent hopelessness as she handed them over. "Your children's?" Tara whispered as she paid. The woman nodded; then she looked fearfully over her shoulder at the Raiders crouched in a circle and betting on dice.

"I'm so sorry," Tara said. "Have they gone to the Light?"

"I don't know," the woman choked. "I lost them in the smoke. I let go of their hands and they were gone, taken in a heartbeat. I lost them." Her voice began to rise and Tara shushed her, but it was no good. One of the Raiders looked up, scowling, and Tara did the only thing she could: she shoved the toys into her basket and walked away. She wasn't even around the corner before the screaming started.

A s King's Second, Valan occupied the large suite of rooms formerly belonging to the dead Prince Janis. Familiar with the palace's layout from the siege, Tara knew exactly which corridors and shortcuts led from the suite to the king's chambers. Handy, for when the time came, and the brief moment with the mason today gave her hope it would be soon. Getting the Rankers on side was easy enough, but they needed every slave rebelling at once, rising in every Circle and every district and causing so much chaos that no one would notice her slipping through the palace and putting a knife in Corvus's heart before drowning Lanta in her own filthy, sacrilegious godpool.

If only it could happen now. Tara didn't do regret as a rule, but right now she was regretting buying those wooden horses with rare intensity. It had taken hard work and luck and the exact right mixture of defiance, ability and humility to charm Valan, but it could all come crashing down around her if he took exception to her decision-making.

Tara had laid out the purchases on the big table in Valan's suite and moved to her place by the door to await his return, when she'd have the honour of taking his weapons and boots and presenting him with wine and food. She got to remove his armour and then pour his bath, a luxury he couldn't get enough of down here in the warm lands.

So fucking honoured.

She also got to tell him about any infractions by the other slaves during his absence, what the kitchens had prepared for him, and any messages that had arrived while he'd waited on the king. She tried to convince herself it was the same as being Mace's adjutant back before the world had gone to shit, but then Mace had never insisted she scrub his back while he sat bollock-naked in a bathtub. She shuddered and reminded herself it was nothing like being an adjutant, because she'd never been one. She was an officer's wife, not an officer.

Her palms began to sweat when she heard his footsteps in the corridor outside. The other five slaves were locked in what must have once been Janis's study. They were always locked away when the second left his apartments; Tara's disguise as the wife of Major Vaunt had convinced Valan that she wouldn't risk her husband's safety by attempting to escape.

"Welcome back, honoured," she said, as she did every single time, an affectation he enjoyed. He shoved his sword at her and strode into the main room, threw himself into a chair. She knelt at his feet and tugged off his boots, put them in the corner and then handed him a cup.

"I got everything you requested," she said and gestured at the table. Valan grunted, rolling the wine around in his mouth as he wandered over. The fabric was arranged in what she thought was an artful sweep that hid the ragged edge where she'd cut it. The four cups and plates occupied the centre of the table along with the linens, and behind them stood the wooden horses.

A muscle flickered in Valan's cheek. "I did not ask for those," he said.

Tara curtseyed. "No, honoured. Forgive me, honoured. The linens were so reasonably priced I had enough left over and more. I . . . was not sure whether your daughters would be able to bring any toys with them and I thought you might want to show you'd been thinking of them."

Valan's expression was unreadable.

"I can try and sell them on, honoured," she added quickly, voice quickening with anxiety, "or. . . . or use them as kindling for the fire."

"Expensive kindling," Valan commented and drank some more.

"Forgive me," she said again, "I should not have done it. I'll get the money back somehow, I swear. I thought—"

"You've done well. Where's supper?"

Tara bit off any more excuses and bobbed another curtsey, hurried to the smaller table set by the window where Valan liked to eat and lifted the heavy wooden cover off the plate. Cold meats, bread, cheese and greens and Tara's stomach gurgled at the sight, wooden horses forgotten.

Valan pushed past her and sat, gestured for more wine and Tara stood by his side and watched him eat and drink food and wine that didn't belong to him while thousands of slaves went hungry.

Her stomach rumbled again and a brief smile crossed Valan's face. He picked up a half-eaten roll of bread and tossed it on to the floor. She stared at it, and then back at him, and then she picked it up and brushed it off and ate it.

I T WAS THREE DAYS before she could get back to the market, but the mason was still there. He'd moved along the wall a little, and while she knew nothing about masonry it didn't look like he'd made much progress. Perhaps Vaunt had managed to get word out to slow the work and it had spread beyond the Rankers forced to do the labouring.

Tara circled the market a couple of times, wondering how best to approach the mason and what she could say, when he solved it for her. She was a dozen strides away when he reared back from the wall with the bellow of a wounded bull, a scarlet spray arcing out of the shade and across the discarded and broken stone.

The man went to his knees, clutching his hand to his chest, and Tara moved for him with the instinct of a soldier to a wounded comrade. "Let me see, let me see," she said, prising at his supporting hand. The slice across his palm wasn't deep but it was long and bleeding freely.

"Merol, son of Merle Stonemason who died defending this wall," the man hissed and then let out another bleat of pain.

"You! What are you doing?" a Raider demanded.

Tara stood up in order to curtsey. "Forgive me, honoured, I have a little skill in healing. I only thought to help so he would be able to continue working."

"Healer?" the Mireces said sharply.

"No, honoured. Just some skills I picked up over the years. I can clean and stitch this. Your will, honoured."

Merol bleated again. "I can't lose me hand, milord, please. Forgive the interruption, I'm sure I'll be able to work again once the bleeding's stopped."

Tara was sure of no such thing but she held her tongue. "Get on with it then," the Raider snapped. "Over there, out of the way of those doing actual work. And I'll be reporting this to your owner, bitch. What's his name?"

"Second Valan, honoured," Tara said and both Merol and the Mireces sucked in a breath. "Come, man. Sit down. You're lucky my master sent me out for needle and thread among other things."

The mason sat carefully on a broken-down crate that creaked under his weight. "Tara Vaunt, wife of Major Tomaz Vaunt of the Palace Rank, currently imprisoned in the south barracks in Second Circle," she breathed.

Merol pulled his hand out of hers. "Know Vaunt by reputation," he said quietly. "Didn't know he had a wife." Tara got ready to run. "But then it's a big city and I don't know everything, do I? I mean, I know about walls and buildings. I know about gates." His eyes bored into hers. "I know about quiet routes from the harbours to First Circle, even, in the slaughter district."

Tara licked her lips. "You know a lot, Merol; you're clearly a useful man. But are you a loyal man?"

"Loyal to who? I got my da's reputation to live up to and that's enough for me," Merol said and put his hand back in hers.

She broke eye contact and examined the cut. "Does it hurt?"

"Nah," Merol said. "Just opened up an existing scar; barely felt it. I saw what you done the other day, how that stall-holder threatened you and you stood up to him. Made me think you were someone worth knowing."

"You cut your hand open for the right reasons then, Merol," Tara said as she dabbed at the wound and then threaded the needle and began to tug it through the flesh. "There are plans. I can't say more now, but I'll come and see you again. Where are you staying?"

"That slimy fucker who was talking to you owns me and another lad. Think he wanted a woman—he's ever so disappointed, keeps threatening to sell us 'cause he knows if he tries to fuck either of we'll squash him like a fucking flea, pardon my language. But we work hard—and slow. Staying in the cloth district."

Tara finished the stitching and bit off the thread, dabbed it some more and then wrapped a new napkin around it. So much for her spare linens—she'd have to tear them up to replace what she'd used here. "Sound out the other big men with hammers and wait for my word. I'll be in touch." Tara stood up and repacked her basket. She turned to his owner and bobbed another curtsey. "He'll need to keep it clean, honoured, or it'll kill him."

The Raider sucked his teeth and then spat, but he didn't contradict her, just waved Merol towards the western wall. "Don't work, don't eat, slave," he growled. "Back to it."

Tara made her way back to the palace and passed a knot of chained Rankers hauling stone in barrows. She slid past one, a man she vaguely recognised, definitely housed in the south barracks. "Mason named Merol's with us," she hissed as she went past. "Tell Vaunt."

She didn't wait for a reply.

MACE

THREE SEPARATE REPORTS OF bands of Mireces, a few hundred strong each, had come in from three locations within a ten-mile radius of the South Rank's headquarters. Whether or not they knew the survivors of the siege were there, they were doing what they could to prevent patrols or intel moving in and out of the forts.

A week of rest had turned into a month as the Rankers finally began to let go of the state of heightened awareness and battle-readiness that had characterised their time under siege and their flight across Rilpor. Exhaustion had bitten them all deep, and for days they moved around the forts like ghosts unless a sudden sound or sight triggered them into violent motion. Mace himself couldn't remember the last time he'd slept so much or his thoughts had been so hard to assemble. As though the siege had stolen his wits.

But now, finally, he felt close to his old self and determined to prove it to everyone by tagging along with Colonel Jarl's Hundreds. The largest reported force was northeast between the forts and Rilporin, with others reported at north and northwest of their position—the three directions from which they were most likely to receive potential reinforcements or vital information. It didn't feel like a coincidence that they'd be there and not elsewhere in the Western Plain.

Hallos had glowered from beneath eyebrows no less fearsome for being more grey than black these days, but Mace wasn't letting the physician talk him out of another patrol and the chance at a scrap, even as he'd ordered the shattered remnants of the West and Palace Ranks to stand down. The fires that had led every one of them to perform extraordinary feats during Rilporin's defence were still banked embers, and they needed time to coax the flames back into life.

Dalli had come too, which didn't surprise him. She'd been spikier than usual since her fight with Rillirin and the girl's removal to Fort Three, and as the days passed the outrage iced over and now they were little more than brittle strangers on the rare occasions they were in the same place together.

All of which Mace put out of his mind as they rode out of the gate in the midst of two hundred marching Rankers. "How are the supplies looking, Colonel?" he asked as his skittish mount sidestepped into Dalli's. He couldn't even remember the last time he'd been on a horse. Somewhere back in the west, he supposed.

"At the current rate of consumption, we'll be on half-rations for all personnel in two moons, quarter-rations in four, and eating our horses and boot leather in six. If we go on to half-rations now—"

"That won't be necessary, Jarl, at least not yet. Once the civilians are gone, even with the provisions they'll have to take with them, remaining numbers will be almost back to normal. We managed to buy up a decent amount of grain before the East Rank garrisons moved into the towns."

"I admit I'm hesitant about sending them so far through hostile territory though, Commander," Jarl said. "Even if the Mireces border is as empty as you believe, that's a two-week march for Rankers, so easily three for civilians with old folks and little ones."

"You're not the only one, but there simply isn't anywhere else for them to go. If we could broker a deal with Krike to house refugees, that would be ideal, but you say we can't."

"Sorry, Commander, if it was possible we'd all be suggesting it. I've served here for six years now and we've never known the Krikites to change their minds about international relations. They said no—they mean no."

"So, we're going to send them to learn to be Wolves instead," Dalli said with half a smile. "Or at least, they're going to occupy our land. Our village in the foothills is small and won't fit them all, but it's empty and the only place without an enemy garrison. They'll have to dig in and build—and try not to strip the land of resources while they're there. Some of us would quite like to go home when this is all over."

"Even once we've cleared out these Raiders it'll be a risk," Mace said heavily, "but there are forty-two pregnant women in the forts and almost six hundred children of varying ages, as well as the old and those who can't move fast. We can't feed them and we can't protect them, not indefinitely." He gestured at the empty, innocent-seeming land rolling away ahead of them. "They're going to come for us. Sooner or later, whether or not they ever learn exactly how many of us are here, the Mireces are going to come. They can't let us live."

It soured the mood somewhat, but it had to be said. They weren't safe down here in the south. Mace's presence and that of the refugees made no difference—Corvus couldn't allow a rested, untested fighting force like the South Rank to live. If he was to have absolute power over Rilpor, they needed to be crushed.

"Let's not forget Colonel Edris, though. He and King Tresh and a Listran army could be just the distraction we need to get the civs safely away," he added in a belated attempt to restore their spirits.

"He'll certainly have some decisions to make about where to attack first," Jarl agreed, "and unarmed non-combatants will be the least of his worries."

"Precisely."

Turned out Jarl was like a dog with a bone, though. "They'll need scouts and guards, too, someone who knows the way, wagons full of provisions. The civilians, I mean—Tresh'll have Edris and his own supplies, of course. Then there's deciding who goes first and how many go at once. Your march here all together was a feat worthy of a song, Commander, but the chances of you managing it undetected a second time, if you even did the first . . ." Jarl trailed off.

"You're not telling me anything I don't know," Mace grunted. He'd already talked it to death with Hadir, but Jarl struck him as the thorough type. It was possible he'd see something they hadn't.

"The first decision is whether we send them in small or large groups, or even one huge one—just get them out and away all together. Multiple groups increases the risk of some being seen and attacked. One large one will be slow and chaotic, hard to control. Exactly how we do it is the focus of the first meeting when we get back, but if we don't make it, Hadir's tasked with ensuring all four thousand civilians, minus those who have joined the militia, get out and get on the road west. Whatever it takes."

That soured the mood even further and they rode in silence for a while, stationed ten ranks back, allowing the forward scouts a clear view not obscured by horses' arses.

There'll be utter fucking chaos when they know we're sending them away. They'll think we can't protect them, or that we're getting rid of them to spare our own lives. All the panic and vicious ignorance from Rilporin will be repeated. And I don't blame them at all. If I were one of them, I wouldn't want to face open country again. Not ever.

He gave himself a little mental shake. *One problem at a time, Mace. Clear the area around the forts so they can get out undetected, and then pray to the Dancer they make it all the way to safety.*

D ALLI HAD DONE THE scouting when the campfires were spotted and Mace had nearly managed not to panic at the length of time she was gone. The sky was a riot of stars that did little to hide any of them, and still somehow she slid in close enough to count their weapons and piss in their stew without anyone noticing.

Mace and Jarl huddled around her so their voices wouldn't carry on the breeze. "About three hundred, maybe more if we assume four to a fire and forty on watch," she breathed.

It was more men than Mace had, but fewer than he'd feared. "All right, we've got the night and the element of surprise, and they'll have shit night vision from standing around the fires. Split up and approach from north, east and west. If they're fleeing anywhere, I want it to be straight towards the forts so our close patrols can pick them off. Pass the word for quiet. I'll draw their attention: try and get in amongst them before the alarm sounds so it looks like we're everywhere."

Jarl showed his teeth and Dalli's face shifted into a feral mask. They faded into the night, Rankers following. Mace took a breath and felt the adrenaline mix with the fear, drew his sword and advanced, moving steadily so his gear made as little sound as possible. At his back crept sixty Rankers, silent, disciplined.

"Who goes there?" came a Mireces voice from out of the blinding light of a handheld torch, flames flickering on Mace's plate and the chainmail of the men who followed.

"For Rilpor!" Mace roared and broke into a sprint. His men followed, screaming, the other two wings holding back in silence until all attention was firmly on Mace. They ploughed into the light and into the line of Mireces scrambling to their feet, fumbling for weapons and screaming questions and alarms and, soon enough, pain.

Mace ducked a hasty swing and carried on past, flicking his sword backwards into the Mireces' exposed hamstring. He went down howling and Mace left him to be picked off by those following. A knot of Mireces charged him and he tightened the grip on his shield, took an axe blow high on its face and smashed the boss in his attacker's chest, pushing him back a step, parried a sword with his own and insinuated his blade past the man's guard and into the side of his neck, a raking slice that put him out of the fight and possibly out of life. Another sword battered into his pauldron and he grunted, stepped back and spun, lashing out with sword and shield, blocking low and cutting high, high, low and then thrusting.

Another axe blow on to his shield was almost enough to break his wrist and he bellowed, kicked the man wielding it in the knee and rammed him off his feet, bringing the shield rim down into his face and hearing the snap of bone and teeth. Screaming filled the night.

"'Ware!" shrieked a voice and he dived, rolling over his shield and into clear space, up between two Mireces just turning to face him, stabbed one and missed, the chainmail turning the point, flicked the blade down and opened the man's thigh instead, kicking into the open wound; he took the blow from the second Raider on the edge of his shield, chips of wood spraying his face and the blade skittering off and squealing down his breastplate.

Spun side on and forced the man back with the shield, herding him until he tripped over a corpse, lashing out with a blow more a bludgeon and staving in helmet and skull. Sucking in lungfuls of air and letting all the rage of Rilporin surge up his throat and out of his mouth in a scream of pure violence, spinning to defend his back when his spine prickled warning, tucked in behind his shield so the attack was a glancing blow off the metal boss and his upward diagonal sweep made it below the chainmail and into groin and belly. Stink of entrails and the scream of a dead man, glimpse of Dalli darting like a fish from the darkness, spear red along a third of its length, twirling and ducking and dealing death.

Another presence behind him and he twisted again, sword already cutting, and Jarl threw up his shield to deflect it. "About a dozen slipped through south if you want them, Commander," he panted when he saw the need for more violence, for release, in Mace's expression, indicating a score of soldiers arrayed behind him with torches and bloodstained faces, ready to run.

Mace took another deep lungful, adrenaline crystal-bright and singing in his veins. "Mop up here," he snarled, bloodlust thickening his voice. "I've got the runners."

THE BLESSED ONE

Seventh moon, first year of the reign of King Corvus
Red Gods' temple, temple district, First Circle, Rilporin, Wheat Lands

LANTA, BLESSED ONE AND Voice of the Gods, and High Priest Gull crouched in the dark of the temple.

They had the beginnings of a plan now, an outline that they were filling in through ritual, through communion and intuition and invention. The godblood Lanta had ingested and which even now stained her skin had lent her wisdom and understanding she'd never before experienced. She understood the gods, *knew* Them, in ways no other mortal could or ever had.

The secret lay in learning how the Fox God had entered the mortal man Crys Tailorson. If they could understand that, they'd know better how to bring back the Dark Lady.

Lanta had already offered her own flesh as host, but the connection had failed. They needed a focus, something for the Dark Lady to sense from wherever She was imprisoned, something big enough, bright enough, to draw Her back past the veil and into Gilgoras. And then into Her new body, mortal and divine mingling into a living goddess to tread the earth among Her children forever. Between them, the Blessed One and Gull were beginning to understand what that beacon might be.

Holy Gosfath. God of Blood and Lord of War.

The sheer audacity, the magnitude, of what they were attempting frightened her, but the alternative—a world without the Dark Lady, the endless agony of abandonment—terrified her far more. And Lanta did not deal in fear of this type.

If they could . . . anchor Gosfath here in the temple, when the time came for the ritual, the Dark Lady would find Her way to Him through the channel of Lanta's soul and the souls of sacrifices, the promise and whisper of blood spilt in Her name, and from there they could direct Her into the Bloodchild—the holy vessel—and restore Her to life and the world. For that, they needed to be able to bring the god to them. They needed to offer Him something. Tempt Him.

Lanta took a deliberate breath of the rank air, the heat and smoke, tasting her fear and embracing it, and then she focused. The knife was sharp, but not so sharp she didn't feel it slice into her arm; what would be the point in not feeling the pain?

"I swear in Holy Gosfath's name that I will not rest until I have brought the Dark Lady out of death and into Her glorious vengeance."

She cut again.

"I swear in the Dark Lady's memory that I will fly past what remains of the veil and search the Waystations and the Afterworld itself to find Her."

Another cut. The temple was thick with tension and the stink of old blood and new, sweat and death and fierce, brittle defiance.

"I swear by my blood and my hope of meeting the gods in death that I will not cease until we have resurrected our Bloody Mother."

She cut once more, the pain lancing through her and making her stronger, more determined. A blood oath, carved in flesh and bone and will, new scars on top of old: a promise to the gods, to the Dark Lady wherever She was; and a promise to Lanta herself.

This is faith. This is determination. This is how we win.

Lanta gave the blade to Gull and he touched its tip to his lips, licking her blood from the steel. And then he swore the same oath, one cut at a time, and the heat in the temple grew, the stinking slaughterhouse smell drifting from the altar and the godpool they'd blessed with the blood of sacrifice, its clotted surface so thick it echoed back their words and the harshness of their breathing.

Beneath Lanta's hands a brass dish full of coals smoked and hissed as her blood dripped into it, filling her head with the path to the Waystation. Opposite her, Gull's nostrils flared as he inhaled the fumes. Lanta's fingers coiled through the smoke, sweat sheening her face.

"Holy Gosfath, God of Blood, lend us your great strength in the quest to return your Holy Sister to you and to the world. Grant us the strength to do your will. God of Blood, we honour you." The glowing coals sizzled and burst into flame. Lanta smiled cautiously; He was listening.

"Gosfath, God of Blood, separated from your loved and loving Sister, we beseech you to search beyond the veil for the Dark Lady, snatched from your loving arms and our yearning souls. We seek your mighty aid in helping us bring Her back from beyond death. Will you come to us?"

A breeze rippled through the dry heat of the room, tickling Lanta's skin, lifting her hair, stealing fingers inside her gown, beneath her breasts and between her legs. It carried the whiff of corruption, the tang of sulphur.

"He's near," she whispered and Gull scuttled further forward, his face a skull ill lit by the glow from the brazier. The heat was so strong it took all her will to keep her palms close to the coals. She sucked in a breath of smoke, held it against the urge to cough, tears stinging her eyes, and exhaled.

"Bring Him," Gull murmured.

Lanta strained, opening herself to Gosfath as she had for years to the Dark Lady. A tickle, a tentative poking, and then nothing. She strained harder, but He wouldn't come. Gull had more experience with the god, but for this plan Gull would not suffice.

"The God does not desire," she said.

"The God always desires," Gull said. He put his hands on top of Lanta's and, with one savage move, pressed them into the coals.

Red screaming agony coursed through her hands and up her arms and Lanta shrieked, fought to pull away. Gull held her tight and suddenly there He was, bright and dark and vast in her head.

Want. Need. Want.

Lanta felt herself pulled along the Path, flying from the temple into the presence of her dread lord, pain and terror mingling into the perfect alloy of devotion.

Heat pulsed around her, fingers of hot air stroking her now naked skin. Ahead, a shadow loomed among the stalactites of the Waystation, massive and misshapen. He was supposed to come to them, not her to Him. It wouldn't work here. It had to be the temple. It had to be. Gosfath's bellow brought her thoughts to a crashing halt and ignited her tongue.

"As we call to the gods in times of pain and terror, so They take as Their due our blood and breath," she chanted. There was no time to worry about what had gone wrong; Lanta was in the presence of the Red Father. "As fear brings us to the gods' presence, I welcome you. Fear is your call; devotion is our answer."

Fear indeed, as the darkness parted to reveal Him sitting on a throne carved from the bones of a mountain. Or perhaps it was a mountain of bones. He rose, head bowed to avoid the cavern's high vault, and stepped down, the black talons on one huge hand skirling across the wall, gouging lines, striking sparks, the noise an unholy screech that made Lanta's eardrums flutter. She dropped to her knees and looked away as He shrank, a giant still but of a size she could comprehend now. Half her height again, three times her weight, muscles rippling like eels in oil.

"Lord Gosfath, God of Blood, most mighty Lord of War and chaos, I am honoured by your presence, and honour you in turn with—"

"Want," the God of Blood hissed, hauling her to her feet with one hand wrapped around her upper arm. "Want now."

"Your Sister wants you too, Father," Lanta gasped, raising her hands in a barrier as effective as a spider's web. "The Dark Lady yearns for your arms around Her, Father, She yearns for you. We must find Her, bring Her back to you and this world, restore the balance—"

Gosfath leant close. "Alone," He grunted and flung her down. "*Want.*"

Lanta cried out as her head struck stone, again as Gosfath threw Himself on top of her, and then screamed as His talons and then His fat red cock dug their way inside her, screamed in an agony so close to ecstasy she understood they were the same. Screamed as the god honoured her.

L ANTA WOKE WITH A wail of mingled pain and exaltation, her consciousness slamming back into her body where it lay in abandon on the temple floor, her head pillowed on Gull's knees and her skirts cast up around her legs. She exhaled a long, drawn-out moan as her hurts made themselves known in a rush that rippled through her body from the back of her head to her ankles.

She gestured with scabbed fingers and carefully, so carefully, Gull undid her gown and peeled it down to her waist. Among the black god-stains and disappearing beneath her breast band, her skin was hatched with cuts, claw marks, bite marks, and at her core throbbed a deep ache that spiked into pain with every movement.

Lanta looked down at herself and a slow smile spread across her face at the ruin of her flesh. She placed one hand between her legs. "The god honoured me," she whispered. Tears started in her eyes.

"Then we have taken the first step," Gull replied. "The next time, you must draw Him here rather than go to the Waystation. We must be able to bring Him through the veil if the Dark Lady is to return."

Lanta forced herself to sit up, groaning against the flare deep within her pelvis. Next time? Even if she could go through this again, there was no saying that Holy Gosfath would come through the veil and into the temple. Not next time, maybe not ever. She breathed through the pain and pushed her doubts aside. It would work. He would understand and He would help them. He would be rewarded, first with Lanta to appease and comfort Him, and then by the restoration of His Sister-Lover.

It *would* work.

Gull scooted around to face her, put his hands on her shoulders, reverence lightening his features. "This is monumental, Blessed One," he said. "We have made great progress here today. No one has ever communed with the god so . . . thoroughly."

"Great progress, yes," she said, "but I will need time to heal before I call Him again. His desire and loneliness were so great, you can see what it has done to me."

"And yet time begins to run short. Perhaps some of the slave women could be trained to pleasure the Father until Mireces women arrive," Gull mused.

Lanta's guts twisted, not in pain this time. "No," she snapped. "It must be me. Only me. I am the Blessed One and this is my task, my holy purpose. I will see it done. I will bring the Father to Rilporin, to this very temple. He will come and we will make Him a beacon to guide the Dark Lady home."

I have known the love of the Father. May it sustain me until our Bloody Mother is brought back.

"Come, let us get you to a warm bath and then the healer. You have done great work."

"It is only the beginning," Lanta stuttered as Gull helped her stand, the pain shortening her breath. "For the rest we need Rillirin and the bairn. We have to have her, Gull."

"I will speak to the king on your behalf, Blessed One," Gull soothed her. "I will inform him of our progress, of the urgency, the need, to find his sister. You should concentrate only on the god for now, on encouraging Him to leave the Afterworld and the Waystation and visit His worshippers here. Visit you."

She paused, tightening her grip on her priest's supporting arm and then hissing as the blisters on her palm ruptured. "He said He was alone, Gull," she whispered, and her tears this time were of sorrow. "It broke my heart."

"You will soothe him, Blessed One, and tend to His divine needs as often as you are able. We must explain all we are doing to return His Sister-Lover to Him. Once He understands, it may be that His demands are less . . . onerous."

Lanta's ice-blue eyes frosted over and she pushed away to stand unaided. "No task performed in service of the gods is ever onerous," she grated. Gull dipped his head in silent apology. "I will rest and sleep, take herbs for these wounds. Our great work begins now. All that has come before is as nothing."

CRYS

ESPITE THE PRESENCE OF the southern war leader and her war-riors, the reception for the Rilporians at Seer's Tor, Krike's capital, was less than friendly.

Warriors picked up their approach when they were still a few miles out and by the time the group had reached the outskirts of the great circular town with the tor rearing from its centre, the Warlord's honour guard were ranged across the main road and the gates were shut tight.

"There's something very wrong here," Dom muttered to Crys as they walked steadily towards the line of warriors barring their way. He rubbed tenderly at his right eye. "Very, very wrong. Be careful." He hissed in pain and stumbled and Ash caught him under the arm, helped him along a few strides until he found his balance again.

Crys didn't miss that Ash let go as fast as he could. Dom didn't miss it either. "Is there anything else you can tell me?" he asked the calestar. Dom blinked, surprised and pleased to be spoken to. Grateful just to be acknowledged. A twist of shame rose up Crys's throat even as his palms dampened in animal instinct at the man's proximity.

"Things will not be as they seem. Truth and lies entwine like mating snakes and faith broken and put back together is stronger than faith for-gotten and remembered." He stopped walking, stopped talking, his neck stretching long and to one side, blank brown eyes staring into the future. Crys and Ash got ready to catch him, but after long moments he came back to them and was still himself.

"All right?" Crys put his hand on Dom's back. "Do you need some time?"

Dom coughed, cleared his throat, spat, and then took several deep breaths. His right eye was screwed shut against pain that writhed across his features, but he began to walk, limping slightly. "Be on guard. We're in more danger here than at any point since we fled Rilporin."

"Fantastic," Ash muttered, but he'd noticed the hand that Crys still had on Dom's back and subsided. Relief, confusion and disgust warred for possession of his expression, but he matched his pace to Dom's and the three of them moved slowly to the line of warriors in front of the shut gate.

"The tor's here," Crys said, though it was pretty obvious, looming over not just the town but the entire landscape, visible for miles. "It's where I was born, you know. The Fox God, I mean."

Cutta stepped in front of them. "Cutta Frog-dream, war leader of the south and confidante of the Warlord, with information about the war in Rilpor and god-news for the Seer-Mother. The Trickster has returned to Gilgoras in mortal form."

Whatever they'd been expecting, it clearly wasn't that. The warrior who she addressed opened and closed his mouth a few times, having no idea how to answer such claims. Eventually he clicked his fingers and sent another back to the town through a postern gate. "You'll wait," he grunted, easing the axe in his grip.

"As you say, honour guard. Two-Eyed Man, are you content to wait?" Cutta asked, voice loud enough to carry to the warriors opposing them. There were startled exclamations and Crys approved the tactic. Whatever happened here, Cutta had both named him and given him authority over her. The rumour of that would flood through the town faster than anyone could think to curb it.

He waved a hand. "We'll wait."

It didn't take long. More of the Warlord's honour guard flooded out to surround Cutta and her warriors, and then the Warlord himself arrived with the gold torc of his office glinting on his thick neck beneath his blond beard and braided hair.

A woman who had to be the Seer-Mother followed him out, dripping in ornaments and beads and charms, tattoos around her eyes.

"Rilporians are not welcome in Krike," the Warlord shouted, his hands on his hips next to axe and knife. "And liars are welcome nowhere."

The Seer-Mother stalked past him and up to the Rilporians standing a little ahead of the others. The Krikites who'd followed Crys stepped away, shuffling their feet like children caught stealing apples. She circled the trio and Crys's back prickled, waiting for a knife. Even without the Fox God's confirmation or Dom's partial knowing, it was clear this woman was not their friend.

Want to come out and wow them, Foxy?

There was a feeling of amusement but no corresponding change in his nature. Still, Crys hoped he wasn't going to have to do this alone.

The Seer-Mother stopped in front of him and peered at his face. He arched his eyebrow and waited. So did she, but if she was expecting deference she'd be standing there a long time. "You have destroyed Krike's priesthood and forbidden the old worship," he said; breath hissed from her. "You have made yourself the sole conduit between the people and the gods. That must be a heavy burden."

"I bear it gladly," she said, tossing her head.

Crys indicated the bronze and brass bracelets and necklaces, the many fine beads threaded into her hair. "So I can see. And do you think people beggaring themselves in return for your intervention with the gods is just?"

The Seer-Mother barked a sharp laugh. "You are the one who is here to be judged. You are the one whose truth is to be discovered—and the consequences of it."

"I don't think so," Crys said softly and felt stillness gather in Ash standing at his left shoulder. His lover was readying for a fight. "I do not need your judgement," he continued, raising his voice for the Warlord to hear. "I am Crys Tailorson, officer, soldier, heart-bound to the Wolf Ash. I am the Fox God in mortal form, the Trickster. The Two-Eyed Man. There is rot in Krike, and though I came here to secure aid for Rilpor's fight against the forces of the Red Gods, I will not leave before I have done all I can to bring harmony back to your land and the gods back to your hearts."

The Seer-Mother pounced on his words. "The gods, you say? *The gods*, not 'Me'. You proclaim yourself our lord and then refuse to acknowledge your place in those hearts you speak of so lovingly." She pointed a finger between his eyes. "I name you liar."

"I name you Tanik Horse-dream, false Seer-Mother," Crys replied easily and a ripple of surprise ran through those gathered.

Tanik scoffed. "Anyone you travelled with could have told you my name. There are no secrets among Krikites, Crys Tailorson, false prophet. I am Tanik: what of it? You think that makes you divine?"

"False," Dom said and his teeth clicked together as he bit off the word. "False."

"See?" the woman demanded, gesturing. "Even your accomplice agrees with me."

Neither Crys nor Ash were listening. "He's going," Ash said, "this'll be a full one, he's too close to the edge after that moment just now." He leant in close, hands on Dom's shoulders. "Let's sit you down, Dom, eh? Come on now, right here, that's it. Come—"

Dom's arms flew up and knocked Ash away and then he stiffened and fell like a tree. Crys slid in behind him and caught his shoulders, but Dom began to convulse before he managed to get him on to the floor and he wriggled, hit the dirt back-first so all the breath was driven free, and then the thrashing started, the arching, the guttural grunts.

A spear appeared in the ground by his hip and Ash spun to face the Warlord's warriors. "Don't you fucking dare," he roared at them, turned away before anyone could reply, and threw himself down at Dom's head, murmuring the old charms to soothe him, let him know he wasn't alone. "Hush, now, hush," he said, thumbs tracing circles on Dom's brow. "We're here; you're safe. You're safe. We've got you."

Crys knelt at his side and studied the writhing face as Dom's boot heels drummed the hard-packed earth, foam splattering from his mouth. He put his hand on the calestar's stomach and pushed. "Be still," he commanded and Dom relaxed, a sudden boneless collapse as though he'd been brained. There was a chorus of murmurs from those around them as all crowded in to see, but Crys paid them no mind.

"Tell me," he said.

Dom's eyes opened, brown and bloodshot, glittering with pain. He spat out pink saliva. "Lies live here," he grated to the assembled Krikites as much as to Crys. The Seer-Mother and even the Warlord leant close to listen, though warriors stood ready in case this was some ruse. "Someone here dissembles, cloaked in lies and false prophecy. Someone tricks."

Sharp looks in Crys's direction that raised the hairs on the back of his neck. *Unfortunate choice of words, Calestar.*

"There is deception here, and it stifles the divine," Dom continued. "Someone lies, someone trusted. The gods are leaking from Krike as the faithful turn their hearts away. Water from a broken bucket. Turn them back, or all is lost. Worship again, worship as your ancestors did, or be lost."

Crys sat back on his heels as Dom rolled weakly on to his side and vomited. Ash snatched a waterskin from Cutta and helped him to drink. Despite the situation, the war leader kept her place by their side and Crys was thankful for it. He had an uneasy feeling he'd need her and her fighters.

"Warlord, is there somewhere we may go so my friend can rest?" Crys asked, standing. "He'll be exhausted after his knowing and in a lot of pain. He needs somewhere warm and dry to sleep. You may guard us however you see fit; we won't resist. And if you'd like to question our presence here, I am happy to come with you."

Ash jerked his head up at that and Crys put his hand out.

"Lies and falsehoods and secrets and fear," Dom mumbled, gazing into some inner vista that haunted him. "Lies, all lies. Only dreams are true here and they forget their dreams."

The muttering this time was angry, hostile.

"See?" Tanik demanded. "They know nothing of us and our way of life to speak so. The Fox God would never allow anyone to speak of the soul-dreaming with so little respect. They are moon-mad; it can be nothing else. This one has been born with the sign of the god in his eyes and uses the blessing to cheat and corrupt the weak of mind."

Ash scowled at the implication. "Fuck's sake, I'm not listening to any more of this shit. Crys, help me get him up; he needs to rest. With luck we can be gone in the morning."

Dom's legs would barely support him and he hung between them like wet washing as they started towards the gate. Warriors shuffled and looked at each other, at the Warlord and the Seer-Mother, at Cutta Frog-dream and her two-hundred-strong war band.

"Let them through. House them in the travellers' quarter and put a dozen guards on watch." The Warlord's voice was clear and he radiated puzzlement more than hostility, as though something didn't quite make sense.

"They will be questioned one at a time," Tanik said. "That one's insane claims will be investigated in the sight of the gods. When his heresy is laid bare, he will be dealt with accordingly."

The honour guard formed up around the three of them before Crys could respond and marched them through the gates and into the town, laid out like spokes on a wheel with roads lined with vegetable plots all leading in towards the centre—the tor. Crys felt it pull at him as they walked, felt a sudden sharp-eyed attention from within.

The tor. It will happen at the tor.

What will?

All of it.

Crys wasn't reassured. He was pretty sure the Fox God had said something similar shortly before he was almost tortured to death.

CORVUS

Eighth moon, first year of the reign of King Corvus
Throne room, the palace, Rilporin, Wheat Lands

T HE FIRST OF THE Evendoom women turned up," Corvus said as
he lounged on the throne, one leg flung over the arm. "Three of
them."

"How'd they look?" Valan asked.

Corvus screwed up his face. "Even when they weren't wailing and tearing their hair and so forth, mostly like the bastard offspring of a dog and a
horse's arse. I got rid of them." He studied Silais, who'd decided kneeling
was by far the lesser evil compared with having body parts cut off. "But
Slave Silais tells me some of the others have reputations for being quite
pretty. In fact, he's staked his other ear on it."

The man twitched and Corvus sniggered. "As for the male heirs,
two currently reside in Pine Lock. Brothers. I don't trust the East Rank
to handle it; sort it out for me, Valan. Silais will give you names and
descriptions."

"Your will, Sire. With your permission, I'll leave at dawn." Corvus
nodded. "Regarding your safety in my absence, Tett's a good man, steady
and loyal and a bastard with a knife. He'll make you a decent bodyguard."

"Hails from Crow Crag, not Eagle Height?" Valan nodded. "Good.
Always easier to trust one of our own. Brief him tonight and send him to
me before you leave. Now, how's the mood?"

Valan drummed his fingers on his knee and stared out of the window for a while. "Worried, Sire," he said eventually. "Now that things are settling down, now that we're consolidating, well . . . some of the men are wondering if our victory was actually a victory? Our enemy is still out there, skulking through Listre or holed up in the South Forts—and we'll have news on that any day now. In the meantime, our allies are spread thin across the rest of Rilpor. The Dark Lady is gone, and while the Blessed One's plan will see Her restored to us," he added hastily as Corvus's nostrils flared, "that plan made no mention of whether or not She will return as an infant. The men worry that there are more battles to come and our goddess will be helpless to aid us while in that form. And the food . . ."

Corvus licked his lips and strove for calm. Nothing Valan had said differed from the thoughts that chased around his own brain each night. Not that he would—could—ever admit that. *And if the Blessed One wasn't being so fucking secretive, so godsdamned stubborn, we could put all their minds at rest. Mine included.* Because the truth was he had no idea if the Dark Lady would somehow transform the infant into a grown woman—a grown goddess—at the moment of Her return. Deep in his heart, he suspected Lanta didn't know either.

"Listre is being dealt with. I've sent correspondence to their government stating we have no quarrel with them—which they're probably stupid enough to believe—and Tresh won't be a problem soon enough. Skerris has scouts on the border just in case. They'll take ship on the Tears as soon as anything untoward is spotted. And I've received confirmation from our friends in Krike that they won't aid any rebel Rilporians."

Valan looked at him steadily. "I know it, Sire, but the men don't. I think that's what has them worried. They know threats are out there and they don't know what's being done about them. The Godblind and the mortal Fox God are still missing, as is your sister. We are . . . forgive me, Sire, we are sitting still. We are shoring up our walls and then hiding behind them. And the longer we wait, the stronger our enemies get. Patrolling the Western Plain is one thing, but why not besiege the South Rank forts? Break the threat on our flank ready to face the Listrans if they come?"

Corvus stood and strode to the window and then back again. "You tell me nothing I haven't thought already myself," he said eventually, and

Valan's shoulders relaxed a little. "And while our warriors are fit again, if we leave Rilporin now, we lose it to our own fucking slaves. Make no mistake, if we abandon this place, we'll have to fight to retake it. If we pull the East Rank back to secure Rilporin, we lose the rest of the country. I've been waiting for Fost. Our women are well used to dealing with rebellious slaves, and with them in place to rule our households for us, aided by a few hundred of the men, we can leave Rilporin in safe hands."

Valan sat back with a soft whoosh of air. "I had not considered that," he admitted.

They were interrupted by a pounding on the door, which was thrown open before Corvus could give leave to enter. He leapt onto the dais, banging his knee into the small table before the throne. "Fuck! Fost? Gods, we were just talking about . . ." Fost's face was grey beneath the sweat and stubble. He looked like a man with a hidden wound. "Tell me."

Fost bowed jerkily, gaze flickering from Corvus to Valan and back. He stopped well out of reach of either of them and weight settled in Corvus's gut, black and heavy. "You don't . . . didn't my messenger reach you?"

"*Tell me.*"

Fost swallowed hard. "Dead, Sire. They're all dead."

Valan grabbed his shoulder and threw him into the chair opposite Corvus. Corvus didn't sit; he leant on his knuckles on the table. "Explain." His voice was quiet, deadly.

Fost's throat clicked as he swallowed and hurried to clarify. "Well, not all. I bring you one hundred and six children and seventy-two women, Sire. The only survivors of all our towns along the Sky Path. The rest are corpses, or missing in the storms in the mountains. A few weeks after we destroyed Watchtown, hundreds of Wolves took the Sky Path and slaughtered every woman, child and priest they could find. Our women and boys fought hard, but they were overwhelmed. The Wolves freed the slaves, who fled with the livestock, and we found a few children who'd survived the attack only to starve to death, it looked like. Those I have with me were clever or lucky enough to be overlooked, and although a few swear they saw the Wolves stealing children —" Corvus's breath hitched. He'd been a stolen child, stolen by the Mireces and brought into the Red Gods' embrace. Saved. "— everyone else — *everyone* — is dead."

Now Corvus did sit, and Valan too, perching on the edge of the table with no thought for propriety. His second breathed as though he'd sprinted the length of the city, greasy sweat darkening his hair. His hands shook.

They stared at Fost, and the war chief swallowed again. "Forgive me, Sire. I did not . . . There was nothing I could . . . They were already dead, months dead, by the time we reached Cat Valley, let alone all the way to Eagle Height."

"Who are the survivors?" Valan asked, his voice hoarse. "Is Neela with them? My girls?"

Fost's shoulders hunched. "The women are all minor consorts from Falcon's Landing and Cat Valley; a storm blew in and they were able to flee, invisible. The children are from all our towns, but Neela's gone, Second, and your girls too. I'm sorry."

Corvus and Fost turned from Valan's ragged grief, shuffling in their seats as he bent double, arms wrapped around his waist as though to ward off a blow. A strangled keening came from him that grated like stone against Corvus's nerves.

"I sent a messenger as soon as we reached Cat Valley, Sire, I swear. If I'd known he didn't make it through . . ." He blinked, then coughed. "We're holding all the survivors outside the city for now, Sire. I wanted to inform you first, before the men see how few they are."

Almost all our women, our children. Our future, gone. We tore apart their people and they did the same to us. So be it. If they want a war of fucking attrition, they've got one.

Corvus's face was hot with rage, but an ice-cold, ice-hard ball of hate sat heavy in his chest. "Fost, you have a list of the women and children, who their consorts and fathers are?" Corvus barely recognised his own voice, it was so harsh with sickening anger. He'd had a few consorts, at least one daughter, both in Crow Crag and Eagle Height. Fost's refusal to even mention them said all he needed to know. The man nodded and held it out. Corvus didn't look at it.

"Bring the men to the women, not the other way around. Women whose man is dead will be reallocated on a merit basis in the first instance. I will announce the . . . tragedy at dusk, and ask the Blessed One to say a few words about what has happened."

"Your will, Sire."

"Valan, I grieve for your loss. Go to Pine Lock for me and kill those Evendoom brothers. Take out your rage on them and make sure everyone knows who they are and why they're dying. I want everyone knowing the royals are dead, that my claim is uncontested."

He couldn't even be sure Valan had heard him, but his second nodded and stalked from the throne room without another word. Corvus pitied anyone who got in his way. He poured ale, drank without tasting, then hurled the cup to shatter against the far wall.

I will kill every last fucking one of them, roast them on spits, wind their guts out, peel their faces off. I will kill them all for this. Dark Lady, Gosfath, God of Blood, witness my oath. Now it's personal.

TARA

TARA STOOD QUIETLY BY the window, sunlight sparking strands of gold from Valan's light-brown hair as he sat with his back to her and the afternoon, staring into the cold fireplace and drinking. He was drinking a lot, and early in the day. Tara didn't like it, or that one of the toy horses rested in his lap. Every so often he turned it over in his hands. Once he'd rubbed it against his cheek.

She didn't dare move. Whatever had happened had made him dangerous and not because he was her enemy. He wanted to hurt something. He wanted to *kill* something and she was the only available target. Violence drifted from him like smoke.

He reached for the bottle on the table next to him and sloshed the last of the wine into his cup. Another, already empty, sat by his elbow. She was surprised he was still conscious. Tara padded silently to the shelf and selected a third, hoping after that cupful he'd pass out. She twisted off the cork, placed the bottle gently on the table and stepped back. Valan caught her hand in his, his thumb stroking along her wrist.

"Fetch another glass and sit. Drink with me."

Oh, fuck.

"Your will, honoured," Tara said. She fetched a cup and then set her chair opposite, out of the candlelight the better to see his shadowed face, poured a small measure and sipped.

"Fill it."

She did as she was told, drinking to quiet the butterflies in her stomach. Valan drank some more, still focused on the fireplace and not her. "Neela's dead." The words were so unexpected in the long silence that she jumped, wine splashing her skirt. "My girls too. All dead. Killed. Murdered. Hacked apart by the cunting Wolves months ago. Months, and only just able to mourn them." He flailed his free hand. "Did all this for them, give them a better life under the blessings of the Red Gods, an easier life down here, and by now they'll have been eaten by cats and crows. They'll never see any of it."

He put his hand over his eyes and she saw the glistening of tears on his cheeks.

"Fuck," Tara breathed and drained her cup. "Valan, I'm so sorry." And she was. She took a deep breath. "Is it . . . just her?"

He shook his head ponderously. "Everyone. All of them bar a couple of hundred survivors. Corvus is going to tell the men at dusk and then this city will erupt. Maybe he thinks they'll be less likely to massacre Rilporians in the dark, I don't know. Fucking idiot. So sure he didn't need to leave fighters back home to defend the villages. Arrogant fucking cunt."

Tara pressed her lips together. Dusk. She had enough time. "Would you like to talk about her?" she asked, taking the cup from his unresponsive fingers and refilling it.

"What?" He sniffed and rubbed his face, downing half the wine when she handed it back.

"Your wife, Neela. Tell me about her and your children. If you wish."

"Why?" he demanded, focusing on her. "So you can gloat?"

Tara lowered her gaze. "Forgive me. I thought it might help." She stood. "I will leave you to your thoughts, honoured."

"Fucking sit," he snarled, so close to violence that Tara was back in her seat before he'd finished speaking, heart yammering against her ribs.

You've got one chance, Carter. Do not fuck this up. And please, Valan, don't do anything stupid. Having to kill you now will ruin everything.

"Neela wasn't so highborn as you," he said after a long silence, surprising her again. The wine was warming her, but she couldn't afford any more of it. "Born and raised in Crow Crag like me, but her father was a low warrior and a thief. Childhood toughened her, taught her guile and strength, enough to turn down consort offers from other low warriors. Lot of the women hated her for that, and one or two men tried to force her. She cut the first one on the face, second in the groin, and then they left her alone."

"I'm not surprised," Tara said with genuine respect. "She sounds formidable."

Valan smiled, sad and full of memory. "She was. She knew what she wanted, what she deserved, and that was a better life than the poorer warriors could give her. I thought I'd lose her to Corvus, you know," he said and met her eyes, gesturing that she drink.

Tara complied, then spat it back into the cup when his gaze drifted away.

"But she didn't want a Rilporian, it seems, even one who'd converted and risen as high as war chief. But his second? She'd settle for that. For me."

"Maybe your gods had a hand in it," Tara said carefully. If he got much drunker and carried on talking about Neela, she'd a fair idea what he'd want from her next. "Sounds like you were a good match," she added. "Perhaps They wanted to reward you with a woman worthy of you."

"Then They did," he said, scuffing a hand through his hair. "I loved her, truly loved her, Tara." Her name in his mouth jolted her. "She gave me three children, though I left before I saw the third born. Wonder if it ever was, or if those motherfuckers killed her before it took a breath."

She flinched.

"I made her my life consort after three months, what you call a wife, took no other lovers, not even on campaign, despite what others thought of me. She'd have loved it here," he added, his voice breaking. "My girls too, Kit and Ede. Five and three, they were. Dead now."

Tara took a deep breath and threaded her fingers together so she didn't drain her cup and then keep drinking until she passed out. She well understood the pain the Wolves had felt when they'd seen the dead of Watchtown, every inhabitant slaughtered or burnt. It was their children too, their future. She understood their need to kill in retaliation. She'd just never put names or faces to the people they were taking their vengeance on. Soldiers didn't if they wanted to carry on soldiering.

Kit and Ede. Five and three. As innocent as any dead Watcher child, at the end of the day.

Gods, the things we do to one another in the name of justice or faith. When does the killing end?

"I'm sorry for your loss, Valan, truly," she murmured. "No one should have to outlive a child." She put her hand on his, warm and rough, but pulled away just as he turned it over so they'd be palm to palm.

"Did you have children?" he asked after he'd stared at his empty hand for a few seconds.

She blinked rapidly. "We . . . have not yet been blessed," she said.

"Perhaps your husband has no seed."

Tara felt herself blush on Vaunt's behalf. "Perhaps I don't," she countered.

Valan smiled drunkenly. "I like you, Tara Vaunt. You will make a good consort one day. Maybe when I get back from Pine Lock. And be careful when I'm gone—it won't be safe out there for a while."

"I—I am already married, honoured," Tara said. He was concerned about her safety?

"For now," Valan said, wagging a finger at her. "For now. Don't forget who you belong to, slave. If you both convert, you may be allowed to stay together. If not . . ."

Tara stood and folded her hands to keep them from shaking. "Speaking of my husband, honoured, is there any chance—"

"Go," he snarled, "go to him while you still fucking can, before he's dead too, dead like my Neela." Valan lurched out of his seat and back-handed her, hard. Tara and the wooden horse both fell to the floor, Tara's head ringing and blood in her mouth. "Go and wind tighter the noose that'll be used to hang you one day."

She lurched to her feet, tripped on the hem of her skirt, and fled the room. "Love is a fucking noose!" he roared after her. As the door closed, she heard the sound of shattering glass.

H E KNEW THE RULES this time. As soon as the cell door swung open and she stepped in, Vaunt swept her into his arms and kissed her, kissed her hard and desperately and not for the sake of appearances, and her mouth opened like a flower to sunlight and his tongue was there, hot and strong and his arms were locked around her so tight she could barely breathe.

He smelt of old sweat and hopelessness, and Valan's words echoed in her head. Tara stamped them into nothing.

She was vaguely aware of the threats and promises from Bern — the fucker was still in charge of the prison and even surlier than the last time — and then her back was pressed to the wall next to the door, pinned by Vaunt's body as he blindly stuffed the blanket into the grille opening, his mouth never leaving hers.

When the window was blocked and no one could see them, Vaunt broke the kiss, though he didn't release her. Her chest was heaving with ragged gasps and she knew well the look in his eyes, knew too he'd step back if she told him to, but she didn't. Cautiously this time, as if she might bite, he pressed his mouth to hers again, almost chaste.

There was a moment of indecision — *this is really not a good idea* — and then she was shoving him backwards, away from the wall and towards the bed, her mouth still on his and her intentions clear.

Vaunt's calves hit the cot and he sat down hard, snaking out a hand lightning-fast to drag her down with him. They rolled on to the mattress, legs tangled, all smacking lips and gasps and Tara could feel his cock, hot and hard, poking into her belly.

She broke away just far enough to suck in air and take in the drugged expression on Vaunt's face and then he rolled, pinning her beneath him and lunging down for another kiss, their teeth banging together and catching the edge of her lip, reopening the cut. He licked the bead of blood from her mouth and wriggled in between her thighs, hands tugging at her neckline, her own hands ripping his shirt out of his waistband and dragging it up so she could rake her fingers across his skin.

Vaunt pulled her skirts to her waist and knelt up long enough to tug at his belt. She met his eyes for a second, panting, and then batted his hands away, ripped open the buckle and dragged at her linens as he scooted his trousers down.

She knew they were both only seeking oblivion, nothing more, and then he was on her, and a second later he was in her and they groaned, kissing again and again, gasping and moving and her hands on his arse and his hands in her breast band, on her face, her throat, her thighs tightening on his hips — neither of them capable of slowness — and it was fucking glorious, and he was glorious, the heat in her belly, his heat inside her, the ridges of muscle in his flanks and shoulders beneath her seeking palms.

Tara threw back her head, fingers hooking into claws, Vaunt's mouth burning kisses on her throat and she could feel him tensing, feel his heart thundering in time with her own and the heat grew, and grew, and then grew some more until it exploded and she arched beneath him, sobbing out breath, her thighs locked shuddering tight, and a heartbeat later he groaned his own release, shaking, their arms so tight around each other, cheeks pressed together, trembling through the aftermath of twitches and little thrusts and dishevelled, rasping gasps for air, the room fading in and out with the pounding of her heart.

Slowly they stilled, and Tara lay in a daze, tranquil for the first time in weeks, her mind a beautiful, washed-clean blank. There were tears on her face and she didn't know whose they were, didn't care. Vaunt went to slide off her and she tightened her arms and legs, shook her head once, wanting his weight on her, pressing her into the cot. A shield. A blanket.

"Hello, Major," he whispered after a while and she sniggered, opened her eyes and looked at him. "I was expecting a knee in the bollocks when I kissed you, to be honest. I just, when I saw you, I just . . ."

"I know. Me too." She smirked and pressed a soft kiss to his mouth, heaving a contented sigh. "But if not, well, you'd have had that knee and more besides. But I have to say, that was just what the physician ordered."

Vaunt chuckled. "Want to go again?" he asked and her eyes widened. "In a while, I mean. Not right now. Gods, who do you think I am?"

"An officer in His Majesty's Palace Rank," Tara said with mock solemnity, "and as such the very pinnacle of soldierly accomplishment."

He wriggled his hips. "Funny you should say that," he began and she kissed him to stop the words.

"If that's a sword and scabbard joke, I'm leaving," she warned.

Vaunt licked his lips. "You have no sense of humour, Major."

"No," she countered with a grin, "jokes like that prove *you* have no sense of humour. Now, do you want to hear my news or not?"

"Not," he said emphatically and put his head down on her chest. "I just want to stay here and pretend everything is fine."

Tara smoothed his hair, relishing the weight crushing her into the lumpy mattress, the contented aching in her hips. "Me too, but we can't and it isn't. One of their war chiefs came back from Eagle Height this morning. Nearly all their women and children were killed by a group of Wolves who didn't come to the siege after Watchtown fell. By all accounts it was a bloody massacre up on the Sky Path. Corvus is going to tell the Mireces what's happened at dusk, at which point there's likely to be a second massacre—of slaves this time."

Vaunt rolled off her. "Gods, they did it then. I heard their chief, Lim, talking about it once, but I didn't think they'd have the . . . well, I didn't think they were cruel enough to kill defenceless innocents."

Kit and Ede. Five and three.

Tara pulled him a little closer. "Why not? That's what Corvus did to theirs. It's what they've done in every town and village they've come across. The Wolves were angry, and they had every right to be."

He made a non-committal sound, his hand tracing the growing bruise on her cheek. He didn't ask about it, and she was glad.

She paused, but there was no good way to phrase it. "We'll only get one chance at this rebellion; I'm wondering if this could be it. If the Raiders go on a rampage, some people will fight back. It could spread; it could be the opportunity we need."

Vaunt was silent, staring through her as he thought. "I don't know," he said eventually. "The Mireces will be looking for blood as it is; if we fight back they'll lose all restraint. It'll be brutal and none of us have weapons. Civilians won't fight but they will die, so many of them that the survivors will never raise their heads again. But if we wait for it to die down and then start a whisper in the market that they're going to pay . . . combined with the rage at the unprovoked deaths, that might be enough."

"You're saying we sit here and do nothing and let innocent people die to make others angry enough to fight back?"

Vaunt winced. "Yes."

Tara blew out her cheeks. "Fuck. It'd crossed my mind too on the way here. The angrier they are, the more injustices piled on them—" She broke off and shuddered. "Gods, I feel filthy even saying it. Mace would kill me if he heard me talking like this."

"We don't have enough on our side. It's only us and the masons so far. We'd be massacred. Besides, this is all to facilitate your assassinations. What are the chances of you getting close to Corvus or Lanta tonight?"

She grunted. "Zero." *And I'll have a drunk Valan to deal with,* she thought but didn't add. Vaunt didn't need to know.

"Well, then. People are going to die tonight and there's nothing we can do to stop it, even if we did fight back. So hunker down and stay the fuck safe, you hear me, wife?"

The corner of Tara's mouth lifted. "Yes, sir, husband, sir," she said, and he surprised her with another kiss. She'd thought, now the deed was done, that'd be it, but his lips were warm and his tongue was hot and she wound her arms around his neck and clung to him, driftwood in a flood, safe harbour in a storm.

Vaunt slid back between her thighs and Tara gasped and curled her legs up, her boots resting in the small of his back. "Just stay safe," she managed when he broke the kiss. "Promise me."

"Don't worry about us," he murmured, kissing her jaw, the corner of her mouth. "We're soldiers; we're expendable. That's how it's always been. You know that as well as I do."

"No," she said quietly, palms on his face so he had to meet her eyes. "You stay alive, you hear me?"

"You first—" he began.

The door rattled and then swung open. "You're done here," Bern said, "less you want to do me too."

Tara tightened her arms on Vaunt before he leapt from the bed to confront the man. "Yes, honoured," she said and saw the twist of disgust on Vaunt's mouth. She pushed him off and he wriggled into his trousers while Tara pulled her linens back on and stood, tucking the long side of her hair behind her ear—the other side, which had burnt off during the siege, was too short for her to do anything but slick down.

"I'll see you soon. I love you," she added for Bern's benefit, but it sparked something in her chest she didn't expect and couldn't afford. She was spared having to think about it by Bern snapping his fingers at her. She fled.

RILLIRIN

Eighth moon, first year of the reign of King Corvus
Fort Three, South Rank forts, Western Plain, Krike border

IT WAS TIME TO leave and, now that it was here, Rillirin didn't want to go. She had trained every day with the civilian militia and the Rankers; she was getting better. She could fight. She wanted to fight.

The wriggling of the life inside reminded her that wasn't the best option. Nearly five months gone and the swelling of her belly was obvious to all now. She was tired; she was grumpy; she was hungry. She knew leaving was the best option but she hated it. Every time she started to find out who she was, who she could be out from under the Mireces collar, her life was turned upside down and she had to start again.

"Not you," she whispered fiercely on a surge of guilt. "I don't hate you, little warrior. I just don't know who I'm supposed to be. I never really have."

"Pregnancy can give you the strangest thoughts," said Martha, the woman who had the next cot over. Her youngest was still on the breast and shared with her, while the older two curled up in the next one. "Me, when my eldest was born, I spent weeks, moons even, convinced I'd drop him or let him fall. Slept in the kitchen because I wouldn't risk the stairs up to the bedchamber with him in my arms. Ben used to have to carry him for me whenever we left the house. I was a wreck."

She indicated the little face attached to her nipple. "This one? Tied him to my back and climbed ladders to escape the Mireces and the flames. You do what you have to in that situation. Not that you'll have to do any of that," she added. "I'm sure this place they're taking us to will be safe."

Martha was one of the few who hadn't fallen to pieces when Mace announced his intention to send every civilian except the militia away from the forts. For days there'd been chaos, some city-folk flatly refusing to leave, others rushing to join the militia in the hopes that would keep them safe.

Rillirin had felt a surge of the same fear—by her reckoning she hadn't stayed in any one place more than a few months since her escape from Eagle Height. The Wolf Lands—their destination—held more bad memories than good, but then so did everywhere. A single night of lovemaking in the West Rank forts wasn't much to stand against the horrors, but it was all she had and she clung to it. They'd make more, once the war was over and Dom was himself again and the babe was here. A lifetime more.

The bell rang the hour and Martha and Rillirin looked at each other: time to go. Socks, waterskins, any possessions or wealth they'd managed to bring with them were wrapped up in blankets and slung over their backs. Martha's babe was strapped to her chest inside her shirt so she had a hand free for each of the other children and Rillirin watched her walk out of the barracks as though they were going on a picnic. Rillirin herself was afraid and her child was yet to be born—what Martha must have be thinking of her chances of outrunning an enemy in the wide expanse of the Western Plain, she didn't even want to contemplate.

"We're not going to have to do that," she reassured herself. "Four hundred Rankers and a score of Wolves are going with us. We'll be fine." Still, she tightened her grip on her spear as she followed Martha out into the morning. Gilda was waiting for her and Rillirin felt a rush of reassurance at her presence.

The drill yard was packed to capacity with civilians, some in sullen silence, others weeping, a few still shouting even now. Colonel Osric stood on an anvil outside the smithy so they could all see him. "Citizens of Rilpor," he shouted, signalling for quiet. "I know you're afraid. I know you hoped that this would be your refuge until the war was over. It is not, and you know the reasons for that. You're scared, and you're right to be—" More muttering. She wondered what Osric's rallying speech before a battle would be like. "—but the Wolf Lands are the safest place you can be. Safer than here, which is why you're leaving. You have supplies for the journey, and you have soldiers to guard you and Wolves to guide you. Dancer's grace."

He jumped down from the anvil and Rillirin realised that was it, that was all they were getting. Be scared. Walk. Pray.

"Well, he won't be earning any commendations for public speaking," Gilda muttered, then patted Martha and Rillirin both on the shoulders. "Not to fret. They killed the war bands out in the Western Plain and the Commander has more patrols scouting. The plain is safe. But if they do come, you run and you don't look back, all right?"

Rillirin's hands went to her belly as Gilda's words loosened her bladder. "Run," she said numbly. "Of course." She adjusted the cord holding her blanket and few possessions. *We will run, won't we, little warrior? Run as far as we need to and we'll hide, and then we'll keep going, miles every day, safer and safer the further west we get, and never look behind us.*

Martha huffed a laugh. "You want to walk with us?" she asked them both. "I'd feel better with a Wolf and a priestess by my side."

"I will," Gilda said, "but the lass should make her own decision."

Rillirin paused, knowing the priestess was trying to give her a way out—she knew the thoughts whirling through Rillirin's head. "We'll go together," she said at last. "It's always a good idea to stick with Gilda."

Martha smiled with relief Rillirin didn't share. She told herself the Mireces wouldn't kill women and children; they were too valuable. They'd be fine; they didn't have a link to the Raiders as Rillirin did. She could leave them if she had to. It'd be fine.

Martha pressed a small hand into Rillirin's. "Ben Junior, you mind your manners and listen to Auntie Rillirin, all right? We've got a long way to walk and you'll be tired, but I need you to be a brave boy and do as you're told. We're going on another adventure."

Ben watched his mother with grave solemnity. "I don't like adventures," he said. "Are we going to find my da?"

Grief flashed across Martha's face and her lip trembled, but she had no words.

Gilda knelt stiffly by his side. "We're going to the forests and the mountains where I come from," she said. "Mountains so tall that they have snow on all year round. So tall that if the sun isn't careful, he'll pop like an egg yolk on the point of Mount Gil and then we'd be in trouble, wouldn't we? This adventure takes us away from the cities and into the wilds. But no, your da won't be there, I'm afraid. But we will."

"Am I the only Ben now, then?" the little boy asked.

"That's right," Gilda said. "You've got your da's job now to look after your ma and your little brothers."

Ben scuffed his boot on the flagstones and heaved a sigh. "All right, then," he said.

Gilda stood back up and Rillirin watched her, swallowing against the lump in her throat. The old priestess nodded once and took Ben's other hand in hers.

All right, little warrior. You and me and Gilda, and Martha and her three as well. But no more. We'll stick together and run from the danger and make it to the Wolf Lands. We take them, but no others. We can't.

And with that, the fort's gates creaked open and they began the march.

T HEY WERE TWO MILES out, moving in a ragged mass thirty ranks wide and more than a hundred long, with four hundred Rankers ahead and to the sides. Twenty provisions wagons pulled by horses the Rank could ill afford to lose rolled in the middle.

Rillirin's heart lurched when a horse cantered up alongside, and then lurched again when she saw who rode it: Dalli. The Wolf chief reined in and dismounted; then she beckoned to her. Rillirin passed Ben back to his mother. "I'll catch you up soon," she promised and dodged her way through the straggling lines.

"Here," Dalli said and held out a leather thong with an amulet dangling from it.

"What is it?" Rillirin asked, not moving to take it.

Dalli ran her tongue over her teeth. "Years ago—you probably know this—years ago Dom and I were lovers. He gave me this. I didn't keep it because I still love him," she added in a rush. "It just became a sort of good-luck charm. I thought you could have it. The charm, the luck, whatever. Gilda said you don't have anything of Dom's and that . . . didn't feel right to me."

Rillirin still hesitated. "I have his child."

"If you don't want it, fine." Dalli reached for the saddle.

"Wait. You said he's a traitor and a murderer. You said our babe will be a monster."

Dalli winced, thrust the necklace at her again and this time Rillirin took it.

"We both know I'm a pig-headed fool at times," Dalli said. "I . . . I thought you were dead, back when you went overboard and it grieved me. Gilda, well, let's just say the priestess and I had words and she made me realise a few things." She scraped fingers through her spiky hair, looking past Rillirin to where the priestess waited, stolid and silent and watchful. "Whatever Dom is or isn't, you're my friend. I mean, you were, and I hope you will be again. If we both live, that is."

Rillirin dragged her into a hug, cutting off her words. She smelt of sweat and horse and she was small and hard, like diamond. "I love you," she whispered fiercely and Dalli's arms tightened around her.

"I love you, too. Look after my home, war-kin." Rillirin pulled back to stare at her and Dalli winked. "We'll make a Wolf of you yet. Now go, and Dancer go with you. I'll see you when this is all over."

Rillirin forced herself to let go. "Dancer's grace. Kill them all for me."

Dalli grinned a wolf's grin. "You know it."

DOM

Eighth moon, first year of the reign of King Corvus
Vision house, Seer's Tor, Krike

I T TOOK DOM ALMOST an hour to walk from the small, heavily guarded house in the travellers' quarter, his guards grumbling at the slowness of his pace and the sun high above by the time they arrived. They were lucky—if he hadn't managed to sleep through the previous evening, night and morning, they'd be carrying him. Even so, he was sweat-slick and wobbling by the time he reached the vision house.

It was a small roundhouse with a low thatched roof and a central smoke hole, the structure nestled at the base of the tor in almost perpetual shadow. The lead warrior pointed. "In."

Dom ducked his head and shuffled into the gloom of the interior. His eyes hadn't begun to adjust when the door was shut behind him and the darkness grew, leavened only by dancing orange flames in the small fire pit. Someone sat in the shadows on the other side.

"Calestar. That's who you are—what you are—isn't it?"

The roof beams were many and low and Dom lowered himself on to his knees opposite the figure. "Seer-Mother?"

She leant forward so the flames touched their colours upon her cheeks and swirled in the tattoos chasing around her eyes. "It is a joy and a privilege to meet one who shares the power to converse with the gods. There is much we can learn from each other."

"The honour is mine, Seer-Mother," he said and meant it. "I have never met anyone else who shares my gift. I'm eager to see how the experience of godsight affects you, and whether you have any particular rituals to help ease the pain of the communion. As you saw with me yesterday, it is unexpected and . . . difficult."

The Seer-Mother watched him through the smoke. "So you do not summon it then?" she asked. "I had thought you called it in order to deflect attention from the fraud whose side you haunt."

Dom frowned. "Fraud? Crys is no fraud, Seer-Mother. It is difficult to believe, I know, but he is the Fox God in mortal form. I have seen him perform miracles; I have seen him do many things. The knowings sent to me by the . . . by the Dancer confirm it. If you would but speak to him instead . . ."

"All in good time," Tanik said smoothly. "I spoke with the lover at dawn; I speak with you at noon. It may be I shall speak with Crys when the sun goes to rest. It will depend on your testimony, Calestar. I have my people to care for—I will not allow them to be coaxed into a war by a false god. You said it yourself, after all—someone here lies. There is nothing to say that that someone is not one of your companions."

She waved her hands as if to bat away her words and the need for Dom to answer them. "But first, let us get to know each other. Your gift, Calestar. Have you had it long?"

He was thirsty, the smoke clinging to his throat. "Since I was a boy. There hadn't been a calestar in a generation by the time I showed the gift, so my parents were unsure how to deal with it. When my mother—my adopted mother, that is, Gilda—when she understood what I was, my birth parents gifted me to her and the temple so that I could be raised as close to the gods as possible. It was a difficult time, but it was the right decision for all of us. Gilda Priestess loved me and raised me and helped me to understand what I was."

"Abandoned by your parents when your power manifested? Little wonder you forsook the Light. Oh yes, Calestar, tales of your betrayals reach even Krike, borne on the breath of the gods. But of course you would give yourself to Blood: you had learnt from a young age that the pursuit of power was to be honoured above all else, including family."

Her words were a hammer blow to the chest and Dom gasped, shocked. "That's not how it was. None of it. My parents made the right choice."

"For themselves, certainly. No doubt it was horrifying to watch you suffer so, and easier to give you away so that they did not have to witness it, while at the same time, I'm sure, thinking they made the right choice for you."

There was absolutely no condescension in her tone, but her words prised the lid off a suspicion he'd buried twenty years before and Dom was light-headed with the realisation of it. *Her power is great indeed.*

She threw a bundle of herbs into the fire pit. They flared in a moment of incandescence and then faded, leaving a thick waft of smoke and scent to billow outwards. Dom coughed.

"And now you return to the Light?" the Seer-Mother asked. "Or just to the side of this man you believe to be a god? Having forsaken the Light for Blood, having ended the reign of the Dark Lady, you now seek yet another higher purpose to which you can dedicate yourself? Are you addicted to the power you gain from walking at the side of such beings?"

Dom's head was swimming—anger, denial, guilt, delight, understanding all bundled together in a tangled mess, his sense of himself crumbling like the herbs in the flame. "Truly you see much," he croaked. "But that is not . . . that's not who I am. In this you see false."

Tanik smiled and waved away the comment. "Don't worry, I won't tell your companions. Your secret remains between us." Dom glanced over her shoulder at the man kneeling behind her. "My brother, Pesh Crow-dream. Don't worry about him."

"You're wrong about me," Dom said again. He was so thirsty.

"Or perhaps you are darker still," she mused as though he hadn't spoken, one finger stroking along her jaw and down her throat. "Perhaps your addiction is the ending of such creatures. Are you a god-slayer by trade, Dom Templeson? Does your friend Crys need to fear you?"

"No!"

Perhaps. I don't know.

The Seer-Mother smiled, as though the words inside Dom were as clear as the denial he'd voiced. "Perhaps if Crys is who he claims to be, his death would secure the Dark Lady's return. Perhaps that is your ultimate aim. And if he is not, well, what's one more death on your conscience? But it may be that the cards will tell us."

There was a slow liquid thudding in Dom's ears as her words insinuated themselves between the spaces in his mind, settling like oil into the darker crevices. Pregnant. Waiting. Not entirely unwelcome.

Tanik Horse-dream drew a stack of large, ornate cards from a small box that Pesh handed to her. There were more leaves in the bottom, glossy and dark, and Pesh tipped those into the fire too. "Bay leaves," Tanik said, "from the far, far south of Krike. They help us to see."

The man retreated and Dom watched as Tanik laid out the cards, face up, one at a time. They were intricately painted with vivid natural scenes, some disturbing and some incomprehensible.

"What are these?" Dom asked, his heart still troubled by Tanik's suggestions and eager to change the subject. The smoking leaves gave off a bright, heady scent.

"They aid my understanding. This is how I learn the gods' will, a way very different from yours, but no less powerful. Please, touch any of those you feel particularly attracted to. Don't think about it, just place your fingers and then move on."

Unease was crawling through Dom's gut as he studied the images, his gaze flicking back and forth and back again, over and over.

This is her version of the knowings? Where is the deep connection, the god-space inside her? How does this work, exactly?

Can I learn this, a pain-free communion? Can she teach me?

Hesitantly, he touched four cards in quick succession and then sat back, his breathing ragged. Tanik and Pesh both leant forward, studying the four, and then removed the others from the layout. They glanced at each other and the knot in Dom's stomach pulled tighter.

"What? Have I done something wrong?" he blurted.

Pesh snorted faintly.

"Many things," Tanik said with a sharp smile, "but in the case of the cards, no. There are no wrong decisions, only those that reveal a person's inner turmoil or worry."

The bay leaves thickened the air so that it felt as if he was breathing water, and everything had a faint golden outline, like flame.

Like fire.

"No," Dom said, "no, not now. Not again." His back arched in a spasm, arms flinging out to his sides as though he was trying to fly. "Help me," he slurred, his tongue thick in his mouth, crown of his head pushing up, fingers seeking as though he was being racked.

"Interesting," he heard Tanik murmur. "Most interesting."

Then all was fire and understanding and pain. Pain.

A H, GOOD. YOU'RE BACK with us."

Dom groaned and forced his eyes open against the spike of agony impaling the right side of his face. He was slumped in the gloom of the vision house, the Seer-Mother seated opposite, Pesh behind her. They didn't appear to have tried to help him, or sent for Crys or Ash. His body was heavy, thick with exhaustion, but he forced himself upright.

Tanik leant forward eagerly, her eyes bright amid the tattoos, heavy brown plaits decorated with feathers and beads hanging either side of her face. "What did you see?" she asked.

"I need to go," Dom croaked. "The knowings tire me; I need to rest."

Tanik shooed away the suggestion. "You can rest here. Just tell me what you saw."

Without speaking, Pesh moved to sit between him and the door. *Oh. So it's going to be like that, is it?*

"I chose the cards first," he said with an effort. "Tell me about them, and then I'll tell you what I saw."

The Seer-Mother hesitated and then inclined her head. "Very well."

Dom grimaced, mouth sour with blood, the thick air scouring his throat and rancid with the scent of vomit. Didn't they have water?

"You are sure you wish to know?" Tanik said and the agony spiked in Dom's head again, but he didn't answer, just gestured with a shaking hand for her to proceed. He needed as much time as he could steal to gather some strength before he made a dash for the door.

"We were discussing your childhood, your abandonment by your family and how you subsequently abandoned your gods—and then your adopted gods. The question was whether you would then abandon, or even hurt, Crys, who you mistakenly believe to be our Holy Trickster.

Those were the thoughts uppermost in your mind when you chose these cards." She pointed to each in turn. "The knife; the child; the divine in man; and the harvest."

The Seer-Mother paused, watching him as though her words would trigger another reaction. Dom held himself still, breathing steadily through the pain.

"That was your interpretation of my situation, yes," he said with an effort. "Now please tell me what your cards say."

"They concur, of course," Tanik said as though that was obvious. "You have chosen a powerful combination, Calestar. The knife: both threat and protection, healing and killing. A double-edged sword or a two-faced man. Trust and betrayal."

Dom concentrated on the itch in the stump of his arm, the flicker of ghostly fingers reaching for a ghostly knife.

"The child: could be you as a boy, betrayed by your parents. Or it could be a child of your own; either the one who died with your wife so long ago, or the one not yet born." Dom licked his lips and swore under his breath. She couldn't have known that. She *couldn't*. "Taken together, you plan to betray your child as you were betrayed, perhaps even kill it."

"Or, by your own admission, it could relate to my deep-buried feelings about my parents," he pointed out. The Seer-Mother smiled and inclined her head.

"The divine in man is interesting, and clearly relates to your beliefs about your friend. Or perhaps the divine spark each of us carries within ourselves. Is yours still lit, or is your spark red and liquid? And the harvest in this context would be the souls of the faithful that you hope to reap here." She paused and rubbed her fingertips against her lips, eyes dancing across the cards.

"It may be the divine in man relates to the child as well?" she murmured and Dom couldn't help his intake of breath or the cough it triggered. Tanik nodded as though he'd confirmed her suspicions. "You will betray your child to the enemy. When it is born it will be special, with powerful magic or magic performed upon it. It has a great destiny and will draw all souls to itself. You know this, and so you harbour thoughts of killing it and so preventing the catastrophe."

Dom had no words, could hear nothing more over the roaring in his ears. He hadn't thought that, not once. He wouldn't. Betray Rillirin and their babe? Never. *Never.* He'd die rather than think such horrors.

But Tanik's words were chiming with something deep inside, something oily and putrescent, a lingering idea that had sparked almost as soon as he'd killed the Dark Lady and knew what an awful mistake it had been, how he needed to bring Her back.

"This is horseshit," he said, as steadily as he could manage. "These cards are toys; you can interpret them any way you like. They're not the gods' words. We agree I likely have deep-seated feelings about my birth parents and of course I don't want my own child to feel the same and so I'll do right by it, and the harvest is the hope for peace! It's not complicated. They're just pictures that tell a story."

Despite his words, he didn't know what to believe, or what he'd been thinking when he'd selected the cards. She'd seeded the thought in his head, yes, but had it found fertile soil?

"Now, we had a deal," the Seer-Mother said as though she hadn't just carved a hole inside Dom. "What did you see during your rather theatrical vision?"

"Is this it?" Dom demanded, ignoring her question and sweeping the cards aside with the stump of his arm. "Is this the only way you see the future? You don't speak directly with the gods?"

"The gods speak directly through the cards," Tanik corrected him, a hint of impatience creeping into her voice.

"And you decide what you think they mean by adding together the pictures into a story? That's not knowing; that's not real. It's—it's pretend. You could say anything that fits those images." He took a breath. "You're trying to discredit me, and you're trying to pretend Crys isn't your god, but you're the one who's a fraud. These cards are meaningless. They can be interpreted in a thousand different ways—there's no chance you could ever know for sure what the Dancer is telling you."

He'd expected Tanik to erupt, but instead she sat serene before him, hands folded together, her many beads and amulets rattling softly as she tipped her head on to one side and watched him along the blade of her nose.

"You are wasting time playing games with me, when you should be on your knees pledging to serve your gods, to serve Crys," he continued, heaving for breath in the dark, close confines of the smoky vision house. "What is it you want from me? Why have you led these people astray?"

Tanik gestured and Pesh slid past her to throw more herbs on to the brazier. A thick grey cloud rolled up to hang among the low roof beams. Dom's head swam. "You're going to give your child to the Red Gods."

"I am not," Dom snarled as images tickled at the corners of his eyes. He blinked them away.

"Lies and falsity, the very things of which you accuse me," Tanik said, tapping a fingernail against the cards Dom himself had chosen. His head was reeling and the tattoos around her eyes seemed to draw him in so he couldn't look away. "Fire," she murmured, "bright flags of fire in your eyes. In your head. Messages in the fire. Messages about your child, about Rillirin. Tell me of her. Rillirin. Tell me."

"How do you know that name?" he managed but again it was too late. Dom's jaws snapped together and he lurched sideways—and fell. Into the flames. Into the images and the pain and the knowing. He could hear screaming.

When it was over, when the world returned to him and he to his body, the ground was pressing into his back. The pain in his head was excruciating and tears were sliding down his cheeks into his hair. A familiar exhaustion, stinking as a corpse shroud, lay over his limbs. Heels and elbows and shoulder blades throbbed with bone-deep bruises from the convulsions.

The words were in his head and his throat was raw, but he had no idea if he'd told them anything. Everything. He forced open his eyes and Tanik and Pesh were there, silent, watching him.

"You make quite the spectacle," Tanik Horse-dream said eventually, and that's when Dom noticed the cards on the yellow silk square before her had changed. He grunted and held his hand to his right eye, trying to focus the left. Didn't work; he couldn't make out the images as they writhed like living things across the cards. Pesh threw more leaves on the fire and Dom suddenly realised what they were doing, how they were forcing the knowings out of him. He hadn't even suspected such a thing was possible; he had no idea how they knew what to do or how he could stop it. A whimper slid from his throat and he tried holding his breath, but his body was so spent it demanded air. He sucked in smoke as well, felt it tingling in his throat, his lungs, into his brain.

"Please don't," he managed. "The Fox God will never forgive you. You're His priestess, His and the Dancer's. Please, no more."

The Seer-Mother chuckled and wafted the smoke in his direction. She breathed deep of it herself, but he knew it wasn't meant for her. "You can feel it, can't you? The lure of the Blood? You can see the Dark Path once more beneath your feet, can't you, Calestar? Serving Blood, always serving Blood."

Dom tried to scrabble backwards but his body was as unresponsive as a sack of meat. And shining bright in the centre of him: memory and loss and love and devotion. Adoration. He tried to push it away but it coated his hands and arms and face and soul, drew him into its red-black vortex. Drew him back in. He wept and struggled and begged and then surrendered and embraced it. Felt it slip around him Blood-warm, Blood-soft. Wept some more.

"Fire and knowledge, Calestar. Such knowledge; enough for us all to share. Where is General Mace Koridam and what are his plans?" Tanik asked, her voice low and coaxing. "You can see him, can't you? In the flames? Go to him, learn his intentions. And tell me."

Teeth gritted, fist clenched at his side, Dom thought of Gilda's face instead, wise and laughing and suffused with strength. Gilda and the Light. He reached for her but the image trembled, shifted, slid into another. A different woman, one beautiful, lustful, and lost. He choked.

The fire roared.

TIME PASSED OF WHICH Dom knew nothing, and then someone was lifting his head and shoulders roughly, shoving a hard cushion under them and letting him drop with little care. The inside of his skull felt as though it had been scoured out with salt and rusty blades and his eyesight, if anything, was worse. Blood and saliva mixed thick and sticky in his mouth and he couldn't spit it out. Couldn't move. Could barely breathe.

Dom had lost count of the knowings, of the questions or the answers he'd given—if he'd given them any. Gods knew he'd tried not to, but his throat was raw with screams, stinging with bile and thick vision smoke, and, for all he knew, from shouting answers at them in response to the incessant questioning.

"Go," the Seer-Mother said, though not to him, and a figure exited the vision house. She loomed over him and there was a sharp sting beneath his ear and then a fierce burning through the skin and into his head and neck. The light filtering in through the wattle walls was a rich golden summer afternoon. Hours, then. Hours in the fire, burning.

Numbness spread through Dom's neck and tongue from the site of the stinging pain beneath his ear, stealing sensation from his skin, his mouth, his nose, creeping towards his eye.

Sound faded in and out and his vision steadily darkened. The numbness moved into his chest, down his arm.

The fire raged one last time inside him, and Dom flung himself towards it, seeking not knowledge but oblivion. An ending. The cushion did nothing to deaden the impact of convulsion, but Dom's body was so drained that he did little more than twitch, weak as a drowning kitten.

He found the fire—the ending—with something like relief.

He fell.

CRYS

Eighth moon, first year of the reign of King Corvus
Seer's Tor, Krike

WHAT THE FUCK? DOM?"

Ash's shout brought Crys at a run from the kitchen, fingers clutching for a sword that had been confiscated before their imprisonment began.

The door was open and Dom lay in front of it, sprawled and unconscious. "He had one of his fits," a Krikite said and walked away.

Ash stared after him for a second and then bent to Dom. The calestar was the grey of a dead fire, his skin waxen with old sweat. "Help me get him inside," he said and Crys grabbed his legs and together they manoeuvred him on to a bed. "He's breathing, but only just. Lie him on his side; I don't want him choking if he pukes. And get all the blankets we have. And make some broth."

Crys did as he was told, moving fast. He handed Ash a cup and the man tried to dribble some into Dom's mouth, but he didn't swallow and they had to tilt his head to get it back out again.

"He's barely breathing," Ash said. "This is bad, Crys. We need a healer."

"Keep him warm; I'll get one." Crys opened the front door again and the guards leapt to attention, brandishing spears. "Our friend is sick. Fetch a healer, please." Nobody moved. "He might be dying." Still nothing. "Then get me the Seer-Mother. Dom was with her when this happened and I've got some questions of my own. Fetch her!"

"Seer-Mother is in retreat at the top of the tor," a Krikite said. "No one's to interrupt her when she's communing with the gods."

Crys's mouth was sour. "Oh, believe me," he grated, "she's not communing with the gods. I'd know if she was. Whoever it is she's talking to up there, it's not for your benefit or your land's. Now get her here."

The warrior who'd spoken blew out his cheeks with affected boredom and then spat a thick gob of saliva on to the grass. "Not happening."

Crys slammed the door on them and returned to the bedchamber. "They're not shifting and they won't send for aid." He stared down at the motionless figure. "All right, move. Let me see what I can do."

He knelt by the bed and put his hands on Dom's brow and stomach, closed his eyes and reached. "Come on, come on," he muttered through gritted teeth. "Foxy, come on. He needs us."

Climb the tor.

Crys's eyes opened. "What?"

Climb the tor and make them all see. Dream with them. Go now.

He rose to his feet. "What are you doing?" Ash demanded. "Crys, love, I know what he did but . . . I think he's dying."

Crys pulled off his boots and socks. "I have to climb the tor. I have to go . . . home, to my birthplace."

Ash gaped. "What the living fuck are you on about? We need a healer, not a fucking picnic with a view."

"I know it doesn't make sense, but I have to dream with them. It's time to show them all who I am. The Seer-Mother's up there and she won't come down, so I'll go to her." He pulled off his shirt, unbuckled his empty sword belt and kept just a knife shoved into the back of his trousers. "Find Cutta and tell her I'm climbing the tor. Tell her the Fox God will dream with them all at dawn, but they have to take the Cunning Way. You too, and bring Dom. I'll see you at the top. Bring as many as you can; tell Cutta to help."

"Dawn?" Ash demanded. "Trickster's cock, man, *what are you going to do?*"

Crys took a swig of water and then shook out his arms. "What I have to. Just get them up there. When they see me climbing, they'll want to come. I hope." He didn't wait for an answer, just ripped open the front door again and stalked out. Shirtless in the bright sun, he knew the spectacle his scars would make and he could feel the heat in his eyes as they began to glow. "Take me to the Seer-Mother."

The Krikites stumbled backwards and half of them set their spears in readiness to run him through. "It is forbidden. You have not been summoned and you are not Krikite."

Crys shrugged and began walking; they scattered from his path and then rushed to catch up, trying to slow him but unwilling to touch. "Then stop me or bear witness."

They wouldn't stop him.

CRYS DUG HIS TOES into a crack in the rock and ground out a curse as a nail split and a hot spike of pain shot through his foot. He spat on his palm, rubbed his fingertips in it, repeated with his other hand and then shook out both arms one at a time. Just dropping his arms below shoulder height was exquisite relief. He stretched out his aching fingers, face and chest pressed to the rock to maintain his balance.

The sun was tumbling out of the sky and he was only a little over halfway up, but his heart was slowing now that he'd made the traverse around the outcrop. The rock face was already in shadow, making it harder to see the route he'd thought to take. *If it was a route. Looks bastard different up here to how it seemed down there. Higher for one. A fuckload scarier for two.*

He took a steadying breath and chanced a look down and then all around, studying the striations and cracks, trying to find a dozen that he could string together to get him higher. Up and to his right, an arm's length distant, was a wide lip of rock. He could get his hands and maybe even his elbows on that, haul himself up to sitting and have a proper rest, and then use it to move up. He squinted. No toeholds to reach it. He'd have to swing, handholds or nothing. If he missed the lip he'd fall, but even so it looked like his best option. It was that or climb back down and start again, and he knew this was his only chance. If he didn't summit now he'd started, the Krikites would kill him.

Hundreds had gathered at the base of the tor, craning their necks up to watch his progress. He just had to hope Ash and Cutta could encourage them to come back at sunrise to dream with him. If they didn't, well, there was a good chance the Seer-Mother wouldn't let him back down alive.

Flicking the blood off his feet and then wedging his sore toes deeper, Crys shook out his arms again and flexed his fingers, got a tight grip with his left hand and then pushed his arse backwards and began to rock from side to side, right hand reaching for the ledge. He swung three times and at the apex of the fourth he let go, drove through his legs and flung himself through space towards the lip.

He missed.

Crys wasn't falling. He absolutely wasn't falling, because that would be ridiculous and terrifying and *oh fuck, I'm falling!*

In fact, once he'd slammed into the rock it turned out he really wasn't falling so much as sliding back down, stone burning his palms and chest and the soles of his feet as he pressed himself against it, scrabbling for purchase. He slid twice his own height before his right foot hit a ledge almost hard enough to break his ankle. The impact arrested his speed just enough for him to find a crevice and burrow his fist inside and then he hung, suspended by his left hand and right foot, panting, bleeding from a score of abrasions and with an insane laugh bubbling through his chest.

Cursing and giggling and drunk on adrenaline and fear, he found a fingerhold for his right hand and, shoulders burning, rock rash scoring his bare flesh, he began again to climb.

CRYS COULD CLEARLY SEE the rock wall despite the dark, and the stir of the wind against his skin was a language he could almost understand. Guiding him, teasing him towards the handholds that would take his weight and gain him another few inches. As though he'd become a part of the landscape, its heart beating in his chest.

His legs were shaking now, his forearms and the muscles in his hands thick and stiff with fatigue, but the stars were above him instead of stone—another half-dozen reaches and he'd have made it.

Sweat stung his eyes and trickled down his cheek to slide bitter into his mouth. He licked his dry lips with his dry tongue, thirst ravaging his throat. Soft and furtive sounds from above—people moving around, talking in low voices, the growing orange glow of torches. It was tempting to call for help, but he'd come this far without it and didn't need it now.

The next few handholds were easy, his toes jamming into crevices and clinging to tiny outcrops as though he was more squirrel than fox, and then, suddenly, he was there. He climbed over the edge and reached flat ground, standing tall despite the urge to cling to the surface in case he inexplicably threw himself off the top after all his efforts to reach it. His belly undulated as he sucked in cool air and starlight.

There was a group of people peering down the tor's side about twenty strides from him; they must have lost sight of him in the darkness. He backed away from the light, around a hump of rock and into the darkness, leaving them to their useless searching, wandering until he found his feet rooted to the stone.

Here?

Here. Sit and listen.

Crys sat cross-legged, feeling the sweat dry on his chest and shoulders and back and his muscles soften and relax, the poisons of exertion seeping away. He watched the night, the sliver of moon and the peeking stars hiding and revealing their faces behind veils of cloud. The wind hummed around the stone, laughing, and bats and owls and night moths rode its currents. Crys listened to the wind and the stone, the moon and clouds and stars, the gentle lullaby of the earth sleeping far below.

The tor connected earth with sky, body with soul, and human with divine. Crys was a knot in the thread between the heart of the night and the soul of the earth. He could reach out and touch . . . everything. He could feel the sanctity of this place moving like a slow ripple through the tor and through him, a constant ululation. It was both ancient and familiar and sparkling with newness.

He inhaled summer night and reached inside himself, probing into the spaces the god inhabited, curling into and around and through what he found there, ivy through a skeleton, binding life with memory.

And the Trickster grew to meet him, a feeling like a beloved's fingers sliding through his in every part of his body so that Crys realised he was laughing and weeping at the same time, quietly so as not to shatter the experience. He was welcomed into his own body, understanding then that it had never really been his, and wasn't his now. It was theirs, a shared and sacred space. A home. The binding of the split souls begun under Dom's torture was completed now with love.

A faint silver net like a tracery of glowing spider webs lifted from his skin and healed the scrapes and cuts from his climb, and tingling at the edges of his heightened senses he knew he'd been spotted, felt the vibrations of approaching feet.

Smiling, Crys rose fluidly and faced the oncoming audience. They were backlit by torchlight but he identified the Seer-Mother and the Warlord among a bevy of guards.

"Who do you think you are? My guards—" Tanik began and they stepped forward, hands tight on their spears.

Crys gestured. "I am the Two-Eyed Man. I am the Trickster. I climbed the tor to my birthplace and I sat here and felt the world move through this place and I felt the rift in it, the jagged edges where the people here have lost their faith because they honour you instead of the gods. Because they have forgotten the Light. I have come to restore their belief, and I have come to prepare you for war."

"You have no idea what you say," the Seer-Mother tried, rattling her beads and strings of bird bones and teeth as she flailed a hand in dismissal. "The magic is strong here; we are strong. And war? You have no comprehension of our world."

"There is no magic," Crys contradicted her. "There used to be sacred spirit, there used to be faith and the joy of the shared dream, but those have been destroyed by your lies about magic, and about how only you can wield it. It isn't magic these people need; it is the gods. Gods you have cut them off from by making of yourself a barrier. Absorbing their worship as though it is yours by right, instead of the gods'."

The Seer-Mother broke into loud discord, shivering the night, and Crys slashed his hand through her words and stilled her. There were murmurs of consternation. "And I understand that if Rilpor is not saved, the Mireces will come for you next. I understand that they will break you, enslave you, kill your children. I understand that if we work together now, fight together now, we can prevent both our countries from falling under the sway of the Red Gods. I ask you to renounce your lies of magic and mystery and restore these people to their true and proper faith. With our help, Seer-Mother, Krike will be strong again, her people and warriors steady in their faith."

"I am the Seer-Mother," the woman said, thumping the butt of her ornate staff on to the stone, "and I see nothing of the sort! No coming war, and no god before me. It is you who lies."

Her words were as the screeching of magpies in his ears. "Have your people climb the Cunning Way at first light, as many as can fit up here, faithful and dissenters alike. By noon tomorrow I will show them all both who I am and who they can be." He spread his arms. "I will see you in dream."

CRYS SAT AND WATCHED the dawn, the slow birth of colour across Gilgoras's sleeping hide, the joyful burst of birds into the pink and peach and golden sky. The sun kissed him and the stone on which he sat, warming his naked chest and back, and inside the Fox God stretched and slid in lazy contentment, as though oblivious of what was to come or the guards who'd stood in a ring around him all night. Or perhaps He was just enjoying the peace while it lasted.

It didn't last long. A growing clamour heralded a crowd ascending the Cunning Way: either Cutta and Ash had convinced the people, or the Seer-Mother had sent out the proclamation as he'd asked, intent on as many as possible witnessing his humiliation. If the latter, she clearly had some plan in place, one he suspected he wouldn't like much.

The stone was beginning to warm beneath him now and he stretched, shoulders popping, and then stood. The crowd was growing, spilling from the path and taking up position all around him, his guards shifting with unease at being so outnumbered. There was an excited buzz of voices as men and women jostled for a good vantage until a gap opened in their ranks and the Warlord and the Seer-Mother approached. Four guards carried a litter in which Dom lay, looking even worse than he had when Crys left him, and three more warriors escorted a grim-faced Ash. His expression didn't lighten when he saw Crys. Cutta Frog-dream and her warriors were there, too; she gave him a tight nod, no doubt hoping her faith in him wasn't misplaced.

Tanik Horse-dream pushed through the ring of guards around Crys and then gestured them away, despite their reluctance. She raised her arms, the staff gripped tight in her hand. "People of Krike, loyal sons and daughters of the gods, you are here because a challenge has been made to our very way of life. A lie has been spread about our faith, about the lives we lead here in Krike at the very birthplace of our Lord Trickster. This *man*"—Tanik swept her staff behind her; Crys leant out of its path— "claims to be the Great Trickster Himself. And so you are gathered here to witness this *man*, Crys Tailorson of Rilpor, attempt to prove himself a god. Our god! He seeks to convince you of this claim to control you, to draw you into a war in a foreign land. A war we have already refused to enter. He will manipulate you—but he will fail."

As introductions went, it could've been better, but Crys could see that most of the witnesses still seemed excited, and the Fox God thrummed with mocking amusement at the woman's clumsy attempts to steer the crowd.

"The man Crys Tailorson's test will take place in the dream world," Tanik shouted. "I will take him through the soul-dream, and there he will be revealed as his true and irrefutable self."

It was a nice touch, the repetition of "man," a subtle reinforcement in the minds of the onlookers that he was a fraud. But Tanik's plan placed all the power with her, and that was unacceptable.

"No." The tor sang beneath his feet; his chest and thighs buzzed with energy. "No. We will all go. Every one of us gathered here will soul-dream together. Then all will know first-hand who I am and what I am. It will prevent . . . misinterpretation of events."

He heard Ash snort.

"The journey is taxing," Tanik said, her reluctance at the admission clear. "Only one can be guided at any time."

Crys nodded. "By you, perhaps," he said, and though his words weren't loud, they carried across the stillness of the tor. The Seer-Mother flushed. "I can take us all. I can show every man, woman and child here present the future, the past, and everything in between."

"This is not a Rilporian custom. Have you soul-dreamt before?" the Warlord asked before Tanik could dismiss his words. "No? Then how will you perform such a feat with no training, no experience?"

"I am the Fox God. I live in dreams. Sit." He settled himself back on the rock cross-legged, early sun gilding his shoulders and hair and sparkling in the silver scars, and he waited in silence. He could feel the Trickster laughing, bubbles bursting inside him. Hesitantly, looking to each other for support, for permission, the hundreds of people crammed on to the summit copied him until only the Seer-Mother was left standing.

"Well?" Crys asked her. "Do you wish to journey with me?"

She looked across the crowd, face impassive, and then she sat, rattling the necklace of bear teeth hanging to her navel. "We come now to the start of your journey," she began, her voice deep and sonorous, "and I will—"

"Everyone close your eyes," Crys cut in, "and listen to my voice." Tanik's stare burnt him but he returned it with equanimity and one by one the crowd closed their eyes. Ash's shut last, suspicious.

"I ask that you all take my path to the dream. The fox-path, through the undergrowth and across the fields and into the woods. See now before you a forest of oaks and chestnuts, birch and ash. Birdsong among bright branches, small glades of wildflowers and lush grass. A soft breeze dappling the forest floor with leaf-light, the laughter of the Dancer on the air, careless as butterflies. Listen to my voice . . ."

THE FOREST WAS SUNNY and warm, bursting with life. Crys had never been here before, and yet it was home—bone-deep, soul-heavy home, a sense of rightness and contentment. A place of peace.

He looked around in awe; every animal around him was a man, woman or child of Krike. A tall roan mare—Tanik Horse-dream—and a white-furred fox—the Warlord, Brid Fox-dream—stood closest, while a multitude of animals ranged behind them. A wave of wonder flowed from them as they saw each other, as they recognised kin and enemies and friends and lovers. As they saw each other's soul animal for the first time.

Crys glanced down at dark paws tipped with sharp black claws, flicked new muscles and felt his thick, brushy tail sweep the leaf-litter behind. He laughed at Ash, an astonished-looking otter and certainly not the noble wolf he had imagined, and then swallowed his laughter when he found Dom. The calestar's form wavered and writhed from eagle into adder and back again, as though his soul had been broken and re-formed in a new guise and didn't know what it should be any more, its pieces jammed back together by a blind man who little cared for the outcome.

But he wasn't here for Dom. Not yet.

"You see me," he said clearly despite his fox-muzzle. "You see what I am. Not a fox; the Fox. You see my eyes are the same: one blue and one brown. You know what that means. You see yourselves, here in the shapes your souls take, here where I have brought you. You see there can be no doubt. I am the Fox God. I am the Trickster."

"We see no such thing," Tanik said, her ears pinned back. "So you are a fox. Our Warlord is a winter fox. Many of our people are foxes. This is not proof."

"I brought each of you here as effortlessly as lighting a candle. Those who had not soul-dreamt are here with us, without thought, without struggle. I—"

"This is not proof," Tanik repeated, her tail flicking and her front hoof gouging at the earth; sparks flared up when she struck the ground. Fire in the dreamworld. Crys looked at Dom and saw him, as the adder, uncoil and move towards Tanik. Ash's otter pounced on him and held him still but that, more than anything, told Crys who he was facing.

His ears pinned back in unconscious response; he forced them upright again.

"You bring us to a place we know intimately, that we learn of in our legends and histories, that we visit in ritual, and you say it is some great thing. This is home to us; of course we can visit it with ease."

There was no more time for talking. Tanik the horse leapt, lashing out with hooves that sparked red fire, her teeth bared. Crys twisted up and left and he bit Tanik's haunch as he skidded past. And then the Fox God blazed into life like a lightning-struck oak and Crys's consciousness was thrust backwards in his own mind so that he was as much observer as any of the souls gathered there.

The Fox God changed shape, becoming a horse to match Tanik but several hands taller. She reared and kicked; he pranced sideways and with a single raking blow of a front hoof cut her shoulder to the bone. She screamed and submitted.

And then He was a fox again, fox-sized. And then an eagle, flitting up into the canopy; a hawk; a swallow; a stag; a hedgehog. Blazing with silver light, the Fox God became the shape of every spirit animal there gathered, appearing next to another of that kind, not to dominate this time, but to touch, fur to fur and claw to claw. Drawing them to Him. Binding with love, not fear.

It took only seconds before He was back in His fox-shape once more and slinking to the front of the group. He leapt lightly into the clearing, and an instant later Tanik's hooves slammed down on to His ribs and back and her teeth tore at His neck. No pause, no breath to think, just impact and red blood and pain.

Deep inside, Crys cried out, fury mingled with terror, and shoved forward, lending the Fox God his strength, his will. And the Fox God retreated a little and Crys surged into the space and now they moved as one, one breath, one being, one will, changing shape swifter than thought—a wren to slip below a slashing hoof, an adder to strike at a muzzle, an eel to slip from between yellow teeth and finally, with a shout loud enough to cow every animal there, He was Crys again, the shape of a man in this place where animals ruled. Not a hunter or trapper, not one who came to tame and pillage the land but a man attuned to the rhythms and seasons of life, who took only what was needed to live.

The Two-Eyed Man, one foot in the wild, one in the city.

With a sweep of one arm he haltered Tanik, the rope in his hands glowing silver as spun moonlight. She fell still, flanks heaving and eyes rolling, but quiet.

"I am the Fox God, the Great Trickster, shifter of shapes and teacher of the cunning ways. I am Crys Tailorson, soldier, heart-bound to Ash Bowman. I have never lied about who I am, about what I am, not since my awakening and never again. Do you accept me?"

All of the animals gathered in the clearing of that sunlit glade, deep inside their own souls and joined for this one perfect moment with the souls of their kin and their god, cried out their faith and lay down, pressing beaks and muzzles to the soft earth.

All except one. Tanik did not—would not—submit.

THE SUN WAS POISED overhead when Crys blinked and found himself on the tor again, his legs numb from sitting so long, his mouth dry and foul-tasting. Weariness weighed on his shoulders like a pair of anvils, and whatever strength he'd expended in the soul-dream, not even the Fox God could replenish it.

Stiffly, he stretched out his legs and sat through the fire of pins and needles, watching the faces of the gathered as one by one they returned to themselves. Some wept, many laughed and talked excitedly, and those who had met a kindred spirit animal sought each other out, the sense of family acute in the bright morning.

Crys pushed himself to his feet and breathed deep, toes gripping the stone beneath him. He heard Ash gasp and looked over, saw the archer's mouth hanging open in shock. Ash patted his own shoulders and Crys glanced down, away, and back again in surprise.

Curled and looped and swirled over his shoulders and down as far as his elbows was a vine-like tracery of red lines amid his silver scars, a plaiting of silver and red-gold, a pattern that was both perfectly comprehensible and a ravelled mystery depending on whose eyes he examined it through. The patterns curled across his collarbones and chest, and he knew instinctively that they slid down his back between his shoulder blades, a mane of russet and silver. Scar and divinity, inextricable.

He looked back at Ash, saw the archer lick his lips and nod his appreciation, felt a grin tug at the corner of his mouth. *We still pretty, Foxy?*

Amusement bubbled up. *Prettier.*

Crys laughed and spread his arms wide as Tanik and Brid made it to their feet. "Children of Light, followers of the Fox God and kin of Krike, welcome. There is much to be done in the coming days and months. Find your priests, relearn the rituals and the stories from your old folk, remember your ways. Tanik Horse-dream is no seer. She is not beloved of the gods"—he met her hateful gaze—"or, at least, not of your gods. Put your faith in the land and each other, in your priests and the Dancer and the Great Trickster. Be Krikite again, dream again, as your hearts dictate."

The Seer-Mother leapt forward, hand going into her robes and coming out with a long black knife with a serrated blade.

"Liar!" she screeched. "Traitor!" She shoved past the hesitating guards and rammed her blade into Crys's gut up to the hilt. "Liar!" she spat again as the crowd stilled, silent and stunned at the ferocity of the violence, its unexpectedness where the rest of them were so filled with elation.

"God, not liar," Crys replied over the sudden beat of blood in his ears and its hot liquid rush down into his waistband. The pain was exquisite, flooding every part of him, bright and beautiful and agonising. Dark with threat. Red with promise. His knees buckled and he locked them before he could fall. His hand brushed Tanik aside, gently, and then he dragged the knife from his belly and gave it back to her.

Light flared and the wound healed, the blood ceased to flow and the pierced organs knitted themselves back together. The woman stumbled back, dumbstruck.

"No!" she screamed and slashed him from throat to navel.

He had a second to wonder what exactly the guards were being paid for, and then scorching, nauseating hurt washed his body and his insides were threatening to become his outsides. He ground his teeth against the scream, hands pressing the mouth of the wound together, muscles tight against agony that demanded he break. He didn't.

"I speak the truth," he gasped over Ash's shouted threats and there was more silver light. His ribs vanished; his intestines retreated. He healed. Didn't matter that he was whole; shock threatened to dump him on the stone anyway and his blood was hot and sticky as it soaked into the wool of his trousers and slid all the way down to his boots. The wound was gone but the pain, and its bright, searing memory, loomed large in his shuddering body.

"I am sorry that you have been brought to this," he said, to everyone's surprise including his own. "You reap what you sow." Sweat sheeted his body and stung his eyes.

Tanik readied her knife again but then the Warlord was wrestling the blade from her and Crys clearly heard the snap of a finger as he wrenched it away. *Could've done that a while back, you know. Would've really made my day, not seeing my own bladder outlined by the sun.*

He swallowed a manic giggle.

The Seer-Mother shrieked, spitting like a cat. There were other acolytes, there were Tanik's personal guards and her brother Pesh, who Crys couldn't see but who rarely left her side, but none of them moved except to kneel. Like a wave on a shore, from the front ranks to the rear, the people of Krike knelt as they had in the forest, though this time in their mortal skins. Ash hesitated a second, wanting to be ready to dash to Crys's aid, but then he too dropped to one knee.

"I am the Fox God," Crys said, his voice only a little stronger than his wobbling knees, but his will stronger than both. "I do not ask you to worship power, as Tanik did. I do not ask you to worship me. I ask you to think for yourselves, to question what you know and what I am showing you. The Light waits for you; turn your faces to it. Remember who you are and the things you are capable of."

"Kill him," Tanik roared and Crys tensed, but no one came at him. He smiled then, his teeth bloody, willing himself not to fall. If he fell it was over, regardless of all he'd done and shown them. *Just a little longer, legs. Don't fail us now.*

And then the Warlord stepped forward. Crys blinked, dizzy, and licked dry lips. Hadn't expected that. "Do you challenge me?" Brid demanded. Crys shook his head. "Do you seek to rule my people?"

"I seek to lead them, both back to the Light and then in war. You are the Warlord; I do not seek that position. But if you need to prove the Seer-Mother's words to be a lie, then do it. I won't stop you."

Ash's face was just visible over Brid's shoulder, panicked, frantic. He was shaking his head and Crys felt a little courage leak away. He sucked in a shuddering breath, not sure he could stand another. It wasn't even the pain so much; it was looking into their faces when they did it. And choosing not to fight back.

"Brid Fox-dream, you who share the fox shape with me, of all people should understand. Your life has always been mine. Shall mine now be yours?"

The Warlord twitched. "What?"

"You didn't just dream of the fox, did you, back when you were a boy? You dreamt of me. A warrior with one blue eye and one brown, sitting on a rock with a fox in his arms. You never told the Seer-Mother, who saw only what she wanted to in your soul-dream; you never told anyone, so afraid were you that you'd done something wrong. You saw me." The Fox God put His palm on the man's chest. "See me again."

Brid stumbled backwards. Then he knelt. "I knew it was you," he whispered hoarsely, hand going to the fox amulet around his throat. "I knew it, I just—I couldn't believe it. Forgive me for what I have allowed to be done."

"It was I who allowed it, Warlord. And it was necessary."

The Fox God faced the crowd and raised His arms again. "Do any here contest my claim?" The summit of the tor echoed with silence. "Then it is done. Warlord, if it be your will: send out riders to summon the warriors. Gilgoras stands on a knife edge. I ask that you help me bring her safely from the precipice."

The Warlord stood tall. "We fight by your side, Lord. We are your children." He pointed at Tanik. "As for you, exile is too easy a punishment for your poison."

Tanik Horse-dream, false Seer-Mother, screeched and clawed, but Crys didn't like the triumph that still shone in her face. "It doesn't matter what you do to me," she shrieked. "You're all going to die anyway!"

The Warlord jerked his head and cheers rang from the crowd as the warriors holding her wrestled her to the edge of the tor and pushed her off. She didn't scream.

It wasn't the ending Crys had wanted, but it was probably better than the ending she deserved. And it was done. Ash's relief flicked over Crys's skin like feathers.

He looked at the jubilant crowd and then, very carefully, he sat. For now, at least, they were his.

THE BLESSED ONE

Eighth moon, first year of the reign of King Corvus
Red Gods' temple, temple district, First Circle, Rilporin, Wheat Lands

W HAT PROGRESS HAVE YOU and the East Rank made in finding your sister? We must have that child, Sire, or all we have
accomplished, all we have done so far, will be worth less
than piss in the wind."

"That is what you wish to talk about, with Valan gone and the city a
tinderbox? Estimates suggest as many as a quarter of the city's slaves are
dead."

Lanta smoothed the material of her gown across her legs, taking
her time. "Then that is however many fewer mouths to feed, something
I believe you were concerned about. We have been dealt a heavy blow,
more than one of them. We will deal with this as we have dealt with all
the others—with the strength of character and true belief that makes us
Mireces. The women and children are dead, Sire, and I have prayed with
our warriors several times a day, Gull as well. We have done all we can to
soothe them, but it is time to focus on what we can achieve, what we must
achieve if those deaths are not to be for nothing. Now is not the time to
falter."

"Falter? We were lucky our own warriors didn't tear us both apart for
this! Lucky we only lost a quarter of the slaves. The men are not the only
ones who begin to doubt, Blessed One."

Lanta's breath caught in her throat and she covered it with a low hum of displeasure. "What does it matter if the ritual is complete but the Bloodchild is lost to us?" She showed him her bandaged hands; then she jerked at the neck of her gown so the bruises and scratches were visible. "Which one of us is working harder, my lord king?" she demanded. "Which one of us puts their life at risk for the gods? Find me your whore of a sister."

A muscle jumped in his cheek, but his voice was calm. "You assume that the Godblind spoke true, that Rillirin is in fact pregnant. You put all your hopes in the words of a man who proved false, who turned traitor and committed the most terrible of crimes. Even if he did speak true, I already have men scouring every town and village; she is not to be found."

Anger tightened the skin of Lanta's face. "You think I don't know his treachery? You think it somehow escaped my fucking attention what the Godblind did? You talk of searching the towns and not finding her. Then clearly she isn't in a town. What about the hamlets, the isolated farmsteads? The lands of the nomadic horse herders in the north; the abandoned and destroyed forts? Are your men searching those too? Must I think of all the options for you?" She slapped the arm of her chair in frustration. "Perhaps if you weren't so enamoured with your new crown and those pretty slaves and that ridiculous palace you'd understand your priorities. You think we have won; I know we are still at war and I, at least, am acting accordingly."

Corvus blinked, his eyes blue as a midwinter sky. "We all mourn, Blessed One," he said in tones of ice, "and we all pray for your success. The Dark Lady's absence has broken everyone; I seek to strengthen us again in body, just as you do in spirit. And yet this new catastrophe has weakened us once more. On top of all this, I am working to secure this country against further uprising and prepare it to receive the return of our Bloody Mother. There are many demands on my time—"

"You think I care?" Lanta almost spat. "You think administration is important, that taxes will make us great? You think *Rilpor* matters any more without Her here to rule it?"

"Yes, Blessed One, I do," Corvus said. "Rilpor matters, because when the Dark Lady is brought back, She will be brought back here, to this place. Or would you have us retreat to the Gilgoras Mountains and the frozen, animal-torn corpses of our dead? Would that be more fitting to Her glory?"

Lanta sucked in breath to retort, but Corvus spoke over her. "Are you more likely to be successful up there? Because if you are, Blessed One, I will give the order today to abandon this country and the men will jump at it. They will race back there in the forlorn hope they might find survivors and they will feel the loss anew when they do not.

"You think my priority is ruling Rilpor; you are wrong. My priority is the gods' will—and that, as interpreted by you, was the subjugation of Gilgoras. That is why I concern myself with administration and taxes and slaves. Because that is *my* task in this great purpose of ours."

The muscles in his shoulders and thighs were tense; it was clearly taking all he had not to leap from his chair and shout at her the way he would a slave. She wanted him to try it, could almost taste the satisfaction it would bring her. And he expected her to back down, to acknowledge his efforts and the odds stacked against them; instead Lanta attacked.

"Not good enough. Your excuses bore me. Do better, Corvus, or suffer the consequences."

His cheek twitched again, the only sign of dark emotions running swift beneath the surface. "I understand your frustrations, Blessed One. Indeed, I share them. We all do," he said with a restraint she hadn't anticipated and didn't like, not one bit. She wanted a fight. She wanted . . . a reason to act, to do what needed to be done. It felt as if Corvus was hindering the Dark Lady's return, and hindrance Lanta would not tolerate.

That he would doubt my desire to bring Her back, to see all the gods' plans succeed. That he would think his devotion the greater . . .

"Where before we could have beseeched the Dark Lady for aid in locating my sister, or told our men to pray to Her for succour, now we are lost. You are not the only one who has given everything, after all. We can only search. And so we do."

Beneath the blood-soaked hem of her gown, Lanta's toes curled, the only—invisible—sign of her utter fucking outrage at the king's gall. "You need not remind me of our plight, or the Dark Lady's absence from Gilgoras. I am well aware of those facts, *Corvus*." She used his name deliberately, making it an insult in her mouth. "If you seek to imply our Mother's absence is my fault, or the actions on the Sky Path, then I advise you to choose your words with especial care. Without me—without the gods—you are nothing more than a jumped-up warlord with delusions of grandeur."

Corvus thrust himself out of his seat and Lanta leapt up to meet him, glorying in the challenge, the battle to come.

"If you had not let loose the Godblind on the Fox God—" Corvus began.

"If you had not allowed them both to escape when they were within the grasp of your warriors," she retorted, the words echoing through the temple. "If you had secured the city and all within it. If you had not bickered like a boy with Rivil. If you had not let Rillirin escape in the first fucking place. *If, if, if!* You think to lay this blame on me? It was I who told you not to trust the Godblind, and it was you who saw in him a way to the gods that didn't involve me. You sought to divest yourself of the need for a Blessed One and because of it, you let the Dark Lady die!"

Her chest was heaving, face hot with righteous indignation. The godblood whorls on her skin prickled, urging her on.

"You overstep," Corvus said, and his fists were bunched at his side. "You go too far."

"And you do not go far enough," Lanta screeched, daring him to hit her. To give her a reason. "You argue over slave allocations and harvests, you worry about subduing broken villagers, you waste time building fucking walls we ourselves knocked down. You build and consolidate when you should search and wage war. And then you blame me for not finding Rillirin. Me, when I spend my days and nights in ritual, my soul cast further than you can imagine into the realms beyond this one. When I beg and beseech our Red Father to aid me in my search. *What are you doing, Corvus? What are you doing?*"

Lanta stepped forward and poked him hard in the chest. "This country has made you soft. It has stolen the fire from your belly. It has seduced your eyes away from the gods who are our true reward."

"Take your hand off me," Corvus said, so quietly and with such venom that even Lanta, the Blessed One and Voice of the Gods, felt a moment's pause. Her hand dropped to her side. "Will Rillirin's child make a difference if we have been slaughtered by our own slaves? Will the Dark Lady's return be celebrated as it should if the Mireces are no more? If we are dead, Lanta, how will we bring Her back?"

His use of her name, as deliberate as her use of his, was like a slap of cold water in the face. *This is where we are now. This is how far our alliance has fallen.*

Then so be it.

"I will see every single one of us dead if it brings Her back," she said softly. "I will kill us all for Her, myself included, and I would rejoice in it. If you were a true Mireces you would understand that."

He stilled. Everything about him became the watchful coiled readiness of a predator spotting prey. Sweat prickled across Lanta's palms; she raised her chin.

"And so we come to it at last," he murmured. "Honestly, it took you longer than I'd expected. Is it my faith that you doubt, or just my blood that you hate? Is that why you always hated Rill, because Liris valued her, a foreign bed-slave even you couldn't supplant?"

Lanta found she didn't know what to say.

"Do you doubt my faith?" he asked and rolled up his sleeve to show her the scars of blood oaths and blood promises, the jagged, ugly lines he'd made in his flesh when the Dark Lady first vanished. He pulled a knife from his belt with just enough swiftness that Lanta flinched. His smile was without warmth, without humour. "Tell me, Blessed One, how deep to cut. Tell me that if I kill myself here and now it will bring Her back, and I'll have opened my wrist before the words have finished echoing."

He watched her face, her eyes, as she thought about it. She had no doubt he'd do it, not the tiniest sliver. And despite everything she felt and thought and wanted, Lanta let the moment go.

"It would not serve our purpose at this time," she said. "Though if— when—it does, I will be honoured to perform your sacrifice myself."

"The honour will be mine, Blessed One," Corvus said, and Lanta knew the danger was past, at least for now. Their alliance remained in existence, ragged and under immense strain. When it finally broke, Lanta would need a replacement ready. An acceptable, devout replacement.

"We will find her, Blessed One. We will because we must. The East Rank has her description and knows to question the townsfolk for a red-head with a Mireces accent. Someone will know her, will be willing to give her up in return for some small reward. But with the news of our losses in the mountains, I cannot send the Mireces out looking for her. They would be hasty, and I could not guarantee that Rill would make it back to us unharmed."

Lanta was Mireces; she well knew how hot their passions ran. "I agree, and yet we must act faster. That is not an insult, Sire. Have the East Rank question every pregnant woman they find. Your sister could have dyed her hair, be working hard to change the way she speaks. But the babe should be showing by now—no woman can hide that."

"Your will, Blessed One."

"Not my will. The Lady's." She forced a small, conciliatory smile on to her face. "Thank you, Sire. And now I must pray. I will join you in the square at dusk, and I will offer what succour I may to our people."

Corvus inclined his head and strode from the temple, past the god-pool that reeked and slapped thickly against the sides of the basin, its waters red and scummy.

Gull emerged from the shadows and took Corvus's chair for himself.

"We are surrounded by faithful idiots," Lanta said quietly, "who have no conception of the delicate nature of the work we do here."

Gull nodded, stroking a long finger down his cheek. "They do not. But nor do they need to. They need only obey and believe and, when the time is right, unleash their rage at the losses we have suffered on our enemies. It is we who will change Gilgoras and restore our Bloody Mother to us and to Her dominion. And that one does believe; there is no doubt about that. Despite his secular preoccupation, Corvus believes utterly, as though he was never Rilporian at all. His faith is unshakeable. He was a wise choice for king."

The Blessed One's mouth turned down. *And yet I did not choose him. Though I will choose the next.*

"He will serve," she said shortly, "for as long as he is useful. And then we shall see."

MACE

Eighth moon, first year of the reign of King Corvus
South Rank headquarters, Western Plain, Krike border

EDRIS HAD COME. AGAINST all the odds, and despite the possibility of further Mireces patrols on the Western Plain, Edris had come. The colonel wasn't riding at the head of an army of Listrans and accompanied by Tresh, their new king resplendent in shining plate. Edris wasn't leading a wagon train of supplies or trotting in the midst of a mercenary company sent by their new monarch.

Colonel Edris was alone. He guided his horse through the postern gate and reined in in front of the administration block, where Mace stood with Hadir, Dalli, Hallos and the senior staff.

Mace's stomach was churning as he examined the colonel's blank expression, the sort of face you made when you were about to stand in front of your senior officer and deliver the worst possible news.

Edris unhooked a crutch and manoeuvred himself on to the ground. Mace noted with distant detachment that he was moving well for a man with one leg. He pulled a sack from its place by his saddle and held it in his crutch hand, limped forward and then saluted. The officers returned the gesture, and then Mace smiled.

"Colonel, you have no idea how glad I am at your safe return." He gestured at the sack. "I do hope that's full of letters from Tresh, or promises of aid or some such? Gold wouldn't go amiss, enough to raise an army, perhaps." He knew it wasn't gold; Edris's arm would've snapped off if he'd been carrying a sack that big full of gold. But the man looked so haggard that Mace was seized with the ridiculous urge to try and cheer him up.

Edris licked his lips and said nothing, limping past them towards the door. Mace's mouth opened in shock at his lack of manners but he gestured for everyone to follow and they crowded into his office, jostling to stay out of the way as a stench rose from Edris that was far more than the rigours of travel.

"Colonel? What is going on?" Mace demanded when Hallos had slammed the door on Hadir's curious adjutant.

Edris wedged the crutch deeper into his armpit, untied the neck of the sack and upended it on to the table. The object within tumbled free and rolled to a stop, staring at him from rotting eyes.

"Behold King Tresh," Edris said, throwing the sack on to the floor. "Corvus's men reached Highcrop sixteen days after us and massacred everyone on the estate, my men included. The king is dead and our Listran alliance with him. Long live King Corvus." Edris's tone was black and bitter as gall.

Mace's guts turned to water. "So they know we're not in Listre?" he asked in a hushed voice.

He gestured them all to seats and poured wine despite the earliness of the day.

Edris stared at the head until Dalli used the sack to scoop it up and placed it gently on Mace's desk instead, no doubt staining his paperwork with its . . . juices. Out of sight, if not out of stench. Hallos's eyes followed it, and Mace knew the physician was desperate to inspect it. He'd have his chance.

"They know we're not there," Edris said after a deep draught of wine. "The sheer fact no army came to Tresh's aid when Highcrop was attacked tells them that. Tresh's household guard fought hard, and my lads too, but everyone bar me was put to the sword and then Tresh himself was beheaded. Right there in the throne room, amid the cloth of gold and the fine jewelled cups, they kicked him to his knees and hacked off his head. Ugly, too, poorly done. Four blows it took, Tresh alive for all of them."

Edris's laugh was mirthless, and he cut it off with a trembling hand pressed to his lips. "Forgive me. I'd taken a cut across the chest—a scrape really, little more—but there was enough blood and bodies around me they thought I was dead. It's the only reason I'm not, the only reason I'm here." He gulped again at his wine and Mace wanted to scream at him to tell him the rest, but didn't. Instead he thought of the soldiers he'd sent east with the man.

"He was going to send us troops. He knew he was our king; he'd been mustering men, paid for out of his own purse until he could claim the royal treasury. He'd been seeking aid from the Listran government, promises of support, of trade and suchlike. As soon as it was known Tresh was dead, the army disbanded, faded into Listre as though they'd never been. I laid low until the Mireces had left, then followed, made my way here as covertly as I could. Though I can't say for sure whether I've been tracked. It may be I've led them straight to you, sir."

We nearly had it. We were this close *to aid, to outnumbering them enough to guarantee victory. This* fucking *close.*

"Is there any hope at all of a Listran alliance?" he asked instead of commenting on Edris's last statement. Now that the civilians were safely away from the forts, it was a waiting game until the next engagement. And they'd already done enough to provoke a response by slaughtering the war bands in the Western Plain.

Edris shifted. "I don't know, sir. Tresh was murdered on their soil; they may seek to make amends. I could've gone to the Listran capital and begged for aid—I still can, if you wish—but in the aftermath I thought informing you as soon as I could was more important."

Mace sipped more wine, feeling it go to his head, and stared around the table. Hadir's face was rigid, Jarl's expression was unutterably weary, Hallos was scribbling furiously in his medical notebook, probably about the smell of Tresh's head, and Dalli . . . looked as though she was trying not to giggle. The corner of his mouth turned up without volition; when faced with such monumental fuck-ups as these, the dashing of almost every hope they had left and the only certainty further conflict, laughter seemed as good a policy as any other.

"I don't suppose Tresh had children, did he? A bastard son or half-brother we could use? Gods, a daughter'd do," Jarl asked. That stole Dalli's humour and Mace winced, but then she exhaled softly and let the moment go.

BLOODCHILD

Edris came back from some inner vista of horrors. "No, no offspring. There are distant relatives scattered through Rilpor, of course, but Tresh was the closest to succession. Perhaps we could rally around one of them."

"Anyone know who they are?" Mace asked. "Hallos? Surely you had access to records in the palace?"

The physician pursed his lips. "Two brothers in Pine Lock, I believe, several ladies on estates scattered through the Wheat Lands, but the names escape me. And at this point in the war, Rilporians need more than a stranger they've never heard of to be held up as a figurehead. They need someone they know, someone they trust, who's already been fighting the Mireces."

Mace gestured when Hallos paused. "Yes? Go on. Someone in the Ranks? An officer?"

"Something like that, yes," Hallos said and Hadir and Jarl were already nodding. "When we first learnt of Janis's death and Rivil's betrayal, a proposal was put to your father that he take the throne. Durdil, may he rest in the Light, refused and named Tresh. It seems only fair, as Durdil's son and heir, that the responsibility now passes to you."

The silence was thunderous as Mace's eyes bulged and his ears got so hot they nearly burst into flame. And then, in fits and starts and hiccups, the silence was broken. Dalli began to giggle, and then snort, and then to roar with laughter, flapping a hand in front of her face in apology as tears ran down her reddening face. She scraped back her chair with enough force that the legs squealed over the stone and fled the room, trailing hoots of jagged, hysterical mirth.

"I think Dalli speaks for all of us," Mace said. "As you said, there are still Evendooms and Pine Lock is a reachable distance for a strong enough force. We can—"

"After Rastoth the Mad and Rivil the traitor? Perhaps it's time the Evendooms were laid to rest," Hallos said. "New blood. A new line. An honourable line."

"We need a figurehead," Hadir agreed and Mace had to stop himself from lunging over the table and grabbing the general around the throat.

"We have the Fox God," he said instead, a tinge of panic in his voice.

"No one knows where the Fox God is," Hallos said, quite unhelpfully, Mace thought, though the physician didn't register the sour look turned on him.

"And there's still a fair amount of doubt around the authenticity of the claim," Jarl put in mildly, "especially among our South Rankers, many of who know Major Tailorson from when he was stationed here some years ago. Understandably, they're having trouble reconciling the rather wayward young officer they remember with the god they've grown up worshipping."

"Have to say, I wouldn't believe it myself if I hadn't seen some of the things he did on Rilporin's wall," Edris added. Mace gave him a baleful glare the colonel completely failed to recognise.

"No one goes into a war without telling their troops the gods are on their side. We need more than that," added Jarl and Mace had the distinct impression he was being backed into a corner. Mace didn't like being backed into a corner. It made his fingers itch for a sword.

"Which leads us back to the nomination of your father," Hallos said, "and so to you, as his son and heir, Commander."

"No," Mace said, the denial somewhat ruined by the strangled tone. "This is preposterous. I won't do it. I don't bloody well *want* to do it."

"You get my vote," Hadir said. "You'll have the vote of every officer in the South, and you've clearly already got the support of your own."

"Edris is the only officer I have left," Mace snapped.

"And Edris supports this proposal," Edris said.

"Bastards," Mace muttered. He stared at his cup, wondering whether he'd drunk too much wine and this was a fever-dream. *I'll wake up in my cot soon, Dalli next to me and a war to plan. And everything will be normal.*

"You wear—and have used—the heir's sword ever since Major Tailorson . . ." Hallos paused and a sly smile curved his mouth. "Ever since the Fox God presented you with it. Your father himself bade you keep it, I understand. And you're from a long line of honourable men and women, the latest in a noble family that has served the throne for generations."

"I'm not doing this," Mace snapped, but all the officers were radiating approval and Hallos was being the implacable physician who ignored his patient's screams in order to cure them. Mace felt like shitting screaming himself.

"You would fail in your duty to Rilpor?" Hallos snapped. "Betray your oath as a soldier, to make any sacrifice for king and country?"

"There is no king," Mace almost shouted.

"Precisely."

Mace gritted his teeth, but whichever way he looked, however he flailed, the noose was tightening. He twisted his hands together, noting distantly that they were clammy, shaking. "What would you have me do, ride in procession around Rilpor proclaiming myself king? You think Corvus will just hop off the throne and let me sit in it, say he was just keeping it warm for me?"

"Word will spread," Hallos said. "Faster than plague, once it's known. Think how fast the populations will begin to resist when they know the hero of the West Rank is their king."

"Hero? *Hero?* I have lost every engagement I've fought in this gods-damned fucking war. I should be court-martialled, not bloody crowned." The weight of the admission was a wave breaking on Mace's head, roaring so loud in his ears he almost missed Hallos's next words.

"You won at the Blood Pass Valley."

"Yes, and then we fucking ran away and have stumbled from disaster to defeat ever since," Mace retorted and the shame of it was a stone on his chest.

"And yet here you are, our last and best hope," Hallos said. Mace wondered if the man would shut up if he shoved his head in the sack with Tresh's. Probably not.

"We are at war, Commander," Hadir said. "Difficult decisions must be made in time of war. Even if you were just to be made regent until the crisis is passed—"

"That's exactly it." Mace grabbed at the lifeline with both hands and clung on. "If you insist on forcing this upon me, I will act as regent until the Mireces are defeated. That long and no longer. I am not equipped for ruling, gentlemen."

"It's like commanding, Commander. Just a few more things to think about, that's all," Hallos said, but he was grinning because he'd got his own way. "As far as we know, those of noble birth gathered here, plus those good men who have risen to prominence through their own skill and intelligence, represent the last of the Rilporian ruling class. All those who agree that Commander Mace Koridam be crowned Rilpor's king—"

"Regent, *regent*," Mace insisted. The clamminess had spread from his palms up his arms and across his back, cold sweat forming as though he was about to face an enemy in single combat that he knew was better than him.

"Say aye," Hallos finished.

It was unanimous.

"Bastards," Mace repeated bitterly. "Absolute bastards, the lot of you."

Hallos leant forward with a conspiratorial smile as the table erupted in cheers and hope, missing for far too long, was rekindled. "I can't wait to see what they make of a Wolf chief as queen regent," he whispered, and Mace was suddenly light-headed as the blood drained from his face.

"Oh gods," he said. "Dalli's going to fucking kill me."

"Well, Sire, now that that's settled, with your permission I will arrange for the burial of Tresh's remains with all honours." Hallos picked up the sack and exited before Mace could think of a response.

Sire. He called me Sire. This is what it must feel like to go mad. Focus, focus on what's real, what needs to be done. This is just—just a publicity stunt. Propaganda. And breathe.

Mace sat in numb silence and let his officers release some pent-up tension at his expense, barely listening. He weighed the relative merits of throwing up in the corner and getting blind drunk, and decided reluctantly he could afford neither. The war was what was important now, that and nothing else. Stupid political manoeuvring he'd leave up to others. None of it would affect him, not really.

Queen Dalli, he thought, and despite himself the corner of his mouth turned up. *She's going to fucking kill me.*

DALLI HADN'T FUCKING KILLED him. She'd done something much, much worse.

"Announcing yourself as regent but not as king isn't enough. Rilpor needs a figurehead, someone to rally behind. You have to claim the throne."

Mace flung himself on to the bed and stared up at the ceiling. "I can't believe you're siding with them. I don't want to be the shitting king!"

"And we don't always get what we want in this life, do we?" Dalli snapped back, folding her arms in that way she had that told him he was in trouble.

He sat back up, met her glare for glare. "So you'd be happy being Queen of Rilpor, then, would you? Prancing around in posh gowns and eating from gold plates all day? That the future you want?"

"I'm not going to be queen, love. I never will, and not just because we both know how bad I'd be at it."

"Then, no," Mace said with flat finality. "If I take the throne, I lose everything. I lose you. I get the job Rivil killed for and Corvus is messing up, but I lose you. This may come as a surprise, but that's not a deal I'm prepared to make. I don't want to be king, but I'd do it—if you were at my side. But you won't be, so I will govern only until a replacement is elected. Then I'll go back west, rebuild the forts and we can live there. Or I'll retire from soldiering altogether and live wherever you live. But I'm not losing you."

Dalli grabbed fistfuls of her hair in frustration. "You're a fucking idiot, Mace Koridam! You can't give up the throne, the country, your career for me. I'm nothing, just a Wolf with a smart mouth."

He stood and crossed to her, pulled her hands free and held them in his own. "I can and I will," he said softly. "If this war, this . . . whole mess has taught me anything, it's to keep hold of what means most in this world and fight for it, no matter what. I'll give it all up for you, Wolf chief."

"Don't ask me to do this," Dalli pleaded.

"I'm not asking. I'm simply saying that without you, I won't take the throne."

"Yes, which means you're giving me no choice." She pulled a hand free and punched him in the chest. He grunted. "You're backing me into a corner."

Mace grabbed her and, lifting her feet from the floor, strode across the room. "No," he said with sudden passion, "this is backing you into a corner."

"Stop changing the subject," she tried, but he could hear her smile as he pressed kisses down the curve of her throat. "We need to talk about this, Mace. About what's best for the country," she insisted.

"No, we really don't. You don't want to be queen; I don't want to be king. Conversation over. Besides, I'd be a terrible king. I'd rule as though the entire country was one giant Rank. It'd be a nightmare. And I'm probably going to die in the next few weeks anyway, so it's a moot point. Now stop wriggling, woman, and kiss me."

She did, and things were just getting interesting when she pushed him away, both of them flushed and breathless. "No, stop. We *have* to talk about this."

"For the gods' sake, Dalli," Mace grunted, adjusting the bulge in his trousers. "What more is there to say? I failed to retain Rilporin, your entire people were wiped out at Watchtown, I lost half my Rank in the Yew Cove tunnels and I've recently sent thousands of unarmed civilians to wander the entire length of the Western Plain in the vague hope they don't die. And let's not forget I'm about to order an offensive that is going to result in the deaths of thousands of civilians and soldiers. Think about it. Whoever survives—assuming anyone does—won't appoint me king. They'll fucking execute me for genocide of my own people. And I'll deserve it."

The flush in his cheeks now was that of shame. He sat back on the bed and put his head in his hands. He was unutterably weary.

There was a long pause and then Dalli crouched between his knees and pulled his hands from his face, replacing them with her own, fingers in his hair. "Yes, civilians are going to die," she said, and he flinched. "But, Mace, civilians always die. So do soldiers. *It's a war.* Watchtown wasn't your fault; the tunnels weren't your fault. Losing Rilporin wasn't your fault. Can't you see what you've given us? The hope you've given us? Why do you think we're all here, why do you think we follow you?"

"Because for good or ill, I'm all that's left," he mumbled, and the thought sickened him. Of all the great officers, of all the leaders Rilpor had had, it came down to him. "Every man has his limit," he added. "This is mine."

She slapped him, and it wasn't a love tap either. Mace's head rocked sideways and he had the distinct impression she'd torn his ear off. His eye watered and he gasped in outrage. Dalli shook the sting out of her hand.

"Then you damn us all," she said, and her voice was very cold. "You insist you've failed us; you haven't. But you will, if you refuse the throne. That will be your failure, Mace Koridam, and it could well be the end of Rilpor and the safe, bright lives we've fought and died all these months to preserve. Right now we back your decisions, knowing we all share the responsibility for the lives that will be lost. And that's why you have to be king, because you can talk about the death of innocents and we can both believe in its necessity and help you shoulder the blame for it. We want to share the blame. You *make us* want to."

His mouth opened to protest again and Dalli put her finger over it. "This offensive is the biggest risk we've taken so far—win or die. If we didn't believe in you, we wouldn't agree to it. So take the throne and make us believe in you some more."

Her chin trembled with sudden emotion. "Take the throne and I'll stand by your side," she said, taking away his last excuse and looking as miserable about the whole situation as he was, as though the throne was a death sentence, not something men fought and slaughtered for.

"I've talked myself into this as surely as I have you. So if that's what it'll take to make you do what we all know is best for Rilpor, then Trickster preserve me, but I'll be your bloody queen."

CRYS

Eighth moon, first year of the reign of King Corvus
Travellers' quarters, Seer's Tor, Krike

"CRYS?" A GENTLE HAND on his shoulder and he jerked out of sleep, nearly fell out of the chair pulled up to the edge of the bed. "Crys, I think he's waking up."

Crys knuckled his eyes and leant forward, his spine crackling protest. The amount of healing he'd had to force into the calestar so soon after the soul-dreaming, plus the wounds he'd sustained in Tanik's attack, had tested the depths of his strength, and for the first time he realised that it wasn't a bottomless well of power. The Fox God—he—had his limits and they weren't as far out of reach as he'd thought. Not by a long way. Foxy had nothing to say on the matter, and despite how they were almost one these days, Crys got the sense the god was keeping something from him.

It probably had to do with . . . the end, something Crys refused to think about. As he and Ash had promised each other, it was one day at a time with no eye for the future. Still, the sense of secrecy in his own skin was unsettling.

Despite all of that, despite everything he'd done, Dom had slept for a week, a sleep that hovered like a kestrel over the cliff edge of death. Every breath could have been his last. Whatever had happened to him in the knowing had almost broken him, and it had almost broken Crys to save his life.

But now the rhythm of Dom's breathing had changed and his fingers were twitching on the blanket. His right eye opened, closed, opened, and then his left, more slowly.

Crys and Ash craned their necks, manic grins stretching their mouths. "Hello, Dom," Crys said softly. "You've decided to join us, I see." Dom's eyes were vague, anxiety building in their depths. "You had a violent knowing a little while ago when you were with the Seer-Mother and you've been asleep for a few days. Don't worry, you don't need to try and talk yet. Just concentrate on getting better."

Ash slid his hand beneath Dom's sweat-lank hair and lifted his head, pressing a cup to his mouth. "Drink," he whispered. "Just little sips, that's it. Not too much." Whatever animosity had been between the three of them had burnt away in the last days as Dom lingered within death's shadow. Not forgiven, exactly, but accepting.

"Here," Ash said, swapping the cup for a shallow dish, "chicken broth. It's not very hot, so don't worry about burning your tongue. Now that you're awake, we can finally get some food in you. We had to massage your throat just to get you to swallow water, so I'm looking forward to you doing some of the work now." He grinned, but Crys could hear the strain in his voice.

The archer half filled the bowl of a spoon and dribbled the contents into Dom's mouth; they watched him swallow, a little better each time, but slow, so slow.

"Can you tell us how you feel?" Crys asked when he'd finally finished. Not the question he wanted to ask, but the one he needed to. The rest would just have to wait that little bit longer.

"See . . ." Dom mumbled.

Ash screwed up his face in thought. "Seriously tired? Seriously pissed off?" he guessed, working hard to raise a smile.

"Tan . . ."

"Tantrum?" Ash tried. "Tangled? You're worried about your hair? Tankard? You want a drink?"

Crys grabbed Ash's forearm. "Seer-Mother? Tanik?" he asked. Dom blinked in acknowledgment. "Don't worry, she's dead. The Krikites follow the Fox God now; they know who I am. We found a mark on your neck—looks like you were poisoned, though why she did that we might never know. Unless you can remember."

Dom's right hand cut weakly through the air. "Tanik . . . forced knowings." The words were more breath than sound, but they slid across Crys's skin like a snake, leaving chills in their wake. Dom's breathing was ragged. "Saw . . ." he managed and coughed, the sound pitiful in his weakened chest. "Made me tell."

"Made you tell? Tell what—what you were seeing? And what did you see?"

"Everything. Mace. Rillirin."

"Mother-shitting bitch," Ash breathed. "Not that it matters now, she got what she deserved."

"Pesh."

Crys frowned, the name familiar. Then he swore. "Tanik's brother. We haven't seen him since the tor. No, wait, he wasn't up there. Did Tanik tell him what you told her?"

"He was there. Heard it all. Saw him leave."

Crys and Ash looked at each other; there was no point pretending they didn't know where he'd gone. "All right, Dom, I know you're tired, but it's very important that you tell me everything you remember. Where exactly is Rillirin?"

HE'S GOT A WEEK-LONG head start, Crys. We're not going to catch him." Ash's hands were firm on Crys's shoulders as if to hold him in place in case he leapt up and started running for the border. The thought had crossed his mind.

"If Lanta gets her hands on Rillirin and the babe it's all over, no matter what I do, no matter whether we win the war." He kept his voice low, though Dom looked like he was sleeping again. "If she puts the Dark Lady into that infant, I really don't think I can kill it, no matter what it becomes. I won't kill it, not a babe."

"Of course not," Ash said, even as Crys remembered the Wolves' promise of vengeance up on the Sky Path. "But you've got Tara in the city to prevent exactly that happening. Can't the Fox God go to her, tell her to get her arse moving?"

Crys stepped out from beneath Ash's hands and threw his own out from his sides. "If I could do that, don't you think I would have by now?

If I had that sort of influence, I'd have reached out and stopped Lanta's heart and Corvus's too." He paused to compose himself, knowing that yelling at his lover wasn't going to help either of them—or Rillirin. Or Gilgoras. "Sorry. If it's possible, I don't know how to do it, and Foxy isn't giving away any secrets."

"What I wouldn't give for a bloody messenger pigeon right now," Ash muttered. "So you're telling me Rillirin's on her own?"

"For now, yes. Which is why we need to move out. Pesh might have a week-long head start but he needs to find allies among the Easterners or the Mireces, convince them he's got valuable intel and get them to act on it. That gives us some time. Not much, granted, but maybe enough."

"Fewer than two thousand Krikite warriors have arrived so far. That's not enough to aid Mace. It's not enough to win." Ash winced as he spoke, knowing that wasn't what Crys wanted to hear.

Crys rubbed at the red markings tracing his collarbone, weighing up their options. "It's going to have to be, love. We need to march for the Wolf Lands. If Rillirin's there or on her way there, then we can protect her. If we're too late and Corvus gets her, he's going to think he's invincible and that belief might just be enough to gift him victory. Either way, Mace is going to need whatever warriors we can bring him. The longer we delay, the more likely we are to lose."

"And the sooner we leave, the smaller our numbers," Ash pointed out. He sighed. "All right, I see your point. I'll find the Warlord and tell him we need to leave tomorrow."

He glanced once at Dom, pressed a kiss to Crys's eyebrow, and ducked through the low door into the warm sun. Crys watched him go until muffled sobs told him that Dom was awake again.

He took a seat in the chair and clasped the calestar's hand and the squeeze Dom gave it was less pressure than a butterfly's kiss. "Don't worry," Crys lied, "we've got plenty of time. We'll find her."

"My fault," Dom breathed, haunted. "My fault. You should kill me."

"What?"

"Kill me. Please."

"You asked me this once before and I told you then: your task is not yet complete," the Fox God said while Crys was thinking of a response. "It is still not complete."

Sobs racked the man on the bed, energy he didn't have expelled in shaking, heaving gasps. "Please kill me," he begged again. "Can't do this. It's too much."

"Yes, you can," the Fox God said. "And you will. You are needed, not just by me but by Rillirin and your child. Do it for them if no one else."

"I'm trying," Dom whispered. "But I haven't the strength. Dying . . ."

"Dying would be easier, yes. And as for strength, you'll find it when the time comes. You'll have to."

Crys put his hand on Dom's shoulder to take the sting from the Trickster's tone, but the calestar shrugged it off and turned his head away. Quietly, so as not to disturb him, Crys emptied the room of knives. And then, doubting his decision but with no alternatives presenting themselves, he began to pack.

RILLIRIN

Eighth moon, first year of the reign of King Corvus
West of Fox Lake, Western Plain

THEY'D BEEN ON THE road nearly two weeks and, despite everything, they were making good time. The long days and longer miles of walking had led to an increase in querulous adults and whining children, so to maintain the peace the Rankers let the youngest ride the provisions wagons for part of each day.

Rillirin hadn't realised the group would separate—she didn't think the soldiers had told anyone, not wanting to cause more panic—but when they reached the start of the great marsh between the southwestern foothills and the plain, they'd been split down the middle, two groups of a little under two thousand each, with one soldier per hundred civilians to protect them. It didn't seem enough, but so far there'd been no sign of the enemy.

It had taken most of the afternoon after the group split for Rillirin to realise she'd lost both Martha and her children and Gilda. A spasm of worry had rippled through her, but it was too late now. Gilda's group had headed straight into the foothills and Rillirin's party was taking the easier—but longer—route between the marsh and Fox Lake, the great expanse of water shielding them from view from the rest of the Western Plain. She sent a prayer after them and concentrated on walking.

Sore feet and lack of food were familiar complaints, but the ache in her back, the growing discomfort in her hips and deep in the bowl of her pelvis, was new and unwelcome. Her body was changing to accommodate the ever-growing babe and she was starting to feel as though she were slowly spreading apart, everything settling into new configurations that supported her child but hampered her ability to walk.

She'd begun leaning more and more on her spear as the hours and the days went by, but the pace was never allowed to slacken. The Rankers seemed to be everywhere, marching at their sides and front and rear, jogging back to the stragglers and hurrying them back into the column, encouraging adults to rotate the carrying of small children and bags of provisions so everyone got a chance to walk unencumbered. They had to be marching half as many miles again each day as the rest, but she never heard them complain. They had the safety of two thousand civilians to ensure; they couldn't afford to favour blisters or strained muscles.

Fox Lake was a glittering blue expanse under a sky almost the same colour, its shores thick with reeds and mud banks, great stretches of land soft and boggy and sucking underfoot. The going was slow and hard and the wagons had stalled three times, the weary horses straining in the harness until dozens of hands helped shove them free to muted cheers.

By mid-afternoon the day after the group had split, they reached a fast-flowing river that pounded down out of the foothills towards the lake and were forced to unhitch the horses and swim them over, stringing guide ropes between the banks to help people cross and then hauling the wagons over by hand.

Captain Sadler was as wet and exhausted as the bulk of his two Hundreds as they made multiple crossings to assist the refugees. Two-thirds of them had made it to the other side when the first arrows flickered out of the trees covering the uneven ground leading to the foothills.

Screams rang out and those who'd already made the crossing, Rillirin included, milled in confusion, seeking the source of the danger. Many threw themselves back into the river, clinging to the guide ropes and thrashing towards the other side, but then screams rose from that bank too, more arrows finding homes in flesh.

Sadler and his Rankers drew swords, but most of their bows were on the wagons, still on the other side of the river, and the few soldiers there were already being cut down. "Scatter!" Sadler roared, one of the handful of orders the civilians been forced to memorise and the one Rillirin had never wanted to hear. Her clothes were heavy with water and chafing as she leapt away from the rest and began to run, not thinking, just running, spear tight in her slippery hand. Towards Fox Lake and the stand of willows and silver birch lining its closest edge.

She caught a glimpse of Rank uniforms with the blue armbands that meant the enemy East Rank—and ignored the shouts and screams rising like a storm behind her. *Run, just run. Protect the babe. Fucking run.*

An Easterner came alongside her when she was a few hundred strides out from the tiny wood at the lake's edge. Rillirin skidded as she slowed and he turned with her. She lashed her foot into his knee and rammed the tip of her spear into his belly as he stumbled. His chainmail turned the point, but she swung into the next blow, a whining arc that drove the butt into his jaw and smashed it like eggshell. He went down choking on blood and Rillirin spun in a circle with the spear whirling around her as shield and weapon both. She opened the arm and chest of a second soldier and took off again.

Her breath whistled in her throat and her legs were heavy as the ground grew softer, her lower back and pelvis jarring up to her skull with each footfall, but still she ran. Too scared not to.

Rillirin focused on the trees getting closer with each jolting stride, the lake beyond them serene and shattering sunlight down its whole length until it blinded her, her footsteps slowing perceptibly despite her best efforts and now the fear was closing her throat further, making it harder to drag in air as the shouts from behind got louder and more strident, and her back was spasming with pain, the babe kicking its indignation up under her ribs, into her lungs and heart, adding to the misery. Telling her to stop.

If I stop they'll kill me. They'll kill you, little one. I can't stop. I can't.

Someone grabbed her jerkin and hauled her to a halt, and Rillirin pivoted on her left foot and rammed her spear towards him, barely fast enough but barely would do. He folded up around the point, the breath grunting from him. She yanked back on the spear and rammed it in again, missing his throat but opening his cheek instead so she could see teeth and tongue and pink gum. He sprayed blood as he screeched and fell, kicking like a rabbit in a snare, and she was off again, the single glance behind her enough to show more coming, and more engaged in battle and slaughter on both sides of the river. The trees were close, so close now, her only refuge.

She ducked under the branches of the nearest willow and into its long feathered fingers whispering and sighing in the breeze, incongruous beauty of pale leaves backlit by the sun. Rillirin wove past a stand of birch, staggering and panting, heading for the darkest heart of the little wood. The Rankers were shouting, angry now, crashing through the trees behind her, snarling their frustration as she wormed ever deeper beneath the low-hanging branches. Why were they after her? There were thousands out there they could take. Why her?

A shock of birds flew up, piping alarm calls, and Rillirin hunkered down in the gap between the boles of two trees, dizzy and frightened, gasping at the air, spear shaking in her fists. She just needed a few seconds, a few deep breaths.

Someone must have signalled for quiet, because the voices died away and the wood fell into the unnatural silence of any wild place invaded by people. In it, the furtive sounds of approaching footsteps were clear. Rillirin tried to quiet her breathing, her thighs beginning to cramp. She slid out of her refuge and across and around roots and underbrush, thick ferns tangling in her hair, the shock of purple foxglove in a shadow making her flinch.

The ground was getting wetter, softer, and despite her best efforts Rillirin was leaving sign, the imprint of hands and knees as she crawled, the drag of spear and toes behind. Maybe if she stayed still they'd give up; there were more than enough civilians out there to be captured. The thought of trading her life for theirs made vomit burn the back of her throat, but the shame wasn't enough to make her give herself up. She hunkered down low, sinking very slowly into the boggy ground. She had the babe to think of.

"Rillirin? It is Rillirin, isn't it?" a voice called. Not Rilporian, not Mireces. "My name's Pesh, Rillirin. I'm from Krike and I have news of Dom. He sent me to find you."

Rillirin sat up on her heels without thought, staring back in the direction of the voice. "Dom?" Why would Dom send a friend to the East Rank to tell them of her? Unless . . .

"Come on now, girly, there's nowhere to go," a soldier called, definitely Rilporian this time. Definitely an enemy. "Corvus himself sent orders to find the pretty redhead carrying a babe. Fucked the king, did you? Well then, he won't hurt you if you're carrying his child, now will he?"

"Shut up," the Krikite yelled, angry, but the words were ice down her neck. If Rillirin had needed any reminder of what awaited her at the hands of her enemies, this was more than enough. Unbidden came flashes of images: Liris, not the king in question but the one who'd raped her, drunk and pawing at her flesh; the pinches, slaps and casual punches of his second and war chiefs; the Blessed One's calculating stare, weighing her life in the scales of her foul gods.

I won't go back to that. I won't see you raised like that.

She crouched lower, but there was a subtle slide of movement off through the trees and Rillirin knew they'd find her soon enough. They knew her name; they weren't going to leave her be. Corvus would kill them if he found out they'd let her escape.

There was no escape. Rillirin's breathing steadied and a quiet certainty grew in her stomach—they wouldn't take her. Not again. *I'm so sorry, little warrior. I would've dearly loved to have met you. I'll see you in the Light, I expect, and I'll explain then why I had to do this. It's not your fault; please know that.*

It wouldn't be easy with the spear, but it'd be easier than seeing her child as Lanta's plaything. And it was the child she did this for—not herself. She reversed the weapon and wedged the butt in a knot of roots, shifted up on to her feet and placed her throat against the tip of the blade. Left hand holding it in place, right hand on the curve of her stomach.

"Dancer's grace, my child. I love you." Her voice was breathy against the pressure of the sharp, bright steel.

A sudden gust of wind and the drooping fingers of willow parted ahead of her and there was the lake, right there, only strides away. *Get in the lake, hide in the rushes. Swim.* Rillirin leapt forward, crashing heedlessly through the mud as shouts went up around her, grunting as she pulled her boots free one at a time, step after desperate, laborious step until her foot went in up to the ankle.

She splashed forward another few steps, tripped over a thick tangle of water weed and fell, hands breaking her fall but sending up a splash that pinpointed her location to everyone within fifty strides. Rillirin flailed onwards, spear gone somewhere in the water, her only thought to get out deep and then move parallel to the shore. The reed bed was thick and tall, bulrushes standing proud above her head, and she was half crawling, half paddling, chin just above the water, but there was splashing behind her and more shouts and she floundered on, just about deep enough to swim, and she stretched out, cupped palms seeking open water and distance and speed and someone grabbed her by the ankle.

Rillirin screamed and kicked, her head going under and half her breath lost to the water, surfaced and kicked again, thrashing, felt her boot come off in his hand and flapped another stroke before he got another grip, on her calf this time. She twisted on to her back, took a breath and kicked with her free foot, aiming for his head and letting the motion carry her beneath the surface again. She felt impact, not sure whether it was his face or shoulder, and his fingers loosened, but then more hands, two-three-four as more Rankers piled into the shallows and she came up and screamed and screamed and screamed, blinded by her hair, by the water, by terror.

"Get off me," she choked, spitting water. "*Get the fuck off me!*"

Hands on her hips now, grasping her shirt and jerkin, reeling her in like a desperate fish, and as soon as she could she added punches to her kicks but there were four of them and they dunked her, held her down until her struggles were to grab their arms and pull herself up to breathe. And when they jerked her upright and she couldn't think about anything other than sucking in air, her wrists were already tied.

A strange-looking man in animal skins and covered in tattoos stood on the bank, victory beaming from his face. "Didn't I tell you?" he demanded. "My sister sent me on ahead to bring you this gift and here it is."

The Ranker captain turned a disgusted look on him. "Fuck do you want, a reward? We'd already had four separate reports of this band moving to the foothills and had an ambush planned."

"We have captured the Bloodchild and its mother," Pesh said as though the captain hadn't spoken. "The Dark Lady will be reborn." He looked into Rillirin's eyes. "And my feet are on the Path."

They stood her up in the shallows and Rillirin fought them until a soldier stepped behind her and pulled her hard against him, head tucked between her ear and shoulder, one arm looping across her chest, the other across her belly, his touch a foul invasion.

"None of that now, girly," he whispered. "You'll upset your child."

Rillirin screamed again, loud and full of hate, thrashing against the restraining hands, legs scissoring. None of it made a difference. "Please," she wheezed. "Please don't take me back. Please." The captain stepped forward, pulling a ring of metal from its place tied on his belt. "*No! No no no!*"

He snapped the collar around her neck, hammered the pin through the lock. It was just a symbol—there was no chain—but as its weight settled on her collarbones and the back of her neck, Rillirin wept at its awful, heart-breaking familiarity.

They led her carefully out of the water and past the wood and into the sun and on to firm ground where more soldiers cut down or captured the last terrified members of her group, once thousands strong, now just piles of meat. Old folks, children, it didn't matter. Some of the Rankers laughed as they hunted down the defenceless; some of them were silent and grim.

Sadler and the soldiers who'd been under his command had fought well and fought to the death, piles of Easterner corpses littered around their broken formation.

"Fetch the horses," the captain called. "Me, the savage and these two here will take her to Rilporin." He laughed, boyish and full of delight. "Might be on for that reward, lads!"

Cheers erupted from those soldiers within earshot.

As if the collar had stolen Rillirin's strength, or her will, she followed the man towards the horses with her head down, bound hands resting on her belly and the still, quiet, sheltered form within.

She just followed.

TARA

Eighth moon, first year of the reign of King Corvus
Night kitchen, the palace, Rilporin, Wheat Lands

THE VIOLENCE THAT HAD spread through the city in the wake of the revelation of the Sky Path killings had claimed more than a thousand lives. Tara and the other slaves belonging to Valan had been lent to his friends while he was away in Pine Lock. Friends who had worked them hard and fed them little but not killed them, at least. Or not killed Tara, anyway—she hadn't seen any of the others since Valan had left, but she doubted anyone would harm the second's slaves.

Her temporary owner was War Chief Fost, the man who'd travelled to the Sky Path and discovered the carnage. He'd lost two consorts and seven children, apparently, and perhaps it was only the weeks of his journey with the survivors that had hollowed out his rage and grief into something crystal-sharp and brittle, lethal but not to her. She'd survived the weeks of Valan's absence so far with nothing more than a few casual slaps and kicks, though the violence throughout the city continued unabated. Each day saw new corpses and not all of them were slaves: Mireces women were now a commodity and men killed to possess them. Tara was too busy serving Fost and making contact with potential rebels to wonder what the women themselves thought of the situation.

Back resting against the wall, she sat on the stool with her eyes closed. The heat from the ovens beat against her skin, bringing a light sweat to her palms and brow, but she ignored it. Ignored the quiet industry of the cooks and cook boys and the frail, incessant whimpering of a baby strapped to its mother's back as she pounded dough.

Tara was exhausted by the stress of sounding out palace slaves, of maintaining her cover, of finding plausible reasons to go to the market where she could pass word to Merol or the Rankers, who toiled now on rebuilding houses in the merchants' quarter. As they'd hoped, more and more slaves were open to the idea of rebellion and fighting their way free to flee the city. They'd slowly set up a network of people who knew people who'd pass along word, so that nobody—not even Tara or Vaunt—knew exactly who was on their side.

Not that she'd been allowed to see Vaunt in Valan's absence, though the order gave credence to her swapping a few words with the labouring Rankers. He was alive and as well as could be expected. And so was she.

Tara yawned and scratched at the raw skin beneath her collar and it was then she became aware of the quiet. Even the newborn had ceased its complaint. Her eyes opened on the dim kitchen, deserted but for three figures standing opposite. At their head was the prison guard, Bern. The one who'd assaulted her so many weeks back. The one Valan had punched and threatened in consequence. The one who she knew had lost his consort in the Sky Path massacre and demanded another from Fost, who'd refused him.

Tara stood fast, crossed to the table and snatched up the bottle the war chief had sent her to fetch, grabbed a glass as well and turned to leave. A hand closed on her shoulder.

"Now, now, pretty," Bern said, "don't be rude. It's our night off."

Cold flooded Tara's stomach. *Stupid, stupid, stupid!*

"Forgive me, honoured," she said to the floor as he tugged her around to face him. "War Chief Fost awaits his wine, but I'm sure anyone else here would be happy to serve you a hot meal. Please excuse me."

A second man slid around behind her, cutting her off from the exit. Her heart began to thud. Chances were good she could kill or disable all three—she certainly had the rage for it and the element of surprise—but that would be the end of her cover. Then again, she knew from their expressions what they wanted, and she wasn't giving it to them, disguise be fucked.

"I must go, honoured," she tried again, bobbing a curtsey and backing to the door. As expected, the man behind her wrapped an arm around her waist, hand grabbing her right wrist. She struggled, testing his strength, but fell still as Bern approached.

"You are rude," Bern said, running a finger down her cheek, "and you haven't learnt your place in the world, despite this." He flicked his fingernail against her collar. "Best you learn the lesson now, with us, so's you're broken in for Valan. We're doing you—and him—a favour, really. Hold her, Ram." The man behind tightened his grip on waist and wrist as Bern began to unlace his trousers.

Tara struggled a bit more, whimpering for the look of the thing, and when Bern opened his mouth to laugh or speak, she rammed the glass in her left hand into it so hard it shattered against his teeth and ripped his lips and tongue open as she ground it deeper between his jaws. A short kick to his groin, using Ram as a support, and then her hand came up with the splintered remains of the glass in it and she stabbed blindly backwards. Ram screeched and let her go, hands going to his face, and she stepped around the keening, blood-drooling Bern to accept the third attacker's rush, waited until he'd committed himself and then clubbed him on the side of the head with the wine bottle.

The heavy glass held and he went down without a sound. Tara hesitated for a second; if she left them alive, they'd never stop hunting her, but if she killed them, Corvus would tear the palace apart looking for the culprit, and although they were all slaves together Tara didn't doubt that one of the kitchen workers would sell her out, rebellion or not. Slavery and loyalty were uneasy bedfellows.

Bern's hand snaked around her ankle and tripped her; she fell heavily, shoulder blades hitting the flagstones, the back of her skull a second later. The bottle did break this time, but by the time she'd blinked away the lights in her head, Bern had twisted the shattered remnants from her hand and was dragging her away from the debris. Towards him. Beneath him.

Her right hand was bleeding, splinters of glass in her palm; Tara gritted her teeth and hooked her thumbs, going for his eyes. He reared back, slapping them down, and then headbutted her hard enough to stun.

BLOODCHILD

Blood burst from Tara's nose and mouth, bubbled hot and salty into her throat, and she gathered a mouthful and coughed it hard in his face, slammed her undamaged hand under his chin as he jerked away, his centre of balance shifting so she could squirm out from beneath him. Not far enough.

He scrabbled, caught a handful of neckline and flesh, tore her hand from his jaw and slammed her back down on the stone, lifted her, slammed her down again, and once more. The impacts drove the air from her lungs. Tara fell limp, the pain in her back monstrous, vision bleary and thoughts muddled.

"Fucking. Little. Bitch," Bern slurred through his ruined mouth, blood spraying with every word, every breath. He paused a second to pick slivers of glass from his mouth and tongue and she stirred, trying to slide away again.

Ram appeared in her eyeline, his cheek and ear pouring blood, and aimed a kick at her head, missed, and slammed his boot into her shoulder instead. Tara grunted, the new pain restoring a little clarity. Bern was straddling her thighs, so she grabbed his jerkin, slammed both knees up as hard as she could, dragging him forward and twisting her hips at the same time. He tumbled off her and towards Ram, who skipped back out of the way.

Tara scrambled to her feet but tripped on her skirt; she went back down, putting out her hands instinctively to break her fall and screeching when the glass and cuts hit the stone. The pain was dizzying, lightning bolts shooting all the way up to her shoulder, and involuntary tears sprang to her eyes even as she got a foot under her and lurched back upright, right hand held protectively to her chest.

Ram came in low, shoulder driving into her stomach to throw her and she managed to get an elbow strike down into his back before her feet left the floor and she was hurled backwards again. Tara tucked her chin to her chest, shoulder blades hitting the stone and left palm slapping the ground to break her fall and then swinging back to grab the back of Ram's head, pressed to her belly. She pushed him down and herself up, scissored her legs around his neck and one arm, his face lost in the folds of her skirt somewhere by her groin, and then she squeezed with every ounce of strength in her thighs, left hand twisting the wrist of the arm scrabbling for purchase across her stomach and chest.

"The fuck?" Bern bubbled, trying to get past Ram's thrashing legs.

Go to sleep, fucker. Go to fucking sleep. Sleep! It only took seconds for Ram's thrashing to lessen to twitches, but he wasn't quite out when Bern came at her again. And he wasn't playing any more, a knife longer than Tara's forearm clutched in his hand.

"Let him go," he lisped. Tara kept squeezing but Bern roared and lunged and she had no choice—she kicked Ram away and rolled, crashed into a stack of barrels and then was being dragged backwards by her collar, choking.

Bern hauled her into clear space and put his knee in her back, pressing her into the stone until her ribs creaked and she couldn't breathe. The point of the knife was very, very cold beneath her eye. "Bitch," he hissed again, blood and saliva stringing from his chin on to her cheek. Tara could feel her heart thudding against his knee, he had so much weight on her. Tiny sips of air, rapid and not enough, and pain everywhere as it all caught up with her and adrenaline even now brightening everything so she could see the dust in the cracks between the flagstones, the glitter of glass fragments, could hear the pat-pat-pat of Bern's blood over her own heart and gulping, whimpering lungs.

The knife dug in, sliding through the delicate skin down into the socket in preparation to shuck her eye like an oyster and the only sound she could make was a thin mewl like a starving kitten, no breath for more.

"What are you doing?"

The knife slid out of her face, the knee released its pressure and Bern began to babble. Tara sucked in three breaths deep enough to make her dizzy and then the animal inside her slipped its collar and she climbed to her feet, snatched up the knife he'd dropped, wrapped an arm around his neck to pull his chin up, and sawed through his windpipe and half his neck.

Valan stood in the doorway to the kitchen. "Fost said you'd be here," he said, the words so incongruous in light of it all that she just stared at him, panting, bleeding, and ready to kill him too. And Ram. And every last motherfucking Mireces in Gilgoras. Every exhalation ended with a soft growl as she brought the knife up ready.

Ram groaned and rolled to his knees. "Second? Second, this slave, cunting bitch, she attacked us—"

Valan took three long steps into the room, drew his own knife and stabbed him once in the chest.

Ram fell back, his face comical with surprise as he pressed his hands to the small, neat wound that was shortly going to kill him.

Tara moved into clear space where the bodies wouldn't trip her; Valan followed. "Why did you do that?"

"Because they tried to hurt you and they failed," Valan said and pushed her knife down—didn't take it from her—then put a finger under her chin and examined the injuries. His eyes were dark with unnamed emotion. "Because if they were incompetent enough to lose to a woman, they didn't deserve to live. And because they touched my property without permission."

Tara didn't know what she'd been expecting, but it wasn't that. She slid back another step, pulling out of his grip. "Are you going to kill me too?" she asked, bringing the knife back up. None of this made sense. He'd walked back in after weeks away and found her murdering Mireces and he looked . . . worried for her.

Valan sheathed his blade. "Not right now," he said softly, "though I need you to give me that." She licked blood from her lips, hers or Bern's, and handed him the knife hilt-first, smothering the voice inside that screamed at her to kill him.

Valan examined the blade and put it down on the table. "You remind me of her," he said, radiating both pain and approval. He opened his arms, a clear invitation, and if she wanted to live Tara had no choice. Limping and bloody, she stepped into his embrace and stood rigid while he comforted her.

VALAN WAS DIFFERENT NOW. He did his duty for Corvus, settled the disputes among the men and kept the violence that was their nature to a minimum; he petitioned the king when necessary and said his prayers before bed, but he was different. The hard edges had been rounded by grief, a softer, warmer grief for real people rather than the brittle, spiky-edged thing that was the loss of the Dark Lady and which all the Mireces shared.

His grief, his distraction, got under Tara's skin. It made it harder to hate him. *You remind me of her.*

No need to ask who he meant, and no need to guess what he'd be expecting of her soon enough. Expecting or demanding. Forcing.

Valan claimed the deaths of the three men as his own, retaliation for walking in and finding them assaulting his property and so furthering Tara's debt to him. The one she'd hit with the bottle, whose name she didn't know, had never woken up. Fost apologised for the oversight; Corvus didn't even acknowledge the deaths. The second didn't ask where she'd learnt to fight or how she'd managed to survive; he just treated her cuts and bruises himself and put her on light duties.

Tara was more scared than she'd ever been in her life, more out of her depth than when she'd been drowning in the Yew Cove tunnels. And a tiny, tiny bit grateful. She knew that was how they got to people: they took away everything that made a person who they were and then gave parts of it back until the slave was so thankful they became complicit in their own captivity. She swore not to be like that, told herself Valan was as much her enemy as ever, and didn't allow herself to wonder if she lied.

Tara thought of Vaunt and their brief, beautiful and savage fucking, and her hand strayed to her belly and the cramps twisting it. *One less thing to worry about.*

She wondered if she lied about that, too.

CORVUS

Eighth moon, first year of the reign of King Corvus
Assembly place, Fifth Circle, Rilporin, Wheat Lands

CORVUS DUCKED THE BLADE, parrying it upwards with the rim of his shield, his own sword clattering off Tett's shield and spraying chips of wood into the air. The man grunted and gave ground and Corvus charged, eating up the ground until, somehow, Tett wasn't in front of him any more and the pressure against his shield was gone and he was stumbling forward and then, a heartbeat later, the kiss of cold steel on the back of his neck.

"Shit." He shrugged the shield off his arm and hurled it down, only just managing not to do the same with his blade. "Show me."

Tett paced out the footwork with him, showed him the half-moon step that made him seem as though he melted away, the pivot to bring body and blade back into line with his opponent for the killing strike.

They practised it until Corvus had learnt it, and then he nodded, clapped the man on the back. Even though Valan had returned from a successful hunt in Pine Lock, he'd kept Tett around. He liked his quiet competence and watchful nature—since the killings in the wake of the news about the Sky Path deaths, the city had been on edge. Brawls between Mireces, and the odd Raider corpse that no one seemed to know anything about, had lent a sullen, suspicious air to Rilporin. Corvus knew what a brewing slave rebellion felt like, and so did the rest of the Mireces. Most of them had taken to wearing their mail in the streets again.

They were standing in the shade, drinking well-water so cold it made his teeth ache, when the messenger cantered up the King's Way, his horse's shoes sliding on the cobbles as he hauled it to a halt and tumbled from the saddle to salute and then bow awkwardly.

"Your Majesty? Corporal Hooper, Sire, East Rank's Third Thousand late out of Pine Lock with news of movement in the Western Plain and intelligence regarding your sister, the Princess Rillirin." The long string of words finally came to a halt and Hooper blushed and snapped back to attention.

"What movement?" Corvus snapped, wiping the sweat from his face and feeling a lurch of excitement. *Chance of a fight? About fucking time.*

"Several patrols on long recon saw what looked like thousands of civilians marching northwest from the direction of the South Rank forts. Major Baron was going to set up a large ambush party, take as many captive as possible and extract information from them about—"

"About my sister?" Corvus interrupted.

Hooper looked longingly at the bucket standing on the lip of the well, but knew better than to ask. "Initially, yes, Your Majesty. Then just as I was about to leave to bring you word of the civilians, a stranger gallops into town in weird clothes, furs and skins and the like. Says he's Krikite, of all things. Says the princess will be travelling with a large party of civilians heading for the Wolf Lands. Seemed too much of a coincidence—had to be the same party."

Corvus felt some of his excitement shrivel and die. "So you don't actually have word of my sister, then. You haven't actually seen her—no one's actually seen her?"

Hooper shifted from foot to foot. "Not as such, Sire, or not by the time I'd left. The Krikites said the intel came from the calestar," he added, wary, expecting anger. "Dom Templeson, he said his name was. He's there at Seer's Tor along with, with Major Crys Tailorson, who professed to be the Fox God."

There was a long silence as Corvus digested the news. He wasn't sure which was more important, Rillirin's location or that of the Godblind and the Fox God. The civilians could be dismissed as slave fodder for when the time came to replenish numbers, and if it wasn't for the fact his sister was supposedly among them, he'd have ordered them left alone for now. Tett was at his shoulder, poised for whatever order he gave.

"And Major Baron was definitely proceeding with the ambush?" Corvus demanded. "They're going to get her, yes? They understand the importance, yes?" Hooper nodded with every question, each more definite than the last. Corvus clapped once, loud. "This is it, then. We're about to lay our hands on her—and in good time, after all. The Blessed One may actually fucking smile for a change."

Tett shifted at that, uneasy, but kept his mouth shut.

"If the non-combatants at the South Forts are those who fled with Koridam on the ships, then that's the proof we need he's not in Listre," Corvus mused.

"Aye, Sire, which answers your question about why they didn't come to Tresh's aid when we took Highcrop," Tett murmured. "Koridam and the Rankers must've doubled back with the civilians, fled to the South Forts and have been holed up there ever since."

It was almost too much to take in. Corvus wondered whether to send for the Blessed One and Valan, but decided against it. It was a military matter, so Lanta didn't need to know immediately, and if Valan couldn't be arsed to attend him as a second should, he didn't deserve to know. "You, Hooper, how's the mood in Pine Lock and Yew Cove? Slaves compliant?"

Hooper worked his tongue around his mouth before he spoke, his voice raspy with thirst. "Things have settled down, Your Majesty, yes. Very quiet now, which is why we've been able to send patrols into the Western Plain and even up into the Cattle Lands some way. We . . ." he trailed off at Corvus's scowl. He was a wordy fucker and no mistake.

"Good. Get your arse back there and get me half the garrisons from Yew Cove and Pine Lock. March them to the South Forts and burn them to the fucking ground. No prisoners. No survivors."

"At once, Your Majesty."

AND SO YOU SEE, Blessed One, all the pieces are falling into place after all. Rill will be with us in a matter of days, perhaps, and the threat of a Rilporian uprising will be crushed just as quickly. We can then bend all our efforts towards the return of the Dark Lady and the conquest of all Gilgoras."

"And the issue of the Fox God and the calestar in Krike?" Lanta asked him. Corvus's eyelid flickered. Was the woman ever fucking satisfied with anything?

"As long as they stay in Krike, they are no threat. We will consolidate our hold on Rilpor. With the Dark Lady's return, conversions will increase and every convert strengthens us in case of Krikite hostility. In due course I will send envoys into Krike and Listre with offers of truce, allowing us to strengthen ourselves further. When the time is right and our forces are replenished with newly dedicated warriors, we will begin the conquest once more."

And that's all you need to know for now, Blessed One. You have your secrets; I will have mine.

"And how will you know if they don't stay in Krike?" she asked.

Corvus controlled his temper, only his flared nostrils indicating the sourness within. "We will patrol the border," he said. "With the South Forts destroyed, we need not fear reprisals. Do not concern yourself with such matters, Blessed One," he added with honeyed malice. "You have my sister's arrival and a ritual to prepare for. Speaking of which, how goes the rite?"

"According to plan," Lanta snapped. She wasn't as good at hiding her ire as he was. "There is unrest in the city. Be sure your sister doesn't fall victim to it on her arrival."

"No harm will come to her," Corvus said with the supreme confidence that he knew annoyed her. They probably shouldn't be baiting each other when the situation remained so volatile, but perhaps that was the exact reason they did. Ordinary Mireces got to vent their fury on slaves and each other. The king and the Blessed One had no such luxury.

"I must pray," Lanta snapped and rose to her feet. "See that your sister is brought directly to me the moment she arrives."

Corvus waited—and waited—for her curtsey, and then he bowed his head to hide his smile when it came. "Your will, Blessed One."

MACE

Ninth moon, first year of the reign of King Corvus
Southwestern foothills, Western Plain, Rilporian border

THEY'D HEADED SOUTH OVER the Krike border, risking the wrath of neighbours who'd said they wouldn't help them defeat the invaders, and force-marched west into the foothills, crossing back into Rilpor only when the terrain shielded them from easy view or tracking.

It was good to be moving again, even if a forced march was Mace's idea of hell. And not just his, judging by the sour faces. Still, no complaints. They were Rankers with a job to do, and for as long as they were marching, no matter the speed, they weren't bastard fighting.

They'd kept the plans for the march—for their entire, risky offensive—secret until the refugees had left for the Wolf Lands. If any of them were caught during the evacuation, they could say nothing other than that Mace and the soldiers from Rilporin were at the South Forts, but not where they were going. And now, of course, they weren't at the forts. It was also why they were bypassing the Wolf village where those same refugees should—gods willing—now be safely ensconced.

Outriders led by Colonel Edris rode the few cavalry mounts the army had, scouting the flanks and the trail ahead, while Dalli's Wolves were the second line of screens between the world and the Rank. The civilian militia had the centre of the line of march, ragged lines straightening day by day as they adjusted to the discipline. Didn't mean they'd stand in a fight, though, but the extra numbers warmed his tired heart a little.

A shout had him whirling to the source of the sound: a rider cantering from their rear. "Contact south," he called and officers began roaring orders as the militia came to a panicked halt. "At least a thousand, some cavalry, mostly on foot. No uniforms, no blue. Maybe Krikites."

"Distance?"

"Couple of miles, Commander. They've picked up our trail."

"Bollocking fuck," Mace muttered and then raised his voice to battleground level. "Thatcher, Osric, deploy your Thousands across the flat there. Captain Kennett, I want archers on that hill. Militia, you're in the rear. Hold between the line and the field hospital. Hallos, you know the drill." He sucked in a breath as men began to move. "Hadir, Jarl, you've got the rearguard. Dalli? Where's Dalli? Take your people and find out who they are for me."

Half the Wolves were deployed as advance scouts, but Dalli gathered those closest and they loped off through the grass, threading around the Thousands who'd already flowed into position with drill-yard speed, while Hadir sent riders to alert those ahead.

The air was thick with tension and the ill-at-ease muttering of the militia, and Mace wondered again how quickly they'd break when it came to battle. *Just not today. Krike isn't the enemy. Don't be an enemy, Krike, please.*

As always before battle, seconds lasted hours but minutes passed in seconds. After an eternity that was all too soon, Dalli reappeared. And she was grinning. "All clear!" she yelled. "They're friendlies. Allies."

Mace was a suspicious bastard, so he held formation as the first ranks marched into view and refused to let his hopes rise. Definitely Krikites, and led by . . . he squinted. *Tailorson? Crys bloody Tailorson?*

The man was carrying the yellow flag of parley just to be safe, but he was grinning as widely as Dalli was. The archer was there too, Ash, and a man who could only be the Warlord, but it was Crys who Mace couldn't stop staring at.

He wore shirt, jerkin and chainmail in the Krikite fashion, but there was something feral about him he'd never noticed before. Not the eyes, which weren't flaring yellow for once, or the strange red and silver markings showing at his neck, some sort of tattoo, perhaps. No, it was something . . . other, something Mace couldn't identify no matter how hard he tried.

His sandy hair had grown almost to his jaw since they'd met last, and there were beads woven into strands of it, though he remained clean-shaven, unlike the Krikites ranged behind him. The man had never looked less like an officer, or more like himself.

Mace wrenched his gaze from Crys. "Stand down," he ordered and the Rank visibly relaxed. The Krikites did likewise a moment later, hands drifting from weapon hilts only when the Warlord's did.

The Warlord himself was tall and broad, a checked cloak hanging from his shoulders and his long yellow hair braided and hung with feathers. There was a glint of gold at his neck and his weapons were well used but well cared for, too.

Mace stepped forward. "Warlord of Krike, I—"

"You should address the Lord Trickster first, not me," the big man rumbled, gesturing deferentially to Crys.

A smile twisted Crys's face and he stepped forward. "Well, this is awkward, isn't it? How about you let me start?" He went to one knee in the wet grass and bowed his head. "Long live the king."

Mace blinked, heard the rattle of harness as his staff knelt, the louder clatter behind him as the Rank and Wolves followed suit. "Long live the king," they bellowed, and the Warlord gestured for his army to salute.

It was everything Mace had tried to avoid since announcing his intention to take the throne. Even bloody Dalli was kneeling, her expression proud and anxious and a little bit sad.

"How in the gods' names do you know that?" he snapped, taken aback.

Crys pointed with his chin and Mace turned. The royal standard was flying over their army. "Thought if we were going to die, might as well do it for king as well as country," Hadir said. "Brought it from the forts."

"I—You . . ." Mace stammered, and Crys stood again, the armies rising with him. He hesitated a brief second, perhaps wondering at the protocol of confronting a king—Mace snorted—and then stepped forward, hand out as the Rank moved back to attention. Mace took it in the warrior's grip, held on tight. "What now?" he hissed.

Crys jerked his head. "Now greet your allies."

"But what do I call you?"

Crys shrugged. "Major Tailorson works for me," he said with a wink. "Don't know about you, but I'm sick of titles. Crys is fine. Lord if you need to be formal."

"Lord?" Mace's voice was a squeak.

"People can . . . usually tell when that one's appropriate. Rest of the time, it's just Crys or Major—if you still want me as an officer, that is," he added with a sudden nervousness that was almost ridiculous and which served to restore some of Mace's wits.

"Ah yes, you deserted, didn't you?" he said in a neutral tone and Crys flushed bright red. He snapped into parade rest, the pulse jumping in his throat. "But you did also heal my future queen of a fatal wound. Welcome back, Major Tailorson," he finished and Crys huffed with relief.

He saluted and stepped back and let the Warlord take his place. The Krikite was unimpressed at this treatment of his god, it seemed, and Mace wondered how fragile this alliance would prove. *See us to victory, Warlord, and then if you want to go back to arguing over lines on a map, I'll oblige you. Just not yet, eh?*

"Warlord, I am Mace Koridam, Commander of the Ranks and—and King of Rilpor. General Hadir and of the South Rank"—the two men exchanged stiff nods—"and Dalli Shortspear, Chief of the Wolves. Your aid is more appreciated than I can say, especially as it is so unexpected."

"Brid Fox-dream, Warlord of Krike," the blond warrior said. He indicated the woman to his left. "Cutta Frog-dream, war leader. We have fifteen hundred warriors and our aid is given because the Two-Eyed Man asked for it, our great Trickster. We fight for him, not you."

Well, that puts me in my place, and while fifteen hundred isn't many, it's fifteen hundred more than I had this morning.

"I understand, Warlord. Still I thank you. Not just Rilpor but all Gilgoras stands in the shadow of the Red Gods. Together, I hope we can bring her back into the Light."

The Warlord grunted. "Fine words. I hope you fight as well as you speak."

Mace pursed his lips. "Better," he said and knew he'd judged right when the man grunted a reluctant laugh. "How did you know we'd be here?" he continued as Ash slid past with a respectful nod and into the knot of Wolves.

"We didn't," Crys said. "We were coming for Rillirin, but Dalli says you don't have her."

Mace frowned. "We don't. She was sent with the civilian refugees to the Wolf Lands a few weeks ago. This is about her child, yes?"

Crys nodded. "The calestar, you remember Dom?" He pointed to a litter pulled by a brace of horses. "I know you struggled to believe the knowings, but he's been right every time, Sire, and, well, in light of every-thing else"—he jerked a thumb at himself—"I hope you can believe him now. He's told us the Blessed One plans to resurrect the Dark Lady in the body of Rillirin's child. If she does, us winning the war won't make a scrap of difference."

Mace hesitated. More bloody divine intervention. Couldn't a war just be simple any more?

"As far as we know, they made it to the Wolf Lands," he said, "though we're not going there ourselves. In fact, Warlord, if I may be allowed to give your army a target?" he added as an idea came to him. The Krikite nodded. "We're heading for Sailtown. That's where Skerris of the East Rank is based, and as the biggest city outside of Rilporin itself, it has the largest Eastern garrison. We're going to take it, and we're going to take Skerris. We're going to capture or kill every Easterner in the city and deprive Corvus not only of his only ally who understands Rank warfare, but deprive him of as much of that Rank as possible."

Both men were nodding. "The Mireces fight more as we do," the Warlord said. "We've had our skirmishes with them in the far west of our country over the years; we know how to kill them." He showed big white teeth in a sudden smile. "And, of course, we're good at fighting Rankers. But where do you want us?"

"A second attack on this side of the country will throw Corvus's defence into confusion and stretch his already thin resources. Can you take Pine Lock for me?"

Crys nodded. "Yes, Sire. But we could be there in a week, whereas it'll take you far longer to reach Sailtown. How do we co-ordinate?"

"Choose a date. Say . . . Mabon, the autumn equinox? That gives us just under three weeks to get there. You'll need to stay out of sight until the day. Use the time to check on Rillirin. If she's not there . . ."

"If she's not there, she'll be on her way to Rilporin or already in the city. But we have a spy—and an assassin if necessary—in place, with orders to take out Corvus and Lanta." The way he was looking at Mace sent a sudden chill up his neck. "Major Tara Carter of the West Rank."

Mace rocked on his feet. "*She's alive?* When was this order given? By who?"

"Forgive me, I had no way to inform you. She and Ash came looking for me, the day before Rilporin fell. The Fox God gave her her orders."

Mace's fingers were hooked into claws, but then he realised he wasn't looking at a man any more; the hairs on his forearms stood up as though there was about to be a storm. Crys's words of earlier came back to him. *People can usually tell.* Mace could very much tell.

"I needed someone to attempt the kills, someone they wouldn't suspect," the Fox God said. "A warrior, but not a man who they'd never let get close to them. And not a Wolf, either; they'd recognise a Wolf from the tattoo. Tara was my only choice. But she too had the choice, I promise you that, Sire. She knew, she accepted, the risks."

"Of course she bloody did," Mace said bitterly. He'd spent the last months trying not to think of her dead or captured, knowing all too clearly the fate that would await a woman—and a woman soldier, no less—in the hands of the enemy. "Of course she accepted, that's exactly the sort of thing she'd do."

Mace breathed deeply. It was a bold move and Crys was right—Tara was the only one who could manage it. And she was good, very good. He didn't like it, but he couldn't argue with it. And even if he did, what was the point? It was done. Still, Tara, alone in that nest of degenerates. A slave. He winced just at the thought.

"Thank you for informing me," he said, aware the stiff formality only proved his worry for her. "So, Mabon. Take Pine Lock and kill or capture every Ranker there. We want to prevent news reaching the capital for as long as possible. Give the population the Rank's weapons and tell them to hold, then meet us at the western edge of Deep Forest in the Cattle Lands. Once we've regrouped, we'll offer battle and force Corvus's hand, destroy his army and push on for Rilporin and this mad priestess of theirs. Six weeks and this will all be over."

"Six weeks," Crys echoed, but he didn't look relieved. He looked sick, as if he didn't want the war to end. He excused himself and Mace watched him go, frowning.

"Prophecy says the Fox God must die to end the war," the Warlord murmured. "You've just told him how long he has left to live."

THE BLESSED ONE

*Ninth moon, first year of the reign of King Corvus
Red Gods' temple, temple district, First Circle, Rilporin, Wheat Lands*

"HOLY GOSFATH, RED FATHER, I have come to serve you. If it is your will, tell me your desires and let me fulfil them. I am yours, Lord."

The god was propped in His throne, His eyes dull with apathy and world-ending grief. He didn't bother to look up as she spoke, or answer when she finished. The walls of the Waystation were lit with a red light that glowed from everywhere and nowhere, while the brighter gold of fire licked around Gosfath's legs, sparking from His talons, His horns.

Again she had summoned Him to the temple and again she had been brought into His presence instead. But it had felt different this time. He'd approached, she was certain of it, had drifted right to the edge of Gilgoras, ready to set foot inside, before retreating. Perhaps next time He would honour them with His presence in the temple. In the circle. Another step in the spiral path to resurrection.

Lanta approached the throne and the massive red form slumped upon it, nerves fluttering in her belly. "Holy Gosfath, Lord of War, I have come to you. I, Lanta Costinioff and your Blessed One, have come to offer you succour. We are lost without you, Lord, and we are doubly lost without your Sister-Lover."

Gosfath twitched, and His head swung slowly until those black eyes were spears impaling her.

"Gone."

Gosfath's hurt swept over her like a black wind and Lanta shuddered, a sob escaping the prison of her lips. Her own pain was as a leaf bobbing on a torrent when compared with what He had lost and her hands ran across His calves and knees, giving—and taking—comfort. Yes, His grief was immense, but so was Lanta's. As was her determination to reverse the horrors of the Dark Lady's loss.

"We are doing much to bring Her back, Father. In the temple in Rilporin, dedicated to you and to Her, we pray and sacrifice and commune. In the temple, Father."

"Gone."

Gosfath twitched His leg from beneath her hand, the loss of contact an unexpected blow, a rejection that stung. *This is your fault*, it said. *You did this, you left me here alone.*

Lanta forged on, needing Him to understand. "She is gone, Father, but not forever, I swear it. I work tirelessly, day and night, to bring Her back to you and to us, to all Gilgoras. And when She is returned, we will wreak such vengeance on the world as has not been seen in millennia. You shall have blood and screams as your bounty, my god. We need your mighty strength in Rilpor, in the temple, if we are to bring Her back. We . . . need you to come to us, Lord. There is flesh there to slake yourself on, flesh for pleasure and flesh for pain."

Tentatively, Lanta reached out and touched Him again. His skin was hot, a slow increasing heat like a pot put on to boil, but she didn't pull away. If this was a test, she would not fail it. If her hands were to be the sacrifice Gosfath demanded, she would burn them in His fires and glory in it. She took a slow breath. "May I serve you, Lord? In the temple? Will you come?"

Gosfath leant forward and ran a finger down the soft skin of her neck, the talon scoring a bright line of blood. She didn't flinch, though the muscles around her eyes tightened at the sharpness of it. And then He sat back. He licked the drop of blood from His talon, and then sighed like wind howling through a tree canopy.

"Gone."

There was no warning, no way to prepare herself; Lanta was flung back along the pathway from the Waystation to her body, thrust back into it like a man attempting to stuff an eel in a jar. She reeled on her knees and Gull, taken by surprise at her return when he'd expected her to be lost in the rapture of communion, failed to catch her as she collapsed. She lay there, sucking in the scents of old blood and damp stone, her thoughts whirling.

Rejected. He does not want me, not as servant, nor as vessel. He is undone, and so are we because of it. He will not come.

Lanta wiped her cheeks with the back of her hand; her palms were newly blistered beneath the bandages, burns upon half-healed burns, a gnawing insistence that ate at her mind.

"What happened?" Gull demanded, pale, the pulse jumping in his throat.

"The god did not desire. Gone, He said. The same word three times, to every question about the Dark Lady and about our efforts to bring Her back. I asked Him here, more than once. He did not acknowledge it."

She stared sightlessly past Gull's shoulder as a sick dread swamped her. "If we cannot summon Him here, the Dark Lady will have no guiding light to steer by. She won't know that we have a host for Her, a life for Her to take and use to remake Herself. We could fail."

Gull licked his lips and pressed them, wet and cold, to her cheek. "We will not fail. We cannot. We must not. If it is not pleasure our Lord seeks, I will go to Him. I mean no offence, Blessed One, but I have served the god directly for years. We are old acquaintances. Perhaps I can use that."

Lanta rebelled against the idea, but she knew it made sense. It wasn't about pride or position or power, not any more. They were so far beyond such things now, a thought Corvus would no doubt be shocked to learn. The truth was Gosfath was attuned to His priest, as the Dark Lady was attuned—had been attuned—to Her Blessed One. It might be that Gull could persuade Him where she couldn't.

"Go, my friend. See if you can learn anything; see if He will speak with you. I have another matter to attend to. Will you need me?"

"Thank you, Blessed One, but no."

"Then I will leave you to your rapture."

And as for me, it is time to move the pieces on the board.

BLOODCHILD

THE BATTERED SLAVE FLINCHED when she opened the door before jerking into a curtsey. "Blessed One."

"Where is your owner?" Lanta pushed past without waiting for a reply, into a suite lit with bright sunlight from the empty windows. The rooms were fresh and clean, luxuriously appointed, but she knew instinctively that this was left over from Rilporian occupation. As King's Second, Valan had resources and opportunity to surround himself with wealth and had not done so. The man was a good son of the gods and a devoted bodyguard.

Valan stood when Lanta swept into the room and inclined his head. "Blessed One. An unexpected surprise. Is everything well? The king is not here."

"I'm not here to see Corvus," Lanta said. "My days are trying enough without his carping."

Valan ducked his head again, unspeaking, and gestured her to a chair. "Tara. Food and wine for the Blessed One."

Lanta raised an eyebrow. "You gave it a name? Did you also give it those cuts?"

Valan had the grace to look uncomfortable. "I was blessed with a large allocation of slaves," he said when she was seated. "All of them new. It seemed reasonable to use their names until their talents—or otherwise—were established. Tara is . . . different. Clever, for a Rilporian. Organised. She runs my household and anticipates my needs. When she converts, I will free her. She will cast off the soldier she professes to still be married to and make a fine consort."

The woman in question carried a small table to Lanta's side and placed a cup full of dark wine on it, handed another to Valan, and then put a platter of plums, cheese and sliced pork on the table. She curtseyed and moved to stand by the fireplace, her every action neat and silent despite her bandaged hand and the sweep of bruising curling up from the neckline of her gown.

"Consort? To you?" Lanta asked with the smallest touch of alarm.

Valan made a wry grimace. "I mourn Neela and will do so for some time. I doubt this one will still be available when I am ready to take another, not once she has placed her feet upon the Dark Path."

"She could warm your bed in the meantime," Lanta pushed. "You have been alone too long, Second. A bed-slave would ease your cares." She didn't give him time to respond. "You, slave. Anything the second wants, anything at all, you provide. If he honours you by taking you to his bed, you will pleasure him as you pleasure your consort, do you understand?"

The woman gave a jerky nod, her ridiculous hair—cut short on one side, long on the other—bobbing into her eyes. "Yes, Blessed One."

Valan's face twisted, a hint of revulsion, a hint of embarrassment, as though the idea wasn't new. As though he both wanted it and was repulsed by it. Lanta wasn't surprised—the woman was pretty in a way, strong-featured and broad-shouldered, bred for hard labour, but nothing like the spite-filled waif she remembered as the dead Neela. And besides, Valan was well known for his strange, un-Mireces-like prudishness, a source of much amusement among his fellow warriors. Something else that suited her.

"Your hands, Blessed One. You are hurt?" he asked, a clumsy changing of the subject that she allowed. She'd got the information she needed, after all.

"The rigours of my calling. It is nothing to concern yourself with," Lanta said easily as she made a show of grasping her cup and sipping. "Now, to the purpose of my visit, Second. I have doubts, grave doubts, and must share them with you."

Valan put his cup down and shifted to the edge of his chair. "I am yours to command, Blessed One."

"Doubts about Corvus," she said, not bothering to break it gently. How Valan reacted now would determine everything, her actions in the coming months, the coming years.

His face went still, wary but not angry. He folded his hands in his lap and sat straighter. "I am King's Second, Blessed One," he began and she felt a flicker of doubt; perhaps she had misread the situation after all. "I am a good son of the Red Gods. My feet are on the Path, and all I do is dedicated to Their glory. My king acts in the gods' best interests—to my knowledge. And it is to the gods that we ultimately must answer, Their judgement higher than that even of kings, for kings make mistakes and gods do not."

BLOODCHILD

Mistakes like your dead consort and children, Valan. Mistakes like letting the greater proportion of our blood be wiped out so that we must dilute it by rutting with these heathens. Yes, King's Second, yes. I know your heart.

Valan took a breath, knuckles turning yellow. "How may I serve the gods, Blessed One?"

RILLIRIN

Ninth moon, first year of the reign of King Corvus
Red Gods' temple, temple district, First Circle, Rilporin, Wheat Lands

RILLIRIN HAD NEVER SMELT anything so disgusting in her entire life. Not the cave-temple to the Red Gods in Eagle Height, not the stink of corpses in battle or the overflowing latrine pit from the overcrowding in the South Forts. The captain of the East Rank, whose name she had stubbornly refused to remember, and Pesh, the Krikite dedicated to the Red Gods, marched to either side of her as they proceeded through the smoky stench of the temple towards what had been—once—the godpool, where a familiar figure dressed in blue awaited, the torchlight throwing glints of fire into her hair.

The Blessed One stood with her arms crossed and her head thrown back with the old imperious arrogance Rillirin had always loathed, though her expression changed when she recognised her: ugly triumph blossomed in its place. "At last!"

The three of them came to a halt, Rillirin wheezing gently, her legs heavy from the brisk pace, the weight of collar and chain. The weight of her pregnancy—the babe seemed to have doubled in size in the last few weeks.

"The vessel, Blessed One," Pesh said before the Ranker could speak. "The Godblind proved his worth to the cause a final time."

"And where is he now?"

"Dead, I presume. We poisoned him and, in his already weakened state, I suspect he died, though I left before it happened. Time was of the essence to reach Pine Lock and find soldiers willing to stage an ambush on the word of a"—he glanced at the captain—"savage."

"Dom isn't dead," Rillirin said, more calmly than she felt. "You know nothing about him if you think something like poison could stop him."

"I understood her importance," the soldier interrupted, keen for his share of the glory in her capture. "We killed as many as we had to and captured as many as we could safely transport, Blessed One. As soon as I identified the woman, I brought her here."

"Aye," Rillirin spat even as Pesh opened his mouth to argue, "and aren't you the fucking hero for dragging a pregnant woman across half the country, causing who knows how much damage to the child? Pair of fuckwits, both of you."

She was sure her babe was in robust health, but Gilda's warning all those months ago—that Lanta wanted it—was echoing in her head as it had done every day since her capture and through both failed escape attempts. Perhaps if the woman thought the babe was useless she'd leave them be. A vain hope, a fool's hope, but all she had in the circumstances.

"She's a mouth on her," the Ranker added. "Been listening to it for a fortnight and I'm about sick of it, being honest."

"Then feel free to listen to it no longer," Lanta said. "Leave us. Both of you."

They both gaped and Rillirin tutted. "Oh, did you think you'd be getting a prize?" she asked sweetly. "Some gold or slaves of your own in appreciation? That's not really how the Mireces do things, is it, Lanta? In fact, you should probably both give thanks to your dead goddess she hasn't just killed you." She cocked her head at the Blessed One. "I need to piss, by the way."

A man stalked out of the shadows and Rillirin recognised Valan, the king's second, just before he slapped her across the face. "Address the Blessed One with respect." He snapped his fingers and the men who'd accompanied her all the way from Fox Lake melted away like snow.

Lanta put her hand on Valan's arm and steered him gently to the side, then stepped forward until her flat stomach brushed Rillirin's round one. "Such defiance," she murmured, her breath tickling Rillirin's face. "Such fire."

Not really, Rillirin wanted to tell her. *I need a piss because I'm scared. But I'll never let you see that, not ever again.* She forced a sneer on to her face. "Such filth," she replied, pointing with her chin over Lanta's shoulder. "Do you bathe in it?"

The Blessed One's face was cold, but then a smile warmed it. "No. But you might, if you don't watch your tongue." She put both palms on Rillirin's belly, the gesture possessive, almost hungry. Valan moved around behind Rillirin and prevented her from recoiling as Lanta's fingers roamed over her, measuring, gauging, one sliding down between her thighs.

Rillirin released her bladder and laughed when the other woman jerked away in disgust, an involuntary yelp bursting from her throat. "I did warn you," she said, even as Lanta slapped her other cheek with her wet hand. She was light-headed with hunger and exhaustion, fear crowding the edges of her thoughts, but she knew if she gave in now, gave in to the collar or the threats, that she'd never pull herself and her child free.

Valan's hands on her upper arms squeezed hard enough to leave bruises, but they did nothing else. They couldn't, not while she was pregnant. A few slaps, a few pinches, but no more. She was safe until the babe was born. Sort of. Rillirin vowed to make the most of that time—she'd find a way to escape; she'd find allies in the city somehow, among the slaves perhaps.

Lanta dried her hand deliberately on Rillirin's sleeve. "Liris never minded your smart mouth, as I recall. I, on the other hand, am less forgiving." She nodded and Valan grabbed a fistful of Rillirin's hair and yanked her head back. He put a knife beneath her chin and pressed until a bead of blood welled up.

"You carry the seed of the Godblind? The *deicide?*" he snarled into her upturned face. "You, the sister of our king, lowered yourself to rut like a *fucking animal* with the madman?"

"Aye," Rillirin spat back, though she was trembling, "and I enjoyed it!"

Lanta clapped somewhere out of sight, her pealing laughter echoing through the temple. "He put spirit in you as well as a child," she said. "I look forward to breaking it. Again."

"You can try," Rillirin snarled, her eyes rolling. "He's coming for me, the calestar, you can bet on that, and we'll kill you all. Best lock up

Gosfath while you're at it; you wouldn't want to lose another god, would you?"

Valan dragged on her hair again, the skin of his face tightening until it was pressed against the bones of his skull. Death was in that face and, despite her conviction, Rillirin felt a new surge of fear.

"Do not dare to threaten your betters, slave, or the Red Father," Lanta snarled. "I don't care if you are Corvus's sister—I can and will make you suffer in ways you cannot imagine should you test me."

Valan's knife slid from her chin, clanked over the metal collar, and swept down to press against her stomach. Rillirin's gasp was loud in the still air as the point dug in. Her brain knew they wouldn't, but her body knew no such thing and she writhed with animal instinct to get away.

"No, please, please, honoured. Please, Lan— Blessed One. I'm sorry, it was just talk."

"Then maybe you shouldn't talk, eh, Rill?" Lanta said. "Because we have options that won't harm the child. The water barrel. The branding iron. Some of the men."

Do your worst, bitch. Go on, do it. But the words were stubborn, refusing to leave Rillirin's mouth, cowering behind her teeth. Her bound hands were shoving at Valan's fist; she felt a hot sting as the knife edge cut the side of her palm.

"Now, Valan," Lanta said in gentle admonishment, "please remove the knife. Our guest must be healthy and whole to deliver her daughter."

He did as he was told and Rillirin straightened up, grunting at the flare of pain in her back. She shifted her weight to ease it and Valan's hand found her upper arm again. He squeezed, adding another layer of bruises.

Lanta cupped Rillirin's face in her palm. "Do you even know who this babe is, Rill? Do you know her destiny? She will belong to the whole world, and she will walk in glory all her days. In glory and in Blood."

"We are children of Light," Rillirin croaked. "My child will never be yours, never. And it could be a boy."

"Hush now, girl," Lanta said, her voice tender and even more frightening because of it. "Let's get you fed and rested." Her nose wrinkled. "And bathed. There is much to do to prepare for the birth. So much. Valan, that slave of yours—bring her."

"Your will, Blessed One."

Rillirin raised her chin, refusing to echo the words. Lanta's smile was indulgent, as at a precocious child's antics. "Valan will look after you for now, Rill. But we will talk soon, you and I and Gull and Holy Gosfath. Talk of the resurrection of the Dark Lady—and your role within it."

The Blessed One's fingers trailed across Rillirin's belly again and she went cold. She didn't know exactly what was planned, but she knew enough. She lunged with her bound hands for the woman's throat; Valan hauled her back. "Don't you touch my baby," she screeched, kicking out. "You won't have it, you won't. We are children of Light and nothing you do will change that. Keep your bloody hands away from us!"

Lanta dismissed them with a small, cruel smile and Valan began dragging her back towards the exit.

"See you soon, Rill," the Blessed One called as they burst into fresh air.

Tears tangled in her throat, shortening her breath, though she refused to let them brighten her eyes. "My name," she growled, "is Rillirin."

DOM

Ninth moon, first year of the reign of King Corvus
Watcher village, southern Wolf Lands, Rilporian border

WOLF SCOUTS CHALLENGED THEM five miles from the village. Not civilians, but actual Wolves. His people. Their presence unnerved him.

Ash let out a happy yell and dashed forward, calling out names as he recognised war-kin and friends he hadn't seen for months. Crys was soon absorbed into their number, and introductions were made to the Warlord and war leader, while familiar faces glanced at Dom and then away. The rumours had spread, then.

Dom stayed on his horse, grim-faced, and paced the Krikites advancing into the village. At least he'd recovered enough to ride now, to not have the humiliation of the litter added to the rest. His home had been overrun with hundreds—thousands—of civilians. Bursts of voices shattered the peace beneath the trees and pathways that had been little more than trampled grass were now mud-slick roads, wide and slippery, meandering among houses full of strangers, and more houses, and lean-tos and shelters and tents in between the permanent structures. The sounds of chopping wood and sawing and hammering, the creak of ropes and timbers hauled into position echoed among the trees.

His home was no longer his.

Dom dismounted near the Krikites; the new villagers were watching them, not daring to approach, while the Wolves—his kin—were gathering a hundred strides away in the main clearing that had served as training ground and celebration ground both. Scores of them. They must be those warriors who'd taken the Sky Path and the bloody road of vengeance, back after Watchtown burnt. Maybe some of the injured from Yew Cove that Ash had told him about, who'd been left behind to recuperate. They'd come home, even if he couldn't.

"Hello," said a little voice. "Are you new?"

Dom looked over his shoulder at the two small figures standing hand in hand. "Hello there," he said with an effort, frowning at the harsh Mireces accent. "No, I'm not new. Well, I mean I grew up here, but I haven't been back in a while. It's changed."

The little girl's eyes were round; the even littler one had backed behind her sister and was clutching the back of her dress, peeking under her arm. "What's your name?"

Dom crouched and cradled his stump in his other hand; it was suddenly very important that he didn't scare them. "My name's Dom," he said quietly. "How did you get here?"

"Can I stroke your horse?" the smallest girl said and Dom managed a smile. He was all too familiar with that sort of conversational evasion.

"We can do better than that," he said, standing again. "You can both ride him if you want. Would you like that?"

"Auntie Gilda says we mustn't bother the warriors," the taller one said and Dom's stomach cramped with sudden tension. *Auntie Gilda?*

He showed his missing hand. "Well, as you can see, I'm not a warrior, so it's no bother at all. Would you like to?" They both nodded, their eyes now even bigger. The youngest kept looking around them, as if half wishing someone would come and take them away. "Up you get then," he said and reached for the biggest, hoisted her up in his right arm and draped her legs either side of the saddle.

She sat and he placed both her hands on the pommel. "Don't move," he said sternly. "Let me get your . . . sister, is it?" The girl nodded and sat still, barely breathing, while Dom scooped up the littlest and placed her in front of her sister. Both of them began to grin.

"We're so high," piped the youngest. "We can see everything." Dom felt a smile tug at the corner of his mouth. He had a vague memory of his birth father putting him on the back of their old carthorse, how scared and exhilarated he'd been.

The horse shifted and both girls squeaked and then giggled as Dom calmed the animal, stump against its chest to still it, hand hovering just above their legs, ready to grab if they began to slide.

"I'm Kit," the older girl said suddenly. "I'm five. This is my sister, Ede." Kit pointed dismissively to the little girl clutching handfuls of mane. "She's only three."

Dom swallowed another smile. "It's a very great pleasure to meet you, Kit who is five and Ede who is three."

"Do you know Auntie Gilda?" Kit asked.

"As a matter of fact, I do," Dom said, working hard to maintain his breezy tone.

"Good," she said, "so you won't let us get in trouble?"

"Trouble?" he asked and then he felt it, the glare blistering the skin of his back. Slowly he turned his head and there she was, arms folded, on the path to the clearing.

"She's very old," Ede piped up, a little hand making a grab for Dom's long hair, plaited behind his head. Kit pulled her back and they both rocked in the saddle until he steadied them.

"She is," he said around the constriction in his throat. "And if you want to grow up and have children and learn to fight and hunt and weave and cook and live to be a very, very old woman like her, you best do as you're told, hadn't you?"

Dom swept Ede out of the saddle and on to the ground so fast she whooped in a breath and wrapped her arms around his head. He did the same to Kit, who tried hard not to squeak.

When they were both down, Dom made a claw out of his hand and pulled a monstrous face; Kit pulled Ede back, both of them squealing with laughter. "Because if you don't, Auntie Gilda will eat you all up!"

"No!" Ede shrieked and they ran away laughing, looking back multiple times, half in fear, half in the hopes Dom would chase them. He very much wanted to, watching their sturdy little forms vanish into a house.

Past lives already a fading memory, past horrors a fading dream. "Kit and Ede, five and three," he muttered. "How did you get here?"

"Turns out vengeance for our dead's not so clean-cut when it's infants and bairns you've to put your knife into," Gilda said from behind him. Dom smoothed his shirt before he faced her.

He saw the moment when she spotted his missing hand and the merest flicker of sadness crossed her face, but then it was gone and her eyes were hard in their nests of wrinkles. She was thinner than he'd ever seen her, bruises under her eyes and her mouth a thin slash in a face crafted for laughing.

"With me, lad. You and I've things to discuss."

H E EXPECTED GILDA TO lead him to Cam's old house and was bracing himself for the flood of memories that would accompany stepping beneath that lintel, but instead she took him to one of the newly built structures on what had been the outskirts of the village and now appeared to be nearer to its centre.

It was little more than a shack, a roof and walls, a blanket for a doorway, packed dirt for the floor, but it had a bracken bed and some pots and bowls stacked in a corner, and a ring of stones containing a cookfire outside. Gilda gestured him in and he preceded her, his heart in his throat. When she let the blanket fall behind her, the single room descended into guttering darkness.

By the time she'd lit a few candles, Dom had his back pressed to the far wall, blinking at the shadows as if they were alive. His left leg began to shake, threatening to dump him unceremoniously on the dirt.

He gestured deliberately with the stump of his arm. "I love what you've done with the place."

"Sit down before you fall down, boy," Gilda snapped and lowered herself with a grunt on to the bracken and then rootled around until she was comfortable. "Well? Are you going to stand there all day?"

There was nowhere else to sit except the floor. Carefully, as if she were a wild bear, Dom approached and sat at the far end of the heap of bracken, almost wedged into the corner. The silence stretched until he wanted to scream.

"Village is full," he said when he couldn't take it any more.

Gilda licked her teeth and then sighed, as if to say she knew he was stalling. "The Wolves who took the Sky Path didn't slaughter everyone; they freed the slaves and brought back as many children as they could, those young enough to forget the evil they were raised in, those who could embrace the Light. The youngsters will be raised as Wolves, perhaps, or by the former slaves. Either way they'll live, and live in the Light. Our villages may never be what they were, but the Wolf Lands are still a hive of free folk, living clean and happy beneath the trees. That counts for something. For a lot in these times."

"Rillirin's not here, is she?" he asked, though he wasn't sure how she'd react to the question. Did he even have a right to ask? But Gilda just shook her head.

"No. Her group never made it here from the South Forts, none of them did, and—"

"Then Lanta has her. She'll use our daughter to restore the Dark Lady."

Gilda's nostrils flared. "So how do we get her back?"

Dom shrugged. "We don't. She's on her own."

Gilda turned to stone at the pronouncement. Gimlet eyes watched him. Silent. Patient. All priestess, all mother. Demanding better. Demanding an answer that wasn't his to give, a promise he couldn't make. A life he couldn't save.

"What?" he snapped when he couldn't bear it any longer. "What do you want me to say? I don't know how we can save her and that's the truth. If I did I'd tell you. I'd go and rescue her myself if I knew how, if it was possible. But I can't, and she's carrying my child and there's nothing I can do to help her, nothing any of us can do. I wish there was."

"*Do* you wish there was"—Dom's breath whooped into his chest—"Darksoul?"—and back out with a strangled croak. There were no words to refute her implication. Dom had no words.

Gilda steepled her hands before her chin. "How about some fucking honesty, boy? You know, for old times' sake."

The stump of his arm throbbed with anger and the need for violence. He could taste blood on his tongue—his, hers, it didn't matter. He wanted to rend and scream and kill. He wanted to *make them understand.*

"You want to know if I'm sorry? Well, I am. I'm sorry. I'm sorry I told Corvus how to breach the city and I'm sorry I tried to kill you and I'm sorry for all of it, *all right*? I wasn't exactly myself at the time and if I hadn't done what I did, the Blessed One would've had me killed instead. Then you. We'd both be dead now."

I wish we fucking were. I wish I was.

"The Blessed One? Her name is Lanta; try and use it. There's nothing blessed about that woman." Gilda put her head on one side and glared. "And that's your excuse for attempting to murder me and all the other despicable betrayals you've committed, is it? That you weren't yourself?"

Dom waved his left arm in the air. "You did all right at defending yourself, if I remember. And anyway, as you can see I've been heartily punished for my myriad crimes. I've spent the last half-year living with two men who loathe me and not long ago I was poisoned by the Seer-Mother and forced into the knowing more times than I can remember until I had a stroke. The Fox God saved me though I begged Him to kill me. I still don't know exactly what I told her, but I suspect it was everything. So yes, I've damned us all for a second time. And I'm sorry about that, too, but I can't change it and I couldn't help it."

He stabbed the stump into the wall, relishing the spike of pain. "I've been crippled, physically and with shame, since we last saw each other, and I killed the Dark Lady and in so doing I destroyed myself in this life and the next. There's nowhere for me to go when I die; there's no one who'll have me except maybe, maybe, Rillirin, and she's lost to me as well. Is that enough for you or should I get on my knees and beg?"

His chest heaved as he gulped air, but the only change in Gilda's expression was a slight narrowing of the eyes. The fury was building now that he had to defend his actions. Now that his words seemed to bounce off her as though he wasn't even speaking the same language.

Everybody knows what I went through, but nobody really understands it. Nobody can find it in themselves to forgive me. I had my fucking mind broken by fucking gods and they still judge me for it!

He plunged on, the dam of his anger bursting and sweeping all before it. "I won't live to see the outcome of this war so, you know, you only have to put up with me for a few more months and then you can just move on, you and everyone—"

Gilda lunged forward and slapped Dom across the face so hard his ears rang and he fell back into the corner, skull clonking against the wall. He lay there for a few seconds and then sat up slowly, stump pressed to his cheek, tasting blood again, and he stared hatefully at the woman who'd raised him—and now damned him.

"Grow the fuck up, boy," the priestess snarled, on her feet and shaking with rage equal to his. "You did your damnedest to destroy this world and you failed. Now you'll work just as hard to save it, or so help me, I will kill you myself and make you wish it was a god doing it—They'd have more mercy."

She shook the sting from her hand and rubbed at her shoulder; the one he'd stabbed. "You think you're the only one who's suffered, the only one who's hurting? You are the only one of my family still alive, and believe me, there have been days when I wish it had been otherwise, but there it is. You live while Cam and Lim and Sarilla do not. You live while kings and princes die, while good soldiers breathe their last, while officers and warriors and even *gods* die. And all you can do with the gift that is life is wallow in self-pity?"

She tutted and shook her head slowly. "You've been many things in your life, Dom Templeson. This is the first time I've realised that you're a coward."

Dom's heart stopped and a flood of outrage rushed through him, followed just as quickly with humiliation. He lurched to his feet. "I've done things—" he tried and Gilda waved him to silence.

"We've all bastard done things, Calestar," she growled, sounding so much like Lim for a second that Dom's throat constricted. "I stood and witnessed Watchtown's death. I stood and listened to the screams of our people. I watched them run, human torches, out of the gates: my kin. I watched them fall burning from the walls and throw their children from the allure in a desperate attempt to save them from the flames, knowing they'd be butchered by the Mireces and counting that the lesser evil."

Gilda paused, her eyes glittering with unshed tears held back by an iron will. "And I watched you give yourself to the Mireces and the Dark Path. I watched your soul blacken within you, and now here you are at the Fox God's side and He's put a little Light back inside you, a tiny candle flicker, but it's up to you to tend that flame and you won't. Will you?

Because you're so consumed with being the victim of your own story. And when that Light dies again, you'll no doubt blame the people around you for not saving it instead of taking responsibility for your own soul."

She'd never spoken to him like this. No one had ever spoken to him like this. Dom's mouth opened and closed like a landed fish's, but he couldn't think of anything to say. Maybe there were no words to deal with the hate of a parent, with the pain of abandonment, of betrayal . . .

No. No. I'm the one who abandoned them, and the Light. I'm the betrayer. Not Gilda. This is all down to me.

Tears welled and he lowered his head, putting his hand to his brow.

"And none of that shit either," Gilda snapped, stepping close and slapping his hand away. Dom rocked back in shock again. "For the gods' sake, pull yourself together. I cannot stand self-pity. Don't be a coward, and don't feel sorry for yourself. Neither of those things will change what you've done. Nothing you can do now will change the past. But you can attempt to put it right. The question is whether you will."

Dom couldn't bear the challenge in her eyes, because the truth was he didn't know if he could put it right. He turned his back on her, unable to stand the accusations in her face.

"I'm waiting, boy," she growled, and now she sounded like Cam used to when Dom did something particularly stupid—which was often.

The edges of himself were ragged, threads loosening one by one in the wind and threatening to unravel, and it was taking everything he had just to hold himself together and Gilda had come along with a big pair of shears and she was cutting, cutting . . .

He knew Gilda didn't want to hear that, either. But if he spoke the words she wanted to hear, he couldn't be sure whether they'd be a lie or not.

He held the image of Rillirin's face in his mind. *Only one way to find out.*

"I'll make . . . I'll try and help make things better," he said, haltingly, to the floor. "I promise, Gilda, I'll try not to let you down."

His hand was squeezing the cup covering the end of his other arm, squeezing hard until the cuts from his last visit to Gosfath stung and throbbed and he wished to be anywhere, *anywhere*, else. There was a flicker of heat on his face—an instant of Waystation sulphur and red light, just a heartbeat of seduction and promise and the lure, the musk-scented, heart-stopping lure, of the Blood. There and gone, teasing him with the knowledge he could always go back. Asking, begging, inviting him back.

"What was that?" Gilda demanded. "Where did you just go?"

"What? I don't —" he began and then she was tearing the cup from his arm with such force the leather thongs stretched and snapped and there they were, the clear straight cuts dug into his twisted flesh. Almost healed but an indelible reminder, like the scars on his right wrist, scars of a blood oath, scars from his teeth. Scars scars *scars*.

"You traitor," she breathed and her pupils were wide and black.

"It's not what you think," Dom begged.

Gilda didn't slap him this time, oh no. Gilda bunched her fist and punched him so hard that he was on his arse and staring at the pretty lights as blood gushed from his nose. "You make me sick," she said, her voice flat, dead. "All your promises, your apologies and justifications, all just lies to make me look the other way, to fool us all."

The curtain was ripped away and Ash leapt into the room, axe in hand. "What's going on? Gilda, are you hurt?"

"I'm sorry," Dom yelled from the floor. "They *ruined* me, the Dark Lady and the Dancer both. They chewed me up and spat me out and it's like my back's broken but everyone expects me to just get up and get on with living. I can't! *I'm dying!*"

The hut fell silent, as still as the air before a storm and carrying as much malevolent weight and promise of catastrophe. Dom pulled his knees up to his chest and wrapped his arms around them, letting the blood patter between his thighs on to the earth. "I'm dying," he repeated. "And I'm lost in the dark and I just need a torch. I just need someone to show me the way so I can at least say my goodbyes."

Gilda knelt stiffly opposite him as Crys ducked into the room to stand with Ash. Dom ignored them both. He started as Gilda winked and all the hardness in her was gone. "That's all you needed to say, son. Fortunately, I'm pretty good at lighting torches for those as can't see."

Dom wiped his nose, dumbfounded. She pulled him into an embrace and this time she let him cry, knowing that he needed it now he was him-self again—or as much himself as he could be. She even shed a few tears of her own, and she hushed him when he began to apologise again for all he'd done, the monstrous things for which he was responsible. Instead she held him, rocked him, and crooned over his missing hand.

The afternoon sun was slanting through the doorway and the others had left when she finally pushed him away and looked into his face. Dom's eyes slid from hers.

"Look at me," she commanded in a gentle voice. "You've begun to heal, but there's a long way to go and the path behind you is dark and slippery, beckoning you back. This is the only chance you get, son. Take a single backward step, so much as glance over your shoulder at where you've been, and I will have you killed. You're all that's left to me, but I won't let you jeopardise Gilgoras again, and I won't lose you a second time. You're better off dead than going back there. Do you hear me?"

Dom swallowed hard; even now, despite his words and promises, he could feel the pull of that path. But Gilda's lined face had no pity and no weakness in it; she might have been carved from beech.

There was only one answer he could give her; he nodded. In that moment, he even meant it.

CORVUS

Ninth moon, first year of the reign of King Corvus
Red Gods' temple, temple district, First Circle, Rilporin, Wheat Lands

HE'D TOLD THE BLESSED One that his sister would be sent to her the moment she arrived, but in the end, it was Lanta who sent for him. Apparently, Rillirin had arrived in the city and no one had thought to tell him. He knew Valan had had something to do with it. His second was far too friendly with the Blessed One these days.

He mentioned his concerns to Tett who, after a promise to find out which gate she'd come through and which Mireces were on duty when she did, kept his habitual silence. It was something Corvus had come to enjoy. Valan's opinions were usually valid, but he had a lot of them and rarely recognised when Corvus needed some peace and quiet.

And every time Valan couldn't be found because he was with the Blessed One, Tett was there instead, waiting to serve, to protect his king. To earn his trust. Corvus glanced at him now, walking on his right where the second—the heir—usually was. It was something to think about. Tett was steady, competent, an excellent warrior, respected by the men and dedicated to the Dark Path. More than that, he had a head for numbers and was a born organiser, unlike Valan, who relied on flair and a quick tongue, an easy charisma that made men like him.

He wouldn't make the decision yet. See how Tett handled himself in the next few months until the Dark Lady was restored. Plenty of time to decide the future once that future was secure.

There were Mireces on watch outside the temple; they leapt to attention as he barged past and flung open the door, boot heels echoing in the vast building. The main worship space was empty; they'd be in Lanta's private quarters. There weren't guards there, so Corvus slammed back the door and strode in.

Lanta jumped and Valan kicked out of his chair, a dagger appearing in each hand at the intrusion, so Tett shoved past Corvus and drew his sword. "Weapons up," he snarled.

"Your Majesty? Forgive me, Sire, you startled me," Valan said, hurriedly sheathing his knives. "We have been—"

"Rill?" Corvus wasn't listening, didn't have eyes for the Blessed One and the faint stain of blush in her cheeks as if he'd caught her doing something illicit, didn't care about Valan's garbled excuses. Knowing she was here and seeing her were two different things. His sister hadn't stood when he entered, instead sitting composed and calm in a cushioned chair, a glass resting on the mound of her stomach. She was big already, with a three-moon still to go.

"Brother," she said. "I'd get up but, you know, it's a little difficult to curtsey these days." He blinked at the casual disdain in her tone.

"Shut your mouth," Lanta snapped, the anger in her words far outweighing the insult. Corvus held up his hand, stilling her, and stepped past Tett, took Valan's chair as his own and dragged it closer. He sat, his knee touching Rillirin's, and took the hand not holding the glass, filled with tenderness and something akin to pride. *You will be the instrument of the Dark Lady's return. Your child will be glorious.*

"You're here," he said, almost wondering. "Finally you've come back to me."

Rillirin's lip curled and she threw her wine in his face. "I wouldn't exactly say I'm here of my own free will," she said as he spluttered and Lanta shouted at her again, more strident this time. They both ignored her. "Your pet soldiers kidnapped me and slaughtered all the people I was with, hundreds and hundreds of them. And it's apparently because you believe my child is somehow special. You're all insane."

Her confidence surprised and intrigued him and he was frankly delighted at how it incensed Lanta, even after only a few hours. Still, he'd need to break her before the birth. Rillirin's mouth tightened and she pressed her hands to her belly. She'd been dressed in a gown that was too small so that the material was taut and he watched, fascinated, as the babe writhed and moved inside her. His sister's child. The Bloodchild.

"When did she get here?" he asked Valan, using his sleeve to wipe the liquid from his face and neck and acting as if Rillirin were no more than a precocious child.

"An East Rank captain and a Krikite named Pesh brought her in just before noon. Yesterday." Lanta's voice was cold and precise, but with a hint of satisfaction she couldn't quite hide.

A full day and a half before you think to inform me? I weary of your games, Lanta.

"And what have you three been up to since she arrived? Catching up on old times?" His sarcasm brought a flush to Valan's face and tightened the muscles around Lanta's mouth.

"They stole my clothes, forced me into this sack and then made me stay in this cesspit until the fucking stench made me puke," Rillirin said. "You think I've got a magic baby but it doesn't occur to anyone that it could be harmed by being in this place. You're so bloody—"

"Be quiet," Lanta said, the words grated out between her teeth.

Corvus leant back in his chair and gestured. Tett filled a glass with wine and passed it to him; it didn't escape him that Valan had neglected this most basic duty. "Perhaps," was all he said. They were all uncomfortable at that, expecting more, expecting anger or interrogation or threats. Not calm.

None of them know the first thing about me. Not even Rill.

"Oh," he said, as if he'd only just remembered, "I have a gift for you. Tett." He gestured and the warrior moved to Rillirin's side. She tensed, but he just brushed the mane of her hair back and used a small pair of pliers to tug the pin out of the collar so it fell open. He took it from her neck and now Rillirin was surprised, her brittle confidence melted like salt in blood. Her hand went to her neck as if she couldn't believe it; on Corvus's other side Lanta radiated frozen outrage.

Corvus passed his cup to Tett and pulled the new collar out of the bag the man held. Slender and light, shimmering. He'd even had it decorated.

ANNA STEPHENS

"Silver, to reflect your station as a member of the royal family," he said, and shifted to the edge of his chair. Rillirin stiffened and there was a wordless plea in her face. He leant forward and clipped it shut around her throat, fitted the slender steel pin through the hasp and then held it still while Tett used the pliers to bend it over so it couldn't be removed.

He sat back and examined her. "Beautiful. Like its wearer." He winked, but the fire—the wonderful, infuriating fire—was gone. Part of him hoped it couldn't be so easily extinguished, that it was merely banked and waiting fresh fuel. He poked the coals. "Fox-bitch, Liris used to call you." Lanta was stony, Valan glancing between king and Blessed One as if not sure which way to jump. "Wildcat."

Rillirin's fingers tightened at mention of the dead king's name, the man who'd owned and used her body, but when she replied her voice was even. "I prefer Wolf now. They're my war-kin. I fought with them, and I killed alongside them. Killed Mireces."

"And now you are a princess," Corvus said with a grin, "and one of the most powerful Mireces alive."

"I am no Mireces," she said with quiet venom, delighting him, "and my child will not be either. Dom will come for me, for us both. He'll kill you; maybe I'll kill you."

"You will be Mireces," Corvus promised her and now the flames were back, licking high and hungry and glowing in her face. "You will come to the Path with your whole heart, because your child will already be standing upon it. And what mother abandons her child?"

"I will not, and neither will—"

"If you cannot control your tongue I will have it burnt out of your head," Lanta said, sharp and angry. "We need your womb and your babe, not the rest of you."

"You're not getting my child," Rillirin said again, and the fire was roaring now. If the Blessed One's words had touched her, it didn't show. Corvus could have clapped; he knew how much grit it would take for a former slave to contradict the Blessed One. "Dom will come; the army will come. You're all going to die. And if not? I'll just have to do it myself."

"You should concern yourself only with a healthy pregnancy, Princess," Valan said smoothly, and with every appearance of honesty,

—200—

and it was like a bucket of cold water over them all. Rillirin twitched, confusion sliding across her features.

She didn't answer, just held out her cup to Corvus for a refill.

"You're not going to throw this one over me, are you?"

Rillirin found a smile and gave him a non-committal shrug, though Valan's calm concern had clearly rattled her. Corvus filled her cup and thought again of his earlier plans, that he'd take her as consort to honour the sibling union of the gods, then make her his queen as the Mireces kings of old had done. Once the babe was born, she'd do anything to be near it, even if it was the Dark Lady reborn. Women were sentimental like that.

"Do you have everything you need for the rite, Blessed One?" Corvus asked in a belated attempt to heal the cracks in their relationship.

The tilt of Lanta's chin told him it was too late for that. "Our preparations to place the child on the Dark Path continue. We are ready; we need only for your sister to push it out."

Rillirin rubbed her palms over her belly and smiled sweetly. "Keep waiting, bitch," she said with friendly malice. "I'm weeks away yet. Plenty of time for you all to die screaming."

Corvus's mouth fell open but then he burst out laughing, his amusement increasing at the blistering anger radiating from the Blessed One. Rillirin grinned at him, lifted her glass and saluted, and then swallowed. He returned her gesture, aware of the whiteness of Lanta's knuckles. No one laughed at the Blessed One. No one.

"I am glad your failures thus far sit so easy on you, Sire," Lanta said with brittle ice coating each word. "I, for one, have found little to laugh at in the months since our Bloody Mother was taken from us."

"Oh, Blessed One, you misunderstand," Rillirin said, still smiling. "My brother the king laughs only because otherwise he would weep. Is that not so?"

"Careful, Princess," Corvus said, his mirth withering. "You may be my sister, but my loyalties are firmly with the gods. The Blessed One has my full support. In fact, I have selected a dozen of our surviving women to train with you and Gull in the priesthood, Blessed One. You take too much upon yourselves," he said with false solicitude. "I would not see you exhausted beyond reason when it can be prevented." *And I will have a replacement Voice of the Gods ready for when this is all over.*

He turned to Rillirin before Lanta could splutter a reply. "And as for rescue, Rill, best you face up to the facts: there's no one coming for you."

Rillirin stroked her belly again, an intimate, soothing gesture. Her gaze was even, confident. "If you say so."

RILLIRIN

Ninth moon, first year of the reign of King Corvus
Heir's suite, the palace, Rilporin, Wheat Lands

I F SHE'D BEEN A slave, Rillirin would've known how to behave. If she'd been free, she could have dealt with that too, strange as it would have been in a city run by Mireces. But this . . . this was beyond anything she'd experienced or could understand.

They called her "Princess" and "milady." She ate more and better food than she'd ever had in her life, and slept in a clean, warm bed the size of a house in a suite of rooms big enough for a hundred—the queen's wing, adjacent to Corvus's, at his insistence, far better than the first night of her stay, which had been in a small room in the temple where the stench of hopelessness and dead blood made her nauseous.

She wore Corvus's silver ceremonial slave collar, and while it didn't have a chain attached to it, she still couldn't remove it. Lighter and looser than the cold black iron of the previous collar, it told her two things: she was special; and she was nothing.

She spent her days forced to participate in rituals to the Red Gods, in the awful sacrifices that dedicated new converts to the Dark Path, for despite the Dark Lady's destruction—or maybe because of it—every day slaves came to offer up their souls to Blood in exchange for freedom. The tired, the hungry, the hopeless. Feeling that moment of envy when the collars were taken from them, when they were given a house and food and weapons—still watched, of course, and would be for months—but free. Free.

She spent her evenings with Corvus in his chambers, listening to reports and orders while drinking exquisite wine and nibbling on oatcakes dipped in honey, the babe stretching and twisting in delight at the comfort and the food, all the food. Learning more about the state of the country and her brother's plans than she'd ever expected to know. As if he wanted her involved. As if he trusted her.

She was royalty. She was a slave. She was a child of Light. She took part in Mireces rituals. She had the run of the palace. She was a captive.

If they were trying to keep her off balance, they were succeeding; she didn't know what they wanted of her from one day to the next other than the babe and her conversion to the Red Joy. Both things she swore they'd never have.

And then there was Tara. Of all people, of all the places to discover such unexpected, such sudden flaring hope, there was Major Tara Carter, soldier, officer and killer of men. Now one of Valan's slaves, so changed as to be almost unrecognisable, all her fire banked down to embers hidden beneath cold grey ash.

Tara Vaunt, not Carter, wife to Major Tomaz Vaunt. Both of who are strangers to me, Rillirin reminded herself for the fifth time that day. Betraying Tara's cover story was unthinkable, and she'd nearly done it the first moment they met out of sheer surprise.

Tara stood opposite, hands clasped in front of her, face impassive as Valan and Lanta sat at the table among papers and candles and cups of wine. Rillirin herself sat in a hard chair against the wall farthest from the fireplace; even so, sweat misted her face and the babe stirred, restless at the inactivity.

Rillirin tried not to look at Tara, but couldn't help herself. Every time she did, the woman was watching the pair at the table, alert for the smallest gesture that would indicate a need. Rillirin marvelled at her efficiency, how she anticipated her orders so easily. Tara was a far better slave than she had ever been, though she reminded herself not to congratulate the woman on it if they got out of here. *When. When we get out of here.*

"Rill," Lanta snapped, so abruptly she squeaked in shock, "serve Second Valan his meal."

Tara took a step forward but Rillirin shook her head. "Your will, Blessed One," she said softly. It was part of Lanta's insatiable quest for power; she was proving she had more authority than the king's sister or the mother of the so-called Bloodchild. While Rillirin was brave enough these days to challenge the priestess, she made sure only to do it when Corvus was present; her brother seemed to enjoy them pecking away at each other and he wouldn't let Lanta punish her.

Tonight, though, he and Tett were poring over the giant map of Rilpor painted on the wall in the war room and, as Rillirin was never allowed to be alone, she'd trailed the Blessed One to the second's quarters and there been confronted with this intimate, secretive conversation between Lanta and Valan. A conversation she couldn't hear and to which she wasn't allowed to contribute.

Still, word of her food cravings had spread through the palace and Tara had given her a plate of honeyed oatcakes shortly after her arrival and a smile that promised her she wasn't alone, even if it felt like it. A smile that had nearly made her burst into tears.

"Rill!" Lanta snapped again and she started, realising she'd been sitting lost in thought. She flushed, heaved herself out of her chair and paused to press a hand to the small of her aching back, just for a second. She took three steps towards the table and a pain surged through her, from her back into her belly, heavy and brooding. She grunted and bent forward, then let out a long, drawn-out groan as the pain only increased. Her belly was as hard as a stone. Her legs wobbled and, to her surprise, it was Valan's hands that appeared to support her.

"Easy, sweetheart, easy," he murmured, holding her elbows and hooking her chair with his foot, pulling it towards them. "Just breathe. There you go, breathe. Good. Chair's behind you if you want to sit."

Tara was on her other side now and Rillirin squeezed her hand hard, taking and giving comfort. The touch of a friend.

She groaned again as the pain crested. Gods, she needed to piss.

"When are you due, milady?" Tara asked and Rillirin would've laughed at the title if she'd had the breath. Valan's hand was on her belly and the slight smile on his face was so private she had to look away. "It's likely just a practice pain unless you're near your time."

"Eleven weeks at least," she gasped as it began to ease. It had happened before, though not with such intensity. "It's passing. I'm fine. Get your hands off me."

Valan let go with something like reluctance, his eyes suspiciously wet. He cleared his throat and backed to the table, leaning his hip against it.

"Shall I fetch water, honoured?" Tara asked. "She shouldn't have wine, really."

"Don't leave me," Rillirin begged and Tara flicked a glance at Valan. "Please, honoured. Please let her stay."

"I'll get the water," Valan said, surprising her again. He left.

Lanta was muttering foul prayers, her fingers curling and writhing over Rillirin's stomach and the babe kicked hard, and then kicked again.

"No," she cried. "No, stop. You're hurting it!" Lanta slapped her across the cheek and Rillirin felt yet another pain as she did, that of Tara's grip tightening so hard on her hand that she gasped. She squeezed in response, a desperate voiceless plea not to do anything stupid, because Tara was looking at the knife next to the bread on the table.

Valan returned with the water a moment later, ending whatever murderous plan Tara might have had. Rillirin drank, the cup trembling so some of it spilt down her chin and then her muscles hardened to stone again and she gasped, thrust the cup at Tara so she could clutch at the tightness. Valan rubbed the small of her back.

"Better?" he asked when it passed. Rillirin nodded, but his hand didn't stop rubbing, teasing away the dull ache with patient fingers, and though she should tell him to stop, the relief was exquisite.

This must've been how he was with his consort, what was her name? Neela? It seems even the adder has a heart.

"You, slave." Lanta interrupted her thoughts, addressing Tara. "Do you have children?" Tara shook her head, mute. "You said this was a practice pain. How do you know?"

"I have assisted at births, Blessed One, here in the city. Many births." Tara was lying and they both knew it. But why?

"Then you may assist Gull and me when Rill does go into labour."

What? "Blessed One, forgive me," Rillirin protested, "but surely I need a proper midwife? What if there are complications? What if something goes wrong?"

Lanta put her head on one side and pursed her lips. "Then we will cut you open and pull forth your daughter. We don't need you, Rill. Have you still not worked that out?"

Rillirin's heart gave one tremendous, liquid thud and then began pounding wildly so that within seconds her head was spinning. "Who . . . who will feed the babe? It'll need milk. You need me. My child needs me!"

"There's a woman who works in the night kitchen who has a new-born," Tara said and Rillirin sucked in a breath of utter betrayal. How could Tara mention a wet nurse in her very presence? Tara was supposed to save her! "She could assist at the birth, or tell us who helped her, at least."

Not betrayal after all, though ambiguous enough to seem that way, perhaps. To slide a little further into the circle of trust. Rillirin let her chin wobble and deliberately shoved Tara's supporting arm away.

"Stop staring at me, all of you," she snapped. "I feel fine and there's weeks yet. And you don't know it's a girl. How's your dead goddess going to feel if you try and stuff her into a boy, eh?"

Lanta flushed with anger but Valan stayed her. "She's frightened, Blessed One. Let her have her little victories. Once the child is born, she can live the rest of her life under your punishments." A threat like that would've carried more weight if he hadn't been soothing her back pain when he said it, but it settled Lanta's ruffled feathers.

"She shouldn't be here," the Blessed One grumbled. "She should be staying in the temple so that everything can be prepared in good time."

"Corvus won't allow it. As long as he controls her, he controls you," Valan said, finally stepping away. He gulped wine before passing the cup to Lanta. Rillirin felt a little bloom of surprise—the Blessed One sharing a cup as lovers did? And talking of the king as if he was working against the two of them? What was going on and, more importantly, how could Rillirin use it to her advantage? "Or thinks he does, anyway."

"Slave, find that woman and secure her help. Where and how she birthed, who assisted her, how much milk she has in case there is a need for a wet nurse," Lanta ordered. Rillirin gritted her teeth, but Tara curt-seyed and left the room.

"You'll be fine, Rill, when it comes. Just keep breathing through it and you'll be fine." Valan's voice and expression were rich with wistfulness, but then it vanished as he rubbed the back of his neck and shifted his chair so he faced away. She watched them, heads close together as they murmured, Rillirin forgotten again. Forgotten until they needed the babe.

She stroked her stomach. *I think you and me and Auntie Tara have some plans of our own to make, little warrior. They're not the only ones who can keep secrets.*

THE BLESSED ONE

Ninth moon, first year of the reign of King Corvus
Red Gods' temple, temple district, First Circle, Rilporin, Wheat Lands

YOU HAVE HEARD THE latest in his list of failures, I presume?" Lanta demanded as soon as Valan walked in. "You have heard how he jeopardises our country and all our plans with his incompetence?"

Valan twitched at that, but then he nodded. "Yes, Blessed One. That he missed his opportunity at the South Forts—"

"Missed his opportunity?" she demanded, incredulous, and then bit off the words to gesture him to a seat at her side. "The South Forts were found abandoned and emptied of all provision. No clear sign of where they went or how many they numbered, even. Apparently they just vanished. There is an enemy on the loose in Rilpor, Valan, and we have no idea of his strength or where he will strike next. And it is Corvus's doing."

"I advised him to attack the South Forts, Blessed One," he said. "Said the time was right, that we needed to end the threat. He refused."

"And he told me he had many demands on his time. That I shouldn't bother him." Her upper lip drew back from her teeth. "What those demands were, who can say. They certainly didn't include securing the country against our enemies."

"Enemies that are now at large, unwatched, able to strike at us where and when they please," Valan agreed. The tension in the room wound a little tighter.

Lanta clicked her tongue. "Perhaps the time has come," she said. She let her calf rest against his; his lashes flicked shadows on his cheeks as he glanced at her and away. He didn't move his leg.

Valan ran his hands through his hair and then down over his face; he was worried, uncertain. "Now that we are here, I would be lying if I said I wasn't uncomfortable at the thought of your—our—plan. Corvus is my friend."

Lanta licked dry lips. "And that, of course, is why you are a faithful son of the gods," she said smoothly and took his hand. Her thumb traced small circles on the back of his wrist and she noted the faint flush in his cheeks. "That you can make this sacrifice for Them, that you can regret the loss of a friend for the greater good, shows your strength of character. He is your friend, but he is not fit to be king. War chief, yes, that he excelled at, but not this. Not governing. He must be replaced."

"And that replacement will need to be Mireces," Valan said.

Lanta blinked. "Valan, you are King's Second. We both know what that means. Besides, I would not discuss such things with you if I had not intended for you to replace Corvus."

"Whereas, I had thought to suggest you take the throne, Blessed One," he murmured and Lanta froze. The seed of her queenship that she'd planted among her priesthood had died with them, or so she had thought. Now it seemed it had found fertile soil after all.

He seized her hands. "As queen you would rule us more wisely than Corvus ever has. As Blessed One you already guide us through the world and safely to the shore of the Afterworld. To do both would be a heavy burden, but I would support you, Blessed One. I would be your strong right arm, your executioner. None would rise against you and live, I swear."

"Valan, dear Valan," she murmured. "We need a king. You are King's Second. This is all so unexpected, a possibility that I had never considered. But, perhaps, if it is your wish, I could stand at your side and help you rule."

He blinked, swallowed hard, swallowed again. "It would be my honour," he managed, his voice hoarse.

Her hand rose to the side of his face. "It is you who honour me and, as always, the gods," she breathed, and leant in to kiss his forehead. "And worry not. I know you mourn Neela; I will not ask of you . . . There will be no need if you do not want . . ."

Pain and anger flashed in quick succession across his features, both emotions part of the reason he had chosen her over Corvus, Corvus who had made the decision to leave the women and children behind and unprotected. And dead. His eyes flicked to her mouth and then away.

"You were a good match, good parents to the girls . . ." She searched her memory. "Kit and Eve?"

"Ede." His hand twitched in hers.

"Ede, yes. Forgive me."

He bit his lip; the golden flags of firelight danced across the planes of his cheeks. So young. "I know they are happy in the Afterworld, Blessed One. I know they are content and they are waiting for me, that if they knew of my actions here they would be so proud. But . . ."

"But you miss them." His head jerked in a graceless affirmative. "As you should. We are put on Gilgoras for twin purposes—to serve the gods, and find happiness. You did that. And while we will rule together to the gods' glory, I do not expect you to, ah, to love me. You gave Neela your heart; I would not ask for the same."

It wasn't all an act; Lanta felt uncommonly anxious. Despite the rumours both she and Liris had allowed to spread, she had never shared the old king's bed. Though she blushed to acknowledge it, Lanta had never shared anyone's bed. Her body and mind were tools of the gods, sacrosanct. The only love she'd ever known was Holy Gosfath's, brutal and uncaring of her needs. Perhaps it would be better if Valan didn't want her, though as she studied his face a warmth grew in her belly that had nothing to do with wine.

Valan snapped out of his reverie. His hand shifted beneath hers, turning so that their fingers slotted together. He raised it to his lips and pressed a kiss to the inside of her wrist and her stomach fluttered. "Believe me, Blessed One . . ." he began and paused. "Lanta. Believe me, Lanta, it will be the easiest thing in the world to love you, once the pain of Neela's loss has faded." And then, as if he'd read her mind: "Though I do not know how I can ever compare to the love of a god."

She found a gentle smile for him, one so lacking in artifice or arrogance or power that it sat strange and light upon her lips. "Do not worry about such things," she managed, nervous anticipation thrilling through her. "We will learn each other. All else will come from that."

"You . . . do not mind about Neela?" he asked.

"You would not be the man all Gilgoras needs as its supreme ruler if your heart was dead," she promised in her turn. "Grieve as long as you must. I will be here when you are done, and so will the world."

She sat back, breaking physical contact with intense regret and ending the moment, beginning another. "Now, Second, I am afraid we must to business. The . . . transfer of power needs to be accomplished and Corvus removed. What are your suggestions?"

He adapted to the change in topic with something like relief, though whether thoughts of Neela or thoughts of kingship worried him, she couldn't tell.

"There's the Krikite, Pesh. He mopes around the temple and the palace like a ghost, expecting some reward, some acknowledgment of his actions in bringing Rillirin here. His sister was supposed to have joined him and has not; he grows increasingly worried. It would be easy enough to manoeuvre him into making the attempt. As you said, he is expendable—deal with it."

"Hmm, perhaps. Though he is an unknown quantity. We do not know him, his loyalties, whether he will betray us rather than aid us. I cannot trust him. In fact, he is expendable—deal with it."

"Your will. I would not recommend we bring another Mireces into our confidence. I can do it myself, of course, whether in a formal challenge or something more circumspect. Poison, perhaps."

Lanta dismissed both ideas. "We must be clean of this, and poison is beneath us and not guaranteed."

"Then a more unusual option, Blessed One, but one I think will work. My slave, Tara. She can kill Corvus."

"EXPLAIN," LANTA SNAPPED, AND all intimacy fled. She reared back on the seat and folded her arms, donning the Blessed One's guise like the armour it was. "I said someone we can trust."

Valan nodded. "I do trust her, despite that she is Rilporian. The day I returned from Pine Lock after killing the Evendoom brothers, I went to Fost to retrieve her. He told me she was in the kitchens. I was hungry anyway, so I followed her. I could hear a fight so I approached with caution, stood in the shadows and watched. There were three of them trying to rape her. She killed two."

Lanta's mouth fell open; she snapped it shut, gestured for him to continue.

"She's more than just a fighter, Blessed One. We've all seen women fight off drunken advances—gods, Neela was no stranger to it. This wasn't that. The way she moved, the way she weighed up her attackers, how she flowed between them not giving them time to regroup or rush her or come at her from behind. Even when they had her on the floor they couldn't best her. She's highly skilled—and she's never used that against me or anyone, not until she absolutely had to. As a slave, she can get close to him and it will look—it will be—a simple revenge killing that he didn't see coming."

"She's your slave and you're named as second," Lanta pointed out, but more from curiosity as to how he would overcome it, not to curtail his plan. It had a simple elegance that kept her name far removed from the whiff of suspicion.

Valan spread his hands. "I won't be in the city," he said. "When we are ready to act, you will send me away on business. When that happens, I will lend Tara to Corvus and I will leave a knife lying in my quarters before she goes. I saw the look in her eye when she was fighting those men: savagery, yes, but joy too. She's a killer and I don't think she'll waste the opportunity."

He paused for her reaction. Lanta stared into the fire, thinking it through. "You cannot guarantee she'll take the risk, though," she said eventually. "You said yourself she only fought because she had no choice. If she didn't make an attempt on Corvus then, why would she this time?"

"Tara's husband is an officer in the Rank; he's a prisoner in the south barracks and she'll do anything to keep him safe. So we—"

"Make her a willing accomplice," Lanta interrupted. "We tell her she has to kill the king and if she doesn't we'll kill her husband."

"Or we promise them both their freedom," Valan said. "Whichever one we think is more likely to make her comply. We give her motive and we give her opportunity and then we sit back and mourn the tragedy."

A slow smile spread across Lanta's face. "I like it," she said. "Where is she now?"

"In the south barracks with her husband. I had . . . anticipated that our conversation this evening might turn in this direction. I thought an early reward for her could make her more amenable. It'll be the last time they ever see each other, after all."

Lanta laughed low in her throat and patted his knee, letting her fingers linger for a moment. *Sentimental as well as ruthless,* she thought approvingly. *I like it.*

"All right, prime her for the act. The sooner it is done, the better."

Valan bowed his head. "Your will, Blessed One."

TARA

Ninth moon, first year of the reign of King Corvus
South barracks, Second Circle, Rilporin, Wheat Lands

ND HE KILLED THE third one for you? I don't understand."

"I wouldn't say for me. I was capable of doing that on my own, thank you," Tara said.

Vaunt growled. "You know what I mean. He took your side. He watched you slit a man's neck and didn't punish you. Didn't kill you. Slaves die for less than that, they die for nothing. Yet not only does he know you can fight, he allows you to live and he allows you to come here."

Tara felt a faint blush stain her cheeks. "He . . . likes me, I think. I remind him of his dead wife in a way. He's warier around me, gets a bit jumpy if I'm carving meat or whatever, and he watches me a lot more but . . ." She waved a hand helplessly. "It's hard to explain. It's as though now I've shown him who I am, he actually trusts me more. As if we don't have secrets."

"I don't like it," Vaunt said and anger washed through Tara's chest.

"Should I have let them rape me to maintain my cover then?" she hissed, jerking out of his embrace and rolling to the edge of the bed, her back to him. The bruises were fading faster than the memories and it had taken an act of will to respond to his touch. Now she was regretting having made the effort.

Vaunt leant up on his elbow and put a gentle hand on her shoulder. "Absolutely not," he said with enough vehemence that she twisted back to face him. "You kill anyone who touches you without your permission and fuck the consequences. It's all well and good you being sent here by a god, but not even He would expect you to make that sort of sacrifice. And I'll fucking kill you myself if you let it happen."

"Because I'm your wife and your honour would be stained by my shame?" she asked and the mockery had an edge to it sharper than any blade.

"Because you're a godsdamn soldier and you protect yourself by killing your enemies. With extreme fucking prejudice."

Tara bit her lip at the surge of relief that he wasn't a prideful, pompous cock after all and pulled him into a hug, hiding her face in his chest. She let him hold her, the steady beat of his heart beneath her ear an unexpected comfort. His skin was salty against her lips, which she liked, but his ribs pressed into her cheekbone, which she didn't. The Rank prisoners were on half-rations despite the hours of building work they carried out, and Vaunt and Colonel Dorcas next door were on even less, seeing as they weren't allowed outside the barracks.

"There's more news," she said eventually and Vaunt groaned. "Rillirin's here."

"The sister? Shit. What can we do?"

"Get her out. What Valan told me—that they're going to use her babe to somehow bring back the Dark Lady—well, I think they really are. I've heard Lanta and Corvus discussing it. It's common knowledge. Crys—the Fox God—whoever, wanted me to ghost Corvus and Lanta, cut the head off the snake. Now I'm wondering whether killing Lanta and getting Rillirin out of here will be as effective. It'd be as likely to stall their consolidation of the country. She's getting big, but she's still got eleven weeks to go, she reckons. That said, she'll run if she has to—and she'll have to if we're going to get away."

Vaunt ran his fingers between her shoulder blades as he thought, raising goosebumps on her skin. "Can you get her alone?"

"She spends all her time with Lanta or Corvus, from what I can tell, except for at night. She's sleeping in the queen's wing and there are half a dozen Mireces on guard when she's there. But I might be able to use this new trust of Valan's and kill Lanta when Rillirin's with her in the temple."

Tara tipped him a wink. "A slave rebellion would come in handy right around then, wouldn't it? A rebellion that would require Corvus's attention—and Valan's—leaving me free to ghost the priestess and grab the girl."

Vaunt's grin turned feral. "Funny you should say that," he murmured and darted his head down for a kiss. "I think I might be able to help you."

"Then the faster we do this, the better. Rillirin's only going to get slower and more tired as the days pass, and the Rankers are getting weaker by the day too."

Vaunt's face went hard. "I know. Mireces bastards are working them to death and don't seem to care. But they'll fight," he added when he saw Tara's worry. "Believe me, they'll fight."

She hoped he was right. Whenever she was allowed to visit, she had to school her face to impassivity so as not to shame them by retching at their stench. They were chained in squalor when they weren't working, movement limited to the small few steps their shackles permitted between their beds and their shared chamber pots. Hours of back-breaking labour followed by hours of stinking, flea-plagued hunger, broken by the screams of nightmare and the low, shame-filled weeping of men who'd long since run out of hope. Corpses were left where they fell, sometimes for days.

"Do you think it's like this in the north barracks?" Tara asked.

"Worse. They've had an outbreak of fever. Scores dead, the whole place in quarantine. Mireces are mighty pissed off about it, and scared, too. Your friendly mason told Salter a few of his lads were sent there to look at bricking up the doors. Might be they're just going to seal them in and leave them to die."

"Gods," Tara muttered, sitting up and pulling the blanket up to cover her nakedness. "Those poor bastards. Is there anything we can do?"

Vaunt scratched at his beard. "Pray. Could be a strange sort of blessing. I don't imagine whatever it is they have planned for the rest of us will be pleasant. A few days of fever and then drifting off into the Light seems like a pretty decent outcome these days."

She shuddered and lay back down, pressing her length against him, warm and alive still, the circle of his arms a haven. His feelings for her were complicating matters. Or was it her feelings for him?

"We'll need a signal," she murmured, smiling as his hands began a leisurely exploration of her skin. "Some way for you to know when I'm going to make the attempt."

"Any slaves in the palace working with us?" he asked, distracted, and she smiled again, shifting a little closer.

"A few, but doing it in the temple would be wiser. Closer to the South Gate." She inhaled sharply. "Are you paying attention?"

"Mm-hm, to every line and curve. And listening, definitely. Lots of listening."

"All right, I'll send word when I know I'm going to the temple. It could take up to an hour to reach you, so that's how long I'll have to kill Lanta and get Rillirin hidden. Once you've got this city on its knees, we'll slip out and away."

"Be careful," Vaunt whispered without warning. His hand came up to cup her cheek. "Promise me."

Tara bit back the offhand comment that sprang to her lips. "I promise. You too. Don't fucking die on me, Major."

"Not part of the plan, Major."

She wrapped her arms around his neck, his beard scratching against her cheek. "I don't know when they'll let me visit again, probably not before we do this. So I guess I'll see you on the other side. I'll have a very pregnant woman in tow."

Vaunt winked. "I'll have a slave rebellion at my back," he said.

She managed a smile. "Show-off," she said, but he was distracted again. A long, low growl of pleasure eased between her teeth even as she told herself to focus on the mission, because despite their promises neither of them expected to see each other again.

Only it wasn't that easy any more. She'd told Crys she didn't expect to survive this, and she didn't. She'd been at ease with that knowledge, before Vaunt, because she was a soldier and it was her duty. Not now, though. Now Tara wanted to live, and for Vaunt to live too.

She grabbed him around the waist and hauled him on to her, lifted her hips and drew him in, giving him—giving them both—a reason to cling to life. To keep on fighting.

It was all she had to give, so she gave it all, with reckless abandon.

BLOODCHILD

TARA. SIT. TELL ME, how is your husband?"

Danger prickled along Tara's spine. Valan was sitting to one side of the fireplace; he gestured at the empty chair opposite, giving her no choice. The chair's position put her back to the door and her palms began to sweat.

She sat. Valan raised an eyebrow. "Forgive me, honoured. H-he is well, thank you. As well as can be expected, that is. He hasn't seen the sun in months."

"And what would you do to ensure he did see the sun again?" Valan asked. He poured her a cup of ale, handing it over with a polite smile. She took it on reflex, but didn't drink. The smell of the hops made her nauseous.

"I don't understand, honoured."

Valan watched her over the rim of his cup. "It's a simple question and you're a clever woman," he said, wiping foam from his upper lip. "What would a woman of your unique talents do to ensure dear Tomaz's survival?"

She sipped the ale, forced herself to swallow. "You told me that if I worked hard and did as I was told, I would be allowed to visit Tomaz. I have done as you asked and you have kept your word, for which I am grateful. What more would you have me do?"

Valan put his cup down, leant forward and took hers out of her unresisting hand. He laced his fingers together. "Tell me how you learnt to fight," he said instead of answering her.

Tara didn't try to hide her confusion. "Three older brothers and a husband in the army," she said, sticking as close to the truth as she could manage. "My ma wanted me to be strong enough to look after myself instead of relying on the restraint of men. Tomaz . . . liked that about me and kept teaching me after we wed."

"Interesting," Valan said after a silence so long she nearly screamed. "Could actually be true." He slashed his hand through the air when she tried to protest. "I don't care. Darling Tomaz is hostage to your good behaviour and, so far, it's been effective. I need more than good behaviour now, Tara, and Vaunt's life—more than that, Vaunt's *pain-free* life—is dependent on you. Let me down and your husband will die screaming. Do you understand?"

Tara glanced behind her; the door was still closed, the room still empty. She wiped her palms on her skirt as Vaunt's words came back to her: *kill anyone who touches you without your permission and fuck the consequences.*

The question, of course, was whether she'd give that permission to save another's life. Vaunt's life. The ale was bitter on her tongue. "I understand."

"At some time in the next few weeks, when I tell you the time is right and not before, I want you to kill the king."

Every bell in the city could have been ringing and Tara wouldn't have heard them over the roaring in her ears. *Does he know? Is this a test?*

He was calm, allowing her to process what he'd said. Tara wiped her palms again, licked cold sweat from her upper lip. "Forgive me, honoured," she said carefully. "I . . . don't understand."

"Which part? That Corvus is going to die by your hand, or that your husband will be tortured to death if you refuse?" She said nothing. "I watched you saw a man's windpipe open with every sign of enjoyment. I would think the opportunity to do the same to our king would fill you with delight."

"If I have offended you, honoured, please allow me to apologise," she began.

"Stop. This is a simple transaction. Corvus's life for Vaunt's. If the price is too steep, say so and this conversation is over."

He's handing me Corvus on a silver fucking platter, practically guaranteeing I get a shot at him and keeping his own hands clean at the same time. Of course he won't free us afterwards, but he won't need to, because Corvus's death will be the spark that sets this city on fire and we'll all be free by the time it burns itself out. I fucking guarantee it.

Tara inclined her head. "Your will, honoured."

MACE

Mabon, first year of the reign of King Corvus
Outskirts of Sailtown, the Tears, Horse Lands

I T WAS THREE HOURS before dawn on the autumn equinox, the date Mace had agreed with the Krikites for the offensive to begin. They were a mile from Sailtown and had moved into their final positions through the night.

They were all about ready to drop, and the battle hadn't even begun. The forced march the long way round, through the foothills of the Gilgoras Mountains and past the ruins of the West Rank forts—a pang in his gut at their sad dereliction—and over the Cattle Lands to Sailtown had taken longer than anticipated, and by the time they reached the target, they were in danger of missing Mace's own deadline.

He tapped his fingertips to his heart, commending his soul to the Light and adding an unspoken prayer that far across Rilpor, in the prosperous river town of Pine Lock, his allies were also moving, descending upon the occupying East Rank like a flood.

Under a sky too bright with stars, they began to move, shadows against the silver landscape. It was a straight run and sentries would see them soon enough. Mace had a thousand men with him, running swift and silent through the stubble of harvested crops. In the third rank from the rear was Hallos. During the course of the siege and the summer in the South Forts he'd found a hitherto unexplored physical strength and determination. He'd kept up with the forced march with minimal complaint despite his advancing years. Now he looked like an ageing bull, all hard planes and enormous shoulders, small black eyes and wild, grey-shot beard.

Mace couldn't see the other wings of his army from this vantage, but he wasn't supposed to be able to and he trusted them to have deployed in line with his orders. The eruption of violence as they stormed for the main gatehouse would be the signal to the rest to begin the count to three hundred before launching their own attacks.

Mace was in the front rank, of course, despite arguments to the contrary. He might be king-elect, he might even be Commander of the Ranks, but he was a soldier first and foremost, and a leader of men. He knew Dalli would be leading her people too, future queen or not. It was who they were—what they were.

They were three hundred strides out when a scrim of cloud darkened the field and Mace dared to hope. Moments later it was gone and the starlight seemed brighter in comparison, and soon enough fires bloomed along Sailtown's city walls and thin, distant shouts of alarm pierced the night. Mace sped up, his men with him, and they thundered across the fields, little point in stealth now. Over the pounding of feet came the humming whine of arrows, barely visible. Mace wrenched his shield high and kept running.

The first screams, the first tumbling men and those who fell over them, and then fifty paces on and more men falling—but not because of arrows this time. Cries of alarm and men vanishing into the ground at either end of the line. Leg-breakers: shallow pits dug and covered with wattles and dirt to disguise them, located on the edges of the field to bunch his men together, force them into one narrow channel, one churning mass that could be raked with sustained volleys.

And so it proved. Mace's shoulder was aching from the weight of the shield, but he daren't drop it; the arrows were relentless and his numbers were thinning as they slowed and filtered through the safe ground deliberately left for them. It'd open into a killing field soon enough.

He'd a few archers on his flanks loosing volleys of their own, and it kept the defenders' heads down for a while, but still his losses were too big too early.

Less than a hundred strides from the wall and suddenly the black blobs on top of it were milling and running, confused shouts echoing up and adding to the cacophony of screaming civilians. Figures streamed away north and Mace's step lightened; his second Thousand were making their approach.

He picked up the pace again, the gatehouse visible now. A Fifty headed straight for it and began hacking with axes while the rest flattened against the walls, out of eyeline unless the defenders leant right out over the battlements and presented themselves as targets to his archers. A few did and were shot, fell screaming. The rest kept their heads down, the volleys from both sides faltering.

Mace led his own Fifty to a point at the base of the wall where the torches were further apart. The defences were only twice the height of a man and it was easy enough for them to boost each other to the top, even in armour. The third Thousand were making a howling attack from the southern sward closest to the river, causing more confusion, diverting more attention.

Sailtown was nearly surrounded, the river the only way out now. And Dalli and her Wolves had the river.

Mace stepped into the stirrup formed of a man's hands and threw himself upwards, armour dragging at his shoulders as he got his elbows over the top of the wall and scrabbled for purchase. A hand grabbed inside the neck of his breastplate and heaved, the leather straps and buckles straining. He rolled over the wall on to the allure, up to his feet and ran for the stairs down to the gatehouse.

There were three of them on the steps, Easterners all, blocking his way. He didn't bother slowing, or doing anything much other than tensing as he kicked out at the first and caught him in the chest, the man's sword too close to do much damage other than thwacking into Mace's inner thigh blunt-edge first. Still bloody hurt though. The Easterner rocked back, missed his footing and was gone, felling the two behind, all three of them hurtling down the steps with a sound like someone throwing pots down a well.

Mace charged after them, dragging free his sword as he went. He leapt over one, clearly unconscious, and a second, very dead, his neck at an unnatural angle, and met the third's sword with his own. This man was groggy and bleeding, but he was up and he was fast—would have been even faster if he weren't so dizzy. Mace didn't let him find his equilibrium, launching a flurry of attacks and forcing him back. The Easterner thrust and Mace slid his shoulder back out of range and then grabbed the blade in his gauntlet, hung on and chopped his own sword downwards, bludgeoning the man on to his knees and opening a deep gash in his shoulder.

Mace pulled on the weapon again, jerking him forward and exposing the back of his neck to his sword. He killed him, turned back and stabbed the still-unconscious Ranker at the base of the stairs. No time for mercy, and no desire for it either.

His men were nearly through the gatehouse with their axes, but Mace threw the bolts and heaved the crossbar free and the shattered remains swung inward, then pressed himself against the inner face of the wall as they streamed past, filing left and right for the storehouses and communal cellars, the key buildings and areas they needed to take and then hold. Enemies within and without; if the Easterners weren't stupid, they'd see it was hopeless and surrender.

Mace suspected the Easterners would be stupid—or at least too afraid of the Red Gods to surrender without a fight.

Smoke was already drifting up from sections of the city and everywhere rang with the sounds of fierce fighting. Mace followed the last stragglers to clear the gate along the central street towards the town square. He'd left his shield at the bottom of the wall, so when a flight of arrows hissed down from the roofs, there was nothing he could do but tuck and run, slamming his shoulder into a door and through, falling into a large kitchen with a banked fire and narrowly avoiding being stabbed by a woman brandishing a filleting knife, standing between him and two small children.

"Dancer's grace," he gasped. "We're here to help. Friendlies, friendlies!"

She sagged, all the fear and the fight rushing out of her. Then she pointed the blade up. "There's men up there," she hissed, and that's when Mace noticed the slave collar on her neck, and on the necks of her children. He went very cold. He'd known it, of course, known that that would be the fate of his countrymen when Rilporin fell, but he'd never actually seen it. Didn't want to see it, and certainly not encircling the throats of children.

"How many?" he asked, barely recognising his own voice. She held up three fingers and he nodded, rolled his head on his neck. "Gate's open," he whispered. "Get your little ones and get out. Run. Once we've secured the town you'll be safe; until then this isn't the best place for you. Any soldier you see who doesn't greet you in the Dancer's name"—he crossed to her and lifted the hand holding the knife, placing it against his inner thigh, his armpit, the notch of his collarbone—"you aim for one of these. Understand?"

Her eyes were huge in the paleness of her face, her lower lip trembling, but she bit it hard and nodded, and the hand he held shook a little less. "Thank you."

"Go now. It's going to get noisy in here."

He waited until they'd slipped through the door and then took the stairs, step by stealthy step. The upper floor was divided into two luxurious bedchambers, and he had time to wonder whether this had been her property once, before the Easterners had taken up residence here and made her a slave in her own home.

Voices in the closest room, the one that would look down over the road. Mace drew in a deep and silent breath, adjusted his grip on his hilt, blinked away sweat and then barged inside.

The door gave too easily and he stumbled through, went sprawling so the man swinging the axe missed him, and so did the follow-up spear thrust from the room's second occupant. Their bows and quivers were on the floor beneath the open window and Mace had a split second to acknowledge his luck that they'd tried to take him hand to hand instead of just shooting him as he entered, and then he was up on his knees and spinning to parry the axe, his blade thunking into the haft. He twisted his wrist and slid his sword over the man's guard, got one foot planted and shoved forward. The tip just entered the middle of the man's throat, not enough to kill him—not fast, anyway—but certainly enough to panic him; the axeman dropped his weapon, eyes goggling and both hands going to his neck. He gurgled and a faint red mist plumed in the air; Mace had nicked the windpipe. That'd do for now.

The spearman was good, so Mace hooked up the axe in his free hand and did his best to get inside the Easterner's reach. It was almost impossible, and both of them knew it was just a matter of time. Mace backed slowly, senses straining around him for some advantage, a moment, an object, anything that would help. He was nearly at the window and about desperate enough to throw the axe and charge after it when the second Ranker gurgled again, louder and more urgent this time. Mace flicked his eyes over his opponent's shoulder and widened them slightly. The ruse was enough—the spearman spun to the imagined threat behind him and Mace chopped through the back of his knee with the axe, then through the back of his neck as he fell.

He stepped over the dying man and killed the one he'd injured. She'd said there were three up here, the woman whose children wore chains. Mace took a deep breath, cuffed the sweat out of his eyes, and kicked open the next door, ducking in case of arrows.

WHAT HAD BEEN A rampage through the streets eventually became the sort of battle they were all familiar with. In Sailtown's big assembly place, at least five hundred Southerners stood against almost the same from the East, lit in garish orange by fires, torches, burning thatch, burning wagons.

Dawn was a promise in the east as the superior numbers began to tell—Mace had hundreds more lining the roads to the square that he could rotate in whenever one of his fell. General Skerris, by contrast, had only the minimum number of soldiers to garrison the town and those civilians greedy enough or stupid enough to convert to the Red Joy in return for power and the removal of their collars.

As if it had been ordained, the two officers came face to face in the melee. Mace had taken a shield from a dead Ranker and he snarled from behind it when he recognised Skerris's huge bulk shoving through the line towards him.

"You traitorous bastard," Mace yelled and swung. The first shattering clash of their blades had men on both sides of the conflict scrambling for cover and a space opened up around them, though to either side the battle raged on. Mace ignored the rest of the fighting, focusing only on

Skerris and the ground and any Easterner who looked likely to try and stab him in the back. "Let's dance, fucker."

Skerris grinned, tucked as much of his bulk as he could behind his shield, and attacked. He came in low, then flicked his wrist at the last instant so that the blade arced up. Mace's shield was dropping to cover his legs when the sword tip gouged across the top for his face. He slipped the blow, hoisting the shield to bat the blade up and away. It blocked his view of Skerris for a heartbeat and the general used it to ram his own shield rim-down on to Mace's foot. There was the distinct crack of bone and pain shot up his shin.

Mace roared and thrust over the top of Skerris's shield, his blade screeching off the general's breastplate and skidding sideways into the inside of his elbow. Skerris hissed but the wound didn't hinder him.

The East Rank general pulled back behind his shield, resetting for the next attack, and Mace copied him. He could hear renewed fighting to his right and left, but refused to let his focus be drawn, teeth gritted at the hot, throbbing agony in his boot.

He caught the slight shifting of weight that indicated the attack just before it came in hard and fast on Mace's right side. He defended, feeling from the pressure in his blade that Skerris was trying to turn him, to get him side-on to the battle and expose his flank to the enemy. Mace resisted, stepping into the attack instead of away, closing down Skerris's strokes before they were complete and forcing him into short, defensive parries.

Younger, fitter, Mace had Skerris on the run and only a few exchanges away from surrender or a killing stroke when a spear shot past the Easterner's meaty shoulder and slammed into the top edge of Mace's shield, splinters jagging up into his mouth and eyes, the spear itself stuck deep in the wood. A young lieutenant dashed to his side and offered his shield in its place. Mace threw his at Skerris, slipped his hand in the straps of the new one, and shoulder-barged the boy out of the way before he got skewered.

Mace slipped, his broken foot grating agony. He went to one knee. Saw Skerris's attack coming, unstoppable.

The world slowed; his breath stopped. He could see the sweat on Skerris's florid face, the rime of flame reflected on the edge of his sword as it arced downwards like solid lightning.

Mace shoved his shield up above his head and thrust in turn.

Skerris's sword came down and metal screamed and wood shattered and Mace screamed too, bracing himself. Impact. The shock of it running through his sword arm as his blade slid up beneath the breastplate into the gut and on, all the way nearly to the hilt. Simultaneous shock through his left arm and the awful sound of a shield smashing apart and exposing him, leaving him defenceless.

And then stillness, the moment a perfect tableau.

A pause that lasted a lifetime before Skerris fell like a fucking tree, the crash and clatter of his over-sized armour and the thud of all that flesh smacking the stone enough to steal the heart from the nearest East Rankers and prove to Mace that he was still alive, at least for now.

He clambered to his feet, shaking the broken shield from his arm and wincing at the click in his elbow as soldiers leapt forward to protect him.

Skerris was bubbling blood out of his mouth, more of the same in a steady flood from beneath his breastplate. Mace contemplated letting him bleed to death and knew not even a traitor deserved that much pain. He put his sword tip on the fleshy throat.

Skerris bared red teeth. "My feet are on—"

Mace rammed the sword home, cutting off words and air and life, then slid it free and flicked the blood from its length. "Throw down your weapons," he bellowed through a raw, stinging throat. "Surrender and we'll show you clemency. Resist and you'll be cut down to the last man. Choose."

THE SUN ROSE ON a town devastated and burning and strewn with corpses—and on a town that was free.

Dozens of East Rankers and scores of townsfolk who'd converted had barricaded themselves into a ropewalk. Civilians, venturing from their homes as the battle raged in the centre of town, had surrounded the building and thrown lit torches on to its roof and into the bales of dry, inflammable hemp stacked outside and burnt them alive, beating to death any who tried to escape the flames.

But the losses weren't all Easterners. Skerris had seeded the whole town with firing platforms, concealed alleys and traps, bigger and nastier than the leg-breakers outside the walls, and in the dark and the confusion they'd done their work too well. Mace didn't know yet how many he'd lost, but it was more than he'd expected. More than he could afford.

But Corvus has lost his only Rank general. He's lost hundreds of soldiers here, either dead or surrendered, and he's lost the initiative, too. He's lost the illusion of victory, of invincibility.

And I've finally won a fucking fight.

Mace snorted exhausted amusement. He sat on a water trough in the square, weary down to his very marrow and trying not to think about how many miles he had to walk on a broken foot. Townsfolk and soldiers were rounding up those Easterners who'd surrendered, and others were dragging forward more men—and a few women—who'd converted and been put in charge of working and punishing the slaves. When the town was lost, they'd thrown down their clubs and thrown themselves on their community's mercy. As with the folk in the ropewalk, they were learning how much that mercy was worth.

Mace had the blacksmiths cutting off the slave collars as fast as they could, but if anything that was fuelling the people's anger. No longer slaves, their need for vengeance burnt hot inside them. And Mace knew he couldn't allow them to give in to it. He didn't need a massacre here; he needed them to be Rilporian again.

But that meant the prisoners were his to punish and Mace had no idea what to do with them. In the heat of battle, yes, he knew what he was fighting for. When he'd sounded the all-out in the battle of the Blood Pass Valley, knowing he was ordering a Mireces massacre, he'd known then, too, that it was the right decision. Now, here, craving only food and sleep and something for the pain in his foot and side and elbow and every other bloody fucking body part, actually, he'd no idea what punishment to mete out to fellow Rilporians.

"You best get used to it," Dalli said when he confessed. "As king you'll be dispensing justice every day." She gusted a sigh and ran a filthy hand through her hair, then his, tidying it back from his brow. "So regal," she muttered and he managed a weak chuckle.

He sent for Hadir and then made his decision. "Do we have any priests here?" he called. He wasn't executing surrendered men, even if they did deserve it. "Priests of the Dancer? And any town elders too, please."

Eventually a priest and two elders were found. Mace forced himself to stand and gave the old priest his seat: the man looked even more unsteady on his feet than Mace himself felt.

Best get straight to it. Hesitating won't make them like it any more.

"Elders, gather your people, gather your possessions—everything you can carry. Gather your livestock and harvest whatever you can. Make all haste for the abandoned town on Dancer's Lake."

The three of them gaped at him. "Impossible," a woman spluttered, though Hadir grunted his agreement and gave him an approving nod.

"You have until dusk," Mace said. "I'm sorry, I know this is difficult, but we cannot spare the soldiers necessary to protect you. The Mireces will retake the town and enslave you again. They may execute every last one of you. Your only option is to leave."

"That's impossible," the male elder echoed. "We'll never get everyone ready in time."

"The Rank will do all they can to assist you, but the order will be better accepted coming from you. Thank you."

They gaped some more, but a couple of Rankers escorted them away, giving them no more chance to argue.

The priest was watching him in horror, no doubt fearing what it was he'd be asked to do. Mace tried for a reassuring smile; from the man's reaction, it probably looked as strained as it felt. "Priest, I'd like you to do something for me, and for these benighted fools who were tricked into a false faith. I'd like you to save their souls."

The old man pursed his lips and then sucked at his remaining teeth. "I can do that, but then what? Will you recruit them into your army or free them to prey on us as we flee?"

"Neither. My Rank will collar and chain them much as you were and you will take them with you to Dancer's Lake. They can dig the latrine pits and haul the wagons and carts, then labour to rebuild the town ready for winter, should this war drag on."

He got another grunt from Hadir at that and felt a little better. "Feed them and water them, do not beat them. Treat them better than they treated you, and ensure your people do too. If I hear otherwise . . ."

The priest stood and peered up at Mace, and though his eyes were rheumy with age, he radiated approval. "Threats will not be necessary, Your Majesty, though they may not eat as well as the rest of us."

"Understood. And for those men who refuse the offer of redemption, place them into the custody of the Wolves over there. Though I hope there won't be many."

Because those are the ones I'll have to execute.

"And where are you going if you're not staying to protect us?" the old man asked.

"To win the war," Mace replied and then waved him away. When they were alone, he looked at Dalli and Hadir; the wiry general had made it through the battle with little more than a strained shoulder. "Help anyone who needs it today and ensure they all leave by dusk, General. We'll stay here tonight, leave at dawn tomorrow. I want to make sure none of the townsfolk try to return. And before we set out, burn the town and any crops that remain in the ground or stores in the barns. Leave nothing for the Mireces to utilise when they get here."

Hadir grimaced, but saluted and left him to pass on the orders. Mace lowered himself stiffly to the water trough again, wincing as his foot blared its protest. Dalli sat next to him, a strange look on her face.

"What?"

"So that's what a king looks like," she murmured and nudged him. "I've never seen one close up before."

CRYS

Mabon, first year of the reign of King Corvus
Pine Lock, northern side of the River Gil, Cattle Lands

THE RAIN WAS HEAVY enough to drive all but those who were commanded to be out into shelter. It hissed through the air and roared on the surface of the Gil, reducing visibility to mere strides from the bows of the boats and rafts. It hid Crys and his Krikite army from the sentries huddled into their sodden cloaks in the rickety watchtowers they'd erected along the river.

Pine Lock was a split town, half on the southern side of the Gil in the Western Plain, half on the northern in the Cattle Lands. The river that cut through its heart made for good fishing and excellent trading—and now it bore upon its waters the men and women who would descend on both halves of the town to free it from the mailed fist of the East Rank.

Crys wished the rain had been his doing as the Krikites were whispering, but the truth was it was just raining, as it was wont to do in autumn—a stroke of luck he was taking full advantage of but hadn't influenced. He was in the lead boat, a fishing skiff packed tight with warriors, Ash at his side. They rode low in the water, as did all the vessels they'd scavenged and built in the last frenzied few days since leaving the Wolf Lands.

He had fifteen hundred proven warriors under his command, half on the water, the rest split to come by land north and south of the town.

BLOODCHILD

The equinox thrummed in his veins, Gilgoras balanced between equal lengths of day and night, as Crys was equal parts human and divine. He was so full of energy he wanted to leap from the bow and swim for shore, swarm up the bank, up the nearest watchtower and in, armed with only a knife and the righteous fury of the night, the downtrodden, the Light. He didn't. He sat still and composed, eyes flickering between the banks, awaiting the first shout of alarm, as the rain pounded his head and shoulders, soaked through chainmail and gambeson and shirt, trousers and socks and linens until he squelched as he moved.

Somewhere towards the rear of the fleet was the boat containing Dom and Gilda, who'd come to lend her skills in healing and to comfort the townsfolk; they couldn't be sure any priests of the Gods of Light had been left alive.

Crys couldn't leave the calestar behind, not when he still had a role to play, but nor would he risk him in the forefront of the battle. Dom could move and run and even fight, but slowly, clumsily, and only as a last resort. If it came to it, it'd be Gilda defending him, not the other way around.

The northern half of Pine Lock was the largest, and they'd guessed that would have the bigger complement of occupying forces, so Crys indicated the boat should turn for that shore. They were running with oars and the current, no sails to creak and flap and draw eyes, but even so the water slapping the hull over the sound of the rain echoed harsh and loud in Crys's ears.

The first watchtower loomed out of the night, barely there in the darkness but for the wavering blob of orange at the top. *Don't be looking, don't be looking, don't be—*

"What's that? Who goes there?"

Shit.

A second shout of alarm, from the other side of the river, no doubt alerted by the first. Only half a dozen boats were in range of the town so far, not enough to steer for shore. A sudden scuffle, the thud of something heavy hitting planking from both of the watchtowers, and then silence. Crys grinned. A few of the Wolves who'd recovered from their injuries and returned to their summer village had elected to join his army, and he'd given them the task of eliminating the sentries. It'd taken them longer than he'd hoped to get through the town unseen, but with luck they'd kill all the lookouts before a full alarm could be raised.

"Four more towers to go," Ash breathed into his ear, thinking along the same lines.

"But we'll only be in the eyeline of the next two; we'll dock before nearing the last ones. By the time they notice us, it'll be because we're standing behind them with swords drawn." He caught the glint of Ash's teeth as he grinned.

Of course, it didn't work out that way. The initial challenge must have been heard by a foot patrol, because there were pitch torches hissing and spitting along the southern bank, moving fast as men ran to and fro, and then the northern bank lit up too.

"Archers," Crys said, and the word was passed quietly from boat to boat. Stealth was gone, but no point letting the enemy know what they were planning. "You've got the call," he added to Ash, who was braced against the boat's rail with his war bow at full stretch. The strings wouldn't last long in this rain, but a dozen volleys would likely give them enough time to reach the shore.

"Loose," Ash roared and shafts flew north and south, arcing through the night towards the torches and the watchtowers, most shooting blind. Tillers were forced across and the boats began to split for each bank. Everyone knew what they were doing; the orders had been given hours before. There was nothing left to do now but execute them.

And avoid getting executed ourselves.

Hilarious, Crys thought, but a smile quirked the side of his mouth. His skiff scraped the dock wall and Crys was up and out, hauling on the bow line to bring it fully alongside. The anchor dropped and the Krikites leapt to shore. Leaving a rearguard to hold their escape route and protect the boats, he led the rest in a dark tide up from the docks, fanning left and right and into the town.

A knot of Easterners pounded through the puddles towards them, and Ash dropped to a knee and took four despite the gloom and wavering orange torchlight. The remaining three came on, bellowing wordless cries of rage and alarm, and Crys surged to meet them, Krikites following and Ash covering the buildings to their left.

"King Mace," Crys bellowed. "For the Dancer!"

"Fox God, Fox God, Fox God," came the Krikite chant, as satisfaction coursed through Crys's limbs.

He spun beneath the first Easterner's spear, using the thick mud to slide beneath his guard, stabbed upwards and felt a spray of hot liquid across his chin and neck. The man reeled backwards, somehow holding on to his spear and his footing, the weapon rootling in the mud for Crys and he blocked, blocked again, lashed out with his foot and connected with the Ranker's shin. A solid enough blow that the man shrieked, slipped and went down.

Crys scrambled to his knees, sword hilt slippery with rain and mud, got a two-handed grip and scythed it into the Ranker's thigh, slicing muscle and tendon. Blood burst from the wound and Crys got to his feet, kicked away the man's spear and kicked him unconscious.

Guard up, he spun, but the others were dead, the Krikites grinning at him and each other as if that was it, victory assured. Crys's mouth tasted of mud; he spat, beckoned and set off at a run. They weren't done yet.

"Nice shooting," he said as Ash caught him up.

The archer blew rain off his nose. "You say that like you're surprised," he said; then he clapped him on the back, rested an arrow lightly on the string and took point, leading Crys and his band of Krikites through the black, soaking streets, the squelching of their boots lost in the persistent patter of rain and the grinding churn of a water wheel somewhere in the darkness ahead.

The street leading from the dock on this side of the Gil was wide and looping, following a meandering path that created too many corners and shadowed alleys for Crys's liking. Ash's arrow pointed into each for a second before he moved forward, but their progress was slow—too slow. They were to meet up with the overland troops in the cattle market, so Crys tapped Ash on the shoulder and halted him. "I'll lead."

"Not a chance," Ash began to protest.

Crys gestured with two fingers at his own face. "I can see fine. You're as liable to shoot an ally as you are an Easterner. No offence."

It was true and Ash was professional enough to agree. He slung his bow and pulled his hand axe and knife instead, before gesturing for Crys to proceed. "Fine. But I've got your flank."

"Wouldn't have it any other way," Crys said. They moved like shadows in the rain down the twisting road, engaging a squad of Rankers who stumbled into them. The fight was brief and savage and one-sided, most of the Rankers unarmoured and bleary with sleep, called from their beds into a rainstorm and a battle. Eventually, the road emptied them out into a wide-open area of churned grass and they paused at the edge, squatting low and peering across the open expanse.

"Grain stores are opposite," Crys breathed. "Straight over, no stopping." More Krikites poured out of the roads to join them, and they were within sight of the huge looming barns when torches lit up the edge of the green and Rankers charged them, their lines solid and three men deep.

"Back," Crys yelled, but more Rankers appeared from the north, and then from the east too. West and the river—west and that winding, black and treacherous street—was the only way out. It'd slow the enemy advance, break up their numbers, but it'd do the same to Crys's. West or fight. Run or die.

"Stand," he bellowed as warriors began to shift in a bunching stumble of panic. "Stand. Archers, the east is yours. Pin them down and keep them down. Ash, you're in charge—don't let them flank us. Move."

Ash gave him a look, but did as he was bid.

"Three Hundreds with me. Form line; we've got the southern approach. Rest of you, deploy north." He could estimate their strength now they were closer. "We outnumber them," he bellowed, "so don't let them reinforce each other. Keep them separate, defeat them separately, accept surrender if they offer it. *Move.*"

Though they weren't Rankers, the Krikites deployed with dizzying swiftness, moving to Crys's orders as though they'd been under his command for years. The archers disengaged and formed a smaller block of their own between the two lines. Within seconds they were sending shafts through the night into the advancing Rankers, who threw up their shields and kept on coming. A few sent return flights, and more came from south and north, but they were loosed on the move and in the dark, many going wide.

Crys shoved his way out of the line and jogged its length, checking the ground, the tightness of the shield wall, the readiness of his warriors. A bowstring snapped off to his right and a woman cursed its loss, dropped the bow and shoved her way into the northern line instead.

Stop. Here.

Crys came to a halt and faced the onrushing enemy; the southern advance had the biggest numbers and they thundered and squelched and skidded towards them. *We playing, Foxy?* he asked, rolling his shoulders and flicking rain off his sword.

He felt the smile inside. *Oh, we're playing.*

Crys turned his back to the Rankers and looked over the heads of his line and the line behind. The enemy approaching from the north were further away, slower to advance, picking their way across the grass. Avoiding their own traps, maybe.

Break the southern advance, the strongest force, and the rest will falter. Then wheel the line and reinforce east and north, mop up the remains.

He took three more paces forward and began thumping his sword pommel against the inside face of his shield. The Krikites took up the rhythm, and then began stamping too, the sound building and building, and some of the Rankers began to slow, glancing at each other, their war cries faltering, the line beginning to lag and bulge until—

"South flank," Crys roared, "wedge formation. *On me.*"

Crys's time in the South Rank had seen him fight a few skirmishes against the Krikites he now counted as allies, and he well knew their martial capability, but the speed and ease with which they switched formations appeared to surprise the Easterners. There was a visible ripple of hesitation before they came on again.

Crys pounded through the grass and their line stiffened, soldiers falling into step and shields coming together and he tucked his head and then he was among them, smashing into three men with shield and mailed shoulder, sword bludgeoning like a club and then slicing in, his speed carrying him into the second line and almost the third before the weight of bodies brought him to a halt.

"Fox God, Fox God, Fox God!" came the chant again as the wedge drove them forward and he gained a few more steps and he saw the words light fear in the Rankers' eyes. They'd been in Rilporin; they'd seen what he'd done, who he was. The man who'd fought a god. The man who *was* a god.

Rankers were squirming back away from him, flailing weapons without skill or speed to keep him away, a primal, religious fear glazing their faces. Crys staved in the closest with his shield boss, swept his sword up beneath a guard and into a thigh, back out, into the back of an arm, out again and then he reversed the swing and hammered the pommel into the screeching mouth so far he felt the man's teeth against his fingers. Wrenched it out in a spray of enamel and clubbed him again, between shoulder and neck, dropping him to his knees. Kicked him on to his back and jumped over him, the Krikite behind finishing him off as they pressed forward, parting the Rank's line with the ease of a dog splitting sheep.

He waded on through men and rain and mud and slick grass, moving with a speed born of divinity that the rest of the wedge couldn't match, his legs and arms and shoulders and back tireless, sights and scents combining to alert him to the next threat, the need to duck, where to step, how to move. Crys was alive in the midst of the death he dealt, awake in a way he'd never been, Rankers dying before and beneath him in swathes until, without warning, without order, they broke.

"Take them, they're yours," Crys bellowed to the warriors at his back, heard the wave of affirmation rise like a storm and they raced past him, the formation holding and then dropping as it became a race to reach the fleeing soldiers first.

In the east, the archers were pressed hard, though they'd winnowed the numbers advancing on their position. He slid into place on Ash's left just as the tall archer caught a blade with his hand axe and knocked it aside, knife slicing into his attacker's wrist and spurting blood into the night.

"All right?" Crys asked in the pause before the next one came. Ash swiped at sweat and took his eyes from the enemy to search Crys for wounds. "I'm fine. Can you hold a little longer?"

"Aye, but not too long, mind," Ash warned. "And watch yourself."

"You too." Crys protected Ash's flank through two more short, intense battles, and then slid away during a lull. The East Rank was disciplined and they knew their business, but they were outnumbered and split up, unable to execute a coherent offensive. If the Krikites could break the northern line, they'd have it won.

The rain lessened a little as Crys joined the swaying line shield to shield with the Rankers. They were more evenly matched in strength and the Rank had the impetus of forward movement. He saw a woman go down with a spear in her chest, a man take an axe to the face, and he waited for the silver light to rise, draining him as it healed them. It didn't come.

Foxy? We doing something about the injured?

Foxy?

His sword arm faltered as his attention moved inward. They were together as always, moving and breathing and stepping as one, but there was a . . . refusal to heal, a stone sitting in his chest that couldn't be moved, and beneath it the pool of quicksilver, of life renewed.

A Ranker seized on his instant of inattention and struck hard, so hard Crys's sword jolted in his grip; he tightened his fingers at the last second, fumbling the hilt, but the man's backswing was arcing towards him and there was no time to parry, the blade still not set in his fist. His shield began to come across to intercept, too slow and exposing his left side, no one there to defend it, no Ash in place as an extension of him, his second set of arms and eyes and strong legs.

The shield was across his front, defending neither side, when the blade went in, biting deep beneath his sword arm, the impact through his chainmail rocking him sideways a step—sideways into the blade coming from that direction too, a double impact like a heartbeat, thud-*thud*.

An animal howl went up, not from him but from them and Crys was on his knees, unable to breathe, feeling as though his ribs had been coated in pitch and set alight. His mouth opened but the air was trapped outside him and his sword weighed more than the world and his shield was just resting, rim on the dirt, top edge against his cheek.

The Krikites faltered. The East Rank screamed.

Foxy? Nothing.

Foxy?

The blades came in again.

DOM

Mabon, first year of the reign of King Corvus
Pine Lock, northern side of the River Gil, Cattle Lands

LEFT AT THE BACK of the battle like a boy with his nursemaid.

Dom stood on the dock with his sword in his right hand. It was unfamiliar, awkward, everything about it wrong, throwing off his balance. Still, he'd insisted that Gilda strap a buckler to the remains of his left arm; at least if he reacted instinctively and swung with his left, there was a chance he could smash an enemy in the face with it.

A score of Krikites were fanned along the dock in front of him, guarding the boats that were their way out if they absolutely had to retreat, and Dom knew that if it came to fighting, they'd be the ones to save the fleet, not him.

He tried, again, to swallow the bitterness, but it seemed he was too full of it to force any more down and it bubbled like acid upon his tongue. Off to his right stood Gilda, hunched beneath the rain, gnarled hands gripping the old spear haft she'd begun using as a walking stick. The top, which she'd sanded down to a comfortable roundness, was just the right height for her to prop her chin upon, and she did so now, for all the world like an old woman watching a flock of goats in a summer field.

Dom spat into the mud at his feet, trying to clear the taste of shame. Shame made him angry, and anger made him selfish, and that just reminded him of all he'd done and shame would fill him again. An endless, draining loop of emotion and beneath it all, beckoning, coaxing, waxed the call of the Blood. Growing stronger. Imperious. As always, he put an image of Rillirin's face between him and it, an idea of their child and their future, the life they would have when this was done. It was his way of tending his soul, nurturing the Light in him, that little candle-flicker so small and brave against the darkness that threatened.

Candle-flicker.

A bloom of fire off to his left and Dom twisted his face away, screwing shut his eyes before it could take hold in his mind. Too late. The air left his lungs with a protracted moan as he rose on to his toes, arms outflung, sword spinning away in the mud.

"Nnnno," he forced through a tight throat, a thick tongue and gritted teeth. "Nnnno."

"Dom?" Gilda was by his side. "All right, let's sit you down," she said, but he didn't sit so much as collapse, distantly registering the impact on his tailbone and then his shoulder blades.

Fire roared in his head, boiling his eyes, his brain, roaring until he screamed. He felt himself begin to convulse, his back arching, belly reaching for the clouds, felt Gilda's hands on him fierce with worry, with love, and then She ripped him free and stole him away.

EVERYWHERE, NUMINOUS AND WITHOUT source, a golden glow, as though he were the wick at the centre of a flame. Wildflowers, pine resin, rich earth, the coppery tang of blood and the ozone of lightning all hung in his nostrils, while running water and birdsong and a breeze chuckling through leaves sang in his ears.

"Calestar," She said, Her voice low and loving, and Dom cringed.

"Send me back," he gasped, dread black inside him. "Please, I have nothing to say to you. You've done enough, hurt me enough. Send me back."

The Dancer's eyes were wise and ancient in Her youthful, laughing face, and they stripped away his secrets in much the same way the Dark Lady's had done. Divine violation, over and over, raping who he was, what he was, giving no thought to the consequences or his own needs. Taking what They wanted and leaving him hollow and hurting. Was one really better than the other, when all was said and done?

"You grieve, my child. And you hate."

"Hate you," Dom spat with as much venom as he could muster as the Dancer's love—broad and deep and smothering—seeped into his veins and muffled his thoughts, his emotions. Blanketed him in love. Stultifying.

"We are so close to the end, Calestar," She said. "I just need you to hold on a little longer."

"Can't die until you say so, is that how it is now? Condemned to live until you've wrung me out like a rag, sucked the last bit of joy and promise from my life and left me a fucking husk? Is that it? *Is it?*" He pummelled his fists against Her and She held him tighter, ignoring his struggles until he was snared in Her eyes, a fly in a web. "You're pulling me apart. All of you, over and over, just pulling me to pieces." His voice caught on a sob. "Please stop."

"You must not go to the Waystation again, Calestar," the Dancer said in her sweet, young-old voice.

"I've already promised Gilda I won't."

"And now you will promise me," She said. "Only hurt awaits you there."

Dom's nose wrinkled as the scent of soot—so unlikely here—drifted towards him. He caught what might have been the puff of ash in the corner of his eye, there and gone. Blinking, he focused back on Her, let the anger rise to smother all else.

"You told me once I had a great destiny. You told me I would do great things, but there's nothing great about murder, betrayal and apostasy. Nothing I've done has been great; none of it has helped my people or those who stand in the Light. I've brought us to the brink. Doomed us all. And it was you who set me on this path. You who shoved me into the Blood deep enough to drown and turned away when I begged you to help me out." He wriggled free of Her embrace and raised a shaking, accusatory finger. "You put me in Her grasp and now you tell me I must not go? Where is *my* free will? When do *I* get to choose?"

"You do not truly understand all the things you have done," the Dancer said, "and nor will you in this life. As for those sins you have committed, you still have time. You can change it all, make up for it all. I showed you once the things you would have to do and you fought against them."

"You're fucking right I did," Dom screamed. "You said you'd showed me everything. You didn't, you showed me not even a taste of what I had to survive. Not even a breath of the horror you forced me into."

The Dancer put Her cool palms on either side of his skull, stilling his struggles. "And now I will show you the last of it," She said, and though there was remorse in Her tone, there was no apology. "And if you fight this, if you give up on this, then all is truly lost. Gosfath and the Dark Lady, my wayward children, will be ascendant, while Their Brother and I will be lost for eternity. And despite what you think, precious child, you do not want that for the world or yourself."

"Wait. *Wait!*" Dom took Her wrists and pulled his head free of Her grip, a suspicion so horrifying growing within that he could barely give it voice. "What do you mean, your wayward children?"

Sorrow softened the Dancer's expression and one of the vines in Her hair withered and died. The light in Her face flickered and dimmed, and another waft of burning reached him.

The Dancer sat among Her flowers and beckoned for him to join her. "Millennia ago, the Dark Lady and Gosfath were mortal. More than that—they were my priests and I loved Them well. Over time They positioned Themselves between me and my followers. Over time, They sucked faith and power to Themselves, in secret, and then They came to me—as you are with me now—and They deceived me and stole. Wisps and tendrils and then ropes and cables and great sheets of me, of my essence and my love, and They wove Themselves monstrous shapes to inhabit and They demanded sacrifice, for only blood can sustain Them. And They became."

There was silence as Dom took in the words, silence unbroken now by birdsong or zephyrs. This was the silence of the burial mound, the stillness that falls after violence is done and blood is spilt.

"This . . . this is all your fault?" he whispered, and the Dancer—goddess of Light and love—flinched from his words. "You did this, you broke the world, you caused untold suffering and the deaths of millions over the years? And now you expect us—expect me—to fix it for you? *How? Why should I?*"

"Because I cannot," the Dancer said. "I spent most of my remaining essence on weaving the veil that kept Them out of Gilgoras. Now that essence too is gone and my strength has failed. The veil has torn and though I tried, I could not stop the Dark Lady taking what She wanted from you. And now without you—without men and women and children of faith—I will fall and the Red Gods will rise and not even the Trickster can defeat Them alone. The world will turn to Blood and to ash. Worship and despair will become one, wedded for eternity."

"You did this," he repeated, unable to grasp anything else. "You caused all of this. Your blindness, your desperate need for love, for worship. Like a tick feeding on a dog, uncaring that the animal will die because of you. You're no fucking better than the priests who became gods Themselves. If only we could do away with the fucking lot of you."

The Dancer's sorrow grew until it filled the world and filled Dom and his heart was like to burst and all his angry words flew like bees from his mouth and were gone.

"I loved Them, as I love all of my children and all Gilgoras. I was blind to Their ambition. And I and all the world has paid for it. But now I need you. When the veil failed I marshalled the last of my strength to aid my Son in His battle against Gosfath."

"You sent the lightning."

She nodded, and now he spotted the source of the ashy smell; Her left hand was blackened, tiny flakes of soot drifting from it every time it moved. Like his had been, melted to the knife he'd stabbed into the Dark Lady's heart before the Fox God chopped it off.

"And now I am almost spent," the Dancer said and Her grief was not for Herself but for the world—and for him. "I fear for you, for my Son, for all Gilgoras. That is why I ask your aid, Calestar. Without you, the world will fall. I can do little more. It must be you, and the Trickster, and those you love and who love you. All who stand in the Light must come together and fight. But you must understand how. And what it will cost.

"This is why I come to you now, Calestar, because the final choice must be made. Before, when you were still in the Dark Lady's grip, you would not just have said no: you would have revealed my plan to Her. I could not let that happen and so I had to retreat from you and your actions. For that—for the feeling I had abandoned you—I am sorry. But when Gilda forgave you—when she gave you the courage to begin forgiving yourself—I knew you were ready. And now here we are."

She looked diffident of a sudden, almost afraid Herself, and Dom was seized with a sudden impulse to deny Her. What would happen if he said no? "Why me?"

The Dancer's sorrow swelled further. "Because it must be someone."

It was no sort of answer, and yet the only one She could give. Had She chosen him from birth, or simply picked the closest person as events unfolded? Was he special, or just convenient? And did it matter?

"I just want Rillirin," Dom whispered, as here, in Her presence, he found the simple shining core of himself and saw that it was family and peace. "I don't care about great destinies and divine wars. I've done enough, more than enough. I just want to go home to Rillirin and see my child born. I want to apologise to her for everything that's happened. Will I get that chance?"

"Yes," the Dancer said and Dom's heart stuttered. "May I?" She breathed, reaching out to cup his head again.

Dom ran his fingers over the stump of his sword arm. Even here, in the presence of his goddess, it was gone. "You're asking me to take on your duty," he said eventually. "You're asking me to do what you cannot."

"Yes, Calestar, that is what I am asking."

"And the reward is that I'll see Rillirin again."

"No, my love. You will see her again anyway. This duty must be chosen, not bartered for."

His breath shuddered in his throat. "Will I survive it?"

The Dancer leant forward and kissed his brow. "That depends," She murmured as the knowledge poured into him, a raging torrent of fire and understanding and pain and risk and hope and pain and sacrifice and pain.

"It depends on whether, by the end, you want to."

D OM SUCKED IN AIR and rain and the first hints of autumn. He was a shell filled with poison, filled with knowledge so awful that he teetered on the brink of tantalising, welcoming madness. So easy to fall in. So easy to let go. But there was a gleam, too, the promise of Rillirin and a love renewed. Redemption. It meant so much more than he'd expected and he clung to it as the hurt swamped him.

"Breathe, lad. I've got you." Gilda was using the sing-song tone she always had when he was a boy. It told him the physical toll had been as bad as the rest of it. If he'd had the energy, he might've laughed. If he'd had the time, he would've slept.

"Up," he croaked instead, opening his eyes. Mud beneath his fingers, wet soaking into his back and arse and thighs, the hurts making themselves known with unseemly glee. "Up now."

"You need to—" Gilda began, but the certainty was building in his chest and he struggled on to his side and then his elbow, retching, not pausing.

"Up," he managed again, and Gilda hauled him up to standing, put her walking staff in his hand and took his other side, shoulder in his armpit, a muffled grunt as she took his weight. He swayed, turning his head like a dog sniffing out prey, and then began to wobble along the road. It was only then that he realised how weak his left side was, leg and arm sluggish, unresponsive and barely able to support him.

No time for that either. "Help me."

"What did you see? Where are we going?" Gilda fretted.

"Crys." It was so slurred she didn't understand, the pain in his head almost enough to buckle his legs again; only fear kept him going. To get back to Rillirin he had a job to do, and getting back to Rillirin was all he wanted, a need clean and pure, a love untainted with power or control.

Gilda didn't ask him to repeat it; pulling his arm more firmly across her shoulders, she shuffled with him down the streets, through patches of utter darkness, faster than he could manage and only Gilda and momentum keeping him upright.

Dom couldn't hear the fighting over his own laboured breathing, so when they emerged into a marketplace or village green, where two vicious battles were being fought, the unexpectedness of it brought them to a halt. A brawling melee to their left collapsed even as they arrived, Easterners throwing down weapons and raising their arms, the other on their right raging as the Krikite line tried to bunch around a central point, as the left wing started to buckle.

Dom headed for the knot where the fighting was fiercest, where discordant wailing—of both triumph and despair—was beginning to rise. He took a deep breath and pulled his arm free, dug the staff into the mud and lurched into a limping, pathetic run, a mangled war cry clawing from his throat.

"Dom," Gilda cried, but there was no time. He wormed into the thick of it, wormed past the Krikites in the front of the battle and threw himself over the kneeling figure, knocking it flat and himself to his knees, and he swung the staff right and then left, clumsy and slow but with the element of surprise, right and left again, and then again, sitting on the Fox God's back, shielding him with his crippled body, his dying life. The Rankers reared back in surprise but then recovered, crowding forwards, swords and spears lunging for them both, more sharp points than a hedgehog had spines.

Dom threw himself flat and tensed against the promise of steel. It didn't come. The hot salt of blood splashed the side of his face, one eye, and then the unmistakeable thud of weapons hitting shields as they locked above him and men died so they might not. A severed arm splashed into a puddle.

Hands grabbed him and dragged him off Crys, then more grabbed Crys and dragged him back too, and the Krikites sealed the hole in the line and held it, though he could see—almost smell—their desperation. *Has the Fox God fallen? What's happened? Have we lost before we've even begun?*

Ash whirled past in a fury of bloodied steel. "He lives," he screamed. It was enough for the Krikites.

Dom lay on his back staring into the night as the lines moved away from him. The rain was lessening, patches of clear sky to the east, heavy cloud still in the south. A star watched him as he watched it.

"Crys?" he slurred again, the pain unendurable now and bringing whimpers from his chest, adrenaline unable to temper the poisoned exhaustion of a knowing.

"I'm here," Crys said from above and to the side as the last of the Rankers died or submitted. "As are you, Calestar." And there he was, looming over Dom with blood running down his face and his eyes burning a fierce yellow. He grinned, his teeth sharp and white. "You've chosen then," he added. "I have to say I'm glad. I didn't want to die there because you took a darker path."

Prostrate and hurting, Dom began to laugh. "Trickster," he coughed, knowing Crys would understand him even if no one else could, knowing his choice had been no real choice at all, just another manipulation, this one intended to force him to commit. For all Her apologies and sad eyes, the Dancer had manoeuvred him one last time. "I'm not doing it for you, you bastard. I'm doing it for Rillirin."

Crys winked. "And that's why you'll never falter again, Calestar. Welcome home."

THE BLESSED ONE

Tenth moon, first year of the reign of King Corvus
Private audience chamber, the palace, Rilporin, Wheat Lands

THE SLAVE HAD AGREED, as Lanta had expected. Now all they needed to do was find the perfect opportunity, not only to get Valan out of the city for a few days to alleviate suspicion, but to ensure that the transfer of power was seen by all Mireces as a good thing.

The Blessed One shifted in her chair, biting back a groan. She had communed with the God of Blood two days before and was still recovering, though the triumph of it—for He had come to her in the temple rather than summoning her to the Waystation—had yet to fade. She had invited Him, summoned Him, and He had responded, though of course their union this time had been of the flesh, as well as the soul. The hurts were greater. *The honour is greater.*

With at least eight weeks before Rill gave birth, she had three or four more opportunities to commune, to beseech. By then, the god would be used to coming to the temple, so when the ritual came to be performed, they would be guaranteed His presence, His guiding light to summon the Dark Lady to Gilgoras and Her new body.

"It is time for Rill to move into the temple," Lanta said, and the woman jerked her head up.

"She's got weeks yet," Corvus pointed out, more to spite her than because he cared, she thought.

"I'm not staying in that shithole," Rillirin said. "Bad enough you make me go there every day. It's even more disgusting than the temple in Eagle Height. I won't live in it."

"You'll do as you're ordered, slave," Lanta said, though in truth the thought of weeks more listening to her answer back and being unable to do anything about it would be a trial. "Your child is to become a goddess; what you want is irrelevant."

"My child is an innocent babe and will live its life in the Light," Rillirin started, as she always did.

"Enough," Corvus snapped. "I'm sick of the two of you bickering like a pair of dried-up old consorts. If it's time to take her to the temple, take her and have done with it. I've had enough of the whole bastard situation."

And there we have it: "The whole bastard situation," as if the resurrection of our Bloody Mother is a chore or a whim that he regrets agreeing to.

Valan was watching her, his expression unreadable. She gave the smallest nod of her head: *Soon. Very soon.*

"Corvus, brother," Rillirin began, trading on their shared blood as she had ever since she'd been returned to them. "Surely you don't—"

Three heavy raps on the door cut her off and Tett strode in a moment later. He sketched a shallow bow. "Word from Pine Lock, Sire. Ten days ago a large force of Krikites, allegedly led by the Fox God Himself, took the town and freed the slaves. All East Rankers garrisoned there were killed in the fighting or captured. The town was then evacuated and burnt to the ground, with the refugees vanishing into the Western Plain. Perhaps to Alder Hollow, perhaps just to lose themselves in the wilderness or flee to the Wolf Lands."

Lanta's blood ran cold. They were losing control. *Corvus* was losing control. If they allowed Rilpor to languish under his reign much longer, they wouldn't have a country to gift to the Dark Lady when She returned to them.

"*Ten days?*" Corvus snarled, lurching out of his chair. "Gosfath's balls, why did it take so long for word to reach us?"

"The Ranker was wounded during the battle, which slowed him. And he didn't know whether the Krikites had gone on to Yew Cove, so he couldn't risk taking a boat past the town. He had to march overland."

Corvus swore and began to pace.

"There's more, Sire," Tett said stolidly. "Sailtown fell too, on the same night. A co-ordinated offensive on the autumn equinox, it seems. Mace Koridam and the surviving loyalist Rankers appeared out of nowhere and overran the defences. They somehow managed to get across all Rilpor without anyone spotting them to raise the alarm. Skerris is dead and Sailtown, too, was burnt and its people fled. A patrol out of Three Beeches saw the smoke and investigated, then reported in and were sent on here."

Corvus swore some more, with passion and inventiveness. Lanta could hear her teeth grinding. Skerris was a priest of the Red Gods, as well as a soldier. Skerris was more fucking useful these days than Corvus.

"And Koridam has pronounced himself king."

That brought all movement, all speech, to a clanging halt. The room was silent but for the crackle of logs in the fire, the snorting of Corvus's breath, and Rillirin's smothered laughter. The identical expressions of violence on all their faces as they turned to her only made her laugh more.

She pointed at Corvus. "You're so fucked," she giggled. "Oh, you're so fucked now. The Fox God's back and he's coming for you, and the whole country will flock to Mace's banner when they find out he's king." She laughed some more, going red. "You're so fucked."

Lanta looked at Tett and at Valan; neither of them seemed inclined to disagree. Corvus spun away, grey with fury or with shock, and retreated into the shadows at the corner of the room, snagging a cup as he passed the table. It got halfway to his mouth before he flung it at the opposite wall, dark wine spraying across the plaster and dripping like blood to the flagstones. The cup itself was made of soft, heavy gold and crumpled on impact, though without the satisfying sound of shattering he no doubt wanted.

While his back was turned, Lanta gave Valan a nod. *This is it. This is our chance.*

"Sire, I will ride at dawn for Sailtown to pick up their trail and prevent them from attacking us here," he said as if it had all been rehearsed. "With enough warriors I can bring them to bay and defeat Koridam, end his bid for your throne before it has even begun. I would suggest sending Fost to Pine Lock to do the same. It is best we know exactly what we are facing. Tett, how many men did Mace have?"

"No," Corvus interrupted, and Lanta didn't miss that he looked to Tett for support. Tett, not Valan and not her. "It's time this farce was ended. Tett, get me the map." The man dragged it off a shelf and Corvus pointed to the floor in front of the fire where the light was best. They squatted either side of it and Valan moved to Corvus's left. Lanta shifted to the edge of her seat and peered down.

"Sailtown," Corvus said and put his dagger on the symbol.

"Pine Lock," Tett said and did likewise.

"They've split their forces, but it was ten days ago, so we can't capitalise on it. The messengers moved through Yew Cove and Three Beeches, yes? Those towns remain productive and under control?"

"Yes, Sire, they're fine, or they were when word came through. Jumpy with the news, but holding firm."

"So where have they gone?" Corvus mused, tapping a finger against his lips as he examined the map. "Will they regroup or come at Rilporin from two directions?"

"That would leave garrisons at Yew Cove and Three Beeches behind them," Valan pointed out. "They'd need to take out those positions to guarantee they weren't caught between our walls and a second attacking force. The fact they left them indicates they feel the need to consolidate troop numbers."

"Yes," Corvus said and Lanta felt a flicker of disquiet at how easily Valan had been pulled back into the king's circle. Even now it could all slip through her fingers. Goddess, country, power.

Tett drew a straight line with his finger from Pine Lock to Sailtown. It went directly through Deep Forest, with the lake called Silent Water in its midst. "Seems a likely staging point. They can conceal their numbers in the forest and use it as forage. The lake will keep them in fresh water. Sit tight and wait for us to come to them."

"Then perhaps you should not. Surely they will have laid traps," Lanta said. "You wouldn't know what you might be walking into."

"The longer you leave them out there, the more damage they'll do to your pet Rankers and your grip on ordinary Rilporians," Rillirin said as if she had the first fucking clue about military strategy. She shuffled to the edge of her seat and pointed. "Maresfield's an easy win for them if they are in Deep Forest. Then they may as well carry on to Three Beeches. After that—"

"Shut up," Corvus snapped, his voice cold, but he didn't contradict her because she was right. "They know we know where they'll be. And they know we'll come for them."

"We could march wide and flank them," Valan suggested and Lanta noticed the use of 'we'. Her jaw tightened.

"We'd have to come at them through the forest," Corvus said. "No. Straight approach is the simplest; we'll put Rankers out as screens to trip any ambushes they've set. Tett, send word to Yew Cove, Shingle and Three Beeches to strip their garrisons, leaving the smallest possible number to control the populace, and to march or sail to Rilporin. I want them here in ten days at the most, so send those messengers now. I'll take as many Mireces as I can and we'll march together for Deep Forest. One final battle and it's done. Tett, you'll ride as my second."

Lanta's breath caught in her throat and she looked instinctively at Valan. He'd paled at the pronouncement, but she thought it the pallor of anger rather than shock. Good. She could use anger.

"And me, Sire?" he asked with stiff formality.

"You stay. Protect the Blessed One and keep an eye on my sister; don't let the slaves rise in my absence."

"Your will, Sire." Spots of colour danced high on his cheekbones, but his voice was tightly controlled. Still, the shame of it was obvious to them all.

"Blessed One, would you or Gull intercede with Holy Gosfath for me, see if there is anything else we can learn?"

Lanta stood, willing herself not to look at Valan and the ashes of her plan. "I will do so. Rill, with me—you cannot stay here with the king absent and he will have much to plan in the coming days. He doesn't need you under his feet. *Second*," she emphasised the title, "perhaps you and I should discuss how best to manage the slave population."

Tett stared at them without speaking, Valan hesitated and then stood, and Corvus pretended not to notice. Lanta snapped her fingers and Rillirin heaved herself out of the chair, apparently deciding not to risk angering Corvus or Lanta herself any more this night, and together they left. The king didn't even watch them go.

Lanta pointed at the guards who stood at attention outside the room. "You two, take the princess to her quarters and help her gather up whatever she needs; she is moving into the temple. Second Valan will escort me." She didn't wait for a response, striding along the corridor with her skirts boiling like a blue wave around her ankles. "This is a catastrophe," she muttered. "I do not have a legitimate reason to send you out of the city, yet we must do it before he leaves. Let us find your slave. The sooner this is over, the better."

"Blessed One, perhaps this is a sign from the gods that this is . . . not the right choice." His tone was hesitant, as it should be. "We are still far from sure of victory."

Lanta wanted to scream. "You believe I have made a mistake in this?" she demanded, her voice a low hiss. "No, Valan, the choices we make in honour of the gods are not always easy, but they are always right if it is Their will. And Their will shall manifest in the success or failure of the attempt—all we can do is make it." She pressed her hands to her heart. "I have told Holy Gosfath what is happening here, told Him what I think we should do to secure His ascension and His Sister-Lover's return. The god agrees."

The words were not a lie; at no point had the God of Blood indicated that He did not agree with Lanta's plans to replace the king with Valan and rule alongside him. The God of Blood had not indicated displeasure at her proposals, because He concerned Himself with issues far greater than petty power struggles. As such, his silence was tantamount to agreement. Still, the validation straightened Valan's shoulders. The god approved his claim to kingship.

He put his hand on her arm, slowing her. "Then, Blessed One, forgive me but even with such divine approval we cannot act now. This new intelligence proves the country is too unstable for a change in ruler. Let Corvus go and fight Koridam and his Krikites. Let him go and secure Rilpor on our behalf," he murmured, "while you and I remain here and together effect the return of the Dark Lady. If Corvus lives, we kill him on his return. If he does not . . ." He shrugged. "Then Tett will be king, a nobody, a stranger to most of our warriors. I was second to Corvus as war chief, I am his second"—his face twisted with anger—"*was* his second as king. They will support me if I challenge Tett on his return. But whether it's Corvus or Tett who marches through Rilporin's gates after their victory, Blessed One, he will not live out the night. His victory over

Koridam will give us the country—and then his untimely death will *give us the country*."

"Very well," she said eventually. "The situation moves more swiftly than I had hoped, but we can still seize the initiative and bring Gilgoras on to the Dark Path." She stopped. "The gods want you as king, Valan, and that is why they have seen fit to have you remain here, out of danger. There is no shame in it; it is divine intervention. And I want you . . . as king," she added and gave him a smile he'd feel all the way down to his toes. "Adapt or die, as the gods decree. We are Mireces. We overcome."

"Corvus is not Mireces," Valan added, confidence and contempt weighing equal in his voice.

"No," Lanta said. "He is not."

TARA

Tenth moon, first year of the reign of King Corvus
Heir's suite, the palace, Rilporin, Wheat Lands

THE NEWS OF THE fall of Pine Lock and Sailtown had stormed through Rilporin, trailing worry and excited speculation behind it. The Mireces had tried to suppress the revelation that Mace Koridam was setting himself up as a rival king, but there was no stopping it.

It was exactly what they needed, stirring up the slaves, giving them hope. Every one of them knew Mace had come to Rilporin's aid despite all his Rank had endured, and they knew what he'd done, how he'd managed to get thousands of refugees out of the city even if they themselves had been trapped. He was a man, a soldier, a commander who had fought and nearly died multiple times to bring them victory. The revelation he was taking the crown put them on a cliff edge of rebellion and Tara was about to push them over the edge.

Valan and Lanta weren't the only ones who could plan a coup, after all.

As the days passed while they waited for the Easterners to arrive, Tara paced Valan's suite waiting for his signal to take out Corvus. It didn't come, and although she made a show of being vocal about Vaunt's freedom and the promises she'd been made, she stopped short of pushing the second too hard. He told her the plan would still go ahead when Corvus was back, and he might even have meant it, but Tara's own plans had moved on and her impatience was for Corvus and his army to leave. She trusted her general, her Commander of the Ranks—*my king!*—to deal with Corvus as he deserved.

And then, finally, the Mireces and East Rankers headed out into the Wheat Lands towards the distant Deep Forest, eight days after they'd learnt of the twin attacks by Mace's forces. A wave of punishments and killings preceded the march—those slaves who weren't deemed cowed enough were executed and Tara knew some of the men and women she was relying on would have lost their lives. She couldn't afford to change her plans. The vast majority of the north barracks Rank prisoners were dead of fever, and Vaunt's in the south barracks were weak from lack of food, but the slaves still outnumbered the remaining Mireces and converts five to one. It was fear that kept them in place. Fear, starvation and the lack of weapons. Vaunt's job was to take away the first and procure the third—they'd just have to deal with being hungry until the city was secure.

And then they were gone, and Valan hadn't gone with them. Another unforeseen complication. And not only that, but he'd seconded her to be his informal aide, trailing him around as he inspected walls and stores, meted out punishment, even visited the temple and Lanta. But she couldn't risk taking on Valan, Lanta and whatever guards the priestess had until she could get word to Vaunt or any of the rebels to say they were ready to go.

Corvus had left three days before and the remaining Mireces were beginning to relax, making it the perfect time for the rebellion to begin. If they delayed much longer, some of the slaves would take matters into their own hands, and if Tara wasn't in place when it started, she was unlikely to get to Lanta and Rillirin before the city went into lockdown.

Until, on the fourth morning, it was there. Her chance. Word came shortly after dawn that a section of the western wall had suffered a partial collapse in the night, and before the sun was more than a finger over the horizon, they were striding down the King's Way to First Circle.

"Explain," Valan snapped to the masons gathered around the small drift of rock and dust. A few had already started tapping and chipping at the stone around the collapse, but everyone turned to face him as he spoke. Merol was there; Merol saw her. She gave him a small nod.

"Cracks inside the wall," a mason said. "Too deep in to see from out here, no way to tell they're there. So much shifting and hammering at that end it caused a collapse up here."

Tara suspected he was making it up as he went along, but the Mireces didn't do a lot of building with stone—with luck, they'd get away with it. She knew, too, that word was passing without her involvement, that the rebels had realised they needed to get her here and so they'd had to do something big enough to attract Valan's attention. It was a huge risk, but if she could phrase this right, it would pay off.

The mason who'd spoken turned to the wall and started gesturing, and Valan stepped forward, wary because the men were bastard massive and armed with hammers, but they all shuffled back out of his way. Merol ended up next to Tara.

"Looks like a god took exception to our wall," he rumbled and she frowned at his peculiar choice of words, then understood.

"A message from the gods, perhaps," she murmured, the code the rebels used to identify each other. He nodded, thoughtful. "And will you have it ready by noon, do you think?"

"Noon today?" he asked, startled. Tara nodded, not daring to look at him or Valan or anyone. "That's a tight timeline to rebuild a wall. Will need a lot of men."

"I'm no mason," Tara said, "but I think there are enough to get it done. And, well, it needs doing, doesn't it?"

Merol glanced at her sidelong. "Aye, it needs doing. I think noon will work just fine."

NOON CAME AND WENT and the city remained worryingly quiet. Valan was at his desk with the one they called Slave Silais, the nobleman Tara had last seen trying to escape the city and the Mireces invasion, the pair of them discussing the need to re-establish river trade with those towns that still survived after Mace's scorched-earth approach to Pine Lock and Sailtown. Silais was the one who had helped let into the city the very people he was now collaborating with. Silais was the one who had tipped the scales in favour of the enemy.

She'd stood opposite him for an hour and his gaze had travelled through her several times. Despite his position, despite the metal collar on his neck, he still acted as if he had a royal sceptre up his arse. And he didn't have a clue who she was, either. It infuriated her.

The sun moved on, an hour past its zenith. They'd caught Merol. He'd been discovered as a rebel and executed. The rebellion she so desperately needed wasn't going to happen.

The door burst open. Silais shrieked, Valan leapt up, knife glinting in his fist, and Tara flinched, hand groping for a weapon, her tension releasing in a great wave of adrenaline that nearly made her stagger, the world coming into painful focus.

"Second! Slave riot in First Circle. Bunch of soldiers, looks like, and some masons, but it's spreading."

"Shit," Valan said. "I knew it. I knew something would happen. Stay here," he snarled to the room in general and was gone, slamming the door after him. Tara heard the turn of the key in the lock.

"Thank the gods we're safe," Silais babbled as the other slaves began whispering. "Thank the gods for Second Valan and his quick thinking. It'll be carnage on the streets, you mark my words."

"Lord Silais." He turned to face her. "You don't remember me, my lord? During the siege, at the tunnel entrance leading to the East Gate just before you let in the invaders and damned us all. Your friend Lord Lorca called me 'woman'. He should have called me Major."

Silais gaped, then gaped some more when Tara slid the stolen skinning knife out of her sleeve. He held up his hands in front of his face. "No, no, don't! Guards, *guards*!"

The knife went into his neck and back out, an effortless puncture that nonetheless went deep, and a thick scarlet jet pulsed into the air when the blade unplugged the wound. Tara leant away from the blood and lowered him to the floor with a muffled thud. His mouth was opening and closing like a fish's and Tara felt nothing. It was an effort to say the words: "Dancer's grace, Lord Silais."

She stepped away before he was dead, back to the door to listen—still quiet. Valan had taken the guards, presuming the lock on the door was enough. Tara undressed while the other slaves watched in mute horror, probably expecting her to begin bathing in the man's blood or something. She hadn't realised how heavy her skirts were until she slipped into an old shirt and pair of trousers belonging to Valan and secured them with a belt. The freedom was exhilarating. She bundled up the gown, secured it in a roll by tying the arms around it, and then wrapped a short scarf of blue linen around her neck to cover her slave collar. A half-cloak with a hood completed the disguise. She was armed, just, she was in trousers, and she had her orders: she was a soldier again.

Tara cleaned the knife on Silais's shirt and then knelt and slid the point into the lock. It was a slender blade, made for getting in beneath the legs of game, and the lock was big. It didn't take long to slip the catch.

She faced the slaves bunched together at the back of the room, as far away from her as they could get. "Listen to me. This whole city is going to explode into violence any minute. You can join the uprising and help to overthrow the Mireces. If we fight back together, they won't be able to stop us. We can take the city, take these fucking collars off, end the war." She held out a bloody hand, imploring. "Come with me. Fight with me, fight for our new—our rightful—king."

They shrank back together, a herd instinct she couldn't break. "Y-you can't," one stuttered. "They'll k-kill you."

Tara flipped up her hood. "We all die. This is my chance to die free, on ground of my choosing and not at another's whim. I'll leave the door open—even if you don't fight, try and run. Get out while you can. Dancer's grace."

She didn't have time for any more. The Rankers would push through First Circle and into Second, working their way towards the centre of the city and encouraging every slave they found to fight back. They'd free Vaunt and Dorcas from the south barracks to co-ordinate the uprising. They'd kill every Mireces they found without mercy and without regret. The whole city was going up in righteous fury and Tara had a mad priest-ess to kill and a heavily pregnant woman to rescue. Thrumming with energy, she slipped the gown under one arm and left Valan's apartments.

THE CITY WAS FULL of running figures, some in Mireces blue, some in collars. Screams and shouts spilt across the sky from far behind her, thin and high and distant. Tara ignored it all, slipping from house to shadow to building to wall, sliding through the district gates like mist.

Wearing the hood up in the streets was conspicuous, but so was her hair so she had no choice, hoping the blue of her shirt would stop anyone looking too closely.

She was in Third Circle and moving steadily, not in the centre of the road but no longer skulking through the shadows now she was away from the main action. She strode as if she had orders to be somewhere.

The gate into Second Circle was unguarded but locked. Tara checked her surroundings. Gosfath's tantrum in the city had caused a lot of damage around here and it didn't take long for her to find another way through; part of the wall collapsed behind the ruins of a burnt-out building.

Second Circle was the one Vaunt should be even now lighting up, far around its circumference to the west. Random shouts up ahead, co-ordinating movement, and she broke into a run. She only needed to cross Second Circle and reach the gate into First and the temple district, then lose herself among the buildings until she reached the grand temple. She was close, but if she was mistaken for a Mireces at a distance and they ordered her with them to help quell the rebellion, she was dead and those even now dying were doing so for nothing.

She ducked out of sight as another shout went up, unsure whether it was aimed at her and not waiting to find out. Two rights into a small alley, sprinting its length, out the other end and an immediate left, in through a broken window and down, pressed against the wall out of eyeline. A scrape and shuffle in the darkness and she was up and in a corner of the room, knife in hand and wishing it was a sword. A huddle of faces and protective arms, the glint of metal at their necks.

Tara hid the knife, then tugged at the scarf to show them her own collar. She held her finger to her lips. "Head for the South Gate after I'm gone. Get out and run and don't look back. Dancer's grace."

She waited a little longer and then slid back out through the window, catching her shirt on splintered wood and ripping it, grazing the flesh beneath. She retraced her steps and peeked from the mouth of the alley; the road looked clear and the gate into the temple district was right there. Tapping her fingertips against her heart, Tara went for it, bursting out of the mouth of the alley and running hard.

She was across the open space in seconds and through the gate, turned immediately left and wove into the temple complex, thinking only of losing any potential pursuit. Within minutes the grand temple loomed into view, its pale marble columns formerly a beacon for the faithful and now degraded by the foul rites that were performed inside its once-hallowed walls.

Whatever Vaunt was doing, he was making enough noise about it to have drawn off most of the Mireces. Five were stationed outside the temple's main doors, but Tara wasn't going in that way. She moved towards the back. There was a smaller entrance the priests used to and from their accommodation.

Sure enough it was there and it was guarded, but only by a single Mireces: a mistake, but a fortuitous one for Tara. She threw a stone that attracted his attention to his right, his sword side, then leapt out on his left and ripped the skinning knife through the side of his neck. The return strike thudded into his chest. The blade was wicked and tore him open easier than breathing. Tara clapped her free hand over his mouth and wrestled him down to the ground, punched the knife through his ribs two, three, four more times until he was too weak to make a sound.

No point dragging him out of sight—there was blood everywhere. It was about speed now. Tara unclipped his scabbard and fitted it to her own belt, the weight on her hip an almost religious comfort. She drew the sword and tested its balance: not great, but serviceable.

She slid the knife back into her sleeve, then slipped into the temple's gloom and the stink of fear and the overwhelming, gagging stench of old blood. Her nose wrinkled and bile rose; she forced it down, mouth watering. The temple's main space was for devotions, but there were almost a dozen smaller rooms for private ritual and consultation and Lanta could be in any of them. Rillirin too. She scanned the open space and saw nothing, so she moved towards the first of the private rooms. She'd have to clear them all, one by one, to kill the bitch.

AND THERE SHE WAS, in a small devotional room, kneeling in prayer with bandaged hands outstretched in supplication to evil. Even better, she had her back to the door. Tara checked both ways along the corridor, but the Mireces didn't go in for candles, it seemed, and she could barely see anything. Still, the longer she waited the more chance of being discovered, so she pushed the door just wide enough to slide through — bastard thing creaked like a ship in a storm — and slipped in.

Fortunately, Lanta's prayers consumed her and she didn't hear. Tara crept forward, ignoring the tremble in her sword hand. Part of her wanted Lanta to hear her and make a fight of it; it'd be easier to kill her if it was self-defence. Tara blinked sweat and doubt from her eyelashes. The Fox God had given her this mission, had trusted her with these assassinations. All Rilpor needed Lanta to die. All Gilgoras. She took another step, focused on the angle between neck and shoulder, down behind the collarbone to sever the big veins and open the lung, nick the heart.

"Forgive my intrusion, Blessed — Who are you?"

Tara spun and lashed out, her boot catching a man in the gut and flinging him into the wall by the door. She didn't wait for him to get up. Lanta got a bandaged hand in the way of the first blow and screamed as the sword took off a finger and opened up whatever wound was already there. She punched with her other hand, a glancing strike off Tara's cheek that did nothing but make her a little warier. She fell into a fighting crouch and began to circle, Lanta twisting to keep her in front and pulling a hammer from her belt. She was grey with surprise and pain, breath coming in sharp hard pants, and though her eyes glittered with unshed tears, they danced with fury, too. Tara kept circling until she could see the man, Gull, over the priestess's shoulder.

"Rillirin," Tara bellowed in her parade-ground voice, the name echoing through the temple. "It's Tara. Get your boots on; we're leaving."

Lanta swung the hammer and it clanged off the sword. She leapt back from the riposte. Gull was on his feet now, one hand on the wall for balance, the other pressed to his chest.

"Blessed One? Blessed One, where are you?"

Oh, you are fucking kidding me. Valan?

She'd been hoping to have a crack at the king's second for everything he'd put her through, so on the one hand, it meant both Tara's targets were in the same place. On the other hand, it meant both Tara's targets were in the same place.

Gull charged her and she sidestepped, raking him across the arm with her sword, but then the hammer smashed into the outside of Tara's left elbow and she screamed as pain erupted through the joint and she and Lanta came together, chest to chest with Lanta inside her guard. Tara headbutted her, heard the crunch of cartilage and shoulder-barged her away, stepped back to bring the sword into range when Gull grabbed her ankle and jerked. She hit the ground on her left side and her elbow blazed agony at her so that her vision flashed white for a second. When she could see again, the sword was gone and Lanta was coming for her, hammer raised and blood pouring from her nose and mouth.

"Tara?" Rillirin appeared in the doorway.

"Behind you!" Tara screamed as a shadow moved. Rillirin threw herself sideways and a man stumbled into the room, arms flailing as he missed his grab at her. A converted Rilporian. *Fuck.*

The distraction cost her. The hammer came in again, into her flank, her kidney, and she grunted as the hurt exploded in her, deep into her core, and stole her breath.

"Valan!" the Blessed One shouted through a mouthful of blood. She raised the hammer again and Tara knew she was going to be battered to death. *Fuck!*

Rillirin grabbed Lanta's upraised arm and yanked sideways. The convert grabbed for her again and wrestled her away, but it was enough. Tara kicked Lanta's feet from under her so they were all a tangle on the floor, yanked the skinning knife from her sleeve and rammed it into the woman's chest.

"Valan, *help*," Gull called as Tara rolled to her feet, found her sword and ripped it across the convert's gut as her left hand twisted a knife out of his grip, the movement triggering another searing pain through her arm. She'd probably cracked her elbow; nothing to do about it now. She shoved Rillirin through the door.

It had taken seconds, felt like years, but the shouts and running footsteps told Tara she was out of time. She glanced back once at Lanta—the woman was slumped, gurgling, blood soaking her gown—and then she ran, following Rillirin's lumbering form to the rear exit.

Movement in the main temple and Tara grabbed her and dragged her down, sliding into the deepest shadow she could find, hunkered behind a pillar, fighting to calm her breathing. The girl was panting, wide-eyed, but quiet. Footsteps and their echoes, confusing the sound, making it hard to pinpoint direction. Tara held her breath and strained her ears and eyes for the furtive, malevolent creep of movement, of ambush.

She could just see his outline now, on the opposite side of the godpool, but that left an unknown number of guards somewhere in the gloom. But if Valan was stupid enough to get between her and the exit, it'd be rude not to kill him on the way past.

"Blessed One?" he shouted again, doing the same as her and trying to locate allies and enemies among the bouncing echoes. The answering bleat was weak, but it was enough. Valan didn't hesitate. He broke into a run, saw her and possibly Rillirin as he passed and pointed, then was gone into the rear of the temple. *That's it, go and watch the bitch die.*

Three Mireces charged her. Tara rolled to her feet and stepped into the overhead slash of the first that would have cleaved through her shoulder and punched her sword into his gut, ripping sideways and spilling his intestines. It'd take him a few minutes to die, but die he would, and he'd be in no fit state to oppose her while he did it.

His sword arm fell to his side and he sucked in a breath to start screaming and Tara shoulder-barged him into the second, leapt sideways away from the third and was gone, following Rillirin and her mad dash for the exit. One followed, the other racing around the far side of the godpool to try and cut them off. He was faster than Rillirin and he came on like a galloping horse just as Tara overtook her and dropped, knees slamming into the smooth marble and skidding beneath his arcing sword. She chopped her own through his shin as she passed, nearly losing her grip, and he howled as his leg shattered.

Rillirin overtook her again, face hard with grim determination, one hand supporting the bulge of her belly, and then fingers snagged the back of Tara's cloak and hauled. She let it take her over on to her back and brought both legs up, kicking up and back as the Raider loomed over. It was only a glancing blow with the side of one boot, but enough to spoil his aim as he stabbed down. She slashed upwards with her sword and caught the inside of his arm and the tip of his nose, sent him reeling back with a curse, flipped on to all fours and stabbed at him again, low into the gut, ripped off the cloak still in his hand and was gone.

Tara burst out of the temple, caught a glimpse of red hair vanishing into an alley and pounded after Rillirin. She was going the wrong way, deeper into the city, not used to the twisting roads designed to confuse an enemy. Tara caught up with her and then took over, weaving back through the buildings towards the South Gate, halting at every yell and rush of running feet. Smoke drifted on the air and the sound of fighting was loud, close. They could use the confusion.

She quartered the road, scanning the buildings and the doorways and the alleys between them, Rillirin silent at her shoulder. One last dash through the square before the gate and they'd be out. More shouting, more running and the clash of arms even closer.

Tara gritted her teeth, sword arm wrapped around her midriff so she could clutch at her side, where the hammer had smashed into her. She'd be pissing blood for a week, she reckoned. If she lived that long.

A final look, the sounds of fighting too close for comfort now. "Ready?" she breathed. "Out, over the bridge and keep fucking running. Go."

Rillirin ran, Tara on her heels and sword and knife in hand. The gate was there, hanging open. "Go!" Tara yelled and Rillirin managed a little more speed and they were strides from safety when Valan stepped into view. The girl faltered. *"Fucking run,"* Tara screamed and overtook her, moving to engage. More Mireces ran from the shadows but if she could distract them long enough for Rillirin to get out of the city . . .

Valan's face was cold, with a hint of betrayal and a surplus of rage. A Mireces came in on her left and she ducked, knife opening up his thigh while she was low, came up and kept running. And then she was on him.

His guard was high and she chopped for his ankle, forcing him to skip back as he turned the blade to catch hers. Tara let her momentum take her in close, crowding him as he stepped back again and taking a sheet of flesh from along his jaw with the dagger. Valan roared in pain and punched her in the face, knocking her back far enough to disengage his sword and step into range. Tara blinked away tears, ignoring the throb from her nose and mouth, ignoring the blood.

Rillirin bolted past her and she attacked, stopping Valan from reaching her. They fenced, a quick flurry of four, five, six cuts during which he sidestepped, trying to spin her and she moved into it, crowding his sword arm—she had nothing to lose now Lanta was dead. *May as well make the most of it.*

BLOODCHILD

A sudden increase in the sound of fighting, not from Rillirin thank the gods, but behind. The slaves, maybe even Vaunt.

"Protect the Major!" came a strident shout and Tara hesitated just an instant. Valan saw it and put the two together. His face suffused with blood and icy fury, but then Rank slaves armed with stolen knives and swords and staffs and masonry chisels flowed around her.

Valan disengaged, leaping out of range. "Loose!" he roared and all of a sudden it was raining arrows.

Tara caught a glimpse of a figure vanishing through the gate and then she was one of only seven left standing, the rest dead or dying on the stones and archers leaning from the windows to either side with fresh arrows nocked. Valan pointed his sword at her. "Throw down your arms," he said.

Her mouth quirked in amused disbelief. "Fuck you." She brought the knife up to her throat, eyes roaming the bodies around her, desperate not to find Vaunt's face among them. "Dancer's grace," Tara whispered, for them and for her.

Something smashed into the back of her head.

CRYS

Tenth moon, first year of the reign of King Corvus
Western Wheat Lands

"Y EW COVE'S NEARLY EMPTY of Rankers," Ash said as soon as he reached Crys in the small camp and assured himself his lover remained unhurt. Crys didn't mind the mothering one bit, not with only weeks left to live. If he could've sent anyone else to spy on the town, he would have, but Ash was the best tracker and scout they had this far from Mace's army. He reached out and tangled his fingers in Ash's.

"So Corvus has pulled all his troops together after our victories at Pine Lock and Sailtown," Crys said. "Exactly as we'd hoped. Gives us a chance to end this once and for all."

"We could take Yew Cove," Ash said, avoiding the implication behind his words, "free the people, sow some more discord for Corvus."

"Our orders were to scout and come back," Crys said. "I'm inclined to agree with our king. No matter how swift or silent we are, we'll lose some in the attempt and we need every fighter we've got. The remaining Rankers and converts won't risk dealing with the townsfolk too harshly—they know how badly they're outnumbered and won't want to push the slaves into open rebellion. That's a fight they'd never win. They should be safe enough until we have victory."

He let go of Ash's hand to stare southeast to where Rilporin dominated a horizon he couldn't see. If Corvus was coming that meant he was alive, which meant Tara might not be. He wondered if Foxy would tell him if she'd fallen. He wondered if he'd want to know—it was his words that had put her on her path. *And I've ordered soldiers to their deaths before. This is no different.*

It felt different, though. Or . . . something did. He rubbed at an ache in the pit of his stomach, smiled when Ash's lips grazed his temple. They hadn't discussed it, they'd just started showing their love for each other in public and if the Rankers who'd ridden with them didn't like it, at least they didn't comment. It would be over soon, anyway. Crys wasn't going to hide for whatever time he had left. Crys was done with hiding, with not being exactly who he was, man and god and heart-bound.

"All right," he said to the fifty-strong patrol with their borrowed and stolen horses, "we'll ride a deep loop towards Rilporin over the next couple of days and see if we can pick up movement or advance scouts. Let's give the king something definite to worry about, because I for one am sick of all this bastard not knowing."

The mix of Krikites, Wolves and Rankers grinned. They broke camp and soon enough they were on the move again, riding easily despite the snap in the air as autumn drew its cloak of reds and golds across the country, its fine tracery of low mists at dawn, its sudden, chilling downpours that told him summer was a distant memory. The last summer he'd ever see and he'd spent it fighting. An upswell of affection and humour reminded him not to dwell but to live and live well for the time he had.

He scratched idly at the russet pattern curling up through the open neck of his shirt beneath his chainmail as they rode, breathing deep of the crisp air and doing his best to ignore the ache in his stomach. It had begun a couple of days before and was likely just stress, but it seemed to get stronger the closer they rode to Rilporin. As though something in the city was calling to a part of him.

He looked over at Ash, sweat from his run back from Yew Cove sticking his curls to his brow despite the chill. He sensed the weight of Crys's gaze and tipped him a wink; Crys smiled and the ache faded a little, replaced with something warmer, something real.

He clung to it through the rest of the day, and the day after that, as they rode closer and closer to Rilporin and the ache, the sense of something coming, the gloom that hid behind the sun, continued to grow.

"THEY'RE COMING," CRYS SAID to the group assembled in Mace's command tent at the edge of Deep Forest a week later. "Three days behind us, perhaps—we pushed hard to put distance between us. We caught the leading edge of their outriders, didn't get much of a look at the force marching behind before they chased us off, but the estimate is three or four thousand."

"Right, if it looks like four thousand we assume it's eight and plan accordingly," Mace said and the Warlord, Dalli and General Hadir nodded their agreement. Hallos was there too, which meant he was taking a break from drilling the Rank surgeons and Krikite healers for a change. The gods knew they'd need every last one of them when battle was joined, especially now Crys knew his healing ability was more limited than he'd previously thought.

He decided to seek the man out after the council was concluded. The ache was still there, sapping at his energy, quietening even the Fox God. It was a slow poison and he needed to counter it. *Three days until the battle, Foxy. Doesn't seem very long at all now, does it?*

We are together.

I know.

Trouble was, the sentiment wasn't as comforting as it had been months or even weeks ago. Dying alone was terrible, but so was dying when there was still so much living to do.

"Tailorson?"

Crys jerked out of his reverie and blushed. "Sorry, sir. Sire."

Mace's face was unreadable. "I asked if they had cavalry."

"Outriders only, it seemed. Probably no more than a hundred."

"That's still enough for a cavalry charge," Hadir pointed out and Mace nodded. "Pit-traps and leg-breakers like the ones that cock Skerris laid outside Sailtown would be useful to break up the ground in front of our line."

"Agreed: get men preparing it at first light. Until then, gentlemen, dismissed."

They filed out one by one and Crys waited until they were alone. "A moment of your time, Your Majesty?" he asked and managed a faint smile at Mace's glare at the use of the title. "It's about Ash. About what happens to him after I . . . well, after."

Mace gestured him to a seat. "I thought we'd get to this eventually. Let me point out here and now that I am not expecting you to die in this battle. You're too bloody good a soldier and frankly I can't afford to lose you. So do me a favour and stay alive."

Crys managed a mirthless laugh. "I'll be doing my best," he said.

"That said, I will offer Ash a place on my staff after this is all over, or assign him as Dalli's personal bodyguard, whichever he prefers. It would be nice to keep the two of them together, though they'll no doubt make a mockery of the business of ruling. Alternatively, if Dalli passed over chiefdom to another when she becomes queen, Ash would get my vote as a more than suitable successor. And of course, the Crown and the Wolves will forever be closely entwined. Dalli won't let it be any other way, and I'm not stupid enough to argue with that one on a regular basis."

Crys didn't know what to say. He'd expected an argument, awkward questions and perhaps even a reprimand for their public behaviour. He hadn't expected Mace to understand him so well. Hadn't expected compassion. It was an unfamiliar feeling after the months of wary devotion that was all the Krikites showed in his presence. It loosened a ball of tension in his chest that had sat there so long he'd forgotten about it. He let out a shaky breath.

Mace leant over and slapped him on the arm. "As I said, I'm ordering you not to die, Tailorson, but if you do disobey me, I'll see him well looked after."

"Thank you, Sire," he stammered. "It means more than you could know. Your . . . acceptance too."

Mace's mouth twitched but his face was pensive. "Let's just say Dalli is a tyrant and has taught me a few things about not being a prejudiced arse. A few lessons that I—that all of us—should've learnt a long time ago. And besides, it's not easy to love a warrior when there's a battle on the horizon," he added. "With everything on your shoulders, I wouldn't deny you this small comfort. Of course, it requires both Ash and me to live to see it performed."

"You will, both of you," Crys said, an automatic rejection of the possibility of death, but Mace took it with more belief than was wise, as if it was a divine prediction. Crys didn't disabuse him of his faith. He stood. "Thank you again, sir. With your permission?"

Mace stood and Crys saluted him. "Dismissed, Major."

Crys left the king to his planning and went in search of Hallos. The physician leapt to his feet when Crys entered the long, low tent that would be the field hospital once battle was joined. The burly man hastened the length of the tent and ushered him towards the torchlight with unseemly glee. "It is an honour, a great honour," he said. "How may I help?"

"Easy, Hallos," a voice said and Crys recognised Gilda in the shadows; he felt an absurd flush of relief. "Let the lad sit before you start poking him."

"I wouldn't," Hallos protested but Crys thought he looked a little guilty despite his words. He took the proffered seat anyway and Gilda dragged her stool closer into the light, rolling her eyes when he glanced over.

He felt faintly ridiculous now it came to it, sitting here about to complain of bellyache a few days before they'd be fighting and killing. And that, of course, was when the Fox God decided to take over.

"There's something in me that's trying to burrow its way out," He said and Hallos sucked his breath in with a great gasp as the change became apparent. He fumbled for a pencil and notebook without looking, licked the wrong end and began to scrawl across a page already thick with text. "I think it's the Dark Lady's essence," He added and the pencil stopped moving. There was a long pause and then Gilda slid a little closer.

Uh, Foxy? When were you going to tell me about this?

What, did you think we'd just pissed Her back out? Laughter bubbled in his veins.

Yes. Well, no. Well, I didn't really think about it.

We'd never have used our cock again if we'd done that, the Fox God assured him.

"Fascinating. Absolutely fascinating," Hallos muttered. "And tell me, what makes you think it could be such a . . . substance? And why is it trying to, ah, vacate your body now?"

"Because the time is nearly here," said another voice from the shadows and the hairs stood up on Crys's neck. Dom limped into the light between rows of cots awaiting cleaved and screaming patients.

"No," Crys whispered. "The Bloodchild is at least six weeks away, probably more. The battle will have been fought and won by then. It'll be over."

"The Fox God's destiny is to defeat the Dark Lady. How can you do that if you die in three days?" Dom asked. Gilda helped him on to her stool and stood behind, ready to catch him if he moved into a knowing. Hallos's head swivelled like an owl watching two juicy mice, unsure which to eat first.

"So I survive the battle?" Crys asked, his heart leaping. There was still time, there were still days for him to spend with Ash, to wring every last drop from life and love.

Dom's laugh was sly and not exactly reassuring as he pressed his hand to his right eye. "Or maybe that babe just doesn't want to wait," he said. "Who knows?"

TARA

THE WATER WAS SO cold it stung when it hit her in her face; for a few seconds the only thing she could feel as she made her way back into consciousness. Soon enough, though, the vicious, biting pain in the back of her skull roared back, throbbing down her neck and into her shoulders so that she hissed a long breath in through her teeth. Tara opened one eye—the other was swollen shut—and the room swam into view. The barracks. The cells. But not Vaunt's.

Colonel Dorcas stood at attention with fierce, unbending pride despite the blood staining the tatters of his uniform. He'd fought hard then, before he was captured. Could Vaunt keep the rebellion alive without them both to assist? Of course he could. Could and would. She and Dorcas would be in for a beating, no doubt, but—

"I need this room. I don't need you." Valan stepped into view, pulled a knife and stabbed it into Dorcas's throat. He missed the big veins as the colonel got one hand up in an instinctive block, but then Valan was behind him, free hand pulling back on his forehead, knife hand slicing away at muscle and windpipe until a sudden jet of blood vomited from Dorcas's neck and splashed against the wall and floor, spraying into Tara's face.

Tara got halfway to her feet to rip Valan's own throat out with her teeth before the men holding her twisted both arms behind her back and wrestled her back down to her knees. They held her still, a hand on the back of her skull to make sure she watched him die. She held the old soldier's gaze until it was over, silently promising vengeance, and then raised it to Valan's face.

"Leave us," he said. The easy, competent man she'd come to know in the last months was gone. The flash of vulnerability when he talked of his wife and children was gone, subsumed beneath impenetrable ice. He was Valan, King's Second, and her death was in his eyes.

The men holding her wrenched her arms back tighter, eliciting a screech of pain, and then slammed her face down on to the stone hard enough to split her eyebrow and send up a splash of Dorcas's blood. By the time she'd got her hands under her, they were dragging the corpse through the door and slamming it behind them. She was sodden with blood, the cell a stinking miasma of gore and waste and fear.

Slowly, Tara stood, swaying. The blow that had knocked her unconscious—she checked the light from the high window—not long ago had left her dazed, and not even the pain and dawning fear could cut through the fog in her head. "Honoured?"

Valan's forearm slammed into her throat as he forced her back against the wall, pressing hard enough to cut off her breath, his face close enough to kiss. She choked, one hand fumbling at his arm, the other at his belt for the knife. Couldn't find it.

Valan headbutted her. Lightning exploded behind her eyes, cartilage cracking in her nose. Still couldn't breathe, blood gushing over his forearm, heavy leather vambrace jammed up tight beneath her chin.

"Why?" he asked. Tara blinked, scrabbling for air, stars bursting in her vision. "Why, you bitch, tell me why? You knew what would happen if you disobeyed, what would happen to Vaunt, and yet you take up fucking arms against me. Rise against me with the fucking Ranks. *How could you betray me?*"

She wheezed, pleading with her eyes, and he released just enough pressure that she could sip in a little air. "I'm sorry," she choked.

Valan roared in her face, forearm pressing even tighter, and she tried slapping at him, got a handful of his hair and pulled until he drove his fist into her kidney—the same one Lanta had smashed with the hammer— and if she could've screamed she would have. The splintered ends of ribs grated under each blow, agony and nausea and Valan's arm all constricting her throat until she began to black out.

He let her slide down the wall, stepped back and kicked her in the gut, forcing out the breath she'd inhaled. She saw something in him snap and curled into a ball, hands over her head and teeth clenched so she didn't bite off her own tongue.

It had been years since she'd taken a sustained beating. It was harder than she remembered; went on longer, too. It was Valan's own exhaustion that finally stopped him, when she was barely conscious and all she could hear was his panting and her own whimpering. Her ribs were on fire, her face swollen out of shape, and pain everywhere, in her hands and fingers where he'd kicked them, in her legs where he'd stamped, her spine and arse and shoulder blades.

He crouched and got her in a headlock, dragged her to the cot and threw her on to it. He shouted something and the door banged open and three Raiders piled in, pinning her belly down, legs splayed. Adrenaline cut through the fog and she thrashed between them like a fish on the line.

"No. Get your fucking hands off me! *No! No!*"

They leant their weight on her while Valan threaded a length of rope through her collar and forced her hands up to her neck and bound them behind her head. She screamed again as they bent her cracked elbow. The other Mireces cautiously let her go and Tara rolled on to her side and kicked at them, forcing them away. They retreated and Valan dragged her up to sitting. He waved them back out and she saw the disappointment on their faces.

She spat blood at him and worked at the ropes tying her wrists to the collar, but they were far too tight to wriggle free, even if she'd had the strength. All her hurts came back in a rush, breaking over her head like a storm so a long, drawn-out whimper clawed out of her throat.

Valan stood over her and the violence inside him was tethered and dragged back into the darkness as though it had never been. "You could have had it all," he said softly. "Freedom, a good man by your side and in your bed, children. Power and wealth. Instead you threw it all away and sided with the slaves you're so much better than. And you lied to me; for months you lied. *You're mine*, and yet you made a fool out of me."

Tara was bleary with concussion, but she knew she hadn't been out of it for more than a few hours. The rebellion would still be going, gaining momentum every hour Valan was here instead of out there leading the defence. The longer she could keep him occupied, the better Vaunt's chances of securing the city and finding her. She just had to hold on and Tomaz would kill his way to her and together they'd tear this fucker limb from limb.

This is it, Tara. Say whatever you have to, but keep him talking.

She shook her head, letting bloody drool string from her mouth down on to her chest. "I don't belong to you or anyone, not even the Dancer. People are not—will never be—possessions. I'm not yours."

The stretch in her ribs from having her arms up was shortening her breath and blackness threatened the edges of her vision, but she plunged on. "You're a good man, Valan. A great man. Your devotion to Neela, to Kit and Ede, proves that. You loved them, looked after them, wanted nothing but a better life for them and you worked hard to provide that. Because you're decent and intelligent. Because you're kind."

Vomit scalded the back of Tara's throat, thicker than the hypocrisy. "And when they died you mourned them, as any good man would do. I watched you cry over them, Valan. I knew your grief. Yet here you are beating me senseless and threatening to kill my husband. That's not you, Valan. That's not who you are. I know it isn't. You're too good for this."

Valan sucked at a split knuckle as he studied her. "Mention my family again and I'll let the three outside come in here and do what they like to you," he said, his tone so casual it took her a second to process his words.

Tara didn't have to pretend to look frightened. "Your will, honoured," she said.

Valan grabbed her by her shirt and hauled her off the cot, expression twisting to rage again, as fast and unexpected as summer lightning. "Now you play the good slave? Now, after you attacked the Blessed One? After you crossed swords with me and tried to get Rill out of the city? *I would have given you everything!*"

There were tears in Valan's eyes more frightening than anything that had gone before and a cold, sick dread swamped Tara. "Honoured . . . Valan . . . please."

"You've ruined everything," he breathed into her ear, his cheek pressed to hers. Metal hushed on leather as he unsheathed his knife and Tara stumbled back, but the cot was in the way; there was nowhere to go.

She felt the blade, cold as death, slip beneath the hem of her shirt. "I'm sorry, honoured. I'm sorry, I'm sorry, forgive me, I beg you," she babbled, because keeping him talking was one thing, but being carved open was something far different. "I'll do anything."

The knife scored a cut along her ribs and Tara yelled and threw herself backwards on to the cot, got one leg up in a sort of barrier, but Valan scrambled on to her, evading her kicks, and pressed the edge of the knife against her throat above the collar.

"Don't."

The cell door banged open. "We've got him, Second. It's done, over. We've got the leaders and killed those who wouldn't surrender." Valan didn't break eye contact with her.

"Major Vaunt?"

"Yes, Second. Alive as requested."

Valan pressed the knife tighter as she moved on instinct. "Good." He put away the blade and leant forward, his belly against hers. "Take something from me," he whispered and kissed her mouth, "and I take something from you."

T ARA LAY ON THE cot facing the wall, beneath a stained blanket stiff with blood. She was watching the slow and stately progress of a spider as it spun its web in the corner for the flies that came to feast on the filth of the prison-barracks.

She'd been watching it for hours, unmoving as it created intricacy and beauty from nothing. From itself. If she stayed very still, and watched very hard, it was almost possible not to think—about how she'd failed, about what they'd done to Vaunt. How he'd screamed.

Valan was a different man now; there was nothing in there Tara recognised, nothing at all from the months she'd lived with him. All the cruelty and ruthlessness that the Mireces were famous for, which had seemed so lacking in him, the second who laughed and drank with her, who used her name as though she was a person, not an object, who casually asked her opinion and trusted her, was now distilled into its purest, poisonous essence and directed at Tomaz—to punish her.

Tara bit the inside of her cheek—hard—and focused on the spider. A fly alighted on her cheek next to her eye. The lid twitched and it droned away. *Don't go far, little winged nuisance. Spider's hungry.*

Three days so far, three days Valan had made her watch as the Mireces beat Tomaz into broken pulp. Three days during which they didn't even question him, didn't care what intel he had, what Tara offered to make them stop, even when she offered herself.

Three days they had bound her hands behind her head and walked her into Vaunt's cell and hadn't hurt her. Not even when she asked to take Tomaz's place or she threatened to end them all. Three days and Tomaz was barely human. Three days and the betrayal on his ruined face—the blame—had done its work.

She bit again, the skin raw and swollen, soft wet scabs inside her mouth, impossible to heal. The spider had finished another circuit of its web, building it that little bit bigger, delicate hairy feet placed so carefully only on the spokes, never on the veins between.

The sounds he made as they hurt him, as they forced themselves on him, the threats that became howls that became the sobs of a broken, traumatised thing far removed from the man she knew as three of them held him down and jeered, the fourth grunting away with a red face, his gaze locked with Tara's, lips writhed back in a smile, part pleasure, part hate.

Tara's palm slammed into the stone wall next to the web, three times fast and hard, deepening the bruise already blackening and swelling the heel of her hand.

The spider froze, its legs retracting. The web shivered, and Tara imagined that if her ears were good enough, she'd hear it jingle, a soft chiming like moonlight on water. She wondered what it sounded like to the spider when a fly flew into its trap.

Punishing Tomaz to remind Tara of her place. Reinforcing that she was property. A thing.

No. Not reminding me of my place. My place is pissing on their graves that I put them in. They're reminding me who I am. What I am. And what I will do to them.

She could still see Tomaz, still hear the echoes of his screams. One more tally to cross off, one more debt to pay back a hundredfold. Her own injuries meant nothing in the heat of her rage, a rage that would consume everything it touched. Because Tara was a fucking soldier and she would do her duty and that duty was to save Tomaz and kill Valan and every man who had hurt him. Kill them over hours, over days, kill them for every dead slave, every raped body, every lost child. Kill them until even she was glutted.

She blinked, eyes gritty from staring at the spider and its translucent, ephemeral web, its home built in squalor, its private slice of paradise amid her misery.

Duty.

Her spine protested as she rolled slowly on to her back, and all the many deep hurts, inside and out, woke at once and screamed for attention, as they'd done every day since this all began. Since they'd left her alive. Since they'd made her so very, very angry.

Tara gathered them in, all the hurts and humiliations, pulled them to her like armour, and she promised them vengeance.

MACE

Tenth moon, first year of the reign of King Corvus
The hill, edge of Deep Forest, Wheat Lands

"OH AYE, THEY'RE THERE, plenty of sentries, no fortifications as yet," Dalli said when she and the rest of the Wolf scouting party returned to camp. Any relief Mace felt at her safe return dissipated with her words.

She wiped rainwater from her face and snuggled into the blanket Jarl passed her. There'd been no let-up in the weather for three days and they were all of them soaked, cold and miserable, the leg-breakers and traps they'd laid in the ground before the hill filling with water, the grassland between sucking at their boots.

"They know we're here, but they don't seem to have any intention of marching up to meet us," she added. "About five miles south."

"Warlord, Chief, I want your best and quietest warriors," Mace said into the depressed quiet of his council. "Jarl, send a squad of sappers with them to probe the ground, and then get in there and sow a little silent mayhem. I want them waking up next to corpses tomorrow morning. Let's see if we can't provoke them into charging the hill, eh?"

"The Wolves have the trees on the western slope and the base of the hill and you, Warlord, deploy just above them," Hadir continued, pointing out the positions on the crude map they'd drawn on the wall of the tent. "You're the link between the Wolves and the Ranks and we need you to hold that line or they'll be cut off. As for the summit, Thatcher, you've got the centre; Jarl on the east. Physician, we'll require a field hospital on the flat at the rear; you'll have men to guard you."

The Warlord examined the map while he combed his beard with his fingers. "Good plan," he said. "And we hold these positions day and night until the battle comes? These killers we send in at dusk might provoke them a little too well."

Mace gave him an approving nod, more pleased than ever not just to have the fifteen hundred warriors on his side, but that Brid Fox-dream and Cutta Frog-dream knew the business of war as well as they did. He sucked his teeth. "Numbers?"

"Difficult to say," Dalli said. "We didn't get a full look through the weather. But from the spread and layout, I'd concur with Crys's previous estimate—around four thousand."

"Well, no offence but let's assume you're both wrong and they outnumber us two to one, because I think we all know this is the final gambit. We have to win, so I want us going over all the options. How do we neutralise their numbers? And, at the same time, how are they going to try and prevent us using the terrain to our advantage?"

"They'll try to counter our archers for the initial approach," Crys said when no one spoke. "They'll be under sustained arrow volley for most of the ascent, so the main body will carry their shields overhead while the front rank holds theirs to their chests in case we send arrows flat down the slope. They'll have their own archers on the flanks to try and keep ours pinned down. Might even send a second force through the trees first, get us to move our archers around and open up a gap they can exploit."

"Then our archers need to be mobile from the start. If you stick them behind wicker screens, they have to stay there or risk getting shot moving to a new location. Give us some Rank shields we can hide behind and we can shoot from wherever you need us," Ash said.

They went over the details twice more, teasing out plans and options, settling on a series of manoeuvres to counter suggested attacks, though when it came to it, it'd be the officer in the line who made the decisions based on the flow of battle. There was only so much these councils could plan for.

BLOODCHILD

The night was deep and the Krikite and Wolf ambushers had been gone some time before Mace called a halt. He stretched, groaning as his back clicked and a yawn rippled around the group.

"Any final thoughts?" Mace asked.

Ash coughed and held up his hand. "The, er, the other thing, General—Your Majesty? That we spoke about yesterday?"

Mace puffed out his cheeks, caution warring with instinct, but Dalli was nodding at him, her brows drawn together at his hesitation. Her words came back to him: *Tara would want you to, even if you don't. This is for her as much as them. Best to do it before the battle too, in case we're all dead.*

The corner of his mouth quirked at that. Ever the romantic was Dalli Shortspear. A grin spread over her face at his expression. He cleared his throat and blinked away tiredness.

"Gentlemen. And ladies," he added belatedly. *Brilliant start.* "In light of recent events and the sacrifices that are even now being suffered in Rilporin and elsewhere, and in honour and memory of those we have lost, Wolf and Rilporian alike, I have drawn up a law—the wording's a little rough, I have no idea how to properly announce these things—a law, in my capacity as both Commander of the Ranks and king-elect . . ." He stumbled to a halt.

Colonel Jarl and General Hadir exchanged alarmed glances. The Warlord evinced little more than polite interest, but Ash was watching him with unblinking intensity.

"Witnessed and agreed by Gilda Priestess as the only surviving member of the council of priests," he went on doggedly, and Ash's growing excitement was enough to lighten his tone, "I hereby declare that there is no lawful impediment to women joining the Ranks and serving in combat, as Major Carter has done and is no doubt doing even now with honour and fortitude." *And complete disregard for her superiors' orders.*

Ash's face fell and Crys frowned, puzzlement creasing his features. "What's wrong?" he began.

"Furthermore," Mace said, turning to face him and Ash, "the old-fashioned and ridiculous law against the marriage of couples of the same sex is hereby repealed. And I think, Major Tailorson, that because of that fact, Ash Bowman would quite like to ask you something."

The silence that fell in the tent was part disbelieving, part outraged, and a little delighted, but the shock and dawning panic on Crys's face made it all worth it. Ash took his hands and knelt, the effect spoilt as his knee squelched in the sodden ground. "Crys Tailorson, heart-bound, love of my life. Will you marry me?" he asked and there was a tremble in his voice he didn't try to hide.

Crys's mouth opened and closed a few times and Mace couldn't help but smile. Dalli's small, drenched figure pressed to his side and he slid his arm around her blanketed shoulder, pressing a kiss to the top of her head. "What do you think? Us next?" he whispered as Crys nodded in mute agreement and dragged Ash out of the mud and into a tight embrace. There were ragged cheers.

"Still no," she said. "If I marry you, *King* Mace, and it's a big if, you manipulative git, I'll do it after we've won. If I don't marry you, well, I don't have to wear the stupid hat, do I?"

"It's called a crown, my love," Mace said and her lips twitched as she tried to hide a smile, "and believe me, we're getting wed."

"Oh, are we now?" she began and he lifted her off her feet and kissed her, but then Gilda was bustling into the tent and peremptorily ordering everyone around, grinning so wide he was surprised the top of her head didn't come off.

Gilda prodded him in the arm and he put Dalli down with an embarrassed chuckle. "Thank you, Sire; it'd be a shame if the King of Rilpor missed the most significant wedding in his country's history—and one that will set a precedent among Rilporians that Wolves and Watchers have known for generations—because his tongue was down the Wolf chief's throat."

A blush heated his face, but Dalli was laughing and shooing the priestess away. "Go, go, marry the fools before one of them comes to their senses," she said, but from how tightly the two men were holding hands, sense didn't seem to be something they were worried about.

Mace snapped to attention, his staff following suit with expressions ranging from stolid disapproval to open delight, and they all stood quietly—stood as witness—as Ash Bowman, archer and Wolf, married Crys Tailorson, officer and god.

Whatever happened next, however long his rule lasted, Mace knew he'd done something good with his time as king. Or king-elect, anyway.

CORVUS

*Tenth moon, first year of the reign of King Corvus
Five miles from Deep Forest, Wheat Lands*

THE PRETENDER TO THE throne had laid his battle lines with care, expecting Corvus to walk into them and die like an untrained fool. Corvus didn't. He pulled up his army with five long miles between them and Koridam, and he set his own lines, placed his sentries and sent his scouts to check for movement. And he waited.

Koridam wanted to force a swift conclusion to this war; Corvus should probably want that too, but he had time before the Dark Lady's return to play cat and mouse for a while. The East Rankers had brought harvested crops, livestock and flour with them from Yew Cove, Shingle and Three Beeches, and the Wheat Lands were well named; his army wouldn't starve.

Corvus had roughly two thousand Mireces and the same again in East Rankers. Not a huge number, but scouts put Mace's forces at about the same, maybe fewer. It didn't seem like a lot to decide the fate of a country, but neither side had any more forces they could draw upon. This was it, the final, all-in gamble, only Corvus knew he held the winning hand, gifted to him by the gods Themselves. Still, over-confidence was unwise, hence his decision not to rush the enemy's position.

The hill Mace was perched atop like a cock on a shit heap was the only elevation for miles and it was backed by the leading edge of Deep

Forest—a clever avenue of retreat if they needed it. A small outpost of the forest cloaked the base of the hill to the west and that, no doubt, would be where the Wolves and some of the Krikites were stationed. The rest of the Krikites had the slope from the trees to the summit, with the Ranks commanding the top. It was simple and so it would work—unless Corvus could disrupt those lines, draw forces away from each other, separate the Wolves from the Krikites and the Ranks from everyone.

Fortunately, he had a plan to do just that. And afterwards, when the war was won and the Dark Lady returned in the body of his niece? Afterwards, Corvus would focus on rebuilding his army from converted warriors, Rankers and farmers to protect Rilpor from Listre and Krike. He'd rebuild until he was strong enough to take those lands for the Red Gods, for the Dark Lady who would walk this land clothed in flesh and related to him by blood, a link none would dare to question. He and Rill would rule together, united in love of the Dark Lady, reaping the rewards of all She had promised.

And he'd sire himself a few heirs, on his sister and others. That business with Valan had made him realise his legacy needed to be secured. Tett was a good second, but Corvus wanted his own blood to sit the throne after him. A dynasty like the Evendooms had been, only stronger. The line of Corvus, blood royal and blood divine, a line that would last forever.

No, Corvus was more than happy to wait as long as he needed to before the final battle. Everything was falling into place.

The king's good humour vanished as Baron, the new general of the much-reduced East Rank, trotted over. "They have the better ground, Your Majesty," he said, not for the first time. "I doubt they'll give it up."

"If they have the better ground, why the shit am I going to fight on it?" he growled. "We wait."

"Your plan is to lure them here?"

"My plan is to wait and respond to events as they unfold. If they want to force my hand, they'll have to do more than sit on a hill in front of a forest." He stared at the distant green and brown smudge. "That said, if they send scouts, we kill them. Kill anyone who comes within range. We don't want them getting a good look at us."

Baron looked as if he disagreed, but kept his opinion to himself. "Yes, Your Majesty," he said instead, saluted and marched away.

Tett was nearby, fixing the handle on his shield. "Do you have a plan, though?" he asked without looking up.

Corvus paused; he liked the man's silence, liked that he only spoke when he had something necessary to say. If he was asking now, he was genuinely curious—or concerned. He squatted down next to him and steadied the shield. "My plan is to drag this out as long as possible. Koridam did force my hand in this, attacking the two biggest towns outside Rilporin and killing the garrisons. If he'd stayed quiet, we could've waited until the Dark Lady was returned to us. Which is, of course, why the clever shit didn't wait. Even so, I can't say I'm not relieved to be out of that fucking palace. Pretty sure I was closer to death in there than I am out here."

"Valan," Tett said.

"And the Blessed One."

Tett grunted and tied off the leather wrapping the shield's handle. "And you think I'm less likely to stab you in your sleep than they are."

Corvus ran his tongue around his teeth and waited until the other man looked up. "I do."

The corner of Tett's mouth lifted. "Good, because I've no fucking interest in being king. As far as I'm concerned, I'm not your second; I'm your bodyguard. If I fail in my duty and you die, I won't take the throne. You'd do better naming Fost as second. He's slow but he's dependable, doesn't have the imagination to assassinate you, and even if he did, you'll keep me on as bodyguard and I'll make sure he fails."

"I will, will I?" Corvus asked, amused and only a little irritated at Tett's presumption.

The man shrugged. "Why not? You can afford me. More importantly, you trust me."

Corvus clapped him on the shoulder and stood. "I'll think about it," he said. Either Tett was telling the truth, or he was playing a very clever game. It would be interesting to see what happened next.

FORTY-SIX MEN WERE FOUND dead around their campfires and at their posts the next morning. Forty-six killed in silence, without anyone noticing. Not one had drawn a weapon in self-defence. The number didn't worry him so much as how it had been accomplished. There could be—there always was—only one answer.

"Fucking Wolves," he said to Tett and Baron, just the name enough to set his teeth on edge. "Always the fucking Wolves. Baron, get your men digging fortifications. I want a ditch and palisade up before dusk, big enough to shield us all as it's pretty fucking clear the sentries are as much use as Skerris's bloated corpse. Tett, send men out on every horse we've got. Squads of twenty. Kill any scouts or small patrols they come across. Poison the stream between us and them, too—we'll get water from that pond to the east. If they want to play games, that's fine with me."

"And tonight?" Baron asked. "We retaliate?"

Corvus bared his teeth. "Of course we fucking retaliate. I want your best ambush teams and sappers ready an hour before nightfall. They're to disable or destroy the traps dug into the ground in front of Koridam's line and then wreak some havoc among their sentries. I want more seeded between us and them to intercept any of their lot coming this way. And tomorrow night, and the night after and the night after that. And I want double the number of sentries on the palisade once it's up, day and night."

"Your will, Sire," Tett said.

The urge to go himself was strong, the urge to fight and kill again after months of inactivity making him restless, but he resisted. The time for recklessness was when the battle was joined and his blood was up and it was kill or be killed. If he died on some stupid scouting mission, the Mireces would lose the coming battle. And if they lost the battle, it wouldn't matter if Lanta was successful in bringing back their Bloody Mother, because there wouldn't be any faithful left alive to worship her. No, they needed him, his vision and presence, to stiffen their spines and show them how to win. Show them what victory looked like, and what a king looked like.

Tett followed Corvus to the edge of the encampment and around it, examining the corpses. Knife work, maybe spears. His second—*my body-guard*—carried his own shield on his arm and Corvus's slung on his back. He didn't look at the corpses—he looked at the Rankers and Mireces who'd been stationed nearby. He looked for rebellion, for the defiant eye and sullen voice. And he looked out across the rolling fields of stubble, crops harvested, hay stacked ready for winter, to the distant forest, the distant enemy.

Tett watched for danger, from wherever it might come. When it did, Corvus almost wasn't surprised. It was cleverly done, too, he had to admit. A brawl broke out thirty strides away, Mireces and Rankers in each others' faces, punches and insults being traded and drawing all eyes. All but Tett's. The man yelled a warning and Corvus spun and drew, but the Ranker was already dying on the point of Tett's sword. Another came on, another Ranker, and Tett barrelled into him shield-first, knocking him down and smashing the rim of the shield into his ribs, breaking bones and stealing breath. The man whooped, unable to scream or make his lungs work and then Tett passed Corvus his own shield and they stood back to back, waiting for more. There were no more.

The brawl nearby became a slaughter as the Rankers swapped fists for swords and fell on the Mireces. Were they Koridam's men, spies sent to sow discord and execute the high command, or were they Easterners who'd had enough of Mireces rule?

"Stand down," Corvus shouted as Rank officers began sprinting through the camp in their direction, yelling orders of their own. "Back off," Corvus shouted again and the Mireces tried to disengage without getting themselves killed. Others formed a shield wall and battered their way in between the fighters until the two sides were separated and restrained.

"Whose plan was this?" Corvus demanded, sword still in hand, shield ready. He looked at the Easterners first, but then swept his gaze across the Mireces too. An attempt had been made on his life—he'd assume nothing. "Tell me now and some of you will live."

"They just started throwing insults, Sire," one of the Raiders said. "Talking shit about you, about the Blessed One. Saying how the Dark Lady isn't going to come back, that their oaths don't mean anything with Her dead. Next thing I know, that little fucker there's trying to bite my fucking ear off."

The little fucker in question was a Ranker and the defiant eye was strong in him. "It's true, She is dead and nothing I promised Her means shit any more. I ain't dying out here for a fucking Mireces."

"Oh yes you are," Corvus said. "Not only are you going to die for me, you're going to have the honour of dying at my hand. Bring him here."

Three Rankers wrestled him forwards and before they'd even stopped moving Corvus had rammed his sword up under the ragged chainmail shirt. He kept pushing until half the length of the blade was in the man, the tip threatening to pop out through his neck or mouth.

The other Rankers who'd been fighting began babbling apologies and apportioning blame, a few of the Mireces too. Corvus selected the three loudest—two soldiers, one Raider—and killed them. The rest got the message and shut their mouths.

"The enemy is out there," he said when they were dead, gesturing with his red-clotted sword. "Fight them, not each other. If this happens again, you will live to regret it, over days that feel like years. That is my promise to you. I want the dead hung from spears at each corner of the camp for all to see—and I want everyone to know why I killed them. Know that I will not forget your faces. Do not give me cause to doubt you again."

RILLIRIN

Tenth moon, first year of the reign of King Corvus
Red Gods' temple, temple district, First Circle, Rilporin, Wheat Lands

TARA WOULD HAVE BEEN so disappointed if she'd known that Rillirin's escape had lasted only minutes after all she'd suffered and done to free her, but Tara was dead. She'd died trying to save her, trying to get her out of the city that wanted to steal her child and perform blood magic that would see it twisted into something monstrous. And because Rillirin hadn't run far enough or fast enough, that was exactly what was going to happen. She'd passed Tara's corpse, bloody and tumbled lifeless among the others in the square, when Valan dragged her back in through the South Gate.

Rillirin paced the small room in the temple where she'd been confined ever since. There was a tiny window high up near the roof, the opening filled with expensive glass in many colours so that when the sun shone through it cast puddles of rose and sky and forest and sunset on to the floor. It marked the passage of time and the passage of days. Six so far. Ten since Corvus had marched out to fight Mace and the Rank and the Wolves and the Krikites and the Fox God and the calestar—her calestar, her Dom. Would it have happened yet, the battle? How far exactly was Deep Forest? Who would win? How soon would they have news and would Valan bother to tell Rillirin once he did?

And always, over and over in an endless loop in her head: what were they going to do with her now? Valan couldn't perform the ritual; he hadn't the first idea how to go about it. The Blessed One and Gull had kept it secret, although she wasn't sure whether or not Gull still lived. Tara had hurt him, but had she killed him? Rillirin didn't know and no one was prepared to enlighten her. But as much as she told herself it was over, that there was nothing more they could do to her, she didn't believe her own lies. They'd be out for vengeance, one way or another—it was in their nature. She'd dared to run; Tara had dared to rebel. They wouldn't let that lie. Not ever.

The men who brought her food and took away her chamber pot wouldn't speak to her. No one would speak to her. Valan had been tight-lipped with anger and grief, bloody-handed from killing. He'd run her down like a deer and then hauled her back all in murderous silence. The only voice Rillirin had for company was her own, so she spoke aloud to the babe and Dom and the gods and Tara's memory. She prayed and sang and she paced her room until she was dizzy from turning around every six steps and her back ached. Then she lay on the cot and told the squirming life inside her bedtime stories half remembered from when she was a bairn, making it up where she forgot the details.

And she watched the rainbow on the floor as it slid from one wall to the other and then vanished. Another day done.

"Few more days and Mace is going to march on this city and demand its surrender and Valan will have no choice but to open the gates and let him in. And your da will be with him and he'll come and find us, and by the time you're ready to be born we'll be safe at home in the Wolf Lands, in the winter village with Grandma Gilda and Auntie Dalli and all the rest."

The babe kicked in hearty agreement, up under Rillirin's ribs into her heart, and she winced, arching her back to try and shift the foot somewhere less painful. "What are your feet doing up there?" she groaned. "You do not need to be head down yet."

But the babe had other ideas, it seemed, for Rillirin's womb tightened, a ripple of pain from her back to her navel, harder, longer and more intense than any practice pain before. She rode it, trying to remember to breathe. Breathing made it hurt less, they said, as it hurt more, and then more, and then slowly, slowly drained away.

"Well, that wasn't fun," she muttered. She stood and walked, trying to ease the ache low in her back, pausing to gulp water from the pitcher on the table, still cold from the well. "I could do without another one of those until twelfth moon."

But the leading edge of the light pattern on the floor had barely advanced when another one struck, just as long, just as hard, leaving her panting, sweat on her upper lip. "Not. A good. Idea," she grunted, massaging her back and seized with the need to walk again. She padded back and forth, resolutely refusing to entertain the possible. The probable.

Minutes dragged by and then it happened again, pain building at her core and muscles she'd never known she had spasming into life, stealing her breath and drawing her all unwilling into herself so she crouched, hands on the floor for balance, clenched splay-legged around the pain.

Breathe. Breathe!

She tried counting until it stopped but the numbers wouldn't line up.

"Practice pain, just a practice pain," she panted, taking her time getting up. Perhaps walking wasn't such a good idea. She just needed to lie down. Rillirin sipped some more water and retreated to her cot. She started to sing, her voice a little breathy, a trill of anxiety curling through the notes and making them waver. She watched the light cross the room and she counted the contractions until there was no denying it any longer: the babe was coming early. The babe was coming now.

And that's fine, she thought suddenly and struggled to her feet on a wave of giddy exhilaration. She pushed the room's tiny table and single chair against the door in paltry protection. *That's fine. You come as fast as you like, little warrior. Because if they miss your birth, they can't do anything, can they? The Blessed One said it had to be immediately after birth and even if Gull's still alive he won't be ready.*

Rillirin took deep breaths and then removed the too-tight, encumbering gown and wrapped the blanket around her instead against the chill. She rolled the gown into a long rope and wadded it at the bottom of the door to muffle any sounds she might make, and then retreated to the bed.

"Come on then, Wolf cub," she whispered. "If you're coming, come fast. Born and dedicated to the Light before they even know you're on your way. That'll fuck with their plans."

RILLIRIN'S BABE DIDN'T COME fast despite pacing and pleading. It was dusk before her waters broke and dusk was when the guards came with food. And so they did, unlocking the door and shoving on it, forcing away the furniture that blocked it before she could move it away and pretend that everything was fine, that nothing unusual was happening, that she wasn't in the middle of a contraction that made her want to scream.

They piled into the room with shouted threats and were brought to a halt by the pattering of liquid through the straw mattress on to the stone beneath, by the groan Rillirin couldn't suppress no matter how hard she tried.

"Use the fucking chamber pot," one shouted, pointing, but the other knew what he was looking at.

"Get Valan," he yelled. "Get Valan now! Bairn's coming." The first guard bolted as if Rillirin had grown claws and a tail. The second moved in closer and stood watching her as if he was at a difficult lambing.

"It's not," Rillirin tried but the man just smirked. "Please. Please don't let them hurt my baby."

"Shut up." He shifted, glancing back out of the room. Uncomfortable.

"Please. It's just a baby. It's innocent. Valan doesn't know what to do."

"I said shut up," he repeated, but he took a few steps towards the door. Eager for reinforcements.

Rillirin made herself sit up, the blanket falling to her waist and exposing her belly. She put a hand on the top curve. "Please, honoured," she whispered. Her lip wobbled and she dashed away tears and sweat. "Just let me go. Please."

He looked out through the door, looked back at her, and Rillirin's heart lifted. Then shouted voices and he went blank, stood up straight. Moments later, Valan pushed past. "Are you sure? She's early," he said but one look at the strain in her face and he knew. A gentle smile lightened his features. "Come on, sweetheart. Let's get you ready to meet the Dark Lady."

"I'm not going anywhere with you," Rillirin barked, putting as much strength as she had into her voice. "Whatever you think you're going to do, it won't work. It won't work, so just *leave me be*."

Valan crouched at her feet and put his hand on her knee; his knuckles were swollen and bruised, scabbed over. "Hush now, lass. Everything's going to be fine. I know you're scared and I know it hurts, but your body knows what to do. Just trust it."

"You know it hurts?" Rillirin demanded, undermined more than she wanted to admit by his tenderness. "How the fuck do you know how much it hurts?"

He slid one arm around her back and lifted; she had no choice but to stand. The blanket fell from her hips, leaving her clad in sodden linens, breast band and sweat. "I helped Neela birth both our daughters," he said, brushing her lank, damp hair back from her brow. "Let me help you, too. Trust me."

She was leaning on him and trying not to, but it'd been hours already and she was scared and he understood, at least some of it. *He's fucking Mireces. He's Valan, King's Second. He's not going to help me. He's going to steal my baby and give it to Gull who doesn't know what he's doing. What if it doesn't work?* A cold shiver racked her. *What if it does work, even without Lanta?* She couldn't bear the thought of either outcome.

"Leave us alone," she managed but then another contraction took her and she buckled under its strength. Valan held her, his arms strong and warm. He let her dig her fingers into his flesh, murmuring wordless sounds of comfort, counting her breaths with her, and by the time it passed she couldn't have let go of him if she wanted to.

Rillirin sucked in two deep breaths and then met his eyes. "Please, Valan," she whispered, using his name for maybe the first time in her life. Her voice was as cracked as a dropped pot, her words as useless, but she had to try. "Please don't take my baby away."

Valan took a little more of her weight and began walking to the exit. "Oh Rillirin, love, we're not taking her away. You're her mother. And soon you'll be the mother of our Mother and one of the most important people in the whole world. Come on, now, let's get you settled. It's all for the best, you'll see."

They shuffled out of the room that had been her prison for six days and the stench of the main temple, awash in rotten blood, smacked her in the face. She gagged and he paused, holding her while she retched. "We'll burn some herbs," he promised her, his voice gentle and soothing so she clung to it, to him, against her better judgement.

The main temple was gloomy but Mireces were hurrying through the shadows with tapers, lighting candles and rushlights and torches in brackets until the room was leaping with smoky light and the shadows lunged at her and pulled away with every breath of air. To the left of the godpool and its filthy, slopping liquid, two huge chalk circles had been drawn on the floor so that their edges touched. Candles placed at intervals around them awaited lighting and a brazier nearby cut the chill of the big open space.

Valan led her into the circle containing a blanket of undyed wool. "Sit, sweetheart," he said and helped her down. "There, just relax. I'll be back soon." Rillirin's fingers tightened on his arm without volition. "Don't be scared. I promise I'll come back. Stay here, all right?"

He stepped carefully over the chalk line, then gestured and a Mireces lit the candles around the circumference. "Don't leave," he told her and then vanished into the gloom, his hurrying footsteps echoing and bouncing from the walls.

Don't leave? Fat fucking chance.

Rillirin clambered back up to her feet and stepped off the blanket, but when the final wick flared into life the hairs on her arms and legs stood up as though she'd walked inside a lightning bolt. Her fingertips brushed the boundary of the circle and there was a spit and a hiss of sparks like knives rammed into her hand. She shrieked and pulled away and seconds later it didn't matter anyway—another contraction seized her and she was adrift on the sea of it, lost to its crashing rhythms, its great waves rushing down on her. When it was over she was on all fours, panting through the final seconds of the muscles easing.

Footsteps. She looked up, blurry with sweat, and a blue-clad figure stepped into view, moving slowly as if in pain. "So," the Blessed One said, her voice a rasp harsh as a death rattle. "The time has come."

TARA

Tenth moon, first year of the reign of King Corvus
South barracks, Second Circle, Rilporin, Wheat Lands

BEFORE THE DOOR WAS fully open, Tara was on her feet and backed against the far wall. Her fists were up, the fingers bruised and stiff, a couple broken, and her sudden movement had set off a coruscation of hurts inside and out. None of it would stop her fighting them. Nothing would ever stop her fighting.

This was the day she said no.

"No games," Valan said and gestured. Two men staggered into the room with a huge wooden tub between them. Steam rose from the water that half filled it. "Bathe."

She didn't move, didn't lower her fists. "What?"

"Bathe or Tomaz loses an eye, an ear, his tongue, his right hand—"

Tara choked on her helplessness. "All right! Stop, I'll do it." He wanted her clean. It sparked sickness in her, but it also meant Tomaz wasn't being hurt today. Valan and two others stood across the exit and if they thought Tara was going to be embarrassed they were very much mistaken. Moving slowly because of her broken ribs, she stripped the blood-encrusted shirt and trousers, slipped out of her filthy breast band and linens and stood facing them for a moment, head up and shoulders back. *This doesn't break me.*

You can't break me.

Valan was silent, examining the damage he'd inflicted with his fists and feet, the scars that were the legacy of her life as a soldier. He jerked his head at the bath and she climbed in, holding her breath against the glorious warmth. She sat with her back to them and quickly splashed her face, ducked her head under and scraped her fingers through the asymmetrical lengths of her hair. She came back up and flinched when a hand touched her bare shoulder.

Valan knelt at the side of the tub. He dipped soap into the water and then stroked it across her hair, massaged her head with gentle hands while she sat rigid, barely breathing. Had he done this for Neela? She snatched the soap and lathered her skin, ignoring the bruises, cuts and broken bones in her eagerness to keep his hands off her.

The water was filthy when they were done. Valan handed her a rough swatch of cloth and she scrubbed herself dry. He passed her fresh underwear and a gown, a rich purple darkening to blue at wrists and hem. It was truly beautiful and that made her nervous. This felt like more than Valan deciding to make her his bed-slave. This felt ... big. But whatever it was—death, rape or something else—if Valan thought she'd walk meekly to meet it he was very, very wrong.

The other two Mireces restrained her while Valan attached a chain to her collar and manacled her hands together in front of her. They pulled her out of the room that had been Dorcas's for so long and into the main barracks, crammed with every slave who'd rebelled and still lived: Merol the mason, chained at ankle as well as wrist to subdue him; Captain Salter of the West Rank and a few hundred soldiers; a score of slaves from the palace kitchens and more from across the city.

Most of them winced and wouldn't look at her, assuming she was being taken to witness more of Tomaz's torture, the torture all of them heard and none could prevent, including her. Shame wormed in her and she smothered it. Shame was their weapon and she wouldn't let it get its teeth in her.

Tomaz's cell door opened and she stiffened, balked, but this time Valan didn't shove her forwards. They waited as more Raiders emerged, dragging Tomaz between them. He was barely conscious, stripped to his linens so she could see every welt and deformity of shattered bone and torn muscle. A sob burst from her. "Tomaz?" she whispered.

Tomaz's head came up in response and he peered at her from one swollen eye. He tried to smile but his jaw was broken. "Tara," he slurred. She took a step forward and Valan's hand found her upper arm and dragged her to a halt. He shoved her into the embrace of the nearest Mireces.

"You are responsible for this," he said to her. "Your betrayal of me. Your betrayal of him." His knife took Tomaz under the ribs, sliding up into his chest cavity and cleaving stomach, liver and lung as he twisted and shoved. Tomaz stiffened, coughed, tried to inhale but managed only a sick wheeze.

"*No!*" Tara screamed and fought her way free, but Valan dragged her back again and Tomaz smacked into the stone, making no effort to save himself. She fought Valan, manacled hands clubbing at him and it took two more to hold her still. "Tomaz, Tomaz don't go. Don't leave me," she begged instead. "Please, love, please don't go." He was bubbling, hands moving weakly on his chest.

"Honoured Valan, I beg you. I beg you, honoured, let me go to him," Tara said, tearing her gaze from the dying man to plead. "Anything you want afterwards, but please, please let me go to him."

His eyes were narrow with calculation, but something in her face convinced him. "Don't get blood on the gown." He let her go and she fell to her knees by Tomaz's head, cradled it in her hands and leant down to press a soft kiss against his brow, her tears sparkling in his hair. "Hush, my love. Relax. Dancer's grace, Tomaz."

He tried to speak and blood, black and carrying his life within it, flowed from his mouth. She wiped it away. "Sshh, it's all right. Look for the Light, Tomaz. Can you see it? It's right there. Go on now, love. Go and be free."

His lips moved and she pressed close to listen to the last words he'd ever speak. When she sat back he was dead. When she sat back, the last restraint on Tara's vengeance was gone.

"Rankers!" bellowed a voice from the far end. "Rankers, atten-shun!" Dotted among the prisoners, scores of beaten, stick-thin figures rose from their beds and stood, staring straight ahead. The Mireces shouted threats and drew steel, but the soldiers didn't so much as blink.

"Rankers, honour!" Every soldier raised his right hand—or his left if his right was missing—and tapped it three times against his heart.

"Rankers, about face!" With some shuffling, the soldiers turned their backs to Tara's grief, to Valan their enemy, respect for Vaunt perfectly balanced with insult to the Mireces. Slowly, grunting at the pain of it, Merol the mason stood and turned his back, and then dozens of others joined the soldiers. Not everyone—most were too frightened, too traumatised—but some.

"See the honour they do you, my love?" Tara whispered, but Tomaz couldn't see. Tomaz would never see anything again, not this side of the Light. "Wait for me," she breathed. "I won't be long." She kissed his brow and laid him down and advanced until she was toe to toe with Valan.

"King's Second, Valan of Crow Crag, coward and murderer. I am going to kill you."

An unknown emotion flickered across his features and was gone too fast to identify. "And there she is," he said softly. "The real Tara Vaunt. A pleasure to meet you."

"My name is Major Tara Carter of His Majesty's West Rank, though it was my honour to call Tomaz husband in all but name. Now get the fuck out of my way."

"Rankers, about face," Captain Salter shouted again and they moved like a shoal of fish to face inwards. "Officer present. To the front . . . salute!"

She nodded at Salter as she passed and then, for the first time in days, she was outside, in cold wind and grey rain. Tara tilted her head back and breathed in the clean air, unmindful of Valan and the other Mireces crowded around her.

Dozens more were stationed outside and Valan ordered them to bring the prisoners chained in lines of fifty. *It's coming, Tomaz, I can feel it. Whatever this is, it's the final cast of the dice. I'll be ankle deep in their blood before I'm done, I swear it.*

They never should have killed you, my love, not if they wanted to live.

TARA WOULDN'T LET THE ice inside her melt and spill its load of hurt as they made their slow march east through Second Circle. Instead she focused on where they were going, and was dully unsurprised when they took the gate into the temple district in First Circle and headed for the main temple, joining the slow trickle of Mireces and slaves moving in the same direction.

Her mouth was dry as Valan pulled on the chain and dragged her forward. She was going to be sacrificed, then. She flexed her fingers. She was fast, despite everything they'd done and all her wounds, and she was righteous. She'd have his knife out and in his throat before he felt her on him. It didn't matter what happened after that, but she'd taste Valan's death on her tongue before they killed her.

A guttural wail sounded up ahead and Valan quickened his pace and they came to the centre of the temple, brightly lit with flame and bunches of herbs burning in braziers. The light was enough to show her Rillirin, writhing in pain in a chalked circle.

"Rillirin? When did . . ." She trailed off as she identified the woman standing close by, leaning her weight on a staff and sallow beneath the black swirls of blood. Lanta.

The ice cracked and flashed to steam beneath a torrent of red-hot rage. At Valan, at Lanta, at herself. "*No*. You said she was dead," Tara snarled, turning on him.

Valan looked back. "No. *You* said she was dead; I just let you believe it. Like I said, you could have had everything I could give you, a place in our world, a place at my side. Instead you betrayed me. Your own actions led you here."

He unlocked the chain and manacles and Tara snatched for the knife in his belt as she rammed her knee up into his groin. The blade came out and she stabbed back upwards for his throat as he doubled over. Valan swung the chain at the same time she kneed him and the heavy iron manacle smashed into her head and threw off her aim—the knife fish-hooked him, slicing through the corner of his mouth and splitting it wide in a bloody smile.

Three men wrestled her into the circle next to Rillirin's, and another hurriedly put a lit candle in its place around the edge, completing a ring of fire that danced over Tara's skin, a sudden taste of metal in her mouth and a fierce pounding at her temples gone as quickly as it had come.

She lunged for him but fat sparks of lightning erupted and flashed through her bones as she reached the boundary and she fell back with a shriek. She threw herself at the barrier again, and again the shock of light and pain stopped her. She probed the edges, growling and stalking like a caged animal, but there seemed no way through. The Mireces mostly ignored her—they trusted the barrier.

"I thought you were dead!" Rillirin called, sitting up on the blanket. There was such hope blazing in her face that Tara almost had to look away.

"Seems I'm not the only ghost here," she said, trying for confidence and falling far short. "Chin up; it's not over yet." If Valan and Lanta heard her, they gave no sign, but Rillirin brightened. Poor girl obviously thought Tara was here to help her.

"You're sure, Valan?" Lanta was saying. "Once you cross the barrier, you cannot come back until the rite is complete. The circles are tuned to the gods Themselves, but the lightning will hurt to pass through."

"I understand, Blessed One," Valan lisped, hand pressed to his face. "There's no midwife, but I was at the births of both my girls. I know what to do." She nodded and Valan pinched the lips of the wound together, took a deep breath and then crossed the chalk line into Rillirin's circle. Lightning flared as it had around Tara's. Rillirin cried out, but then Valan was by her side and the wound in his face had burnt shut. He was shaking uncontrollably, but he was through. So it was possible—for people, apparently, but not for gods.

Interesting.

"Bring me that babe," Lanta said huskily. "I will bring Holy Gosfath. I will bring the Dark Lady and we will have victory over Gilgoras and the so-called Gods of Light."

All right, Carter, you're a stubborn bitch. You're not going to let something like a blood ritual and an almost impenetrable circle stop you, are you? Get to work.

The rest of the prisoners were shuffling in, in long lines joined by a chain through the loops on each collar, herded by Mireces armed with spears. Each end of the chain was locked to a steel spike driven into the ground: the prisoners could move along the line but not off it.

It was ill thought out with too few guards. Tara could already see how they could effect an escape, but the prisoners closest were civilians and she didn't know how to tell them what she needed them to do.

The first prisoner's collar was unlocked from the chain and he was brought forward and bent back over the altar by Gull. Lanta chanted a prayer as she plunged a knife into his throat and let the blood spill into a wide bronze bowl. A Raider snatched it up and sloshed it into the god-pool. Fast and unfussy, more slaughter than ritual but no less obscene for all that.

Gull tumbled the man off the altar and beckoned for the next, but the prisoners were milling and scrambling backwards to the other end of the chain, those at the front fighting, clawing at their necks.

The next prisoner was wrestled free, those behind beaten on to their knees, dazed and docile for when their turn came. A woman this time and she was screaming before she even reached the altar, writhing in the Mireces' grip and begging, begging. She died.

Tara looked at the faces of the prisoners—individual Rankers separated by civilians. Whoever had chained them had been trying to keep the soldiers apart so they couldn't organise to fight back. Salter was there and he was pulling at the prisoners around him, talking urgently, gesturing at the chain, the spikes securing it.

Yes, Salter, yes. Do it, fucking do it—get off the line and kill them all. Come on, come on!

A guard saw what Salter was doing and smashed his face with his spear, kicking him on to his back, the collar cutting into his neck and the necks of those closest, pulling them all down to the ground. While everyone was distracted another's collar was removed and he was hauled forward, drained and thrown to one side. Lanta's droning prayer had yet to cease. In the next circle Rillirin was on her feet, Valan supporting her and massaging her back. Her red hair had darkened with sweat and her face was shiny with it.

"She's barely dilated," he called to Lanta. "Could be hours yet."

The Blessed One lifted a hand in acknowledgment and signalled for the next sacrifice to be brought forward. There were plenty.

EIGHTY-SIX HAD DIED AND the godpool was viscous with blood. Tara had probed every part of the circle again in the preceding hours and all she'd managed to do was give herself a vicious headache and make her fingertips numb from repeatedly pushing against the lightning barrier. She hadn't found a soft spot in the barrier—it seemed Valan had simply muscled through.

She'd have to do the same, and do it now, because Rillirin needed to push.

Tara glared at Salter; he gave the smallest shake. They still weren't ready. She stalked the circle some more until something grazed her foot. She blinked, rubbed tenderly at her swollen eyes, blinked again, but the haze was still there. Columns of red mist were coalescing, swirling and fizzing with fat sparks of purple lightning darting within them. And they'd touched her.

"He comes," Lanta called, throaty with need, with exaltation, and Gull gave an inarticulate shout of glee. "Holy Gosfath, Lord of War, answers our prayers. He comes to summon His Sister-Lover home." She wobbled away from the altar with a brass bowl brimming with blood and came to Tara's circle.

"Can you feel Him?" she asked. "His presence grows. He has been summoned by blood and answers that summons. He comes to claim His reward." She threw the blood, a great scarlet arc that splashed Tara's face and hair and chest, hot and sticky and clinging. She gasped and reeled back, scraping it from her eyes and spitting, retching. The red columns swirled faster, thicker, blunt questing snouts wavering through the air towards her. Tara skipped away from them, flicking blood from her hands.

"Holy Gosfath, Lord of War," Lanta shrieked, dropping the bowl and raising her arms, "come to Gilgoras, to this holy temple dedicated to your glory. Come for your Sister-Lover. Come for your prize." Her left hand dropped and pointed at Tara. "Come and feed, Red Father!"

"Oh, holy shit," Tara breathed as it all came together: why Valan had left her alone after the initial attack, the bath, the perfect gown. "You are fucking kidding me."

One of the red snakes touched her ankle, oily and cold and hot at once. Alien and foul and somehow *interested*. Tara leapt back and three more slithered for her while in the centre of the circle a shape began to form, twice her height.

"She's crowning," Valan yelled and Rillirin was roaring as she pushed and then the Ranker had the chain free of the spike at the farthest end of the line.

"*Go, go, go!*" Salter screamed and the prisoners turned around and sprinted together, yanking the thin chain through their collars and off even as the Mireces realised what was happening.

BLOODCHILD

It was too late for Tara. Her circle was filling fast, the shape inside the red mist solidifying, a sudden hot wind stinking of sulphur blasting through the temple from everywhere and nowhere and stinging her eyes. The tentacles or snakes or whatever they were nosed across the ground and found her foot. A score more whipped forward and latched on to it, smoke and char rising as they burnt at her boot.

She yelped and kicked free, dodged more that were solidifying from the stone or out of the air, spun to the edge of the circle and there he was, Gull, backing from the onrushing prisoners and the Mireces trying to stand against them, his hammer and knife raised.

You want to eat someone, Gosfath? Here you go.

Howling, Tara shoved her arm through the barrier—purple lightning roasting her bones—and got a finger in his collar. Not impenetrable, just fucking painful.

He was a killer, was the high priest, but he wasn't a fighter. Tara hauled him into the circle, disoriented and shrieking at the fire burning through him. She spun Gull around and slammed her fist into his stomach; he folded like cheap tin over her arm. She tore the knife from his grip and slammed it into his spine, grinding over a vertebra and then punching in midway down his back. His legs stopped working. She let him fall, snatched the hammer from his limp hand and retreated towards Rillirin's circle.

I can do this. I can still do this.

They'd tried to break her. Maybe they'd even succeeded, but it just meant they'd stripped away her softness, her mercy, and fashioned her into a weapon. And it was time. This was her fulfilling the Fox God's requirements. This was Tara's redemption and Vaunt's justice. This was fucking *war*.

Tomaz's last words to her, bubbled up with the blood as he died, more a man then than at any time in his life: "I love you. Kill them all." Tara had sworn she would, and Tara was keeping her promise.

The figure in the red haze was clear now, all slabbed muscle and curving horns and hating, wanting eyes. Hands bigger than Tara's head lifted Gull into the air and the last few smoke-tentacles wrapped around him and began squeezing, probing, *entering* him, draining him of blood and life as he cracked and broke in ways that no body should ever move, Gosfath becoming more and more real with every passing second.

When Gull was a shrivelled husk, the last tendrils absorbed back into His body and the god let out a roar of triumph. He saw Tara and the blood coating her was a beacon, an irresistible lure. He came for her, wading through the rising black smoke while, behind Him, prisoners wrenched weapons from the Mireces' hands and turned them on their owners and Valan screamed at Lanta to come into the circle and take the baby that was even now being born.

And that was the moment she'd been waiting for. Valan and Lanta in the circle together, preoccupied with Rillirin. Ripe for the killing. Tara ran at the intersection of the two circles, arms protecting her face, and bulled her way through. More purple light inside her and outside, her blood boiling in her veins and her eyes, face, world on fire, and she was out of Gosfath's reach. And her targets were within hers.

RILLIRIN

*Tenth moon, first year of the reign of King Corvus
Red Gods' temple, temple district, First Circle, Rilporin, Wheat Lands*

THE URGE TO PUSH was overwhelming, a force that Rillirin couldn't deny, lost in its grip. Movement, downward pressure, fire burning at her centre, in the very core of her and she screamed, guttural as an animal, as she crowned.

She paused, panting, sweat and smoke and blood stinging her eyes. Valan knelt between her thighs as pandemonium erupted throughout the temple. The prisoners were free and Gull was dead, maybe, and there was a god in the next circle with Tara, and Rillirin couldn't look at it or her heart would stop.

The urge to push was building again, demanding the very last dregs of her strength, and Rillirin could do nothing but obey the ancient command. Gritting her teeth, head thrown back and another braying shriek tearing from her throat, she pushed and pushed until something slithered between her thighs and into Valan's waiting hands.

She fell back, panting, but only for the space of a few breaths and then she was struggling on to one elbow, reaching out. "Give . . . give it to me."

Valan was crying as the cupped the tiny form. "A girl," he murmured. "Oh, she's perfect. Oh sweetheart, look what you've done."

"Give . . . please," Rillirin tried, but Lanta thrust herself into the circle with a screech similar to Rillirin's. She dropped to her knees at Valan's side, shuddering through the pain caused by the barrier. Her hands were shaking as she tied off the birth cord and cut it with a knife. She scooped the child out of Valan's hands.

"No," Rillirin croaked, but hadn't even the strength to shout. "No," she tried again and got back to her elbow, drew up her legs and shoved up to sitting. Valan lifted Lanta to her feet and the Blessed One hobbled to the intersection with the other circle, out of reach of Rillirin's grasping fingers. Rillirin's muscles were already shuddering with effort, but she scrambled on to hands and knees and dragged herself forwards.

Valan caught her and drew her to his chest, holding her as tenderly as he had her daughter. "You did so well," he whispered, pressing kisses to her hair and temple. "You did so well, sweetheart. I'm so proud of you."

"Dark Lady, beautiful goddess of death and fear, marshal now your great strength and let your Brother-Lover be your guide. Come to us, come to this circle we have prepared for you, come to claim the flesh that will be yours." Lanta's voice was tremulous with passion and exhaustion as she held the baby out in front of her in shaking arms. The black mist swirled faster but then the circle flared purple again and Tara came sailing through, skidding across the stone and through Rillirin's blood.

Lanta ducked, clutching the baby to her chest, as Tara screamed at the pain of the magic. Valan let go of Rillirin and reached for her on instinct. She rolled to a stop and then threw herself at him, the pair of them crashing into the stone, the ritual itself crashing to a halt.

"Lord, Red Father, your reward is here. Just . . . just give me a moment," the Blessed One babbled. "Valan, get her back through."

Gosfath crouched and watched them, then indicated the babe instead, beckoned with talons as long as Rillirin's palm. "Want."

"No, Lord, this is the vessel that will house your Sister-Lover. This is the flesh that will become the Dark Lady. This one is not for you. *Valan, get her back in the fucking circle now.*"

Tara headbutted Valan and chopped a hand into his throat, roaring curses, and Rillirin was standing, swaying, naked but for a breast band and blood and fluid streaking her thighs. As the Blessed One gaped at the collapse of all her plans, Rillirin prised her fingers away and slid the babe, still slippery with blood, out of her arms.

"*No!*" Lanta screeched, wrapping Rillirin and the child in her arms and throwing herself backwards in a frantic surge. Together, they tumbled into the gods' circle.

The world blared with light and noise and dark and silence, an instant of assault on her senses so complete Rillirin didn't know up from down or life from death. Every bone and muscle juddered with lightning and pain and the babe's scream was sudden and piercing and nearly stopped Rillirin's heart. And then they were through and Gosfath was there, right there, and Lanta too, and Gull's shattered corpse.

Rillirin was on her side, her daughter pressed wailing to her breast and her knees drawn up to shield her, and curling towards them was a thin, questing black filament. She jerked back, scuttled on heels and one hand away, realising too late she was moving closer to the circle's centre instead of its perimeter.

"Dark Lady, beautiful goddess of death and fear, see now your new host, of blood royal and blood god-touched. Come to the world, to us your faithful children, to Holy Gosfath, Lord of War. Come to your new flesh, your new life. Come for vengeance, Lady, come for blood!"

Lanta had hold of Rillirin's ankle and was dragging herself up her leg, face ablaze with foul exaltation. The black smoke was writhing faster, groping blindly ever closer, and Rillirin kicked off Lanta's hands and made it to her feet, her womb tightening again as the afterbirth began to move. She sagged, grinding her teeth as the pain ripped through her, and as she did the black essence struck out, faster than a kestrel's stoop, and speared into her child's tiny, fluttering chest.

Rillirin didn't think: she just grabbed at the black tentacle, shrieking as pain ripped up her arm, and she yanked it out.

"Yes, Mother, yes," Lanta was calling. "There it is, your host. Your flesh. Take it and return to us. Holy Gosfath, your prize is here, right here." Lanta pointed, her other hand up in defence. "*Now, Valan!*"

"Want." Gosfath's rumble became a roar and dagger-sharp talons cut through the air towards Rillirin. His index finger just caught her sweaty braid, snipping it without effort and driving on through her cheek and the bridge of her nose. Rillirin almost didn't feel it, but then blood poured down her face.

She ducked as He took one massive stride across the diameter of the circle and His other hand came for her. Lanta was advancing from her other side, grey, one hand clutched to her chest, her faith all that was keeping her upright. Black smoke writhed around her feet, tangling them.

"Head down," a voice yelled and Rillirin curled in on herself as arms wrapped around her and dragged her through the boundary again. More purple roiling hissing lightning that burnt her skin and ratcheted the babe's cries up into screams again, the unmistakeable scorch of burning flesh and an exquisite pain in her face and hand as they cauterised, and they were falling backwards in Tara's arms.

They landed hard, forcing a pained grunt out of Tara before she shoved them gracelessly away and scrambled to her feet, putting herself between them and Valan. The babe's tiny chest was intact, no blood except the birth blood, though a black mark, its edges ragged and broken, discoloured her skin. And her eyes weren't the blue of a newborn's. They were as black as the Dark Lady's Herself, black and piercing and looking right at her, unwavering, focused.

Oh gods, oh Dancer and Trickster, please, please no. Please.

Valan got one finger in Rillirin's silver collar but then Tara was on him, locking her arm tight around his throat and hauling him backwards and then running him at the barrier. She turned her face away as she shoved Valan's head into the lightning and held him there, her arm in it too but Valan was screaming and screaming and screaming, the skin on his face blackening, cooking, cracking open to reveal red flesh beneath and the circle's barrier began to flicker as his feet flailed and drummed and his thrashing weakened and he broke the magic that tried to contain them. The smell of burning hair, cooking meat, and then purple-edged flames billowed up from his face and head and Tara dropped him and staggered back, cradling her blistered, charred arm against her chest.

"Fucking move," she croaked at Rillirin. The circle was sputtering, flickering, the barrier breaking down so they could cross it without it hurting the babe. Tara spared a glance at Valan's final twitches. "For Tomaz."

"Bloody Mother, I am your faithful servant," Lanta began to yell as Tara put her good hand in Rillirin's armpit and heaved her up to her feet. The Blessed One was stumbling around the edge of the circle, clutching at her chest as if about to topple over.. She glanced down and deliberately scuffed her foot through the chalk line, screeching as her form was outlined in purple fire.

"All this I have done for you," she gasped as she recoiled, "all this, bound your Brother-Lover here as a light to guide you, ripped Him from beyond the veil so that you might find your way to us. Take me. I am your willing servant, will be the body you need, Lady. I will be anything you need."

"Tara, wait. Look." The black smoke solidified into tentacles again, punching into the Blessed One at breast and belly and thigh, in and out like stitches through her torso, her jaw and ear, her left eye until she was pinned, lifted and flung wide, suspended and splayed and screaming. Gosfath lurched back.

"Yes, yes, my lady. *Take me!*" Lanta shrieked, her words distorted by the thing in her mouth and face, but they could hear it in her tone, the ecstasy of agony, of all her plans come to fruition. The Dark Lady returned.

Tara grabbed the knife out of Valan's belt and put herself between Rillirin and the gods. "Move," she whispered, but Rillirin didn't. Couldn't, pinned as surely as Lanta was by the spectacle.

"No." The voice was low and female and hungry, so terribly hungry. Seductive enough that Rillirin took a single step towards the black vortex, to give herself and the babe both to that voice that didn't come from anywhere. Her mind shrieked at her to stop, but her body wasn't obeying. Tara followed; all the survivors did.

Another tendril wrapped around Gosfath's fingers and hand, coiling gently up His arm in a loving embrace as if inviting him to join in while the rest twisted, twining, filling Lanta to the brim as she screamed, not in exaltation now but in fear, in pain, in agony.

A silent moment of stillness, and then the muscular black coils tensed, gripped, *flexed*, and they ripped her apart. Chunks of flesh and bone and a spray of blood erupted from the circle, splattering Tara, Rillirin and the surviving prisoners.

Tara wiped bits of Blessed One off her face and began to laugh, a wheezing, sick laugh, but laughter nonetheless. "That'll do," she choked with approval. "I'm counting that as mission fucking accomplished. It's over. There's no one for Her to—"

The voice came again. "All failed me. All had form when I had none. Now I will take a new one and shape it to my will. So, Brother, serve me one last time."

The tentacles looped around Gosfath tightened and then drove inside Him, more and more seeping from the stones and sublimating from the air, wrapping and constricting, breaking and remoulding, and Gosfath was roaring, tearing at the black stuff but it tangled around His talons and His hands and His arms, smothering until He was the red core of a black whirlwind.

"You are shitting me," Tara breathed, breaking the spell transfixing Rillirin. "Bloody move." Rillirin did, holding her breath as she crossed the chalk line, now emitting little more than a flicker of energy, towards the huddled mass of surviving Rankers and those civilians who hadn't fled.

They got halfway to the exit when Rillirin stopped again, barely able to hold her daughter's delicate weight, let alone support herself on her feet. "I can't," she said, tiredness pressing down, the siren song of sleep echoing in her ears.

Tara glanced at the madness behind them and grabbed Rillirin's chin. "You fucking can, and you know why? Because what you did in there was one of the most courageous things I've ever seen, and I've seen a lot. And because this little one needs you to be that woman again, every day until she's old enough to take care of herself. So start walking."

"Yes, sir," Rillirin said, shaky of voice and of legs. She too looked back as they reached the temple doors, over Tara's shoulder as she herded her on, the woman's expression set in a grim rictus amid the bruising. The circle was a whirling maelstrom of red limbs and black smoke and fat purple sparks, sheets of light so bright they threw everything into stark relief, shadows blacker than pitch, blacker than her daughter's eyes. It crossed the barrier of the circle about where Lanta had scuffed the chalk. It was out. The godpool heaved and cracked and split, scummy water sloshing across the temple floor, driving a wave of sacrificial blood before it.

They piled through the door and slammed it shut on the slaughter-house, blinking in the light of an early morning. "South Gate," Tara said in a voice that brooked no dissent, "and as quick as you like. Salter, you've got point."

"Form up," a man roared in response. "South Gate, on the double."

But they hadn't even made it to the bottom of the steps when the ground shuddered and broke beneath their feet and the temple doors blew open. Tara sprinted back and slammed them, but from the look on her face what she'd seen inside wasn't good.

"South Gate, Salter. That is a fucking order. Go."

The split was widening right in front of them, as though something wanted Rillirin and her daughter, as though it wasn't done with them yet. Buildings were tumbling like stormwrack all around them.

Salter looked at Tara and something passed between them Rillirin didn't understand. He threw the sword he'd taken from a dead Mireces towards her, spinning across the cracking steps. Tara nodded. "Get her to Mace, get her to the king," she bellowed. "Follow Corvus's trail: go."

Some of the soldiers jumped the gap and Rillirin began to protest but Salter wrapped his arm around her waist and flung them both across the tear in the stone. Those waiting on the other side dragged them to safety and, without pause, the soldiers formed up and began to move, Rillirin in their midst. She looked back.

Tara was pressing her weight against the temple doors. "Go, and Dancer go with you," she yelled, waving them off.

"Tara? *Tara, no,*" Rillirin cried, voice so hoarse it couldn't cut through the rumbling of the earth, the sounds of splintering wood and falling stone. "Come with us!"

Salter peeled his filthy shirt off and forced it over her head. She got her free arm through, kept the left tucked inside against the cold, her daughter at her breast, tiny and hot, a mere scrap of life. It cut the wind a little. "Come on, miss," he said, already shivering, "we've clothes, weapons and food to find, then we'll get you safe out of here." He put his arm around her, made her walk away. "Major Carter will find another way around, no doubt. We'll see her soon enough. Come on."

Rillirin, numb with fatigue and an excess of fear, had thought she had no emotions left. But as they staggered away from the temple and Tara, trapped with mad, bloodthirsty monsters, alone but for Mireces and the dead, she found that there were, after all, still tears to be shed.

THE BLESSED ONE

The moment of awakening
The Afterworld

L ANTA SAT UP. THERE was an instant of dislocation, the memory of exquisite agony commingled with unutterable glory as she stood in the very presence of both her gods, and then . . . she was here.

The grass was grey and speckled with sticky red droplets. The sky was crimson, as red as the sun through closed eyelids. The permanent dying of the light. Everywhere Lanta looked she saw people. Souls. Those faithful children of Blood who had died in the hundreds of years before her and now thronged the Afterworld.

Death was not to have been Lanta's fate at this time, and yet here she was. The Lady's will. She brushed herself down and stood, tossing back long blonde hair. When a Blessed One was called to the gods' side, the Dark Lady Herself would greet her. Lanta would sit at the Dark Lady's table with the other Blessed Ones and high priests, and she would bask in the presence of her Bloody Mother for eternity.

But the Dark Lady wasn't here. Nor was Holy Gosfath. Lanta herself had summoned and then trapped Them both in the temple in Rilporin. Lanta was alone until—if—They escaped. She'd scuffed the circle before her . . . death. Would that be enough? Unease crawled across her skin. There was no one left in the temple to complete the ritual. Had the Dark Lady claimed the infant? Was She even now returned to the living world, divinity clothed in mortal flesh? Lanta tried to will her sight back to the living world, to observe the moment of her goddess's triumph—for how could it be other than triumphant—but nothing happened. She was here, and They were there, and there was a distance between them that she'd never before felt.

The horde of souls had grown closer. Lanta could see the divisions, how there were tiny but significant spaces between one group and the next. Allegiances and alliances, in the Afterworld as in Gilgoras.

"I am Blessed One Lanta Costinioff," she said loudly, raising her chin. "I am responsible for the resurrection of the Dark Lady Herself. Even now, beyond the veil, She is cloaking Her divine essence in human skin, to return to us, to guide us as She did before. I have—"

"Shut up, bitch." The voice was loud and generated a spate of ugly laughter. "Resurrecting Her? Meaning She died on your watch, eh? Think we didn't know that, didn't feel Her loss here where always She has walked among us in glory?"

"That's not—" Lanta began, but then a figure burst from the throng, covered the bloody grass in a few strides, and punched Lanta in the teeth. She went over backwards, too shocked to scream, and by the time she'd opened her eyes, the man was busy tearing at her gown and linens.

"What are you doing?" she screamed. "I am the Blessed One. I am Lanta Costinioff, Voice of the Gods!"

"You're a fresh cunt is what you are," the man grunted, "and in the Afterworld, we get all those things we were promised. To kill and run and fuck and die without dying. Forever."

"No," she shouted, thrashing. "No, you don't understand. I'm the Blessed One, the Blessed One. *You don't get to touch me.* Stop!"

The man ignored her protestations and now others were approaching: men, women, hollow-eyed children who'd seen too much and done even more. For this was the Afterworld, and what they did, they did forever.

Lanta screamed again as she felt teeth sink into her ankle, a clump of hair rip from her head, and the tearing as the man got her linens off. *Funny, I still have linens in the Afterworld,* she thought hysterically, until all thought was subsumed by pain. Inch by inch, limb by bloody limb, hour by hour, they tore her to pieces. And she felt it all.

Lanta died.

Lanta sat up. There was an instant of dislocation, the memory of exquisite agony commingled with unutterable glory as she stood in the very presence of both her gods, and then . . . she was here. She scrambled to her feet and backed away from the advancing mass of souls.

"My name is Lanta Costinioff, Blessed One to the Dark Lady and Gosfath, God of Blood," she called, searching for a familiar, a sympathetic, face. To her right, another form sat up in the grass and began immediately to run. Away from her. Scores set out in pursuit and then she saw it, all across the endless, bloody fields. Death and rebirth into death. Chasing. Dying. Killing and rutting and eating dead flesh, cannibals and monsters and sadists, every one.

"Listen, just listen to me. I am—"

"Fresh meat," called a woman who had gobbets of flesh clinging beneath ragged, yellow fingernails. Her throat and chest were wet with gore. It might have been Lanta's, from before.

Turning her back to her sisters and brothers in Blood, Lanta picked up her skirts and began to run. In the distance, the hill of the Blessed Ones, where the priesthood lived. Ahead of her, a running battle between hundreds of children armed with sticks and bones, teeth and fingernails and fists.

Lanta ran faster. A howl rose behind her, and the horde gave chase.

Forever.

CORVUS

Tenth moon, first year of the reign of King Corvus
Five miles from Deep Forest, Wheat Lands

THE MOMENT HAD BEEN everything he'd been praying for these last months—a return to the Dark Lady's embrace—and yet nothing like he'd expected. It was early, for a start, far earlier than Corvus had anticipated, and if not for that bastard Koridam, he'd have been there to witness it, to see Rill give birth to a life that would become divine. But that he was not there was ordained, as were all the actions of a life dedicated to the gods. The Lady's will.

The sense of Her return had grown through the night, a looming glory that lifted the hearts and spirits of the faithful so that they barely slept behind the protective ditch and wall thrown up by the East Rank. And the enemy knew what was happening, too, for they didn't attack that night as they had every other night, didn't pick off sentries or sabotage the palisade, steal inside to kill.

And then dawn, and triumph, the culmination of the Blessed One's plans. The glory of their Bloody Mother filling every heart and soul with adoration, with awe and worship and completion.

And then the fall. Rejection and panic, rage and possession, and behind them to the southeast, a storm gathering black and brooding and pregnant with madness.

The Dark Lady's presence, Her pure and guiding presence, was muted, blurred, mixed like paint with another, the jealous and fearful and angry—so angry!—essence of Holy Gosfath, until they couldn't feel either god distinctly, just a roiling maelstrom of rage and vengeance and lust. They were neither uplifted in adulation nor strengthened with holy purpose. Instead, they were battered and bludgeoned with divine rage, divine pain.

Under the clear sky of Rilpor, the army of the faithful knelt in concentric circles around a small knot of men at the centre: Corvus, Fost and Tett, the surviving or promoted war chiefs, General Baron of the East Rank and his most devoted officers, all of them anointed war priests, as Corvus himself was, all lending their faith and discipline to his as he strove to discover the cause of the gods' fury, the gods' . . . merging.

He focused his breath and his mind on Them, seeking, trying to understand the confusion of impressions and emotions that battered at them, to see through it to the gods Themselves, here in Gilgoras. Here in Rilpor. *It may just take time for Her to settle, to come to understand the limits and abilities of Her new form. A day or so, no more, with the Blessed One there to guide Her.*

An intruder ripped into his mind, enveloping him in a hot, sticky rush of confused emotion. Men cried out in consternation and disgust, in fear, as a slick and oily wetness curled into their heads as it did his, a dripping anger bound up with need and awash with lunacy sliding through their thoughts, searching, picking at them, picking them apart. Part of him knew who it belonged to, but he wouldn't—couldn't—accept the name his mind supplied. It wasn't Her. This was not Her.

Corvus clenched his fists as it touched him, as it rummaged in his head, a hunger to it that only made its touch the viler. It didn't want him, it didn't care for him—it needed something from him, but neither he nor it knew what.

Corvus groaned, pawing at the air to push away the web of madness that clung and stuck, that he inhaled with every breath.

Cries of distress and disgust rang across the camp as the worm in Corvus's head writhed faster, harder, bloated with his memories, with parts of him that it chewed away from the rest and swallowed. It was getting angry now as whatever it looked for inside them it failed to find, angry and more desperate, its rummaging careless, harmful. A man in the third ring out collapsed, a spontaneous nosebleed erupting, pouring crimson down his face as he coughed and choked.

Corvus had the briefest glimpse of . . . something, something that couldn't possibly be his beloved gods, couldn't even be alive. Some amalgam of his memories, perhaps, but he didn't believe his own lie. Multiple arms and screaming mouths, eyes misaligned and bulging mad, spine bent this way and that and . . . bunches of red and black tentacles whipping above its head from the weeping, broken flesh in its back.

"You contacted a monster," someone shouted; he couldn't see who. "What have you done? *What have you done?*"

Corvus dropped forward on to his hands and vomited, trying to push the image from his head as all around him his army did the same, rejecting with frantic force the thing twisting through their thoughts. Malice and lust and vengeance and the urge to kill exploded inside him, so thick he could almost taste it, viscous as phlegm.

It was not in Holy Gosfath's nature to concern Himself with the goings-on of mortals: He feasted when blood and flesh were offered; as Lord of War he lent strength to His armies, but He did not often grace Gilgoras with His presence. But as the worm writhed faster, Corvus began to see Him in there, entwined around and through and within the Dark Lady. They were both there, both inside him at once. His gods. The only gods, joined as They never had been before.

And They were angry.

Corvus wiped a string of drool from his chin and raised his arms to the sky, knowing what had to be done, knowing that victory lay in embracing the madness, that to reject it was to know the void. She was back and he would worship Her. Nothing else mattered but to do Her will.

"Dark Lady, beautiful goddess of death and fear, you are returned to us. I feel you in the wind and in me, and I rejoice, for we have missed the glory of your touch."

The part of him that stood separate in the back of his mind didn't rejoice; it cowered, hands over its head, praying for the monster to go away. Corvus ignored it and Fost's abject terror. If the gods were angry, Corvus would placate Them. That was the way of things. It didn't matter what the gods looked like now: They were still his gods. He repeated that over and over, convincing himself, or trying to.

"Holy Gosfath, God of Blood, of war and mutilation, you are reunited with your Sister-Lover, made whole by Her return. I feel you in the wind and in me, and I rejoice, for we have missed the power of your divine battle lust."

Against the odds, despite every obstacle, every moment of indecision or lack of faith, the Blessed One had done it. She'd brought the Dark Lady back to them. She'd reunited Her with Gosfath, together for eternity as one all-powerful being, unstoppable. Corvus vomited again, unable to stop himself. He spat to clear his mouth and made himself stand and face his army.

"Together for eternity," he shouted. "The gods are returned, to Gilgoras, to each other, and to us. Holy Gosfath, Dark Lady, we are your children, we do your will, satisfy your desires. For you, we march to war. For you, we will destroy our enemies and offer their blood and meat for your rejoicing."

He gestured at the others and the chorus was ragged, unsure. But it was there. "Our feet are on the Path!"

Corvus shook his fists at the sky. "Our feet are on the Path. The Path to war!" he screamed and this time they stood and roared it back at him, the chant growing into thunder as they drank the horror like sweet poison.

He didn't wait for them, just headed for the gap in the palisade and the long, stubbled fields that led to Mace Koridam and his ragtag army. His gods were back and Their rage filled his head and heart. The madness of battle was a madness he could understand and he embraced it with something like relief.

Bloodlust shook him, his own and the gods', and it rose like a tide to consume every doubt, drown every image in his head. It flooded across them all, the need to kill for the gods, the need to wipe the stain of Light from the land, and his army didn't hesitate, rippling over the ditch and wall, madness and rage speeding their feet to the final confrontation.

The gods demanded blood, and gladly Corvus would give it to Them.

TARA

Tenth moon, first year of the reign of King Corvus
Temple district, First Circle, Rilporin, Wheat Lands

THE DOORS SHUDDERED UNDER the impact again and Tara braced her feet and strained, the agony in her burnt and broken arm gnawing at her bright and hard like winter sunlight, and as cruel.

She managed a glance over her shoulder and Rillirin, Salter and the rest had vanished. Relief washed through her chest and lasted only until the doors shuddered in their frames again. A questing black filament eased beneath the bottom edge and wrapped Tara's ankle. She yelled as it tightened, crushing hard around her lower leg, and she stepped away from the door kicking frantically. She hacked down with Valan's knife, half severing the tough muscle. It puffed into smoke and sucked back beneath the door, then the wood exploded and more tentacles felt their way through, the rest of the . . . thing hidden in the temple's gloom.

Tara collapsed, scrabbling backwards out of the way. Her left hand found the sword Salter had left, but what good were a knife and a sword? There was a hissing sound, like bees or steam escaping though a thousand times louder than either, as gusts of foul wind blew from out of the temple, rippling the bloody water dribbling down the steps. Sulphur and rot. Her head began to pound.

Thin screams, high and distant, as more buildings fell, Rilporin once more crumpling beneath the whim of a mad god. The screams of slaves, of Rilporians. Screams of her people. Tara used the knife to hack the skirt off above the knee, transferred it to her left hand, took up the sword and stood. No one else was dying on her watch, not if she could help it. If she was the only one to stand between them, then that's what she'd do.

"All right, soldier, buckle up," she said. "It's time to kill a mad god."

Weapons in hand, she climbed over the shattered wood into the temple's stinking gloom to confront the . . . thing. It was a baffling, sickening, awful being, part Gosfath, part Dark Lady, all nightmare. The God of Blood was no more, but neither was the Dark Lady resurrected. Where there had been two gods, two essences of red and black, now there was one. One thing, monstrous and deformed, one curling horn, three arms, two and a half legs.

Two faces, welded next to each other on one huge misshapen skull, the God of Blood's mouth perpetually open in a snarl or perhaps a scream, the Dark Lady's smeared over it like paint, Her black eyes rimmed in red and rimed with madness.

Whatever She had attempted had failed. If She'd hoped to use Gosfath's essence, His form or very life, to build Herself a new body, all She'd succeeded in doing was melding Herself to Him.

Like Crys. Two souls in one body. Except not the fuck like Crys at all, because Crys is pretty and that's enough to make sure I never sleep again.

And it was growing, its heads—*head?*—nearing the rafters as it bellowed-moaned-roared its hate and struggle. It didn't see her coming, too absorbed in its battle with itself and she realised its attack on the doors probably hadn't been intentional. Tara slid through the shadows and the puddles, the splash of her boots lost beneath the noises the thing was making.

It still had tentacles of black protruding from its spine, whipping back and forth as though seeking support, and a red arm, one of Gosfath's still intact, made a wild grab at itself, ripping at black stuff, gouging for the Dark Lady's eye beside His own. Her arm batted it away and the monstrosity spun, unbalanced and staggering.

"Listen, Fox God, this was your idea, sort of, so if you could lend me a little strength, I'd appreciate it. Or just, you know"—Tara tapped her fingertips to her heart—"watch over me, that'd be great."

Gods, she thought as it spotted her and bellowed, *even by my standards this is stupid. Mace is going to kill me.*

I really, really hope he gets the chance.

A manic laugh burst from her as she raised the sword and knife and summoned the last dregs of energy. The divine atrocity that defied nature and all known laws halted towards her, lurching and keening. "Fox God, you listening?" Tara babbled. "A little help?"

There was no response, so she rolled her wrist a few times to loosen it, tightened her grip on the weapons, and moved to meet it. It was distracted, the Gosfath half still intent on peeling the other from itself, and she used that to her advantage, skipping beneath a flailing arm and thrusting her sword up into its gut. It scraped off the solid, stone-hard red flesh and slipped sideways, shoving into the Dark Lady's pale skin with little more effort than it would a mortal's and opening up a wide red mouth that gouted black.

Twin bleating calls, of triumph and of rage, and a tendril of ebony muscle as thick as Tara's thigh crunched into her midriff and shattered what felt like the rest of her ribs. The floor rose up and slammed her in the back and Tara would've screamed if the pain in her chest hadn't obliterated all thought and expelled what little air she had left. She concentrated on not passing out, fighting to breathe, fighting her body so she could fight the monster.

"Where . . . where are you going?" she croaked as the thing limped past her moments later. She swung her left hand and drove the knife into its ankle; it looked back as though at an insect, and the same foot came up and then slammed down with crushing force on her forearm. Tara heard multiple snaps and the burnt flesh sloughed free, trailing in ribbons across the stone as she rolled on to her side and curled up around the fresh pain.

The god-thing paid her no more attention, still growing—or at least the blackness, the goddess, was growing, subsuming the red skin of Gosfath into itself—until the head wove among the rafters and arms and tendrils alike punched through the roof, letting in shafts of bright autumnal sun and a blast of fresh, cold air to whip away the stink and some of the fuzziness in Tara's head.

Sobbing, she rocked up to her knees and held her broken arm to her broken chest; the fingernails were turning blue and there was a heaviness inside her, a sloshing as her lung began to fill with blood. *All right, Fox God—Crys—I'm not joking any more. I really, really need your help or that thing is going to chase down Rillirin and take the baby. Please?*

She didn't wait to see if He'd answer, but got one foot flat, put her good hand on her knee and pushed up, wobbling. The sword was lost somewhere, so she limped forward with the knife. "We're not done yet," she gasped, dots swirling slowly through her vision like soot drifting on a summer breeze. The light was funny, everything glowing slightly around the edges. Had to stop it. Had to keep it away from Rillirin. Stop it . . .

"Hey," she called and then coughed, coughed blood on to the filthy flagstones, on to her chest and the remains of her gown. Tara dragged the back of her knife hand over her mouth. "Hey," she yelled again, a little louder. "I said we're not done."

The gods' head had vanished through the roof as it continued to grow. It couldn't see her. *Never lose sight of your opponent. Unless you're too tall to see them, that is.*

Another manic giggle stole more of her air as Tara shuffled until she stood between its misshapen, tree-trunk legs. One of the knees bent the wrong way so it flailed and limped as it moved. Maybe it was looking for Rillirin. She stared up at the tracery of veins in the pale flesh, squinting, head spinning as her chest bubbled with every breath. She didn't have long.

Femoral artery. That'll do it.

Dragging together the last of her strength, Tara jumped and struck, the blade stabbing in deep and ripping downwards as her weight pulled it out.

The monster let out a bellow and a scream, twin sounds so loud that Tara's eardrums burst. It slammed back through the roof in a maelstrom of arms and whipping tentacles and fangs and claws, bringing beams and slates and ironwork with it, all raining down to bounce and shatter on the flagstones, Tara protected by the thing's own bulk. Protected, but in its eyeline.

Another gout of blood, bright and arterial this time, splattered from her mouth and down her chest as something shifted inside her, tore her open, and then red, black-tipped hands scooped her up and lifted her, faster than bird flight, through the roof and into the air and up towards its face. Faces.

BLOODCHILD

Tara burst into the sky, the city and the fields beyond glowing under a warm sun, bright golden rays winking from glass and picking out the golds and reds in the trees and the rich brown earth.

A flock of starlings whirled past, their weird, looping calls summoning her to fly with them. "Oh, that's pretty, isn't it, Tomaz?" Tara tried to say through the blood in her throat.

The thing holding her was roaring, but she turned her face up to the sun as the peace of the Fox God encased her heart and held it firm.

She wasn't alone.

"So pretty."

The hands closed, and twisted, and pulled her apart.

CRYS

Tenth moon, first year of the reign of King Corvus
The hill, edge of Deep Forest, Wheat Lands

IT WAS AS IF there was a fish hook in Crys's gut and someone was yanking on the line, trying to rip it out so that he staggered, an involuntary cry breaking from his lips as he stumbled on to his knees.

Dom was nearby and he toppled over and began to convulse at the same moment, cords standing out in his neck, teeth snapping like a mad dog's and limbs flailing without control. And it just kept going.

Minutes passed before Crys could stand against the pain and Dom was still thrashing, weaker as his body burnt through all the reserves it had, his tongue and lips savaged. Most of the high command had gathered at the shouts, the running and chaos, and they watched in uneasy, superstitious silence as Hallos, at the risk of losing a finger, tipped opium powder on to Dom's gums. It was that or sheer exhaustion that finally slowed the convulsions to twitches and then dropped him into a sleep so deep it looked like death. Might have been death if not for the fluttering, erratic pulse in his throat, a tiny movement they all watched with the intensity of hawks, waiting for it to skip and then stop.

Gilda sat back on her heels in the grass, wiping a shaking hand over his brow. "What in the Dancer's name was that?" she asked.

"It's happened," Crys said, kneeling next to her with both arms wrapped around himself, breathing through waves of nausea. "She's back, and She's hungry."

"Hungry?"

"Tried to rip out Her essence that I swallowed. Couldn't get it, not yet anyway, so I'm guessing She went back into Dom the way She used to."

"Guessing?" Gilda asked, furious. "You're a god, Crys, do better than guess."

Crys shuddered out a breath and put a palm on Dom's hot face, felt a shadow inside him, and a seed of Light. Striving. There was a flick of sentience across his mind and he withdrew hurriedly from its oily malice, feeling as though he needed to wash out the inside of his skull just from that momentary touch. How Dom stood it he had no idea. *Unless that was Dom . . .*

"I don't know," he said, rubbing his hand against the leg of his trousers. "Something's not right," he added reluctantly. "She's definitely back, meaning the ritual was performed over Rillirin's babe, but it's all wrong. Something went wrong. You'll need to ask Dom; I can't see it the way he can."

"And Rillirin? What of her child, does it live? Is it . . . Her?" Gilda's voice was pure priestess, but the tremor in her hands betrayed her.

"Again, I don't know. I'm sorry. I felt . . . madness and hate, triumph and then pain. All jumbled together." Ash helped him to stand. Rumour hissed through the ranks of the army like a rising breeze. "But if the calestar and I felt it, you can be sure the Mireces did as well, and with less . . . hurting. They'll know the Dark Lady has returned, and they'll probably understand far better than I what's happened. Regardless, I'd bet my life they're on their way even now. The Dark Lady too."

Mace paused, mouth open to issue orders. "What?" he asked instead. "Rilporin's a hundred miles and more."

"She's a goddess, Sire. I don't think distance works the same. If She wants to be here—and why wouldn't She, with so much concentrated faith from the Mireces and Easterners, faith Her presence will both strengthen and from which She can take strength—then I'm pretty sure She can just appear in our midst."

Mace grabbed him by the arm. "And you're ready for this?" he demanded, before remembering who he was talking to and releasing him.

"I don't think we have much choice, do we?" Crys said without rancour as weariness brushed its poison over him. "I'm ready. Just make sure this lot are ready for Corvus."

Mace spun away and began issuing crisp, low-voiced commands to the runners strung behind him. The army began to move, to stretch and settle back into formation. To prepare.

Crys cocked his head as his awareness was wrenched across the miles in response to a plea, not for mercy so much as contact. Recognition. "Tara?" He bent over and put his hands on his knees, concentrating. *Tara? Tara, can you hear me? It's Crys. I'm here; I'm with you. You're not alone.*

The kernel of her courage was crystal-bright and diamond-hard and small. So small among her hurts. She was scared.

Foxy. Go. Do something, anything.

Such as? I cannot rescue her.

Crys's knees hit the grass again, the impact distant, his awareness turned inward and outward at once, across the leagues to Rilporin.

Fucking go, he snarled in his head. *Bring her peace, if nothing more.*

He felt a hesitation, a protest that thousands had died and thousands more would and should He, the great Trickster, mourn them all, and Crys tensed until his whole body was one roaring imperative, an inviolable command that promised retribution not even a god could withstand. A piece of the Fox God broke away and arced across the sky.

Tara's fear grew until it outweighed even the monstrous weight of hurt, enough that either one of them alone would have crushed Crys flat. *I'm here, my friend. I'm here.* Hands descended on his shoulders. *Mace too, and Ash. We're with you.*

Crys reached up and took their hands and with a sigh and a wriggle, he moved the three of them into the soul-dream, where distance meant nothing, and there was Tara, in the shape of a great cat, all stubby tail and tufted ears and wide golden eyes. Her stone-grey and cloud-white pelt was ragged and bloody and she lay on her side, ribs heaving. Those eyes were misted with pain, but they brightened at the Fox God's approach, a slink of red fur. He settled beside her and nuzzled His head beneath her chin. He licked her throat and face and her breathing slowed, stuttered.

"Peace, Tara," Crys whispered. She exhaled and returned his gift, brushing him with a forgiveness he hadn't expected and didn't deserve. A great cat-smile as her dimming gaze moved to Mace and she made a final effort to stand.

"Stay where you are, and that's an order. Just do as you're told for once." She flopped back with another cat-grin that became a grimace as the light of her soul began to fade.

Mace stepped forward, his voice strong and gentle and the last thing she'd know before the Light. "Dancer's grace, Major. You have discharged your duty with honour; you can stand down."

WHAT HAPPENED TO HER?" Mace demanded back in the world, rocked by what he'd seen, where he'd been taken. "How did she die? *Is* she dead?" His voice was ragged but the words were iron-hard and his expression was implacable despite the shine of tears. The fist clenched in the neck of Crys's shirt didn't tremble.

"She's gone, sir. But she saw you and heard you; she knew she was loved. She went to the Light knowing that she wasn't alone."

A muscle jumped beneath Mace's eye. "And she's in the Light? You're sure?"

"Absolutely, sir. She's at peace."

Mace's gaze could've cut steel, but then he let go of Crys's collar and rubbed his mouth. "Thank you. And for allowing me to say goodbye." He cleared his throat and stared off into the distance in silence for a long breath, flinched when Dalli touched his cheek, and then came back to the world. He went over to Hadir and his senior officers, the Warlord and war leader joining them, putting away the hurt until he had time for it. Becoming the soldier again. The officer. The king. Crys should go too, but they'd laid out the plan days ago—he could waste a few minutes just . . . being.

The pain in Crys's stomach was still there, and Dom was still unconscious at their feet, and the enemy was coming and Tara was dead and something, something indescribable, had happened in Rilporin.

Crys focused on controlling his breathing, on slowing the galloping of his heart and surreptitiously wiping the sweat from the palms of his hands, but Ash saw it all and understood it all anyway. He rested his palm on the nape of Crys's neck and pressed their foreheads together. It was close now, the end of this mad, wonderful, perfect love, close and real, not the distant future event that they'd pretended so hard wasn't coming.

ANNA STEPHENS

Ash hadn't left his side in the last week, and would fight next to him in the battle to come. A second shadow armed with steel. It was both a gift and a burden, Ash's presence, the reminder that Crys's life was almost done, that the sum of his days was nearing its final tally, and that it wasn't enough. This love, this life, it was nowhere near enough. Crys wasn't done with living, wasn't done with loving, with Ash, with all of it. He swallowed hard and breathed in the scent of his husband.

I bet Tara wasn't done with life either, was she, Foxy? You still took her.

There was an uncharacteristic, almost angry, silence inside him, so profound that he began to regret the thought. *She's done more to win this war than she knows. One day, in the Light, we'll be able to tell her exactly how.*

"So, a big fluffy kitty, eh? Kind of wish I'd known that earlier," Ash murmured, interrupting the internal dialogue. "I'd have made her a giant ball of string to play with."

Crys coughed a laugh. "She'd have killed you."

"Yeah, but it would've been worth it."

"Let's get him to the field hospital." Hallos's voice broke in. Crys opened his eyes but didn't move from Ash's embrace. They watched as two soldiers lifted Dom and carried him away down the hill, Gilda and the physician following. *What do you know? Have you seen my death yet, Calestar, beloved of gods? Have you seen me end? Did you see Tara's?*

Crys stepped forward. "I'll come with you," he called after Hallos. "We probably don't have long, but let me see what I can do."

Gilda looked back. "Thank you." They hurried down the slope towards the hospital.

"Cavalry scouts coming in hard," a voice yelled behind them.

"Positions," Mace roared and his staff sprinted to their units, the Krikites and Wolves flowing downhill, the archers—without Ash—hurrying to take their places on the flanks. "Tailorson?"

"I'll be back, sir, I swear."

Mace glared but waved him off and the group broke into a run, Dom flopping and bouncing in the soldiers' arms.

"Here we go," Crys breathed. "Stay close."

"Always," Ash said. "Forever."

RILLIRIN

Tenth moon, first year of the reign of King Corvus
South Gate, First Circle, Rilporin, Wheat Lands

THE MERCHANTS' QUARTER HAD supplied Rillirin with an old gown, some boots that were a little too big, and a shawl to fasten a sling for her baby.

My baby, my little girl. Hello, Macha, my little warrior. Seems like we did it after all.

Salter and the surviving prisoners had raided houses and cellars for food, clothes, weapons, the latter being almost impossible to find. A few wood axes, some kitchen knives, an unstrung bow.

Fortunately, they hadn't yet run across more than a few Mireces, quickly dispatched.

"Gods alive, what is that?" The panic in the voice and the pointing finger had Rillirin wobbling around in an unbalanced circle to peer back the way they'd come. It was hard to see past the crowd of thin, desperate soldiers and over the rubble and the buildings still standing, the smoke and dust clouds roiling, but there was . . . something rising over the temple district. A jarring outline of red and black and whipping tentacles.

"Go," Rillirin said, when the soldiers clumped together and stared back towards the temples. "Let's go," she repeated, a little louder. Salter proffered her a skin; watered wine, heavy with honey. It was like a drink from the gods, replenishing a little of her energy. She shambled on, Salter's hand under her elbow and the rest flooding around them into formation again. So tired.

"It's coming," Salter shouted, yanking her to a halt. "Back into the houses, quickly. We'll be clear targets on the road or outside the city. Take cover!"

Soldiers scattered, civilians following, and Salter hauled Rillirin towards the nearest building. They half fell inside, kicking the door shut. They were in a small kitchen, a jug on the table, a pot still bubbling over the fire.

Salter held a finger to his lips and gestured her beneath the table, passing her the jug before taking up position by the small window to the left of the door. Milk. She drank, poking her tongue through the thick layer of cream to reach the liquid beneath. Like the wine, it alleviated a touch more exhaustion, although that could be yet more fear flooding her veins with the urge to run, to fight, to stand over her cub and snarl her threat at any who came for them.

All was silence. Cautiously, Rillirin slid from beneath the table, wrapped a cloth around the handle of the pot and hoisted it from the fire, before retreating with it and a spoon back under the table. *I should be too scared to eat,* she thought to herself as she shovelled scalding stew into her mouth, *but, gods, I'm so hungry. I could eat a horse.*

That thought triggered another and Rillirin dropped the spoon into the pot and, fumbling with anxiety and the worry of getting it wrong, she pulled down her collar and breast band and guided Macha's mouth to her nipple.

The babe knew what to do, and after the initial sharp pain had faded they were both eating, Rillirin pausing every few seconds to marvel at the sensation of that tiny mouth and surprisingly powerful suction.

Sounds of destruction and the roaring of gods broke their mutual contentment. "Nope," Salter muttered. "We need to go." He looked back, mouth dropping open at the scene, and then dismissing it just as fast. "On your feet."

"We should get supplies."

"We stay here we'll be dead in minutes. Come on."

Rillirin adjusted the sling so Macha could continue feeding and then dragged herself to her feet.

BLOODCHILD

They flattened themselves against the outside wall and Salter let out three low whistles. All along the street the prisoners emerged from hiding. A series of gestures Rillirin didn't understand and the soldiers were moving again, some ahead, others behind, while the civilians huddled around Rillirin.

Quartering the approaches as Dom had taught her so long ago and trying to force down yet more fear, so much swallowed it almost made her sick, Rillirin and the others crept to the South Gate and out of Rilporin. They sidled around the slumped, poorly repaired tower called First Bastion and then they were in the open, in the Wheat Lands with a hundred miles to walk to reach Deep Forest and Mace and Dom. The distance undermined her determination but the Rankers were moving already, checking behind and to the sides and she was in their midst with a score of civilians, and they were out. They were escaping. Free.

The road from the city into the Wheat Lands would curve and split and divert but it would, eventually, take her to Dom, and Dom was home, he was her guiding star and she could do no more than steer a course towards him, and if that meant walking a hundred miles in too-big boots then that was what she'd do, she and Macha, walking home. And when they were all back together, she'd stop moving, just settle, him and their babe and whoever was left of the people she loved. Just stop, and build a home, and be peaceful.

She told Salter as much, and he agreed that that sounded like a good plan, and that the best way to find Dom was to find Mace, because he was their Commander and their king. If there was still fighting to be done, Salter and the rest were Rankers and they wanted to be a part of it.

"But we have to wait for Tara," Rillirin added in an exhausted monotone.

"Major Carter's orders were very specific, miss," he said with an effort, "and I for one am far too scared of her to disobey." Numb fatigue crashed into her like a giant wave and she stumbled; Salter put his arm around her waist and then a huge man, a civilian so big there were almost two of him, scooped her up in his arms and began to walk. "Name's Merol," he said, "and I reckon you could do with a bit of a rest."

She tried to tell him to stop, that they had to wait for Tara. Instead she slept, her daughter pressed warm and vital and alive against her skin.

DOM

Tenth moon, first year of the reign of King Corvus
The hill, edge of Deep Forest, Wheat Lands

*H*ATE WANT KILL LUST *need hate want hate hurt scared kill scared*
want alone need betrayed hurt hate kill . . .

It was an endless barrage, an assault not on Dom's senses but on the very core of who he was, what he was. A battering away of his soul, his mind, a gibbering mad cacophony eating his sanity, his reason.

And he could see Her. Them. *It*.

The Bloodchild offering had failed or been thwarted and the Dark Lady, in Her lust and determination to return to Gilgoras, had taken the closest body She could find and made it Her own. Gosfath's body. But Gosfath wasn't a weak and newly made soul like Dom's daughter; He wasn't giving up His life for anyone, not even the Sister-Lover He missed so much. And so They had formed a new thing, of rage unconstrained, a melded madness. The . . . Blood Lady.

And She'd—or They'd—found Dom again, found the godspace within him, the site of Her former glory. It called to Her across the veil, drew Her. If She could claim that space once more and set up dominion over Dom, She could compel him to kill the Fox God and release the last of Her essence. With it, She could oust Gosfath for good and take control, become Herself again, not the hideous, shambling wreck that Her merging had made of Her.

Remade, She could be the sum and pinnacle of Dom's glory and Dom's depravity.

The idea that Her agony was the God of Blood's fault wasn't Dom's, as the urge to tear himself free of the physician and find the Fox God and bite Him to death wasn't his. He knew the urges for what they were, and for the very first time he had the strength to resist. It wasn't the Dancer's words and love that bolstered that strength, nor the Trickster's faith in him, nor the knowledge Rillirin and their daughter still lived and were the only safe harbour in the storm of Dom's world. It wasn't the task he still had to complete that lent him aid.

No. This time it was simple: the newly formed, newly named Blood Lady repulsed him in a way that went beyond abhorrence. He couldn't lose himself in this thing the way he had when She was Herself. And She knew it. Her lust turned Dom's stomach, the memories of him in Her arms a horrendous counterpoint to what She was now.

He made no effort to hide his revulsion, almost glorying in the hurt She sent him as punishment. *My last fight.* It had a kind of justice to it.

Gosfath's lusts were in there as well as Hers, stronger than Dom had ever felt them, His wanton love of cruelty apparent in the flashes He sent of Rillirin, of her suffering through the agonies of childbirth in a place that would tear her daughter away before she'd even drawn breath. Of Tara's torture and her fate, her broken body lost now in the tumbled ruins of the grand temple, sealed away from sunlight and life and hope by tons of stone. Alone. Of Dom's own hands wielding pincer and knife, chisel and hammer, as they carved the Fox God free of Crys's shivering flesh.

Dom was aware, in a distant sort of way, of his body lying heavy and unresponsive on the cot in the tent, as if unconnected to the battle he fought in his mind. A battle he surged to meet, throwing Her every betrayal back at Her; and the more She wounded him, the brighter shone the Light he'd once believed guttered forever. And in that Light, Rillirin's face and the shadowy outline of their little girl.

I walk with the Fox God, and you will not have Him, he promised. *You have been thwarted, destroyed, brought back by your own followers to agony and degradation. And we're going to kill you again, and keep killing you until you can't come back. There's nothing for you here. Give back the Light you stole and twisted for yourself; give up. Give up.*

Who are you to talk to me? the Blood Lady demanded, and Dom could feel how She tried to control the impulses and wild emotions that floated through Her like poison. *I am your goddess; I own you and I will make you suffer—*

I already suffer, though I am no longer yours. Do what you will, Dom replied with mad glee. *Break me, twist me, torture me, whatever the evil inside you tells you to do. Your selfishness has turned you into a monster and it's not you I'm talking to any more. It's you and Gosfath. Melded and mad. A horror.*

So do what you will to me, make me a horror just like you if it will ease your fright and pain. That you can do. What you can't do is destroy me, or take away the Light that burns inside. I defy you.

The godspace was raw and bleeding, and Dom could feel, on the periphery of his awareness, the slow creeping paralysis sliding through his left arm and leg, numbing the side of his face, a dark and dead weight pulling at him.

Still, the confusion and panic on the Blood Lady's hideous split face was almost worth it. She withdrew from him a little, pulling back as if to observe him from the outside. Dom braced for the mockery and resumption of pain; it didn't come.

My children worship and love me, She tried, and he noted with a spark of hilarity the uncertainty in Her.

Your children worship and fear you, he corrected. *As for me, I just hate you. I don't worship you; I don't love or want you. I defy you, and I'm going to help kill you.*

She slammed back into him so that he bucked and flopped.

You will kill the Fox God!

I will not!

"I will not!" Dom's eyes opened, vision blurry, the echo of his slurred shout in his ears. Faces peered down at him, and he knew them though he couldn't name them. He shied back on instinct, laughed but didn't know why, tried to lift his left arm and couldn't.

"Kill you," he mumbled. An old woman leant over him, concern nestled in the wrinkles of her face. He didn't know her name. He slept.

H E WOKE WITH THE Light shining so bright and hot inside him it was as if he'd swallowed the sun.

Dom let his head slide sideways and found Crys lying on the next cot over, hand pressed to his side. The Fox God was pale, beads of sweat standing proud on His face. When He saw Dom was awake He slumped back, shaking, and let the silver light flow back into Him, slow as starlight.

"Motherfucker," Crys gasped, raising a shaking hand to his brow, "make it easy for me next time, will you, and just have a leg off or something. Gods alive."

"You should have saved that," Dom croaked. He was blind in his left eye, left arm and leg barely there, barely alive.

Crys smiled, drawn and gaunt. "Should I know why?"

"Battle," he replied.

Hallos was on his other side, fingers jammed against the pulse in his wrist, lips pursed among the tangle of his beard. "Remarkable. A significant improvement; thank you."

Crys grunted acknowledgment, eyelids sagging with fatigue. "Thought it best to see what I could do for you now, before the fighting starts." The colour was coming back into his face even as Dom watched, straining to hear him over the stutter-skip of his heartbeat.

"Because my task is not yet complete," he said, throwing the Fox God's words back at Him. Crys winced but said nothing. "You're right though."

"The Red Gods?" Ash asked, pacing like a caged animal. "Tell us what's going on, Dom, please."

"The Red Gods . . . something went wrong when the Blessed One cast her great ritual to resurrect the Dark Lady. There is only one god now—Gosfath and the Dark Lady have merged somehow, become one entity, though not by choice, it seems. Water, please."

Crys sat up, wiping his face on his sleeve. Gilda passed him a waterskin and they both drank. "I felt something was wrong, but I couldn't find out what," he said. "I don't envy you the understanding of it."

Dom didn't either. "I call Her, Them, the Blood Lady," he said and the torches seemed to gutter under the name. "Powerful yes, so powerful, but mad too. Their essences have combined, but They're at war to separate Themselves again. Two minds struggling for control, supremacy over one . . . form." He shuddered. "There's no other body for the Dark Lady to inhabit, but She'll be looking for one."

"And She needs what's inside me to do it," Crys said, arms wrapped around his belly. Ash stopped pacing and stood behind him, hands on his shoulders. "Any idea how soon They'll be here?"

Dom grunted a negative.

"Rillirin and the babe?" Gilda asked. "What happened to them if the Dark Lady didn't get . . . inside her?" She was drawn with worry.

"Rillirin and our daughter live," he confirmed. Gilda's face lit up, Ash's too. Even Crys seemed pleased.

"Oh, I can't wait to meet her," Ash said, rubbing his hands together. "Her uncles Crys and Ash are going to teach her every bad habit they know."

Crys's face became carefully blank; he knew, at least, though like Dom he did nothing to disabuse his husband of his delusion. Better to let him dream and go into battle believing that they'd get to go home afterwards. That there'd be a home to go back to.

"And this thing, this . . . Blood Lady, does it still control the Mireces and the East Rank?" Crys asked.

Dom rubbed his left eye, but no matter how often he blinked, there was nothing but blackness there. He didn't mention it. If the Fox God hadn't managed to heal his blindness, it was beyond anyone's skill. His stomach gurgled, but the thought of food made him sick.

"Dom?"

He focused back on his surroundings. "Sorry. And yes, maybe even more than before. Gosfath's never really been one for interfering in Gilgoras, but now He doesn't have a choice. Besides, He'll be looking for every advantage to free Himself. Their merging has doubled Their influence, though the struggle for control makes it fluctuate. But when that awareness is focused on you, it's almost impossible to disobey—and the Mireces won't want to."

He understood the look that passed between Gilda and Ash: how long would he hold out? Did he want to hold out? His head began to pound and Crys's gaze jerked to him, as if he'd sensed something. Something coming.

BLOODCHILD

Gilda was asking him something and Crys was saying they had to get back, but Dom's head was hurting and it was hard to stay awake. He closed his eyes.

Blood Lady. Appropriate, isn't it? He asked Her, Them, as They pounced. They screamed Their rage at his disrespect, and They began to tear. Dom lay still, focusing on his breathing. He'd try and keep it quiet this time, so that the Fox God or Hallos didn't waste any more time on him. Any more healing.

Any more life.

CRYS

Tenth moon, first year of the reign of King Corvus
The hill, edge of Deep Forest, Wheat Lands

C RYS AND ASH HELD the centre of the line with Colonel Thatcher as the Mireces toiled up the mud and slick grass of the hill towards them, Jarl on their left flank awaiting the advancing East Rank.

The distance had spoilt the archers' aim to begin with, but now volleys darkened the already heavy air and thrummed downhill towards the advancing enemy huddled behind their locked shields. The Mireces prayed aloud, a cacophony of shouted entreaties and threats, curses and expletives spat from slavering mouths as the gods whipped them on, faster, gaining momentum, arrows glancing from their shields and soon too close for archers anyway. Colonel Thatcher pulled them back to the flanks.

Crys could feel the beat of blood all around him, hearts twinned with his, moving as one, a shoal of fish, a flock of birds, an army of the faithful with their god in their midst. On his order they locked their own shields and planted their feet, waiting for the Mireces to smash into them and try to force them on to the summit and level ground to even the odds.

Faster still and holding formation, divine madness sparking like steel on flint from one man to the next to the next, infected with battle lust, a flood rising until they were running, charging, screaming. And driving into the line.

BLOODCHILD

The Mireces pushed, pressing them, harrying them, cracking shield rims down on to feet and up into faces, spears and swords poking through and over the wall and jabbing into Rilporian flesh.

"Wedge," shouted a tall warrior in the front and the Mireces flowed into the new formation as if they'd practised a thousand times. The tip drove at Crys and his lips peeled back. He crouched slightly to accept the attack, shoulder into the back of his shield to brace and felt Ash lock into position by his side.

The lead warrior crashed into him, hooked Crys's shield with his sword and curved the blade in around it. Crys batted it up with his, then chopped downwards into the warrior's arm, but then the wedge's momentum surged on and his foot skidded in the grass and it was step back or fall. He let them past.

Crys roared, the Fox God surging up inside him and bellowing His bloodlust, His battle joy, and Crys stiffened his legs and pushed inwards, straining, the men to either side doing the same.

Another Mireces yelled an order for the flanks to re-form into wedges of their own and now they had a three-pronged attack gnawing away at the Rilporian line.

"Shoulders in," Crys screamed over the din, heard the order repeated and then they were shoving forwards and downwards, flattening the wedges, pushing the enemy back step by step and moving down the slope. It was slow, agonisingly so, with men on both sides slipping in the rain and blood, tripping on the fallen, gaps opening in line and wedge both for an enterprising killer to slip a blade into.

The day was growing darker, not brighter, though it wasn't even noon. Rain fell in sheets until it was impossible to see the base of the hill or the western flank where the Krikites were, the Wolves in the smudge of trees towards the bottom.

They took a step forward, killing those in front of them. Step, kill. Step, kill. The Fox God bellowed His challenge. They stepped. And killed.

THE RILPORIANS WERE HOLDING, just, holes gouged in the front line by multiple wedges that were crushed only to re-form further along, like teeth tearing away chunks of flesh until their front was ragged and bleeding.

The Mireces had finally forced them up on to the flat ground at the top of the hill and there the fighting steadied, swirling madly back and forth with the eddies of war, where misfortune and bad luck were as deadly as spear or blade.

The topsoil was thin so there wasn't much mud, but the scrubby grass was as slick as ice and every time a knot of Rankers went down, the Mireces surged and attempted to force them down the rearward slope. Not even the Fox God would be able to stop it if the Mireces got them on the run.

Crys slid from one almost-rout to the next, rallying the soldiers, killing or assisting in the kills of the fiercest Mireces, stiffening the line wherever it began to twist, encouraging exhausted, soaking, mud-streaked, blood-washed soldiers.

Ash at his left side, always, his hand axe darting like a silver fish even in the gloom, crusted with blood and bone, the cumbersome Rank-made shield floating on his arm as though it weighed nothing.

They rotated out of the front line as another Mireces wedge collapsed, moving three rows back to suck in air, shoulders and backs pounded in thanks, Crys's arms touched with reverence.

The Fox God's call—the triple falling notes of a trumpet repeated twice—that he'd set up with Mace drifted through the rain and jerked Crys around like a horse fighting the bit. "Someone needs me." He glanced at the line; they were holding well here, steady and disciplined. Jarl and Thatcher both had the enemy pegged back, at least for now. The trumpet sounded again. "Let's go."

They shouted encouragement and promised to be back soon, that they were doing great, got them on the run, and then headed across the top of the hill towards the command post.

"Listen, when I'm called to battle the Blood Lady, you need to go wherever the fighting's thickest and rally the troops. They might falter when I leave the field." He winced at the arrogance of it, but it needed to be said.

"Bollocks," Ash gasped, affronted. "I go where you go. That's the deal."

"Not this time, love—"

"You're going to need someone to watch your back. Me." Ash's tone was implacable as he concentrated on his footing, the pair of them moving faster than was wise in the slippery grass.

"This is beyond you, Ash. I'm sorry, there's no other way I can say it. If you stand with me there, you'll die before I do. And the Rank will need you."

"You'll need me, and they don't rally to me," Ash protested, a note of panic creeping into his voice. He dragged Crys to a halt. "They won't fight harder for me; they won't stiffen the line or step into a breach the way they do for you. I'll be useless here. I'm useless without you."

Crys found a heartfelt smile for him despite his dread at what was to come. "Useless without me? You survived thirty-eight years without me, you idiot."

Ash didn't smile. "That's before you were my husband. Like it or not, it's different now. Live together; die together." He reached out and wiped mud or blood or rain from Crys's forehead.

"No," he said, so fierce Ash almost took a step back. "No, we do not die together. You live. *That's* the deal. You live, and because I know you live, I find the strength to do what needs to be done."

Ash began to protest and Crys lunged forward, cutting off his words with a kiss that was full of panicked longing and strangled fear. "Live, Ash. Husband. Heart-bound. Please live." He held Ash's head in his hands, brown curls plastered to his forehead beneath his helmet, water dripping down his face. "You have to," he added fiercely. "You have to give me the courage to do this, or we're all lost. Every man, woman and babe in Rilpor, in all Gilgoras. My loss for their lives. Just one man. Just a man, Ash, against all humanity. That's a price we can afford."

"Is it?" Ash asked. "Doesn't feel cheap from where I'm standing."

"Try standing here," Crys tried, but the joke fell flat and Ash choked back a sob, squeezed him in an embrace so tight Crys couldn't draw a full breath.

"You tell me I have to live, but you also tell me I have to rally the front line until the battle is won. I'm not sure it's possible to do both."

Crys licked his lips, Ash's kiss and cold rain in his mouth. "You were born to do this, love. Hold them. And my heart is in your chest, remember. If you live, so does my heart."

"And when you die, so does mine," Ash countered, the words stealing Crys's breath. "Now come on, let's find out who needs you, because I'm not leaving your side." Crys knew he couldn't argue, but he also knew Ash couldn't come where he was going. There was time yet before that final goodbye, he knew that much. Though they were fighting for their lives, he'd make the most of it.

"Tell me again why I married you?" he complained with a shake of his head.

"Devastating good looks and astonishing in bed," Ash said.

Crys laughed and hugged him again. "Damnit. Can't even argue. Come on." The banter made it easier to ignore the pain in his stomach and the increasing pressure in the air, as though his skin was too tight, pressing in from all sides, shrinking. The slow-emerging presence of another god or gods. The Blood Lady was coming.

The Trickster squirmed in discomfort, adding to Crys's dislocation from the real world.

"About time," Mace grunted when they arrived at his command post, the highest point of the hill, with the royal standard hanging sodden from a pole above him. "Wolves are hard-pressed, calling for reinforcements. Mireces are trying to flank us through the trees and I can't throw in the reserve this early. Lend them a hand."

Another courier arrived, soaked and wild. "Field hospital's under attack, sir. Fucking hundreds of them!"

"Shit, there goes my reserve," Mace said with quiet vehemence. "You two, go. We'll deal with the hospital."

"Understood." They set out again faster than before. The field hospital was out of sight of their position, so they peered over at the front line as they slid downhill towards the woods; it was twisted in places, pressing forwards and being pressed back in a sinuous curve like a snake. The Krikites' line was fracturing into a melee on the downward slope as they crossed behind them, individual fights and small bands working together, gaps opening up. They could do with help too, but if the Wolves got cut off, there'd be a massacre.

Wolves, Krikites, the wounded. Everyone needs us, Foxy.

We do what we can.

Shit! Dom's in the hospital.

We do what we can.

Swearing, Crys plunged into the trees, Ash by his side.

MACE

Tenth moon, first year of the reign of King Corvus
The hill, edge of Deep Forest, Wheat Lands

THE LINE WAS FIRM. Despite the fluidity of the Krikites' formation, they weren't letting anyone past. Mace watched Colonel Osric and the five-hundred-strong reserve stream away downhill towards the field hospital at their rear, out of sight in the driving rain.

Everyone was out of bastard sight—the Wolves in the trees, the edge of the Krikites' line to the west and Jarl's to the east. Thatcher in the middle anchoring the two was all he could really see. If the Krikites lost touch with the woods, not only would the Wolves be lost and Mace's flank with it, but the Fox God too. And Dalli.

"It'd be just like her to die so she doesn't have to be queen," he muttered to himself, "so I'm counting on you, Trickster. Keep her alive." He returned to the command post and the civilian militia milling around it like panicked sheep. He wasn't counting them among his forces, not until he had to. And if he had to, they'd be losing.

Two hundred Wolves and fifteen hundred Krikites on his right facing the Mireces, Thatcher's five hundred men of the Third Thousand in the middle fighting a mix of Raider and Ranker, Jarl's First and Second Thousands on the left, also facing the East Rank. And now more Easterners up his arse and killing the wounded in the field hospital—or trying to.

Hallos's bearded face flashed through his mind, then Gilda's and Dom's. Dalli's again. Dalli's always, though he knew there was nothing he could do but what he'd already done. Hadir and Colonel Edris paced the command post with him. The wiry general was eager to get into the fray, and Edris matched him easily on his crutch. Two steady officers. Maybe he could just take a wander to the woods, lend a hand . . .

The rotate sounded and the fighters in the front line stepped back, allowing the second rank to take their place. A sudden bulge caught Mace's eye—Thatcher's five hundred had lost contact with the Krikites and Mireces were flowing through the gap, turning his flank. He snapped out an order and the herald blared the Krikites' signal, calling them back into the line. Nothing happened.

Fuck it.

Mace hefted his shield and started to run. "Form square," he roared. "Third Thousand, *form square*."

Thatcher had the same idea and the line contracted and deepened even as Mace sprinted and skidded through the slick grass towards them. It opened the breach further, but it meant they weren't presenting a flank to the enemy. There was a rising scream behind him and then Edris galloped past, sword drawn. He drove into the closest knot of Mireces and hacked down into arms and faces, his mount striking out with hooves and teeth, spinning on its hocks and knocking over Raiders. A one-man, one-legged cavalry charge.

It was just enough to disrupt the flood of Mireces and then Thatcher's square began to lengthen again, two lines at right angles to each other and the Krikites were surging into the Mireces from behind. They faltered, milling, fighting on two fronts. Mace slowed, adrenaline juddering through him, but the Krikites pushed into position and sealed the breach. A horse shrilled; Edris was down. Rankers sprinted to his aid, but it was a chaos of flashing blades and thrashing horse and no one was coming out of that alive.

"There'll be a song about that, Edris, even if I have to write it myself," Mace promised the man as he tapped his heart. "Dancer's grace." He waited some more, but the line firmed and slowly drove the Mireces back. Wounded streamed past him towards the field hospital and the reminder had him following them to peer down the northern side of the hill.

What he saw didn't make sense. Despite the hammering storm, there were tents on fire and wagons too, thick smoke oiling its way into the sky. Between the burning hospital and his position there was . . . he squinted. A running battle. The reserve had the Easterners on the run.

Straight up the hill to Mace's rear.

"Shit. They've turned them." He sprinted for the command post, the herald, Hadir. He scanned the battle. Couldn't take troops from Thatcher, he was too hard-pressed. Jarl didn't have many to spare, but he had some. Ran back to the northern slope with Hadir, who swore. The Easterners were fighting a holding action to keep Osric's reserve pinned at the base of the hill while the rest laboured up it, hoping to take Mace's command post—take Mace himself—and then drive into the unsuspecting rear ranks of the line.

His front three rows were fully engaged and his trumpeter had already sounded the rotation three times. Everyone in the Rank had now fought in the front line, and those at the rear—directly in front of him—were the most recent out of the clash. If he had to turn them to face another enemy . . .

Mace pounded his fist on his thigh. "Hadir, deploy the militia on the northern crest. Just their appearance might be enough to break the Easterners. If not, they're to advance. I want them coming in hard, understand? Take a Fifty from the rear here and use them to form a wedge; militia probably won't make a charge on their own, but they might follow one in. And gods, I need them to," he added as Hadir saluted and plunged towards the rear of the Rank.

The general wriggled in towards the middle, where the freshest of the men were awaiting their turn to rotate in again, and started passing orders. Those at the rear were staring up at Mace, grim-faced and tired already, knowing, or at least suspecting, what must be coming. The herald sounded the call for orders and a few men began jogging uphill from the rear ranks to find out what the bastard bloody shit was going on now.

Mace took another look down the northern slope; the reserve was doing its best but it couldn't find a way through and the Easterners were coming on fast. The five-hundred-strong militia shambled forward, an uneasy mix of brittle defiance and outright terror on their assembled faces. Knuckles yellow on their weapons, blinking freezing rain from their eyes, they looked at him with desperation. *Please don't send us to fight. Please.*

Hadir and the Fifty arrived and Mace put them at the head of the militia. "Break their momentum. Slow them down. I'll send men to you when I can."

The Fifty nodded, grim; the militia hesitant. "I'll lead them," Hadir said.

Mace began to countermand him and then stopped. He'd said it himself—if they didn't win here, they weren't going to win at all. Victory or death; if Hadir wanted to fight, Mace wouldn't stop him. *I need every soldier I can get, after all.*

"Honoured, General," he said instead.

Hadir's smile was wolfish. "Honour's mine, Your Majesty. Though don't wait too long to send those reinforcements."

Mace blew out his cheeks. "I'll do what I can. You do the same."

Hadir saluted, drew his sword and moved into the Fifty. "Ad-vance!" He began to run, no time to waste, and the Fifty bolted after him, roaring, and then the militia, caught up in the frenzy of it. He was running out of officers. Problem was, he was also running out of options.

This is it, he reminded himself. *Win or die.*

Mace watched for a few moments. They broke the East's momentum as hoped, but they were outnumbered and the militia were falling in droves, falling or trying to surrender and being cut down. Dying or running, haring across the rain-slick slope and throwing away their weapons, just looking for a way past the Easterners and down to the field.

"Orders, sir?" asked Captain Kennett as he puffed up the slope from the rear of Jarl's position. He looked in the same direction as Mace. "Oh. Shit."

"Shit indeed. They're not going to hold as they are, so who can you give me?"

"Third Thousand under Colonel Thatcher is absorbing sustained pressure, sir. We can probably give you a couple of hundred if we must, but—"

Mace cut him off. "No, Captain. If the centre doesn't hold, we're truly fucked. It'll have to be Jarl's."

Kennett was grey with exhaustion and blood loss but still upright. "We've shortened the line so it's four deep not three. Front two rows are the Second Thousand, rear two are First Thousand taking a breather."

"Give me half the First," Mace said. "It'll take us a couple of minutes to prepare and get down there to engage; plenty of time for them to get their breath back. This section of the East is fighting a running battle and they'll be knackered from climbing the hill at speed, so the First should outmatch them. And, again, we have the high ground."

"And the Krikites?" Kennett asked, clearly hoping Mace could use them instead.

"Krikites are fully engaged and anchoring Thatcher's line; I've got a herald on that side of the hill to relay progress, but we shouldn't expect reinforcements any time soon."

"The Fox God?" Kennett tried.

"Rallying the Wolves to stop us being surrounded on a third side. It's up to us now, I'm afraid. All right? Dancer's grace."

The herald sounded the First Thousand's recall, followed by the signal for half-Thousand, and hundreds of weary soldiers turned, looked up at the command post and Mace and Kennett, shouldered their shields and began to climb. If Jarl had heard it — if Jarl was still alive — he'd know he didn't have the reinforcements and would adjust strategy accordingly.

If he was dead, too . . . "Kennett, get back down to your men and keep fighting," Mace said. "I'll lead this lot."

DOM

Tenth moon, first year of the reign of King Corvus
Field hospital, the hill, edge of Deep Forest, Wheat Lands

THERE WERE SHOUTS AND screams, the clash of weapons and the thud of metal hitting flesh, of flesh hitting mud, at the front of the hospital tents, and the sudden bloom of fire and stink of pitch.

Dom lay still, listening, fighting the grasping-tearing-raping clutches of the Blood Lady, but the sounds were getting closer. He didn't know where Hallos and Gilda were. There was a pause in the assault on his mind and soul and a cool flicker of Light replaced it, just a flash, a moment, and inside it, seedlike, the blossoming instruction to move. That it was time.

He'd hoped the internal battle was his last, but it seemed not. He could ignore the instruction and lie here and wait to be slaughtered by whoever was out there, or burn to death, or have a heart attack brought on by the Blood Lady's ravaging. It wasn't much of a bastard choice, really. Go and die. Stay and die.

The Light dimmed and he reached for it on instinct, hauling himself up out of the cot on to a left leg that couldn't support him, a left arm that swung useless, a left eye that couldn't see. Gilda had left her walking staff nearby and he offered her a silent apology as he stole it, using it to drag and shuffle to the rear of the tent and out through the flap. No burning to death today. Dom chose the Light.

It was getting darker, the rain heavier, colder. He could see his breath pluming with each shuddery exhalation. The wool of his trousers and the jerkin and shirt beneath soaked up the rain until they were cold and clinging to his flesh. As though even the elements wanted him to stop.

Dom's lopsided smile was grim. "Have to try harder than that," he slurred, barely recognising his own voice. Thunder rumbled in response and his humour leaked away. An image of his hand, melted to a knife thrust into the Dark Lady's chest, flashed through his mind like the lightning that had done it. He squinted up at the clouds. "Keep your bolts, please. It'd be far too embarrassing to die with both my hands missing— and it'd make using this staff a lot harder, too."

He knew he was talking to himself, and he could feel the vague unravelling of parts of his mind as the Blood Lady's presence grew like a canker in the godspace. She was getting closer and the urges She sent him were getting stronger and harder to resist as he shuffle-dragged away from the hospital and into the expanse of the Wheat Lands, following the call of the Light, the call of the Blood.

Soon She'd fill the world, the battlefield, drive Her followers mad with violence and fill Her enemies with dread. He was building mud walls against a flood.

"No. I'm going to stop you. I am."

Someone shouted his name, but he couldn't tell which direction it had come from and besides, he was running out of time. They were all running out of time. Even the Dancer. The last of Her strength was in the air, steeling the hearts and wills of Her people even if they didn't know it. But She was waning, and if She faded before the Blood Lady was defeated, She'd never come back.

"And then we'll have no gods. I'm not sure if that's a good thing or not."

"It's not," said Rillirin, pacing at his side. Dom didn't look at her. She wasn't really there. The Blood Lady had sent her, and no doubt she'd be bloody and torn open, his sweet Rillirin, and he didn't need to see that, not now, not ever. Another thread of Dom peeled away, drifted free on the wind, gone.

"We will always need the gods," she added. He paused, gasping in air and rain. Cold, so cold. "And there's still time for you, Calestar, to choose which you will serve. The Dancer will lead you to death. The Dark Lady, once restored to Her proper form, will raise you up as Her consort and give you immortality."

"A new Gosfath? No thanks. I wouldn't suit the horns."

Rillirin stopped him, a hand on his arm he could actually feel, and he had no choice now but to look at her. The rain didn't touch her and she was clean and fresh and beautiful. There was no child, no rounded belly housing the life they'd made together. Her eyes glittered with avarice and lust and with more life than he'd ever seen sparking in their grey depths.

"She can take this form, if it would please you," Rillirin added, her hand sliding up his arm to cup his cheek. She leant forward, lips parted, and Dom leant back, maintaining the distance between them.

"No. Go away. You're not her. Rillirin never looked like that. She certainly never talked like that. Piss off."

He started off again, a slow limp, not waiting to see if the apparition had taken his advice. "You're going to lose," the Rillirin-thing called after him. He didn't look back. He needed to get away from the battle, draw the Blood Lady to him away from the others, and he was running out of time.

"Brother."

"Brother," Dom acknowledged and then caught himself, a sharp pain like a blow to the chest. He hadn't seen Lim since the West Rank forts, the same night he'd loved and left Rillirin. Lim was dead.

Lim was the same: strong and dour, silver at his temples, face marked with strength and too much introspection. But his eyes, too, dark like Dom's own despite not sharing his blood, couldn't conceal the greed and arrogance in their depths. The soul lived in the eyes, and those eyes weren't his.

"You're going to lose. The battle, the war. Your soul. You know who it belongs to, and She'll still have it, if you give it to Her. Not like the Dancer. That one will throw you away like spoilt food, not even fit for the pigs."

"I'm not doing this for the Dancer," Dom said.

"Then why?" Lim asked, such genuine confusion in his tone that Dom winced at the likeness to the brother he'd known, his throat tightening.

His hand slipped on the staff and he stumbled, leg shaking as he recovered. Lim laughed at him and the resemblance was gone.

"Because I've finally learnt what it's all about," he said and staggered on.

"And what is it all about?" Lim asked with mocking amusement.

"It's all about where you choose to make your home. My home's Rillirin and our daughter, and I might never see them again but I can make sure they live. I can give them the world and make it a good one. I choose Rillirin, not the gods, though They all seemed to choose me." He snorted. "Who'd have guessed I'd be so popular? No, all I want now is to put an end to this and if that means ending the gods—all of them—then that's what I'll do. For her."

"The Afterworld—" Lim began.

"No."

Lim skipped ahead into his path; Dom's laboured walk came to a halt once more. "But you don't have to die. The Dark Lady needs a consort." Lim leered. "All those delights and pleasures you but kissed the surface of can be yours. *She* can be yours. Forever. The Dark Lady forgives you, Calestar, and She will take you into Her embrace and raise you up higher than you have ever been. Hale and whole and in Her arms."

Dom could see it now, the images overlaying Lim's face and the grey day. The Dark Lady in a mortal's skin walking at his side as they ruled the land together, governed wisely, justly, and were worshipped for it. They would sit side by side on gold thrones at the heart of a unified Gilgoras and there would be peace. Happy children of Blood. Contented slaves.

Dom's mouth soured and he cleared his throat, spat. "No," he said again.

Lim's face hardened. "You are running out of chances," he warned. "No one refuses the Dark Lady."

Dom shrugged. "Then if She wants me, She should come herself." He leant forward, right in Lim's face. "In all Her hideous deformity." Grunting, he stepped around Lim and left him behind. The sounds of fighting were fading. He didn't look back.

"If you're going to go through the list of the dead or the loved, it'll take you some time," he said as he struggled on. "Or you could just come and talk to me yourself. I tire of your games, and I have no interest in your promises. So just come and let's get this over with."

The clouds darkened still further, thunder rumbling over the hiss of the rain.

Careful what you wish for, Dom thought a little unsteadily. He laughed, the sound mad and cackling as the urges rose up in him again, higher than the storm clouds, fiercer than the wind that blew his beloved Rillirin's image far away. And he brought his left arm up to his mouth and bit.

CRYS

*Tenth moon, first year of the reign of King Corvus
The hill, edge of Deep Forest, Wheat Lands*

THERE WAS ELECTRICITY IN the air, an oppressive weight that hammered at his temples harder than the rain against his scalp and chainmail.

The small wood was alive with the sounds of fighting, the wildlife having fled or hunkered down in burrows and between roots until the madness passed them. There didn't seem to be a line among the tangle of beech and ash and birch. It was just pockets of fighting, small groups of Wolves and Krikites against bands of Mireces.

They were badly outnumbered. Crys drew his sword; Ash's axe was already in hand and he discarded the shield against a tree to pull his long knife. The soldier in Crys longed for shield and helmet; the Fox God yowled His amusement and pushed him into the melee, a fierce joy bubbling up as he matched strength and cunning and wits against a foe.

He skidded under a wild swing as a Raider saw him from the corner of his eye and flailed a spear at him. Crys came up inside his guard, punching his sword into the man's belly even as he retracted the spear ready for another thrust. Sheer luck to make a kill against the longer weapon.

He wrenched it out of the dying man's hands and sheathed his sword, spun towards the backs of the fifty or so enemies facing a mixed force of Krikites and Wolves. Ash was at his side, taking down the Mireces who slipped inside the spear's reach, the two of them moving with one mind, one breath. Lethal. Beautiful.

The falling leaves and falling rain muffled the sounds of combat as they fought on, brief, vicious battles among the trees, random thuds and screams echoing from the trunks, impossible to determine direction.

Progress too was impossible, open ground big enough to make a stand non-existent, and enemies leapt from behind cover and forced him to change direction over and over until he didn't know which way he was heading, the trees all beginning to look the same and every one harbouring danger. Claustrophobia began to eat at him almost as fast as fatigue.

Eventually they paused in the lee of two large trees, watching the flickers of movement in the gloom, Ash panting, sheathing his weapons to flex numb fingers. "Gods, how long have we been fighting down here?" he gasped.

Crys shrugged, tired down to his bones. "It must be noon or past," he guessed. "Hard to tell under these clouds."

"Do you think we've made enough of a difference, given us a chance?"

"Yes," Crys said, though he had no idea. He couldn't bear to think about how many more Wolves might be lying dead, about how few of Ash's people were left living. He'd need family . . . after. A sudden eruption of noise and clash of weapons off to their right, loud enough to be big. "Come on. We still need to find Dalli. I'm not losing another of Mace's women." They exchanged a sad grin—if Tara had heard that, Crys would be wearing his own lungs as a hat.

It was a running battle, and it was the Mireces who had the upper hand, only a score or so Wolves backing, ducking, jumping sideways and behind trees, looking to make their final stand. Was this all there was? A score of Wolves from a once-proud people of thousands? It wasn't a battle so much as a series of small, bloody melees as both sides slipped in mud, tripped over tree roots and scrabbled with their fingernails at the edges of death.

Crys charged the largest knot of Raiders, ramming into four facing off against two, backed against a fallen tree with nowhere to go. One of them was Dalli, her spear flashing faster than a kingfisher but she was hard-pressed, the shadow of death in her face as she thrust and dodged.

Crys leapt to her side with a wild yell and a swordsman faced off against him, cutting hard and low for his shin. Crys stepped back and off-line, sweeping the spear around. It jerked to a halt, fouled in the roots at his feet and Dalli leapt in front of him as he struggled to free it and the sword opened her up, hip to breastbone.

Ash howled and Crys drew his sword, thrust, missed, then parried and cut low, slicing below the chainmail shirt and into the lead thigh. The man fell back, blood spurting. Another took his place, pushing Crys back so he trod heavily on Dalli's leg, his ankle twisting and dumping him next to her, legs splayed before him.

The blade took hair and the top layer of skin, scalping a trench in his crown that pissed crimson, hot blood and cold rain mingling to tinge his vision pink. He thrust upwards, the Mireces blocking and cutting back, Crys deflecting. Ash roared something and his hand axe sprouted from the man's ribs, knocking him off balance and Crys thrust again, caught him in the mouth, sword tip driving up into his brain.

Ash ripped his axe free and engaged the next, and Crys spun to Dalli, ignoring the chaos. A head wound made her face into something from nightmare, sheeted in red, green eyes darkening with each passing moment. So much blood.

Too much blood.

Her lips were blue. "Fox God," she managed. "Or is it Crys Bowman these days? Now you're married an' all."

"For you, right now, it's Fox God," Crys said, "and be bloody grateful it is." He prised her hand away and blood pulsed free, faster and darker than it had any right to be. Dalli shrieked.

"Hold on," he said. "Dalli, you beautiful little bitch, just hold on." He pressed his hand into the rip in her flesh, so deep he could practically feel the silken smoothness of her liver pushing back. The silver light flared, bright and brighter still until the trees and Ash and the corpses were all limned in it and he had to squint. The flesh had barely begun to knit before it faded.

"No," he whispered. "No, *no*! Foxy?" There was nothing and Dalli was unconscious, still bleeding. He pressed on the wound again.

It's time.

Crys had wanted a way to prevent Ash following him to his final battle, but this wasn't it. Not Dalli. And yet if he didn't, she'd die.

"Ash love, you've got to get her to the hospital. I can't do any more for her." Ash backed up to him so he could glance at Dalli, then back into the trees again. Crys used the tree the haul to himself upright. "It's time," he added, echoing the Fox God's words.

This is where we say goodbye, he wanted to say, but didn't dare. If he said that, Ash would protest, and the core of Crys that wanted so much to live would rebel, and he'd never find the strength in his drained limbs to walk away.

"What about here? They called for you, Crys. They need you."

"The woods are lost," he said. "Get your people moving uphill and get Dalli to Hallos."

They were alone but for her unconscious form and the dead. There was still fighting among the trees, out of sight but not earshot. They didn't have long. Ash put his axe down head first, the haft leaning against his leg so he could snatch it up in an instant. "This is really it?" he asked, a crack like a shiver in his voice.

Crys swallowed hard. "This is it." He could almost see the words dancing on the tip of Ash's tongue: *Don't go, don't leave me, let me fight for you, love me.*

Love me.

"I love you," Crys said. "I will always love you. In this world, in the Light, for always. Tell me you know that."

"I know that," Ash whispered, his voice hoarse as the croak of a dying raven. "Can I say I don't want you to go?" Crys took a step forward and collided with him, the embrace more the mutual clinging of drowning men than a declaration of love. "Can I say I hate the Fox God?" he breathed.

Crys snorted, the sound halfway to being a sob. "Right now, you and me both," he whispered, "though we're both lying. That Trickster's a charismatic bastard. Turns out He can get people to do all sorts against their better judgement." He pressed a hot kiss to Ash's ear and pulled away a little. "Don't forget me," he begged.

"Never," Ash protested.

"No, Ash. Don't forget *me*. Me, Crys Tailorson. Soldier, officer, gambler. Your husband. Don't forget *me*."

"I won't," Ash said. "I couldn't." His smile was ghastly, a slash of pain in his face. "Go and save the world then, you bastard. You beautiful, stupid, heroic bastard. Go on, make us all eternally grateful to your skinny arse. Send that bitch back to the Afterworld and lock the gate after Her."

"That's the plan," Crys said and he stepped away, breaking the embrace, breaking both their hearts.

They watched each other, neither willing to move first, and then Dalli's breath stuttered in her chest and they looked down, severing the last link. Ash holstered his axe and then crouched and gathered her into his arms, and by the time he'd stood, Crys had backed away five paces, enough to break the intangible link that drew them together like a lodestone to the north. It was a gulf he'd never cross again. It was the entire width of the world, and yet he was there, right there. Close enough to taste and as far away as the sun.

"Dancer's grace," he choked.

Ash whooped in a breath, fingers white on Dalli's shoulder and leg as he clutched her. "Dancer's grace," he said.

Crys jerked his chin. "Go," he said. "Let me watch you go."

Lips pressed together against any final words, any last protestations, Ash backed three steps, turned on his heel, and walked away between the trees. Head down, shoulders hunched.

Crys choked again, fists clenched by his sides as he swallowed down the scream building inside him. Sucking in a great breath until his ribs creaked and holding it, he turned east and began to walk out of the trees.

He left his sword behind. He left it all behind. He walked to his final battle, stripping his armour as he went.

CORVUS

Tenth moon, first year of the reign of King Corvus
The hill, edge of Deep Forest, Wheat Lands

THE TWO EAST RANK Thousands opposing the South Rank were faltering, skidding yard by bloody yard back down the incline. Where their line joined Corvus's, gaps were beginning to open.

"Mother-bastard-shit!" Corvus roared. He'd been at the front three times but was now in the rear, a dozen strides downhill of the writhing mass, trying to evaluate what was happening. If the Rank faltered now it was over. He needed to steady them, bring them back in step with the Mireces.

"Dark Lady, Holy Gosfath, come to us," he prayed. "Guide our hands, our hearts strong in your glory." Tett was at his side while Fost had the other end of their formation, against the Krikites and the Wolves on the wooded slope. They were making progress there and the Mireces line was curving across the hill—they must've taken the woods.

"Tett, get me a hundred men. We're going to reinforce the Rank seeing as the cunts can't even do what they're paid for without cocking it up." He didn't wait for a response, just began to traverse the slope, boots squelching with each step and threatening to send him flying. The temperature dropped even more and the rain solidified into hail, bouncing from his helmet and chainmail, hitting his face hard enough to sting. "The Lady's will," he panted.

It reduced visibility even further, until it was as if Corvus were cut off from the killing and dying all around him, adrift in an ocean attempting to devour itself. There was movement in the flurry of hail and rain as the wind gusted and twisted the weather into shapes that almost seemed to make sense before collapsing in on themselves.

Ahead of him the East Rankers resting at the back stood in grim, silent lines, shivering in the freezing wind, linen flapping as they bandaged minor wounds. He barged through the first of the recovering men and turned up the incline. "On me," he roared. "*On me.*" He felt rather than saw them come with him. Whether it was because he was their king or because the gods urged them on, they shouldered their shields and began to pound up the muddy, treacherous hill behind him without question.

Ahead, a Ranker came flying down the slope, mouth and eyes wild, preparing to cast aside his weapons and flee. He came to a confused, guilty halt as Corvus thundered past and Tett flicked out his sword as he passed, half-decapitating him. Let those following and those ahead, turning to see who was running, understand what happened to deserters.

"Stand," Corvus bellowed to the dark mass of struggling men ahead of him. He ploughed into their backs, sword sheathed and shield held crossways in front of him. His boots dug in, slipped, dug in again, and Corvus got his shoulder in and just pushed. The two men above him felt his resistance, realised that someone—reinforcements—were there, and shoved back with renewed hope at the enemy pressing down on them.

To left and right, the East Rank crashed into the rear of their own troops and forced them forwards. Forced them on to enemy spears and swords in places, but up and down the line he could hear shouted encouragement, warnings, anything to help the two rows ahead.

The line stiffened. The line halted. The line began to push.

"Let me in," Corvus roared at the soldiers ahead of him. He released the pressure on his shield and slid his sword free, leapt into the gap they made for him before the Southerner facing them could seize the advantage, planted his feet, locked his shield with theirs, and braced. He wasn't a Ranker, didn't have their training, but he understood the need to stand firm and stay in the line.

Opposite in the driving hail was the South Rank, only two rows deep. "Hold the line," he shouted as they shoved and slipped forward. "Brace!"

The shields to either side locked more firmly against his. They couldn't wait; it'd take only one man to slip on the treacherous slope and they'd all be down it. "Advance!"

The soldier behind him slammed his shield into Corvus's back, forcing him forward a single, lurching step and tearing a screech of pain from him. He didn't have a Ranker's plate armour and the shield boss ground into his spine, but there was nowhere to go, no way out from under the pressure. He gritted his teeth, offered the pain to the gods, and pushed forward.

The spear of the man behind found its way past Corvus's ear and up into a face, tearing skin. Corvus's own sword followed it, lower, deeper, punching the man off his feet into the soldier behind, who staggered under the weight hitting his shield and then tipped the body off and tried to scramble over it. Corvus took him through the side of the neck. He fell, choking, and the third didn't step into the breach.

Corvus did, and then realised his mistake. He was surrounded on three sides by the enemy, pressed closer than lovers. His shield covered his front, but his flanks were open. A hand gripped his chainmail and hauled him back so fast he nearly fell, but it saved his life. It was Tett, of course. His bodyguard didn't do more than check he wasn't dying before he jabbed his sword at the next man along, distracting him enough that the Ranker to his right could kill him.

Together they picked at the hole in the front line, widening it man by man, the Southerners in the next rows back trying to climb over the bodies and dying. Corvus took a step forward only as the men to either side did, stamping down on the corpse, feeling around it for a solid footing, fencing away with the spear tip jabbing for him, knocking it up hard enough his man behind lunged in and stabbed into the exposed armpit with his own spear. Another one down.

But the end of Corvus's line was still twisting despite all his efforts, pushed slowly back downhill, breaking the line of shields, the strength of numbers and formation.

"*Hold the line,*" he screamed towards the left, but it continued its slow warp. Much more and the enemy would be able to flood past it and roll up the flank like a fucking carpet. And the baggage train and hospital tents were burning—he could taste the smoke on the wind—so where the fuck were the Easterners he'd sent to fire it? They were supposed to be advancing up the southern slope to take these bastards up the arse.

"On me!" screamed a major next to him without waiting for orders. "Three steps back, on my command. Step!"

The South Rank roared its victory as the line shuffled down the hill, straining to pull the left flank back into contact with the rest. They pushed forward, clambering over their dead, harrying the line before it was settled on its new footing, and another bulge appeared as half a dozen of Corvus's soldiers went down on a patch of ice or mud, were slaughtered where they lay, the South shoving into the breach, barging forward behind their shields. They had the momentum now, were threatening to cut Corvus's line in two.

The rest of the Easterners weren't coming. When Corvus himself reached the Afterworld to take his place in glory at the gods' side, years and conquests and the making of legend from now, he would ensure those who had failed him were daily torn apart for their incompetence.

Corvus's mouth stretched in a wide smile as he killed the next Ranker to dare face him. Tett fought on his left, still alive though missing an ear and part of his cheek, blood misting into the air with every rasping breath, but killing and dodging and saving Corvus's life again and again.

Part of him knew they were losing, but it was a distant knowledge, subsumed beneath something else, something greater and immediate and *right there*, filling him to the brim with bloodlust and fury and righteous, revelling madness—the gods had come.

The gods had come and nothing the fighters did now would alter that momentous arrival. Corvus screamed his raging euphoria as all around him, as all over the hill, every faithful son of the Red Gods was lifted up and filled with reckless purpose.

Kill. Kill them all.

Kill everything.

DOM

Tenth moon, first year of the reign of King Corvus
Edge of Deep Forest, Wheat Lands

HE WASN'T SURPRISED WHEN Crys came up beside him. Or not
Crys. The Fox God. He'd shed His armour, His boots and even
His shirt, seeming oblivious to the bitter wind and the hard,
tiny crystals of hail that blasted like gravel into their faces. It'd snow
soon, if Dom was any judge.

"You ready for this?" he asked the Fox God as the presence of the
Blood Lady loomed closer and darker and ever more imposing. It felt as if
She was going to push through the clouds any second and crush them flat.
"The Red Gods' most wanted, gathered together to defy Them."

The Fox God's smile was feral, His teeth overly sharp. "We're ready.
Are you?" He reached out without looking, put a hand on Dom's arm,
and lowered it from his mouth. Dom could taste his own blood and knew
it was wrong; he leant on the Fox God's strength to stop himself from
biting again.

"You're the one She's inside," He added. "You're the one seeing what
She wants you to see."

Dom stumbled away a pace, clutching his stump to his chest. How
did He know that? Was this another vision, sent to distract him while the
real Fox God faced the Blood Lady on His own? How would he be able
to tell?

The Fox God held His arms out wide. "I'd tell you to stab me, but we know that won't prove anything," He said. He snapped His fingers and silver light arced from them to the bites in Dom's stump. They sealed even as he watched. "All right then, Calestar, now that that's cleared up, what's your plan?"

Dom blinked, brushed the cold flesh of his foreshortened arm against his stubbled cheek. It throbbed, a dull, persistent ache. Maybe the cold; maybe something else. Didn't matter, he supposed. "What? I don't have a plan. You're the Fox God; what's your plan?"

The Trickster rubbed at the red and silver patterns on his chest and upper arms, appearing unconcerned. "I'm not allowed to know the specifics of my fate, remember, in case I run away screaming? I assumed you'd have a plan that saw me kill the Blood Lady and die in the act."

Because I tried to kill you before? Dom didn't say it out loud, but from the knowing look on the Fox God's face, He understood the path of his thoughts. "May as well kiss goodbye to a free Rilpor then," he said instead, "because I haven't got a fucking clue."

"Really? Damn." The Fox God grinned. "Then I suppose we make it up as we go along, don't we? Wouldn't be the first time, and She'll be here soon, anyway. Any. Minute. Now."

Unexpected nerves fluttered in Dom's belly—unexpected because they were the nervous thrill of anticipation, the excited anxiety of meeting an old lover again. He did his best to still them.

Remember what She looks like now, what She is. What She's always been, and you too blind to see it.

Remember Rillirin. Home.

The wind was dropping, though the temperature continued to tumble as the sun moved across the sky, a distant orange glow behind thick snow clouds. Winter was early and savage, and a god rode its back. As the squall lessened and the hailstones became bigger, fluffier, the first flurries of snow, the rumbling clash of metal on wood, metal on metal, and metal on flesh rose from behind, the sound swirling and swooping as the carrion crows would soon enough. Dom shivered again.

"Seeing anything unusual?" the Fox God asked.

Dom stared across the whitening field and around in a circle, studying the ground and the sky, looking for that intangible something which might be the Blood Lady's approach. There. He squinted. "I . . . I think we're on the wrong side of the hill."

The Fox God hummed low in His throat. "And yet you walked this way and I followed you. Trying to delay me, were you?"

"Me? No, Lord. I came this way . . ." He paused, thinking. "I don't know why I came this way."

"Because She wanted you to. She wanted access to Her followers without our interference, I expect." He cocked His head and Dom heard the change in the sound of battle, higher-pitched and strident now. Fear and rage. The last desperate moments of thousands of warriors. "She's already here. Come on."

The Fox God set off at a run directly for the small wood hugging the base and flank of the hill. Dom shambled after Him, fast as he could and not fast enough. But the Fox God needed him, there was no doubt about it, so he limped on, dragging his left foot, lurching on his right.

The Fox God came back to his side. "This is undignified, I know, but I'm going to carry you," He said. Dom's mouth turned down but he didn't argue, and was hoisted up and over the Fox God's shoulders like a sack of grain, the staff falling from his hand.

"Fuck," he grunted as they began to run and his sternum bounced up and down on the Trickster's shoulder, stealing a portion of his breath with each stride until the pain made him dizzy.

They slowed through the trees, picking their way through roots, shrubs and the dead clogging their path, and then they were out on to the plain and he heard the Fox God mutter something and slow again, then pick up the pace. If there was such a thing as running reluctantly, He was doing it. Whatever was in front of them, it'd given Him pause. Cold sweat prickled and Dom didn't look.

The Fox God put him down with his back to whatever was there and held his head in both hands to stop him turning. "Are you ready? Do you know what it is *you* have to do, even if you don't know what I'm meant to do?"

Dom licked his lips, wiped his palm against his trousers. "Yes, Lord. Well, I think so."

"Remember the Light," the Trickster said. "See Them for what They really are, not what She shows you. She won't save you. She doesn't love you."

"Neither does the Dancer," Dom said before he could stop himself.

Sorrow darkened the Fox God's dual-coloured eyes. "You know that's not true," He said softly. "But whoever it is you're fighting for, hold them close." He let go and took a pace to the side. Dom had to screw up his courage and hold it tight to his chest before he could shuffle around in his wet boots and look.

The Dark Lady. The beautiful, perfect, tantalising Dark Lady. Her smile was hot as She beckoned to him, and his feet were already moving before the Fox God repeated his admonition to look, to remember. To *see*.

But he couldn't. It was Her, his love, his perfect goddess, the answer to his every prayer. Love and need rose in him as She stroked his mind and slipped into the godspace as silky smooth as Her tongue into his mouth.

My calestar, how I have missed you. She laughed, the sound jarring and wrong. Mad. Dom blinked rapidly, scrubbing his hand over his face and then biting savagely on his thumb, not because She made him this time, but in order to focus on the pain. *You have come back to me. Despite everything. You are mine again.*

Want.

That wasn't Her speaking; that last word was deeper, lower, a hungry child's demand. *Gosfath.* Dom stumbled in the frozen mud, shaking his head like a dog. "What?" he croaked, and then he saw Her. Saw Them. *It.*

His mouth fell open as he took in the full horror. The Dark Lady was gone, subsumed into something far less than human, far more than divine. A mangled wreck of body parts jammed and smashed and minced together, crooked eyes and screaming mouths with too many teeth, too many limbs, too much sagging, swinging skin. Too much everything rearing as tall as Rilporin's towers once had.

Horror made flesh. Flesh made divine. And divinity made mad.

This is what She'd have done to our daughter, he realised, and it was enough to break Her grip on him. She was still in the godspace, scritching around like a diseased rat, but he could see Her with his own eyes, not the illusion She'd placed over them. He wished he couldn't.

The Fox God was at his side, still bearing that look of sorrow. "Sister. Brother," He said, hands outstretched. "It is still not too late."

The Blood Lady raised a hand, mottled with red, three of its fingers tipped with black talons, and She pointed. "You. You have my essence, my spark. Give it back or I will kill everyone here. Kill the entire world."

"No, you won't," the Fox God said, walking forward with all the nonchalance of a man meeting a friend in the street. "You can't. You haven't the power. It's taking most of what you've got to cling on to your Brother, to meld your essence with His. One single lapse in concentration and He'll oust you."

Dom followed Him, a few paces behind, his heart pounding squirrel-fast, mouth dry with fear, not lust. He held Rillirin's face in his mind as a barrier between it and the Blood Lady. Wind-blown russet hair and grey eyes softening a face that rarely remembered to laugh but was lit from within when it did. She was alive still, their daughter too, and he wondered what she'd named her and which of them she most looked like.

Thoughts to bring him peace. Thoughts to build a wall between him and Them.

The Fox God was still advancing, his arms outspread to the Blood Lady as though to embrace Her horror. Dom knew, fear writhing in his gut, that he couldn't let that happen. Not yet. They couldn't touch yet because despite the madness and the halting, twisted flesh, She was still too strong for Him. *Someone's got to weaken Her. Oh, look, that'd be me.*

"My love," he called, and the Fox God's head whipped around to stare at him, disbelief and suspicion warring across His features. "What has she done to you, my love? How did the Blessed One manage to fuck up so badly? She had the babe; she had everything she needed. What happened?"

"Calestar," He warned, but Dom ignored Him, going closer. On the hill where men and women fought and died, the clash of arms seemed weaker, as if Dom were walking down a tunnel and leaving all the sound behind.

The war had always been bigger than the men and women on each side could understand. It had been fought for a thousand years, not by Wolf and Mireces and West Ranker on the border, but in minds and in hearts, in faith and in blood, and in the spaces between the stars and beyond the veil. Now, finally, it had come to Gilgoras. And it was here, on Rilpor's soil, that the fate of them all would be decided. By Dom, the half-Blood, half-Light calestar, the dying cripple who had betrayed them all, friends and enemies and gods alike.

BLOODCHILD

But not you, my love. The Blood Lady preened at his thought. *Not you, Rillirin. Even though it must have felt like it, I never betrayed you.*

The monster brayed its fury and slammed harder into the godspace, trying to force him to recant, to beg forgiveness. Dom swayed like a tree in a storm but he would not stop. Could not stop. He might not be the heroic, self-sacrificing warrior Gilgoras needed, but apparently he was all the Dancer had, because She'd set him on this path years and leagues and deaths ago, stripping his choices one by one until every twist and turn in the road led him not away from, but towards, this moment.

"And I don't even have the energy to hate you any more," he mumbled to the Dancer and to himself. "Let's just get it done."

He rubbed his chest over his stuttering, skipping heart, its rhythm erratic as the Blood Lady continued to scrabble inside him, looking for his truth. He just had to reach Her before She learnt it.

Rillirin.

"My love," he said, near enough now not to have to shout. Her stink enveloped him—sulphur and mould, sex and fear. "What can we do? How can I help you?"

The blowing snow could no longer hide the extremes of Her hideousness now he was so close. She tried to sneer, but Her features were permanently warped into agonised fury and only one cheek twitched.

"Help? I—We—do not need your help." She eyed the Fox God, predatory. "We have our plans." She laughed, the sound as mad as Dom's must have been for all those months, a file across his nerve endings.

A few more steps and he'd be able to touch . . . It. And the closer he got, the stronger the swirling madness became, emanating from Her like perfume, like rot. More pieces of him unravelled, tugged by the winds of Her lunacy, out and away and gone. He could feel them, strands of being, of identity, tearing away in the breeze.

He laughed, a mad, high-pitched cackle that matched Hers, and he stepped forward into Her arms. "My love," he whispered over the hissing, belching screams and shouts that hooted around her from the Afterworld, "my sweet love, you have returned. To me and to all of us."

"I remember you," She said and what he'd thought was fondness in Her ravaged face twisted into fury. "I remember what you did. Because of you, I am this. Because of you, my Brother suffers. I suffer. *Because of you"* — She leant down close so that one of Her eyes was level with his own — *"the world will suffer.* And you will watch."

There was something that Dom was supposed to do now, but it was almost calm here, almost tranquil, in the eye of a storm that lashed everyone around them with madness and fury and hard white snow. There was a patch of Her face that was still Hers, pale as moonlight, smooth as butter. He put his hand against it, stretched on to his toes to kiss that corner of Her mouth, where it was perfect, before it twisted into a mockery of Gosfath's leer.

Nothing mattered but that little corner of Her, the memory and vision of all he'd lost, all he could have back again. "I can make you whole," he breathed. "And then you can make me yours."

The Blood Lady reared back, squealing Her agony as Her twisted, melted form protested. Those parts that were Gosfath writhed, straining, splitting great wet mouths in Their flesh as He tried to rip Himself free of Her. She squealed again, black and red light flashing around Them as She drove more of Herself into Her Brother-Lover, anchoring Her essence deep within but not before He was able to wrench His head away, ripping the elongated skull in half, tearing Their faces free of each other.

"Stop, my love," Dom shouted over the screaming — high-pitched enough to make his ears bleed and deep inside him too — but the thing before him mangled itself even further, one part desperate for separation, the other for control. It shrank, losing much of its imposing height in favour of healing the tears in its flesh. It had three complete legs now, one bending backwards. The heads remoulded, eyes realigning and bones forming beneath knitting flesh and Dom struggled to get away but black, horn-tipped tentacles held him tight, feet off the ground.

The Dark Lady, head and one arm and torso beautiful and perfect and compelling, examined him and the battlefield from atop a writhing monster. Gosfath kept pulling, and more black tentacles erupted from Her spine and pierced Him, dragged Him closer. Dom could see them pulsating as they drank His strength. The god squealed and battered at Her; She ignored Him.

"I know what I've done, I know you have no reason to trust me, but I can fix this!" Dom screamed. He heard the Fox God shout something behind him, ignored it. He stretched and just managed to put his hand on her chest. "It was here, wasn't it, my love? It was here that I stabbed you." The Dark Lady's mouth stretched wide, wide enough to bite his throat out and She dragged him close enough to do it. Dom grabbed Her perfect face with his hand, wrapped his stump around the back of Her head and kissed Her.

The Fox God, shouting.

Gosfath, fighting.

Dom, dying.

Ecstasy and surrender filled him and threatened to swamp his resolve. He moaned at the rightness of it all, the lust and pleasure coursing his limbs and then Rillirin's face, grave and sad, crossed his inner vision and did what no god's command ever could. It gave him back to himself.

With one savage move, Dom ripped open the godspace inside his head and he gave the Dark Lady everything that he was. *Everything.* A barrage of emotion, of guilt and fear and revulsion, a thousand hurts and little indignities and wrenching losses and more guilt and shame, shame, *shame* all flooding through him and into Her, a ceaseless assault She neither expected nor knew how to withstand. She'd wanted everything and that's exactly what he gave Her.

And from the other side the Dancer came too, both of Them inside him and wrestling for possession of the godspace, fighting and clawing and tearing him and each other apart, and then the Dancer poured Her Light through him and into the Dark Lady. Light to burn, Light to sear and bubble and penetrate. Light to kill.

The Dark Lady wrenched away, braying in agony and one of the tentacles solidified into an arm, a hand, and then a long, tapered finger and She speared Dom through his right eye. The last thing he saw before blindness and agony took him was Light, unstoppable, pouring from his mouth and skin and bathing Her in its awful purity.

"Now," he yelled into the blackness inside him. He saw Rillirin again. "*Now!*"

The Fox God attacked.

CRYS

Tenth moon, first year of the reign of King Corvus
Edge of Deep Forest, Wheat Lands

DOM, NO!" HE SCREAMED, but then Dom was tumbling into the snow and the Fox God was moving, propelling them across the icy ground towards the monster, still twice his height. Gosfath was still preoccupied with ripping Himself free of His Sister, and the Dark Lady was bleating and clawing at Her face—the Light that had shone so impossibly bright from Dom's mouth and eyes had burnt Her and She was mad with it.

Crys launched himself at the Blood Lady, silver light blasting from his skin and staggering Her, adding to the ruin of Her face. Not as strong as *the* Light, but enough to deepen wounds already made. His left foot landed on a knee and he clambered up like a squirrel.

The Blood Lady made a grab for his throat, seeking the rest of Her essence, enough to strengthen Her, enough to cast out Gosfath from His own body and heal Her hurts. Crys swayed beneath the flailing arm, got both hands on Gosfath's neck, then worked one under the god's chin, settled his knee against the slab of His chest, and twisted.

Nothing.

He twisted again, harder, and Gosfath's head juddered around, the neck crunching. Then it spun back, so fast Crys lost his grip and the god's snapping mouth just closed on his flailing hand, severing his little finger.

He screamed and his light flared brighter, sealing the wound and scorching Gosfath, making Him squeal in turn. He flailed away, ripping apart from the Dark Lady, red and pale flesh separating, strings of meat and tendrils of smoke trying to haul them back together again. The opening Crys needed.

He plunged both hands deep into the cavity and more silver light flared and blasted into raw flesh.

The sounds the gods made were distilled madness as the stench of a mass grave enveloped Crys. A red hand gripped beneath his chin, thumb and forefinger grinding either side of his jaw, squeezing so hard he had to open his mouth. His light faltered and the flesh slammed together around his wrists, trapping his hands inside Them. Again They began to shrink, using Their bulk to replace the burnt flesh, using up Their own essences, but now Crys was trapped too and he yelled, straining as the god-stuff tried to suck him bodily inside.

Another hand, slender and feminine this time, small as a girl's, stuffed its fingers past his teeth as he screamed, depressing his tongue and questing towards the back of his throat. He jerked, gagging, but the hand pushed in further, remorseless.

"Where is it? Give it to me. *Give me my essence*."

A wrenching, tearing pop and crunch in his jaw, and Her hand went in past the knuckles and Crys couldn't breathe, trapped inside a writhing, mutating form up to the elbows now and the Dark Lady's hand in his throat.

Legs kicking and making no impression, Crys pulled, felt the flesh give and then suck him back in deeper, planted his feet on Their chests and yanked harder, shoulders popping.

Bite.

If he could breathe he'd have screamed as he forced his jaw to close. His teeth went into the Dark Lady's hand and he ground them together, shaking his head like a dog with a rat. The fingers in his throat paused and then . . . melted into a thick muscular tube that slithered free of his throat with a slurp.

Crys sucked in a breath and headbutted Her, kneed Gosfath in the face, lunged in and bit at His ear. Inside Them, his hands clenched and squeezed and ripped until, with a joint bellow of hate, They ripped open and released him. Crys hit the ground and rolled, his jaw flapping loose. Silver light burnt around his head and he felt the muscles and bones in his face reset, click and snap back into place. He screeched at the pain, there and then gone.

Crys got up and his legs tensed, telling him to run. He even took a few steps away from the cavorting, blood-hungry god-fuck reaching for him. Ash wouldn't blame him—he wanted him to get away. Crys wanted to get the fuck away. The Fox God . . . couldn't get away. The fate of the world sat on His shoulders, whether He wanted it to or not.

Not. So *bastard* not. But that still didn't mean He could run. The Fox God had come here to die, and Crys had to let it happen. Because somehow, their death would save the world. He just hoped it would be worth it.

Life is always worth dying for.

Crys spat in the snow, clearing his mouth and throat of coppery saliva. He breathed deep, bringing the world into startling clarity as adrenaline surged through him and bolstered the courage that wanted only to wane. The Fox God rose inside him and when a black tentacle shot out and wrapped around His waist, it was the Fox God who smiled. "Welcome, Sister. Welcome, Brother. How can I help?"

"Give me back my essence," the Dark Lady said as Gosfath clawed at Her and black tentacles whipped and writhed behind Their heads, a crown of madness.

He grimaced. "It won't heal you. Nothing can do that. It's time to let go."

The Dark Lady's face twisted and She began to laugh, though the words quietened Gosfath, who watched with something like hope. The Fox God held out a hand to Him, and He took it.

"You are not as clever as you think, little god," She said. "You do not see as far as I. But you'll help me anyway."

"Yes," the Fox God said, nodding, "I can do that. It isn't too late, for either of you. Renounce the Path you have walked for so long, return the divinity you stole from our Mother and be welcomed back into the Light."

Dom's blood smeared Her arm, Her perfect face. The Fox God placed His fingers in it. "You have done much evil, Sister. So much. Led astray an entire nation, bathed in blood so long that you have forgotten what it is to be clean. To be loved with a pure heart. This body you say I have hidden in, the heart and soul of this man, they're clean. They love purely, not oblivious to the consequences but accepting of them. Return to the Light and you too can feel that love."

The Dark Lady wheezed her mad cackle again and a thick rope of black muscle slashed down, breaking His grip on Gosfath's hand. The God of Blood growled, a low rumble of threat, and any peace and stillness in Him was gone. Once more He began to tear at Her, seeking division. Autonomy. Freedom. She rammed more of Herself into Him so They both squealed and bucked, the tentacle holding the Fox God shrinking as She spent Her essence on controlling Her Brother.

"I said you were going to help me, you puny godling," She groaned. "You, not your Flower-Whore Mother. But when I'm done with you, the Dancer's next."

Crys surged up in their shared consciousness, screaming a warning, but the Fox God let His head fall back, inviting what He knew was to come.

A dozen more black tentacles whipped from the Blood Lady's chest and impaled Him, through the belly and ribs and groin and shoulder, sinking deep into mortal flesh and immortal spirit. Sucking. Drinking.

Killing.

She found the essence of Herself He had consumed in Rilporin to shatter Her into nothing but a wisp of will, lost in the void, and She devoured it. And then She found His essence, the beautiful silver shimmer that reflected Her twisted, warped body and soul back at Her so She couldn't help but see Herself as others did.

She screamed as the Fox God screamed, Her shame the equal to His grief, and slammed a last, thick tentacle into His mouth and down His throat, sucking out the breath from His lungs, the very life of Him.

As the Fox God was pulled from him in great draughts, Crys slid back into the spaces He had occupied. It was like coming home to an empty house, abandoned by a loved one, a hollow, haunted shell. And with his return came the knowledge of his impalement, hanging suspended by ropes of horn-tipped muscle that pierced him in a dozen places. Bled him. Killed him.

He couldn't breathe, a lung collapsing as She siphoned the air out of him like a monstrous bellows made of flesh. He wasn't even bleeding as She drank that too, but worse than what was happening to his body was the moment by moment loss of the Fox God, the greater, better part of his soul, like having a limb torn off slowly enough he could watch it happen.

And he couldn't scream at the loss. She'd even stolen his voice.

Silver lines and black traced across Her features, replacing the red, remaking Her in pewter and shadow as She emerged from the shell of Gosfath like a reluctant crab. Four arms, four legs, two spines leaching away from each other.

Gosfath's face was twisted with a terrible haste and He pulled, splitting Them, ripping Them apart and roaring at the pain of it, but pulling anyway, desperate to be rid of the parasite that was His Sister.

The Dark Lady's body had been destroyed, but it no longer mattered. She used the silver godlight that was the Trickster, twisting and moulding Him into a shining silver net, a woman-shape, into which the black smoke and fleshy strands of Her essence poured.

Gosfath was pushing Her out and She let him, just as eager to be separate and all Herself again, and through the umbilical cords She had deep in Crys's body he could feel Her. The silver shape wasn't strong enough, wouldn't sustain Her for long, but long enough for Her to execute the next part, the most audacious part, of Her plan.

Tired.

Fading.

Three of the tentacles skewering him popped free and Crys dropped a little, bare toes scuffing the grass, the drop and jerk tearing more things inside and the pain so big there wasn't a word for it. The tube came out of his throat and he managed a shuddering inhalation that might be his last.

There was no more Fox God inside him, no more Dark Lady and She, separate now from Her Brother, let him drop without further thought, a broken doll discarded in favour of a new toy.

Gosfath was whole again, but He was not a happy god. He brayed at the sky and roiled the clouds, churning them like butter until thunder muttered and lightning stabbed into the earth, blasting snow into steam and killing birds on the wing.

The Dark Lady was black smoke within a silver shape, Her face and arms and torso clothed in skin. Her golden eyes met Crys's, so smug that under different circumstances he'd have punched them shut, and then She focused on Gosfath. "Brother," She purred.

The God of Blood roared. "Kill," He bellowed, raising His fists at Her. He slammed them into the ground, knocking soldiers and Mireces from their feet hundreds of strides away on the hill. Crys bounced where he lay.

"Kill you."

The Dark Lady nodded once, not with disappointment but with utter indifference. Gosfath, God of Blood, Her Brother, Her Lover and companion of a millennium, was a mere insect. "So be it."

In His brash confidence, Gosfath was probably the only one who didn't expect it. More tentacles of smoke and muscle, hollow, unstoppable feeding tubes, sprouted from the Dark Lady's silver-wrought chest and slammed into Him. Each time She created one, it used up a little more of Her strength, but the vitality She drained more than compensated.

Crys lay in the snow, turning it red with what little blood he had left, and he watched the Dark Lady consume Her Brother-Lover to finish creating Her new body.

The God of Blood roared and fought, clawing at the flesh and smoke tentacles, but the Fox God's strength bound to the Dark Lady's was too much for Him to overcome and He began to come apart even as She solidified, weaving His essence into Hers, into the Fox God's, a black-red-silver net of divinity: hate and madness and rage, and silver, shimmering love and humour that had no place there and enraged Her further.

She needed Him, but She couldn't bear what He was; His joy and forgiveness burnt Her even as He clothed Her in power. An endless screeching hurt She would never quite be rid of. It brought the faintest of smiles to Crys's bloodless lips.

Gosfath fell to His knees, His roars now wails, the violence in His face subsumed by incomprehension, by sudden, all-consuming betrayal. "*Sister*," He cried, one red and flaking hand outstretched.

Her only response was the disdainful, utterly contemptuous curl of Her perfect lip and then He broke, shattered into a million splinters of red light that winked and faded like sparks whirling upwards from a fire.

Gone.

The Dark Lady stretched and pirouetted in Her new form, learning its limits, its abilities. She was a hybrid, an uneasy roiling mix of three gods, three forces, but She imposed Her will on the other two. Eventually, She'd crush Them into nothing but whispers in the back of Her mind.

Crys wheezed a laugh, found another breath insinuating its way into his labouring lungs. And then another. Not quite dead. Not yet.

She squatted next to him. "You are amused? Perhaps I shall keep you, a living embodiment of agony, a perpetual reminder to those I shall rule of their fate should they do other than worship and love me."

Crys dismissed Her words with a blink. "You are a fool," he croaked with a smile that he knew had nothing of humour in it. Still his mouth stretched and he stretched, inside, for the Fox God. He was there, just, in the silver net the Dark Lady had stolen. Crys brushed a finger against it and the connection solidified—for the last time. His smile became genuine.

"Fool," he repeated. "For we are Trickster, and it is in our nature to deceive."

There was a blast of laughter from inside and all around, and the silver light that was the divine spark of the Fox God, moonlight on gossamer, began to fade.

Fox God, lord of cunning and the once and always Son of the Dancer, played His last and greatest trick: He died.

The Dark Lady lurched to Her feet as She felt the disintegration begin. "No!" She screeched. "Not again. I will not allow it. *This cannot be.*"

"And the godlight will lead us all, to death and beyond," Crys breathed, his heartbeat stuttering in his ears. "Follow Him, Lady. Follow Him to the Light and the Dancer and beg Her forgiveness. Die as He dies. As Gosfath has died. Find some peace."

"*No*," She screamed again, but the silver net rippled, rippled and then blew apart, shatters of light bursting across the field and the hill and the warriors, racing each other, joyful and laughing and gone.

Weakened, with nothing holding Her together, with no more strength to steal, the Dark Lady lashed out even as Her form billowed and deformed. She reached for Her followers and sucked the mortality from hundreds of them, thousands, but it was not enough. She was goddess—mere human life could not sustain Her, not in this extremity.

She roared and wailed and bleated, and Crys lay there and watched Her, and found himself sad, but there was no way back now, nothing that could stop the inevitable. Cracks appeared in Her face, Her form, cracks that opened on to an utter absence of everything, until into that absence She fell.

Consumed, at the end, by Herself.

"No coming back from that," Crys croaked. "We did it."

A gust of wind blew across the fields, a lingering malevolence whispering from it, and then it, too, was gone. In its place, clean and pure and silent, the snow began again and through the white curtain a figure was sprinting towards him, curly hair plastered to his brow. Crys's breathing hitched, skipped, settled.

Ash skidded the last strides on his knees, catching himself before he slammed into Crys's side. His hands slid beneath his shoulders and lifted him to his chest and Crys gasped as his shattered insides ground together. "Crys? Crys, it's me, it's Ash. We won, love. We won."

"I know," he breathed. "Love you."

"I love you. I love you, Crys. Just hold on, Hallos is coming and—"

"Ssh," he managed. "Hold me."

He heard Ash's heart crack and wished he could spare him the grief, could save him as Ash had saved Crys and shown him the world, but he couldn't. Ash pulled him closer, draped one of Crys's arms around his waist and pressed his lips to his temple, his brow. "Rest then," he breathed. "Just rest, my love. I'm here."

Thank you, Foxy. Time to say goodbye was all I really wanted.

The snow fell, silent and serene. Crys Tailorson, major in His Majesty's Ranks and husband of Ash Bowman, fell with it.

MACE

Tenth moon, first year of the reign of King Corvus
The hill, edge of Deep Forest, Wheat Lands

FOR THE SECOND TIME in his career, there were gods on Mace's battlefield. He liked it even less than the previous occasion.

As in Rilporin, the gods' arrival had driven the Mireces and East Rankers into a crazed, reckless bloodlust that nearly carved Mace's army into tattered ribbons. As it was, they were shoved back right to the summit of the hill and once the enemy was on the same flat ground, the tempo of battle sped up, not even the howls and otherworldly roars from the field below enough to deter them. Madness shone in every face and gleamed from every tooth exposed by writhed-back lips.

The Wolves had abandoned the wood and the Krikites had been pushed up the flank of the hill, both too outnumbered to hold any longer. They'd linked up with the Rank and now the ragged survivors were hard-pressed on three sides and nowhere much to go. He called for the square and they put their backs to one another and they prepared to fight to the last.

The Krikites were wavering, on the verge of collapse and the Wolves—pitifully few of them left—were buckling with them under the onslaught when there was a blast of red and black and silver light from the field below and every heathen, Mireces or Easterner, hesitated. The barest breath, the merest blink of an eye. It was enough.

"All out," Mace screamed. "*All out!*"

He didn't wait to see if anyone was going with him. The enemy had paused, they'd lost their focus, broken their own momentum. Mace didn't intend to let them get it back. All along the front, men and women, soldiers and Wolves and Krikites and a few, a very few, civilian militia, saw the same chance he did. The soldiers around Mace were with him, slamming their shields together, ducking in behind them and advancing, more forming up behind and getting into the rhythm, forcing the front row forward whether they wanted to go or not. They slammed into the Easterners that held this part of the line and pushed, pushed, pushed again, and the Easterners took a step back. And another. Their line rippled and then snapped like a bowstring and Mace was through them into clear ground.

"Wheel!" he screamed and, just as they practised in the drill yard, his men split in half and surrounded the two groups of Easterners. "Hold." His soldiers stayed their arms, shields locked, discipline perfect. "It's over," he called over the melee. "You've lost. Throw down your weapons and live."

The Easterners closest began shuffling, exchanging glances; the offer of peace in a war they'd never wanted to fight was enough for many. One of their majors began exhorting his troops to crush the unbelievers, screaming that the Red Gods would be displeased. His words cowed several and Mace signalled; his already tight formation braced in readiness for the attack.

"Those Easterners we defeated at Mabon were offered a return to the Light," he shouted, cupping his hands around his mouth. "We have priests who will rededicate you to the Dancer if you surrender now. It's over. Your gods are dead!" He didn't know if they were, had no idea what was happening down there on the suddenly silent plain, but it was worth a try. Anything was worth a try to end this.

"Lies. Your souls are forfeit," the officer screamed in response, face reddening as he sensed the shift in his men. "The Red Gods cannot be defeated, They—"

A soldier turned to him and bashed his face in with his shield, and then drove the rim through his windpipe as he lay comatose. "Fuck this shit!" he yelled and threw down his weapons.

All through the East's two ragged squares there were ripples and scuffles as officers and those soldiers who must be true believers found themselves slaughtered by their own, while the rest dropped shields and spears and swords and put their hands in the air, their expressions ranging from dazed exhaustion to happy disbelief. The man closest to Mace grinned as though he'd lost a copper and found a king.

To Mace's right, the roar of the battle between the Mireces and the rest of his Rank got louder, stealing the barest breath of relief that had begun to sift through him. While he'd been busy negotiating a surrender, the Mireces had used the ice-slick terrain to spin the battle, forcing the rest of his army back against the steepest slope of the hill. If they tried to retreat down that, it would be a massacre, which was the Mireces' plan. Their line began to curve into the bull's horns formation, curling around the flanks to push in from three sides. The slope was the anvil, the Raiders the hammer.

Mace looked around for an officer. "You, Kennett! Second Thousand to escort the East down to the baggage train. Disarm and chain them. Leave a strong guard and get your arses back up here at the double."

He cupped his hands around his mouth for the next bit. "Any man who resists dies. Immediate execution, no hope of reprieve. The rest, give them water and medical attention if they need it."

Kennett saluted and bellowed for the Second Thousand to begin moving the remnants of the East downhill. There were a few scuffles from those who either had nothing left to lose or hadn't got the message, but they were quelled with savage efficiency. Mace waited only long enough to be sure they were on the move, then he turned back to the waiting soldiers. They knew what was coming.

"First Thousand, with me. We're not done yet." The sweat was freezing against Mace's face, the chill in the air making the moisture beneath his jerkin ice against his back and chest. He shivered once, violently, and glanced left and right at his soldiers; they nodded back, grim-faced against the bitter snow.

"Two-pronged attack," he yelled, and his men deployed with impressive speed considering the terrain, the conditions, and the hours they'd already been fighting. "Ad-vance!" The two points of the formation leapt across the treacherous hill and rammed into the enemy's flank and back.

BLOODCHILD

His own men, seeing him coming, braced their line as best they could and then shoved forward. Between them, they began to squeeze the Mireces into bloody paste.

CORVUS

Tenth moon, first year of the reign of King Corvus
The hill, edge of Deep Forest, Wheat Lands

GOSFATH WAS GONE, THE bloodlust with Him. The Dark Lady was gone, and his heart with Her.

Corvus exhorted them to fight and they did, because what else was there, and the enemy was crushing them and would show no mercy. To stop was to die. It suited Corvus—whatever kept them killing suited him—and he tried not to think about where the gods had gone or why. This was worship, this spilling of blood—this was in Their name.

Corvus's line swayed and crumpled like a leaf in a fire. His own men pressed him tighter against the enemy ahead as they strained to escape the new threat, and Corvus gasped and then began to screech as he was shoved on to his foe's blade. His foe was a Wolf and his face said he knew exactly who Corvus was as he scrambled to set his feet and force his sword through Corvus's—his rightful king's—chainmail and into flesh dedicated to the true gods.

Tett swiped at him, and Corvus slammed his forearm into the flat of the Wolf's blade and pushed it away. He intercepted the next thrust and punched his blade over the man's shield, angled down so it entered at the notch between his collarbones and sank deep into his chest.

Gurgling, the Wolf fell and Corvus dropped back to assess his wound. A few links of his mail shirt had broken and the sword had gone in a couple of fingers' width. Corvus was bleeding but there wasn't any gut bulging through the slit; he'd live long enough to secure the hill and his crown. He could still win. He *would* still win.

But around him his Raiders were slowing, stopping, caught up in the loss that once more tore at their souls. The Rankers continued to press in on all sides, crushing them tighter together until they were barely able to move.

"Fight. Fight, you bastards, fight!" Corvus screamed. The madness that had grown in him was still there, god-born but manmade, and as the empty hole in his heart, so briefly, ecstatically filled by Her return, became once more the howling chasm, he threw himself at the enemy. Not even Tett went with him this time. It didn't matter.

Spitting his frustration, lunging forward to slash his sword through the face of a soldier, his swings wild and unguessable, the King of the Mireces cried and roared and hurled insults and metal at his enemies until they surrounded him, trapping him between their shields. Even then he snarled in their faces and promised them bloody retribution.

"She came back once before; She'll come back again. And this time She'll eat you all, souls first, and make you Her walking corpses. And I'll help Her. I'll help! Because *I'm your fucking king.*" His voice echoed across the still, quiet battlefield. Snow muffled him.

"Kneel before me," he yelled, hoarse now, lunging at the ring of soldiers. "*Kneel!*"

"No." The voice seemed quiet, but it carried across the hill. "Stand for your king."

Mace Koridam, pretender to the throne, nothing but a jumped-up fucking soldier with no faith, no vision, strode through the rapidly parting army until he stood outside the circle where Corvus raged. His armour was splashed in blood, his face daubed with it as though he'd realised his error all these years and pledged himself to the true—the Red—gods.

"Do you surrender?" Koridam demanded.

"Fuck yourself."

The Rilporian's eyes narrowed, though a small smile played for an instant across his lips. "I was so hoping you'd say that. Give us room."

"Sire—"

"Give us room."

Corvus laughed at the irony of it—if they'd just done this at the start, thousands wouldn't have died. *And yet each drop of blood was sacred. Necessary.*

"You want this?" he demanded. "You want to fucking try? Come on then. I'll eat your fucking heart before I'm done."

He burst into a flurry of motion before Koridam was fully into the circle, cutting high and then low, shield punching for Mace's face, who sidestepped. He stamped down at the foot, a trick he'd learnt in Rilporin. Again he missed, the soldier flowing like water around his attacks, inside his guard. Corvus cracked the pommel of his sword into Koridam's face and he grunted as his nose mashed sideways, pouring blood. Stepped back.

The ring of soldiers was silent, intent, every eye fixed on the fighters and Corvus wanted to tell his men to attack now while the enemy was distracted, but he didn't have the breath to spare. He cut down the diagonal, aiming to open Koridam from shoulder to opposite knee, but the Rilporian ducked the blow, shield knocking Corvus's arm away and then pain exploded in his armpit, the sword buried deep into his chest.

Corvus howled as the blade ripped free and fell to one knee, couldn't get air back in after he'd screamed it out. Mace kicked his sword away. Still none of his men, not even Tett who'd made so many promises of protection, came to his aid. His blood steamed as it ran down his side.

"Yield," said Mace Koridam. "It's over."

"Fuck yourself," Corvus said again through gritted teeth. "My feet are on the Path and my gods aren't done with Gilgoras. I'll watch from the Afterworld as all you love is burnt to the ground." He pressed the wound beneath his arm, his chest tight with the searing hurt of it.

"Renounce the Red Gods—your dead gods—and live," Koridam said and Corvus summoned the last of his strength to laugh in the man's face.

"Dancer's grace, Your Majesty," the Rilporian said and he even seemed to mean it. The sword, red with his blood, cut through the snowy air and then cut through him.

Corvus, King of the—

RILLIRIN

Eleventh moon, first year of the reign of King Corvus
Field hospital, base of the hill, edge of Deep Forest, Wheat Lands

THEY WERE DAYS TOO late. It was over, not just the battle but the war, leaving behind deaths beyond counting, horror beyond measure, loss beyond comprehension.

In a quiet corner of the tent, where those who weren't expected to survive rested, she sat on the edge of a cot. Gilda was there too, grey with worry.

Macha lay on her father's chest inside his shirt, tucked against his poor left arm, missing a hand. She lay peacefully, knowing him in the wise and ancient way of newborns everywhere. They watched her for a while, watched Dom's face for any reaction. His head was bandaged, the linen passing down over his right eye.

No one had mentioned Macha's black eyes, nor the fine hair on her head that burnt red like fire. Like Gosfath. Lanta had called her the Bloodchild, but Rillirin had stolen her from her fate and now, with Dom and Gilda and the rest, she'd raise her in the Light and there'd be no room in that tiny form for evil. Rillirin had sworn it on her own soul, and she meant to see it done. Still, it wouldn't hurt to check.

"Can you look at her, Gilda, please? The ritual, the Dark Lady . . . I need you to check her. Please." Gilda nodded and Rillirin reached out and lifted Macha from Dom's embrace. A ripple crossed his face and his arm tightened, just a little. Gilda gasped and Rillirin recoiled as the old woman's hand found her shoulder.

"He hasn't moved since we found him. He knows she's here, he knows Macha—and you—are here. Talk to him, lass. Bring him back to us."

Rillirin swallowed hard and squeezed on to the cot next to him, put her head on his shoulder and her hand on the remains of his arm where it cradled their child.

"Home," she murmured in his ear. "You and me and Macha. Your daughter. Home is where we are together. Here."

The slightest frown creased his brow, his breathing changing. Rillirin pressed a soft kiss to his stubbled cheek and Macha squirmed, burbling a contented series of sounds as though she, too, knew they were home.

"Come on, love, open your eyes. Open your eyes and look at your daughter. She's missed you. I've missed you."

"We all have," Gilda said.

"Gilda needs to look at Macha, make sure all's well with her. I need you to let her go, just for a moment or two. Can you do that?" She blinked at Gilda and the priestess slid the babe from the crook of Dom's elbow. His arm moved again, questing, his breathing rapid now, panicked.

"Hush, love, hush. Gilda's got her," Rillirin whispered. "All's well. Just open your eyes. Look at her. Look at me."

Dom's mouth turned down, lips thin. His chest rattled as he breathed, and then his eye opened, blinked, blinked again. Rillirin squeezed him very gently, eyes darting from Gilda and Macha to Dom, trying to see everything at once.

"Oh," Gilda breathed, and Rillirin was dizzy with it. "I see, yes. The birthmark."

"She wasn't born with it," Rillirin said. "The Dark Lady touched her." Dom flinched, shied away as though the words were poison. "I don't know what it might have done. If she's . . . normal."

Gilda held the infant up to her face and pressed her nose against the black mark spreading across the tiny chest. She inhaled and grunted, then pressed a series of smacking kisses to the belly.

"I'm no royal physician," she said, lowering Macha back into Dom's arm—he inhaled so hard he coughed—"but that there is a perfect baby. Ten fingers, ten toes, two arms and legs. Beautiful. Healthy."

BLOODCHILD

"But the mark. Her eyes," Rillirin protested as Dom lowered his chin to brush at his daughter's head.

"Nothing to worry about, I promise, but I'll bathe her in the nearest pool once I've dedicated it to the Dancer," Gilda said. "After that, well . . . love her, raise her in the Light. That's all any of us can do."

She could have been talking about Dom as much as Macha. Rillirin thought she understood, for the first time, exactly what Gilda and Cam had gone through when they'd adopted him, the new calestar, and he'd become and done all of those things. They'd never stopped loving him, or trying to influence him towards the good. They'd never stopped trying to protect him—from others and from himself.

Rillirin took a breath. "So that's motherhood," she breathed, her voice tight. "And I thought the sleepless nights were bad."

Gilda's laugh was strangled. "Oh, lass," she said, "they're the absolute bloody least of it."

"Rillirin."

Rillirin started, clutching inadvertently at Dom's arm as he spoke. "Dom! Yes, yes, love, it's me, I'm here. Macha's here. Oh gods, Dom, can you see me? Hear me?"

"Hear," he whispered. "Blind. Not Godblind though, not any more. Godblinded." He wheezed and Rillirin realised it was laughter. Her ears roared relief and she laughed too, juddering kisses against his cheek and chin and brow.

"It doesn't matter, doesn't matter," she said. "Here, let me help you." She cradled the arm cradling Macha and shifted it upwards, so the babe's downy cheek nestled against his. "Breathe her," Rillirin whispered. "You don't need to see her; she's perfect."

Tears soaked Macha's fine red hair as he took in the scent of his daughter. Rillirin put his right hand on the baby's head and his fingers stroked, with infinite care and wonder, across her crown and down to feel an ear, a shoulder, an arm. Tiny fingers grasped his and his breath hitched.

Then he frowned. "She stinks," he commented and Rillirin giggled.

"Oh gods, she does. I need to change her. Sorry, love."

Dom smiled, his cheek against his daughter's. "I don't mind." But Macha began to squirm harder, mewling her discontent. "Gilda, would you mind?" he asked when she began to cry after a last, endless moment of his lips pressed to her hair. "And I love you, by the way. And I'm sorry for it all."

"Hush, foolish boy," Gilda said, her voice tight. "Always the wrong apology at the wrong time." She took Macha from his arm and stood, looking long at Dom. Rillirin didn't understand.

"Back soon," she said.

"Keep her safe," Dom replied. "Mother."

Gilda choked back a sob and nodded once, patted Dom's foot, and then ducked out of the tent.

"Now then," Dom said quietly, tightening his arm around Rillirin and breathing her in much the same way he'd done their daughter. "About that knowing I had. It's time you fulfilled it."

"What knowing, love?" she asked, nestling closer, not caring about the words, only that he was speaking.

"Rillirin Fisher, herald of the end. You will bring love to death. And death to love."

A cold shiver worked its way through her from her scalp to the soles of her feet. She'd forgotten. She'd hoped it would have gone away, after everything. He raised the stump of his arm and smelt it, the warm baby-smell Macha had left on his skin.

He pushed at Rillirin very gently. "Sit up."

She was shaking as she did, twisted at the waist so she could watch him, hands on his shoulder and ribs. "What are you saying?"

"Gods, I wish I could see you again," Dom said, his voice low with infinite sorrow. "Do you still love me, Rillirin?"

"What? Of course I do. I love you so much, *so much*."

"Then kill me."

The light in the tent contracted, shadows leaping, crowding close. There was no air, nothing for her straining lungs to find. "What?" Rillirin didn't recognise her own voice. "I can't."

Dom smiled, so tender and full of love she couldn't reconcile it with his words. "I'm dying, Rillirin. Nothing is going to stop that, but you can stop it hurting. If you do it, you fulfil the final prophecy and it's all over. You bring death to love—me. And you bring love to death—Macha, once the Bloodchild, destined to be death itself and saved by you and loved despite who she was meant to become."

He trembled, in pain or fear or just tiredness she couldn't tell. He smiled like a skull, and his breath hitched, and his heart stuttered beneath Rillirin's hands. "Do it now, my love. And then make sure our daughter knows who I was and what I did. Tell her all of it, the good and the bad. She deserves that. Everyone deserves that."

"I can't." She wanted to beat him, to press her hands over his mouth and stop his words.

"You can." He reached for her, hand questing in the air until she took it in hers and held it to her cheek. "You have to." He paused to breathe, fighting pain she finally realised he'd been feeling for years and that built now, wave upon wave, to drown him. More pain than she would ever know. "I'm broken, shattered in so many ways there's no chance of putting me back together. There's only one thing you can do for me. Let me go."

"I can't." The same denial, softer now, a child's plea against the coming of night, as though if she believed enough, wanted it enough, she could summon back the sun.

"*Please.*"

Her heart was burning, her eyes stinging hot, unable to cry. She was numb. "But you're home," she whispered. "You're *my* home, the only one I ever really had. The only one I want."

"Macha is your home," Dom contradicted her. "And Gilda and Ash and Dalli and even Mace. They're all your home. Give me the grace, my love. Let me make my peace with the Dancer, after all this time and all our angry, bitter words. Let me sleep. Knowing Gilda as I do, she'll have left you a knife."

And she had. Rillirin picked it up, the handle smooth and obscene in her palm. And right. "I will always love you," she murmured. "You don't get rid of me that easily. Wait for me in the Light."

"Forever," Dom whispered.

Rillirin bit her lip, hard, until the pain stopped her hand from shaking, and then she pressed a sore and solitary kiss to his brow, heard him breathe her in, one last time. The things he'd done, the people he'd killed and hurt, the betrayals . . . none of it mattered. Her courage was failing her and he knew it.

He raised his poor mutilated arm and she put her face against it. "Best thing I ever did, saving you from the Mireces. It was all worth it in the end. To be with you. To love you."

"Best thing you ever did, Dom Templeson, was make Macha with me, our perfect, beautiful babe," she contradicted him, and the smile that lit his face would warm her for the rest of her life. "Go in grace, my heart," Rillirin whispered, and she sent him home.

MACE

Tenth moon, first year of the reign of King Mace
Freedom Hill, edge of Deep Forest, Wheat Lands

MACE STOOD BENEATH THE same royal standard that had marked his command post on this day the previous year. Around it stood banners marking the Ranks who'd fought and died there: South, West and Palace. A high black flag with a stylised wolf's head picked out in silver to commemorate the many dead and few surviving Wolves who'd given everything in the war. The Warlord of Krike's standard.

Below the hill, two more flags flew proud against the high expanse of emptiness—the Trickster's, a fox with two-coloured eyes—and the calestar's, a wolf beneath a sun and moon, newly commissioned for the memorial.

Everyone who'd fought or resisted, everyone who'd lived and could travel had come to bear witness and pay their respects. Mace looked out at them in silence, Dalli by his side with their baby girl wrapped up in her arms. The ghosts of the dead thronged the hill.

Mace took his daughter from Dalli and looked into green eyes in a tiny face. "Lots of people here, sweetheart," he whispered. "Just not as many as there should be. I can think of a few who should be celebrating with us, can't you?" He kissed the pudgy fist that tried to grab his nose.

Dalli stepped forward. "They're waiting, love."

The host was silent and solemn, retired soldiers standing stiff and straight in uniforms not worn for a year. Gilda, Hallos, Mark Salter, wearing a major's sigil now. Colonel Thatcher, now Commander of the Ranks, and his husband, the promoted Major Kennett. Brid Fox-dream and Cutta Frog-dream, who'd together held the wood and the slope with the Wolves and lost three-quarters of their warriors defending a foreign land. Dalli's Wolves, just over one hundred, all that was left of an entire people. Even Rillirin and young Macha with her blood-red hair and black, black eyes.

Among them, hundreds of civilians from Rilporin, the Wolf Lands, Sailtown and Pine Lock and the South Forts. Soldiers, warriors, survivors all.

The dead were shadows among them, hovering close as their names were whispered, and it seemed there was only one living person missing: Ash.

Where he'd gone nobody knew. What had happened to Crys's body, no one knew that either. They'd simply disappeared into the snowstorm, never to return. Some thought that Crys still lived and together they haunted the high passes of the Gilgoras Mountains, watching Rilpor and all the world, ready to descend and defend it once more when danger threatened. Others thought they'd taken a boat to Listre, or maybe all the way out the other side into the great, endless ocean that Gilda had once seen, sailing for new lands and new gods, where nobody knew them and they could be free.

No one believed that Crys was dead.

Not even Mace could truly believe it.

"We are gathered here today to honour the fallen." His voice cut through the murmurs and the wind. "We are here to remember their sacrifice and yours. One year ago today we defeated evil. One year ago today two men faced down two gods and triumphed."

Mace paused and pressed a kiss to his daughter's forehead before sweeping them all with his gaze. "They were heroes. And so is every single one of you. Do not let your deeds be submerged beneath greater stories. Do not ever forget that your heroism did as much to win the day as theirs. When no one would answer our call, Krike came. When the Mireces killed the Evendooms, the Ranks did not falter—and nor did you. I never wanted to be king," he said and there was a ripple of laughter. "I never wanted to lead this country. But I've never been prouder in all my life than the day you led me—by your example—to victory here on Freedom Hill."

He paused, fighting emotion, and Dalli took the baby from him and handed him a silver cup. "For Durdil Koridam and Tara Carter." He shouted the names, pouring drops of wine into the grass with each one.

Dalli took the cup from him. "Ash Bowman," she cried, spilling wine. "And Dom Templeson."

One by one they advanced, calling out the names of those they'd loved and lost, comrades in arms, friends, family. The ground ran with wine red as blood, staining boots and the hems of skirts. Mace refilled the cup for them himself, over and over and over again as the day progressed. He listened to their voices, listened to the names they called. It wasn't snowing this year and the wind hadn't yet got winter in its teeth, and yet he was chilled to the bone by the sheer multitude of what—of who—they'd lost.

Mace squinted up at the next, a giant of a man with a familiar look to him. "Name's Merol, son of Merle Stonemason. He—"

Mace shook his hand. "I remember Merle well. Your father was a great man, Merol. Pretty sure he saved my life. And I've seen you in the city, helping us rebuild. Thank you for coming."

In the depths of the beard, Merol's lower lip wobbled. "He wouldn't let me fight, Your Majesty," he said. "I wanted to, but he wouldn't . . ."

Mace searched his memory for all the stories that had been told after the war ended. "You carried Rillirin, didn't you, out of the city? Rillirin and her daughter?"

The mason nodded and Mace slapped him on the arm and then winced: it was like slapping marble.

Merol shuffled his feet, embarrassed. "Weren't nothing much, Your Majesty. Not like I carried her all the way. Just a while, you know. Just . . . seemed right."

"Well, what do you think would have happened to her if you'd fought and died alongside your father, eh? No, Merol, the gods saved your life to help her. It might not seem as heroic as some other deeds recounted here today, but you ask Rillirin what she thinks of your actions. She's here, too. Speak to her." He noticed two small faces peeking from behind Merol's massive legs. "And who are these young princesses?" he asked with a smile.

Merol ushered them forward, his massive hands gentle enough to cup a butterfly's wings. "My girls. Adopted after the war ended. They're . . . from the west, if you know what I mean."

"They're Rilporian now, Merol," Mace said firmly. "Now and always."

"Can I see your sword?" the littlest one asked, making a grab for the scabbard.

Her sister hauled her back. "Ede," she said. "You're supposed to curt-sey." She stumbled into one of her own and Mace felt the corner of his mouth lift. "Hello, Your Majesty. I'm Kit. I'm six now."

Mace gave them both a little bow. "Hello, Kit and Ede," he mur-mured. "You know your da's a great man, don't you?" They giggled and nodded. "Be good for him, yes? Promise me."

Merol dragged his fingers through his beard, blushing. "Thank you, Your Majesty, though I doubt even you can command this pair." He took the cup. "Merle Stonemason," he said. "Tara Vaunt."

Mace frowned. "Tara Vaunt?" He put the names together and his eyes widened. "Come and find me after the ceremony is over. It seems that's one story I haven't heard."

Merol bowed awkwardly and shuffled away.

Mace watched him go until Hallos blocked his view. He looked deep into his king's eyes. "You made your father proud this time last year," he said. "And you make him proud today."

Mace coughed and shifted. "Thank you, Physician," he murmured.

"King Rastoth," Hallos said, pouring wine. "Durdil Koridam." He handed the cup back and Mace blinked away the sting. Hallos leant in close. "And I'd like it put on the royal record that I've still got a limp. The next time your wife goes into labour, you can find someone else to deliver her."

Mace pressed his lips together but couldn't prevent a very unroyal snort of laughter. "Duly noted, Hallos."

The afternoon was beginning to gloam when the last person appeared to make her offering. The grey novice priestess robes suited her and Mace squeezed her shoulder, gave the toddler on her hip a little wave. Rillirin's hand shook so hard the wine sloshed and the little girl wrapped her arms around her neck to comfort her.

"Take your time," Mace said quietly. "There's no rush."

Rillirin took in a shuddery breath. "Tara Carter, for saving my life," she said, pouring, and a muscle flickered in Mace's jaw. "And Dom Templeson, for showing me how to live it."

Epilogue

RILLIRIN

Tenth moon, first year of the reign of King Mace
Watcher village, northern Wolf Lands, Rilporian border

"SAY HELLO TO UNCLE Ash, young warrior."

"'Lo, Uncle," Macha said as she scampered in through the archer's front door. She squealed when he swung her up and around, darting in for kisses on her ruddy cheeks.

Gilda followed her in, leaning on the walking staff that was a spear. Rillirin closed the door and watched, arms crossed over her chest and fingers cupping the polished amulet hanging from her neck. It had been Dom's. She smiled at Macha's screams of laughter as Ash tossed her up towards the roof beams and then caught her. "You'll make her sick."

"And then I'll give her back to you to clean up," Ash agreed. Gilda snorted and Rillirin pretended outrage.

"Sleepy man," Macha said, pointing to the door.

Rillirin didn't miss the flash of pain in Ash's grimace and winced. "You should have come to the ceremony," she said softly.

Ash scowled. "And leave him? No."

"Not today, Macha," she said and held out her hand.

"It's all right," Ash said and put the little girl down. "He'd like a visitor and you've learnt lots of new words since you were last here, I expect." He dropped to one knee and brushed back her sunset-red curls. "Go and see the sleepy man then. Give him a kiss from me."

They waited until she'd trotted through the door with a wave. Ash handed out cups of ale even though it was barely noon. Gilda drained hers in one go and smirked as she held it out to be refilled, eliciting a reluctant smile from Ash. She'd always been able to drink him under the table. He watched the door to the bedchamber, swirling his ale in his cup. Brooding. "At least she's not afraid of him."

"How can she be afraid of her uncle Crys?" Rillirin protested, but Gilda gave a single shake of her head and she bit her tongue. Priestesses sought the truth, no matter how hard, and she knew what Ash meant: though he fed him water and soup, vegetables mashed into a paste in tiny, patient dribbles, Crys was a barely breathing skeleton clothed in papery skin. He, and the room, smelt of sickness and shit, no matter how often Ash bathed him. Now the snow was here, Ash couldn't even prop open the shutters to let in fresh air.

"'Lo, sleepy man!" they heard Macha say cheerily. Ash's mouth twitched in a smile.

"That one's not afraid of anything," Rillirin said with a hint of sourness. "I caught her standing on my table this morning. I have no idea how she got up there, but she was preparing to jump back off." Worry vied with pride, the scales evenly balanced. Macha was far too young for most of the things she knew and did and there could be only one explanation for her development, but still, not even Gilda's wise old eyes could see a shadow on her granddaughter's soul.

"She's her father's recklessness," Gilda agreed and winked. "How are you, Ash?"

"I know why you're here," he said, flinging himself into a chair and downing half the ale. "Honestly, I'm glad you went to Freedom Hill for the memorial—you deserved to be there—but you don't need to mother me the moment you get back. It's not as if anything's changed."

Gilda raised a grey eyebrow. "I've been mothering you for bloody years, lad. Not much point stopping now. Besides, Dalli's had the bairn. Thought you'd want to know."

Ash sat back up. "She has? All well?"

Gilda smirked. "She threatened Hallos with a spear up his arse at one point if I'm not mistaken, but yes, she's well. Healthy as a horse, the babe too. A girl." She looked at Rillirin.

"Tara."

Ash's face crumpled. "Good name," he said thickly. "She told me once—our Tara—that if she'd had balls, she'd be King of Rilpor."

Rillirin swallowed. "Well, her namesake will be queen, and apparently she's all girl."

"She'd love that," Ash said, and they fell silent.

Rillirin knocked back her ale, suppressed a burp, and refilled her cup and Ash's.

"They don't know, do they, about us?" he asked. "You didn't tell anyone?"

"No," Gilda said. "Though why—"

"'Lo, sleepy man!" Macha said again, happiness in her voice. Ash twitched again. The lines in his face were carved deeper now; there was the first scattering of silver in his curly hair. His hand went to two scars, one in his jaw, one in his chest. He flushed when he saw Rillirin notice the gesture.

Because you can't go into the Light and bring Crys back as he did you. Because he isn't in the Light. He's somewhere else. Stuck between this world and the next. And none of us can find him, not even Gilda.

And that's why you can't bear for people to know where you are. Because you think you've failed him.

Macha appeared in the doorway. "Sleepy man," she said, pointing.

"Yes, Uncle Crys is the sleepy man," said Ash.

Rillirin could see how much the words cost him. She started forwards to offer some sort of comfort when Macha spoke again.

"Sleepy man 'wake!" They froze, all three of them, as the little girl giggled and bounced up and down, her curls floating into a crazed halo around her head. "Wake," she repeated, and there was a noise from the other room, the slightest sound. A murmur, perhaps, or the slide of blankets on a form that never moved.

Very, very slowly, Ash rose from his chair. Gilda beckoned, and Macha ran to her, holding out her arms to be picked up. Gilda swung her on to her hip and met Rillirin's eyes, the look binding her in place.

They watched Ash creep to the door of the bedchamber, tension and broken hope in his lanky frame. Rillirin heard his throat click as he swallowed, and then he stepped through the door. "Crys?" His voice was unbearably soft.

Rillirin took her daughter in her arms and held her tight, breathing her in. The little girl's black eyes were solemn. "'Wake," she whispered. "Uncle happy?"

Rillirin pressed a kiss to flame-red hair. "Oh yes, little one. Uncle Ash is very, very happy." She looked at Gilda. "But how?"

"And the godlight will lead us all, to death and beyond," the old priestess whispered. "And what is beyond death but the promise of new life?"

From the other room came the sound of quiet weeping, full of joy. Gilda ushered them out into a world of black trees and white snow. "Let us give thanks," she said.

"Happy," Macha repeated, and her high laughter pealed across the clearing.

ACKNOWLEDGMENTS

LIKE MANY OF MY characters, I wasn't sure I'd live to the end of this trilogy when I was writing it and I don't really know what to say now that we're here. It's been such a huge part of my life for fifteen years and now it's finished I'm a bit lost.

If you've stuck with me and my characters this far, thank you, thank you, thank you. You will probably never know just what it means to me. I hope I broke your hearts and made you cry at least once.

To my agent, Harry Illingworth of DHH Literary Agency—and everyone else there and at Goldsboro Books—thank you so much for your support and advice. Hard to believe how much we've accomplished in four short years, but I couldn't have managed it without you. You're the best. Here's to the future!

To my glorious editor Natasha Bardon and all of the HarperVoyager team—Jane, Vicky, Jack, Jaime (amazing publicity), Richenda (copy editor extraordinaire) and Dom Forbes and Mike Topping (that glorious artwork)—where to start with the thanks? You made a dream come true for me and I'm forever grateful for all your efforts to make my little books into the wonderful, beautiful monsters they are.

Thanks also to Cameron McClure of Donald Maass and everyone at Louisa Pritchard Associates and the Marsh Agency for your foreign rights work, and thanks to those foreign publishers: Skyhorse in the US, Bragelonne in France, Blanvalet in Germany, Luitingh-Sijthoff in the Netherlands, Dobrovsky Publishing in the Czech Republic and Papierowy Ksiezyc/Caput Mundi Books in Poland.

To my husband, Mark, even I run out of words to express my gratitude for your love and support. You're absolutely the better half of me and none of this would be possible without your belief and your willingness to put up with my weirder habits. I love you.

To all the family and friends who have supported me, cheered me on and been so happy and proud of what I've accomplished, thank you so much. I know I can be a nightmare sometimes but I do appreciate and love you all!

To the Fantasy Five—Mike, Kareem, Laura, JP and Sadir—I love you guys. Thanks for the support and all the fun times. Bang-average!

"82," as ever your beta-reading and military skillz made this a much better book than it would have been otherwise. Now finish your own, because I need to know what happens next.

To all my Warrior Queens, thanks for always having my back. Here's to more shenanigans and may you all be blessed with an abundance of tales to tell.

And to the instructors and students at Birmingham HEMA Club— thank you for trying to teach me Italian longsword, and for the many, many stabbings along the way. I'm no Tara, despite your best efforts, but I have a lot of fun getting killed.

And again to the readers, because it's all about you: read widely and enthusiastically. I have more stories, and I hope you'll walk them with me. Thank you.